ZANE

THE
GOLD
DIGGER'S
CLUB

Dear Reader:

Golddiggers often get a bad rap with a stereotypical image of using a male's pockets to attain financial freedom and success. But nine times out of ten, the men are willing participants who only cry foul when things go south in the relationship. It's not like they do not realize that they are doling out cash and material things, after all. Whether they do it for bragging rights, competition to see who has the finest dime on their arms, or for the sexual favors that they receive in return, no golddigger shall prosper without a man's consent.

I am pleased to introduce Jaye Cheríe and her debut novel, *The Golddigger's Club*. Jaye is entrenched in her own world of celebrity with her online entertainment site. We follow three ladies, Monica, Deidre and Stephanie, who crave money through the men in their lives. But will their scandalous ways continue to lead them to success or cause their worlds to fall apart? Like they always say: "All that glitters is not gold."

As always, thanks for the support shown to the Strebor Books International family. We appreciate the love. For more information on our titles, please visit www.zanestore.com and you can find me on my personal website: www.eroticanoir.com. You can also join my online social network at www.planetzane.org.

Blessings,

Zane

Publisher
Strebor Books International
www.simonandschuster.com/streborbooks

ZANE PRESENTS

THE
GOLD
DIGGER'S
CLUB

JAYE CHERÍE

SBI

STREBOR BOOKS

NEW YORK LONDON TORONTO SYDNEY

SBI
Strebor Books
P.O. Box 6505
Largo, MD 20792
http://www.streborbooks.com

ISBN 978-1-59309-380-8
ISBN 978-1-4516-4068-7 (ebook)
LCCN 2011928057

First Strebor Books trade paperback edition January 2012

Cover design: www.mariondesigns.com
Cover photograph: © Keith Saunders/Marion Designs

10 9 8 7 6 5 4 3 2

Manufactured in the United States of America

For information regarding special discounts for bulk purchases, please contact Simon & Schuster Special Sales at 1-866-506-1949 or business@simonandschuster.com

The Simon & Schuster Speakers Bureau can bring authors to your live event. For more information or to book an event, contact the Simon & Schuster Speakers Bureau at 1-866-248-3049 or visit our website at www.simonspeakers.com.

To my mother and my father—
who saw that I should be an author long before I did.

ACKNOWLEDGMENTS

First, I want to thank God for giving me the ability to write and the courage to overcome various obstacles to make my work available to the world.

To my family—thank you for your unconditional support. I could not do many of the things I do without it.

Keith—I feel like you took a field trip through my brain, pulled out a computer and went to work. This cover is an excellent visual translation of the story.

Keisha—thanks for the numerous IM and email exchanges. They were a great exercise in my instinct and imagination.

Judy—I don't know where my book would be without your positive critiques and gentle suggestions. Thanks for being the first person to tell me that I might actually have something.

Roy Glenn—I appreciate your input and insight into the publishing industry.

First Coast Christian Writers Group—I hope you can continue to give the same enthusiasm and encouragement to others that you have given to me. It truly makes a difference.

Toastmasters International, especially Lillian R. Bradley Toastmasters Club—thanks for your support in my development. We are awesome!

Yona—Thanks for your ideas.

Charmaine—Thanks for your guidance and patience.

Zane—You are giving me an opportunity to make my dreams a reality. Because of you, I know I am doing the right thing. Thanks for the confirmation.

My English teachers (Ms. Welfare and Ms. Zilahy) and Mass Communications professors (Ms. King)—Thank you for seeing something in me that many people didn't.

CHAPTER 1

Monica

"Hut, hut, hut." The quarterback seized the snap and stretched his arm backward, winding up for a throw. He fired the ball right into the arms of Tampa Bay Buccaneers wide receiver, Tony T. Hatcher. Tony cradled the ball and mustered all the speed and power in his six-foot-five, muscular physique to sprint across the goal line. When Tony stopped running, the head coach blew his whistle. All the players broke their positions, allowing waves of sweat to run down their sculpted chests and defined biceps.

The coach hurled his roll of papers to the ground.

"What are y'all doing? If we practice like this, we'll play like this during the season. Now, pick it up!" the coach shouted. The players trudged back to their line of scrimmage to practice the drive again.

Unlike the spectators perched on the bleachers, Monica Hatcher stood on the sidelines trying to play the supportive wife, but the sweat threatening to escape from her pores made it difficult to concentrate. As she watched her husband practice, she kept lapsing into daydreams of relaxing near the pool with a glass of iced tea at her side. That's where she preferred to spend the day.

Instead, she stood tall, hastily pulling her long, black ponytail behind her shoulders. Tony loved her manufactured mane but she yearned for her cropped haircut. She vowed to return to her signature tresses, at least while the heat index topped out at 102 degrees. In the meantime, she obliged her husband with her hair and her presence at the field. Monica figured this would stop him from complaining. Lately, he had harsh words for her absence at his practices. Tony claimed she was acting like a fair-weather fan because his team had a rough season last year.

While she would admit she wasn't attending like she did when he had first entered the NFL, it had nothing to do with the team's record. It was that practice, home games, and away games got old after eight years. She'd grown tired of feigning fulfillment in the NFL life. She was also tired of moving, tired of politicking and tired of smiling big for the cameras. She wanted to focus on activities more important to her, like planning the dinner for The Hatcher Scholarship Foundation.

The coach blew his whistle for the last time. The players broke their positions as if they'd been carrying a ton of bricks they were waiting to drop. Tony jogged over to Monica, wiping the sweat off his tanned forehead. "Hey. Where the kids at?" Tony asked, out of breath.

"They're with Marianna. I would never bring them out here. Too much open space for them to run or disappear, and I'm not running them down in this heat.

Do you want your son running beside you on the field?"
Monica asked.

Tony jerked his head back and frowned. "No."

Between the look on Tony's face and the looks from
nearby players, Monica guessed she was a little too
forceful in her response.

One player walked by, appearing to scowl at her. Self-
conscious, Monica glanced around, while smoothing out
the wrinkles in her sleeveless dress. She thought about
how another passerby might view her as a bourgeois
witch, but she really wasn't that way. She didn't consider
herself a shallow, irresponsible woman—the type who
let her "help" raise her children because she was too
busy shopping and partying. She did, however, believe
in using nannies and cooks to help her out. But even
with the extra help, her family was still priority number
one for her; the children knew they could count on
mommy.

A tiny bit embarrassed at her own behavior, Monica
dropped her head and sighed. "I'm sorry. It's so hot out
here. I think my brain is sweating."

"Well, it is spring and we are in Florida," Tony said
sarcastically. "If you got a problem with the heat, why
did you come here?"

"I came out here to support you."

"And you're doing that by standing on the sidelines
mean mugging?"

"I wasn't aware I was supposed to be cheesing from

ear to ear. You say I never come out. So, I'm out here."
Monica placed her hands on her hips.

Tony threw his head back and pushed his thumbs
inside of his sleeveless shirt. "All I'm saying is don't do
me any favors."

Monica squinted at him. She'd sacrificed not only her
comfort, but her time to make him happy. He could
have at least acted like he appreciated it. If she'd known
he'd react this way, she would have stretched out at her
pool, or better yet, she could have used the day to check
out a couple of venues for the scholarship dinner in
August.

Now that Monica thought about it, she didn't know
why she thought giving him what he wanted would make
any difference. Nothing seemed to please him these
days, especially since the season started. She knew the
reasons behind his sour behavior—his smaller contract
and unfocused teammates—but it was most disturbing
that his attitude was rubbing off on her. Before she could
address their growing discord, Tony turned toward the
stadium exit.

"Where are you going?" Monica asked.

"I'm gonna shower, pick up the kids and take them to
the park," Tony said.

"Fine. I'm going to meet Dee and Stephanie for an
early dinner," Monica said.

Tony rolled his eyes.

"Don't start, okay?" Monica asked. Tony didn't care

for Monica's friends. They didn't like him much either. She wasn't sure how it started but she was getting real sick of playing referee.

Tony placed his hand on his chest, faking innocence. "I didn't say anything. I'll see you when you get home."

Tony jogged off the field toward the locker room. When he passed two women sitting in the stands, he winked at them. They batted their eyes back and burst into giggles. The shorter one whispered to her friend, who howled in amusement.

The acid in Monica's stomach bubbled over like a boiling pot of water. She didn't attend Tony's practice to see him flirt with other women. Before the end of the day, she planned to read him about his behavior. Annoyed, Monica walked toward the exit, eyeing the two ogling women.

During the drive to meet her friends, Monica was still pretty hot with Tony. So much so she had to imagine the layout of the scholarship dinner to calm down. She envisioned an ice sculpture at the front entrance of the venue. Elegant crystal chandeliers in the dining area. Twenty-five tables with champagne tablecloths and floral centerpieces placed at the center. She'd present a plaque along with a $25,000 check for college to two eager high school students.

Thinking about the dinner instantly put Monica at ease. By the time she reached Henrietta's Bistro, she caught herself smiling. When she entered the quaint restaurant, her friends, Deidre Wright and Stephanie Robinson, were already sitting at a booth. With the Tony incident twenty miles away, she decided to avoid bringing it up to her friends because she didn't want to ruin the positive vibe. Besides, if given the chance, they'd only use the incident as ammunition against Tony's character, which she did not feel like defending.

"Hello, ladies," Monica said.

"Hey. What's up?" Dee said, glancing up from her pocket mirror.

"Same ole, same ole. What's up with you guys? Have you ordered yet?" Monica asked.

"Yeah, but here's a menu," Stephanie said, handing it to Monica.

Monica took the menu and glanced down at the choices, which included a special with collard greens, ham hocks and sweet potatoes. She shuddered to think she considered asking Henrietta to cater her dinner. Henrietta's food was savory in a soul food sort of way but she couldn't imagine serving collard greens and ham hocks to the bigwigs in August. She was going to ask these CEOs and politicians for hundreds of thousands of dollars. They had to take her seriously, and to do that, she needed to produce a high class event all the way—from the venue to the food. *Oh, well. Maybe I'll keep Henrietta in mind for future events, like a small birthday party.* Once the waiter returned to their table, Monica ordered the four-vegetable special and a tea. The waiter took her menu and she shifted her attention back to her friends.

"So, which one of you broads is gonna help me plan my dinner?" Monica asked the two women sitting across from her.

Dee looked up from her mirror with her trademark "no, you didn't" expression. She turned around to glance at people sitting at the tables behind her. "You must be talking to someone else because I know you ain't talking to me like that."

Deidre, or Dee to her friends, shifted her eyes back to her pocket mirror, while fixing her wavy weave with French-manicured fingers. As a fashion stylist, Dee was so appearance obsessed that she wore pricey hair, refused to leave the house without MAC makeup and shopped every week. She even liked donning hazel contact lenses and fake eyelashes. They complemented her face, she said. Today, she was minus the lashes but she maintained her diva mode with the contacts.

"Since you're so style-conscious, I thought you might be able to help me with the decoration," Monica said with a wide smile.

"I do fashion. I don't do confetti."

"You're still styling a room. When you think about it, there really isn't any difference."

"There is a difference and you know it. Now, I'm not gonna sit here and debate back and forward with you about decorations and fashions 'cuz I know nothing about the former. So, I sure hope you have something else to talk about."

Sometimes she is so impossible, Monica thought. She turned to her other friend. "What about you?"

"I would, but I'm not really fashion conscious. I don't even like those kinds of events. I mean, everybody gets all dressed up and acts like they're better than you. It gets on my nerves," Stephanie said, scrunching her round, baby face. The last rays of the setting sun shimmered over her cinnamon brown skin and long, curly hair, hinting to her Afro-Cuban lineage.

"You don't have to be fashion conscious. You can just help me make some calls. Besides, this is a dinner for a nonprofit organization. Nobody's supposed to be acting like they're better than anybody."

"You know those people aren't gonna act right," Dee said, peeking up from her mirror.

Monica shot Dee the evil eye for interrupting her volunteer campaign.

"I don't know," Stephanie said.

"You might meet some nice, rich men."

"When do you need help?" Stephanie asked.

"Well, I could use some help tomorrow afternoon."

"Oh, no. I have to get ready for the show. Natalie's gonna get me back stage at the Jam Fest. I already told her I would go. I need to network for more video gigs. I'm gonna spend the whole day getting ready. Sorry." Stephanie shrugged.

The waiter returned to the table with Dee's pepper steak and Stephanie's chicken fettuccine alfredo. Monica watched Stephanie divvy up the chicken chunks and sprinkle extra cheese over the pasta. It was amazing how much effort Stephanie put into the food on her plate, considering she didn't like putting effort into anything else. Whenever Monica or Dee asked her to do something—if there was any real work involved—they could forget about her. It was like she was allergic to any type of exertion. She knew Stephanie wasn't that sorry for ditching her on the dinner preparation but decided not to press the issue right then. *These chicks are going to help me whether they know it or not.*

"Sure. I'll let you know when I need help with something else." Monica tried her best to look dejected.

"How is the dinner going? Are you gonna use a deejay or an actual recording artist?" Dee asked, biting into a tender piece of steak.

"Well, since you don't intend to help, you're gonna have to wait and see like everybody else," Monica said, smirking.

"That's okay. It ain't that important." Dee rolled her eyes.

Monica shook her head. "Don't you want to be a part of something meaningful?"

"I'm a part of many things that are meaningful. I just think it's time for me to focus on me right now," Dee said, reaching for the barbecue sauce.

"Dang, that sounds kinda selfish," Stephanie said.

"Doesn't it?" Monica asked.

"I don't think so," Dee said. "When I said I wanted to start a fashion magazine, did any of you heifers say, 'Wow! Great, Dee! How can we help you out?'"

"We don't know anything about creating a magazine," Monica said.

"Monica, your degree is in mass communications. Even if you didn't know, I could have used your media knowledge. I could have shown you what to do, just like you were willing to show us what you needed to plan your scholarship dinner but oh, no. Instead, I was greeted with cynicism." Dee dropped her fork on her plate and crossed her arms.

"I wasn't trying to be cynical. I thought you should know magazines are losing advertising money these days," Stephanie explained.

"What did that have to do with me and my dreams?" Dee asked.

Monica raised her eyebrows and looked at Stephanie, who had a similar expression on her face. Within the past two years that they'd known each other, Dee had tried to "come up" so many times. There was the time she bought a lot of stock but ended up losing money because the companies closed or underperformed. Then, she bought real estate from a bank but lost that because she forgot to pay property taxes on it. Actually, she forgot about the property altogether. As expected, they had a hard time taking her next big thing seriously, but Dee's passion for the fashion magazine surprised Monica.

The waiter walked up to the table with Monica's special and laid it down gently in front of her. "Is there anything else I can get for you ladies?" he asked.

"No," the women said in unison.

Monica returned her attention to Dee. "Look. I'm just concerned about your abrupt change in direction," Monica said. "But I like seeing you serious about something. So, I guess that's why I need to be more supportive of your magazine. It's a good match for you, Dee. You're right. I apologize," Monica conceded. Dee smiled and pushed her chin up.

"I am too, Dee. From now on, I promise I'll be more supportive of your dreams," Stephanie added.

"Thank you, ladies. I really appreciate it," Dee said, reaching out to touch her friends' hands.

"Now, will you help me with my dinner?" Monica asked.

Looking up at the ceiling, Dee sighed. "I'll think about it."

CHAPTER 2

Stephanie

Five years after its inception, people still flocked to Jam Fest. HOT 91.7 blasted commercials about it every few minutes for the past two months, but even if they hadn't advertised it heavily, people still would have broken their necks to see the who's who of pop and urban music. As in the past, eager fans circled around the stadium an hour early to see the show. Stephanie bypassed the long line and entered the stadium through a side door to meet up with Natalie, her friend and the event coordinator, who got her into the event for free. The two high school friends had entered the entertainment business together and kept in touch. So when Stephanie wanted to get into an event coming to town, she knew who to call.

Stephanie searched the backstage area for Natalie. It didn't take Stephanie long to find her; she could hear her friend talking on her cell phone from a mile away. As soon as Stephanie approached her, Natalie reached into a box, grabbed a backstage pass and dropped it around her neck without breaking her conversation.

"Do I have to wear this? It's gonna mess up my outfit," Stephanie said.

Natalie reviewed her low-cut blouse and short skirt. "Hold on," she said to the person on the other end. "Girl, you betta wear that thing. You don't want them kicking you out, do you?" Natalie asked Stephanie.

"No, I was hoping I could name-drop my way through this."

Natalie rolled her eyes. Stephanie obeyed her friend, even though she believed her way worked fine. After all, she'd been talking her way into places since she was sixteen years old. Once, she talked her way into a rapper's hotel room. He thought she was cute, but his road manager thought she was trouble and quickly escorted her out of the room before the rapper caught a case. It could have been worse; security could have dumped her out on her head. Although she didn't get the full reception she wanted, that incident gave Stephanie complete confidence in her ability to get next to whomever she chose. She believed this night would be no different.

Outside the stadium, the security team ran Guard Tour Wands over people before allowing them to file into the stadium. It was a good thing they did check for weapons, because the crowd became rowdy when they realized they had to wait another forty-five minutes for the show to start. But when the deejay finally jumped on the microphone and played music, they cheered and all was forgiven.

Stephanie stayed far from the ruckus. While Natalie tended to production issues, Stephanie walked around backstage, chatting with stage hands and dancers. When the show started, she was still talking, trying to sniff everybody out for potential gigs but, to her dismay, they acted like they only had gossip for her. Stephanie's senses told her they had more information but they likely feared she would take their jobs. They were probably right. She did look better than them.

After an hour of getting nowhere, she decided to take a break from her digging and stopped to enjoy the show. Suddenly, Natalie dashed to Stephanie's side huffing and puffing.

"What's wrong with you?" Stephanie asked.

"The lighting guy thinks he knows everything. Meanwhile, he's messing up everyone's set. Look! He's not even putting the spotlight in the right place." Natalie took a deep breath and exhaled quickly. "He is so fired."

Stephanie switched her attention to the male singer performing in front of them. His lights were a little off but the crowd of 10,000 people didn't seem to notice. They sang along with the performer word for word. The women swooned over his velvety notes and seductive movements. One fan, who looked about twenty-five years old, charged the front of the stage, screaming and reaching for the singer.

In response, he walked down the stage steps and took the fan's hand. While she giggled, he placed her hand up to his mouth and then moved it down his chest toward his lower region. The women within eyeshot squealed with anticipation and envy. The singer then sang one last, long note. He finished it off pulling the young woman's hand up to his lips, kissing it and letting it go. She almost fell to the floor as the audience erupted into cheers.

"Thank you. I love y'all," the singing Don Juan said, walking off the stage.

Who exactly is this dude? Stephanie thought. He walked in her direction, where she could see him clearly. All 5'11" of him.

"Hey, Levin!" Natalie shouted to the singer who grabbed a towel to wipe his face.

"Hey, baby. What's up?" Levin's speaking voice was as rich and smooth as his singing voice. Stephanie's spine tingled. Her pulse quickened as she searched her mind for the right thing to say to him.

"Ah, you know. Everything is everything. Oh, I want you to meet my girl, Stephanie. Stephanie, this is Levin."

"Hey. How you doin'?" Levin turned to Stephanie and flashed a dimpled smile. A feverish heat rushed to Stephanie's face.

"I'm good," Stephanie said, toying with the pass around her neck. "I see you're doin' your thing out there."

"Well, it's all in a day's work." He smiled again.

Just then someone bumped Natalie from behind.

"Hey!" Natalie yelled.

The young man slowly turned around to find the angry voice he heard. "Oh, my bad, shorty. I didn't see you there."

He looked over and spotted Stephanie talking to Levin.

"Hey!" the stranger said, raising his eyebrows.

At the sound of his voice, Stephanie felt queasy. She almost doubled over before finding Natalie's shoulder to balance herself. Of all the places for her to run into Jimmy, her music producer ex-boyfriend, she had to run into him here. It had been four months since they broke up and it was the ugliest four months of her life. So far, he'd followed her around. He'd sent other people to follow her around. He even repossessed the Mercedes-Benz he bought her for Christmas. She still had nightmares about sprinting down the street screaming at the tow truck driver.

"Hey," Stephanie said in a small voice she didn't even recognize. She stared at the floor to avoid the smug look on Jimmy's face.

"Aww. Is that the way you greet the man who took care of you for two years?" Jimmy asked. The nearby stage crew and dancers turned around to stare at them. Jimmy's face conveyed calm geniality but his tone revealed a hint of his lingering resentment—the type of resentment that could keep someone up at night thinking about revenge.

Stephanie widened her eyes in embarrassment and looked over at her present company. Natalie's mouth had dropped open, while Levin began backing away.

"Listen. I have to go," Levin said to Natalie.

She nodded.

"Oh no, man! You don't have to leave on my account. Stay. Hey, I'm sorry I interrupted your rap." Jimmy walked up to Levin and patted him on the back.

Levin nodded, obviously confused.

"Just remember one thing, man." Jimmy paused and nodded over his shoulder at Stephanie. "She is not worth it."

Horrified, Stephanie couldn't believe what she was hearing. She pulled the backstage pass from her neck and threw it at Jimmy.

"Who do you think you are?" Stephanie yelled.

As Stephanie tried to lunge at Jimmy, Natalie placed her hands on Stephanie's shoulders, attempting to hold her back. Stephanie's breath became rapid and shallow. She balled her hands into fists to keep them from shaking. Pressing her lips together and looking up, she hoped to stop the avalanche of tears threatening to come down her face. Jimmy walked away, laughing.

"Uh, excuse me, ladies. I really must leave. It was good to have met you," Levin said, nodding to Stephanie. "Later, Natalie." He parted planting a light peck on Natalie's cheek.

After he left, Natalie sighed. "Girl, are you okay?"

Stephanie shook her head and covered her face.

"Aww. What a jerk! I know you're not in the mood to go to the after party tonight. So, Why don't you go home, get some rest and I'll call you later?" Natalie said, as she hugged her friend.

Stephanie nodded and turned to leave, passing people who'd just witnessed the spectacle between her and Jimmy. Many of them were the same jealous gossips who wouldn't tell her about up-coming video shoots. A few of the observers openly gawked at her as she walked by; others turned the other way, pretending they hadn't heard anything.

As her heavy feet beat the floor, she found herself wondering how Jimmy could do this to her. Break-ups were never easy, but he made theirs impossible. She was sick of him bad-mouthing her to anyone who would listen. She wouldn't be surprised if the gossips had talked to him first, but all she could do was hope people didn't take his slander to heart, especially professional and personal prospects. The only silver lining in the situation was her faith. She still believed she would find the man for her in this industry. Just because their relationship didn't work out didn't mean she should give up. Stephanie still had dreams of living in a big, beautiful mansion with a wealthy entertainer husband. And nothing, not even Jimmy, could change that.

It wasn't her fault she deserved the best and it certainly wasn't her fault Jimmy didn't have enough money to give it to her. Maybe if he spent as much time getting to know people as he did spreading lies about her, more artists would seek him out for music and he'd have more money, kind of like Levin.

Levin. He seemed really nice and he was cute. He had

the most gorgeous dimples. She would've liked to have seen him again, but she could tell by the look on his face as he walked away that he wasn't interested. She wished he hadn't seen all that drama. Now, she could only imagine what he thought of her. As she trudged down the long hall toward the side door, Stephanie took another shallow breath but promised herself she would not cry until she left the building. This way, she wouldn't have any more witnesses.

∞

A couple days later, Stephanie still had trouble pushing the night at Jam Fest out of her mind. She regretted so many things about that night. For one, she regretted allowing Jimmy to talk her down but she also regretted failing to get more professional contacts. Stephanie couldn't believe she didn't find one person that knew anything about upcoming video gigs. The lack of contacts meant she had to turn her attention to looking for auditions, which irked her but she had no choice. Her agent was too busy riding his new pony—upcoming video girl, Alexis—to focus on finding her work. Stephanie didn't see the big deal about her. She was taller but Stephanie had the curves. That alone should have kept her as the priority.

If the situation with her agent didn't get better soon, she would have to look for another agent. In the meantime, she'd heard about a local audition at the mall and decided to check it out. She doubted anybody with real connections would be there, but at this point, she couldn't afford to pass it up. She was going to need more money soon. *I'd rather be home watching Maury Povich.* She pouted.

Before she could grab her purse and walk out of the door, her phone rang.

"Hello?"

"Hey, girl. How you feelin'?" Natalie exploded onto the phone.

Stephanie rolled her eyes as she contemplated a conversation with Natalie. She did not feel like rehashing her humiliation from Jam Fest and she knew that was exactly what her friend wanted to do. As it stood, it took everything for her to push it out of her mind so she could participate in the audition. Stephanie was ready to forget the night ever happened. She preferred to rush her friend off the phone before she could get started on the incident.

"Oh, great. As a matter of fact, I'm on my way to an audition," Stephanie said in a hurried tone.

"Oh. Cool. I didn't know they had one today," Natalie said.

"Yeah, at the mall. I'm running late. So, I need to leave now. Did you want something in particular?" Stephanie clipped her words even more for effect.

"Yeah. I wanted to say you made a big impression on ya boy the other night."

"What boy?"

"Levin!" Natalie shouted.

"I made a big impression? Don't you mean I made the wrong impression?" Stephanie frowned.

"No. I talked to him yesterday and he was all about you."

Stephanie's ears perked up but she refused to reveal her interest in Levin. Sometimes, Natalie jumped to conclusions, and Stephanie did not want to look like a fool because Natalie misunderstood him. She sucked her teeth. "Girl, I'm not interested in him."

"Yes, you are! I saw you two flirting," Natalie said.

"Was not."

"Was, too."

"I was not flirting. I was being friendly. I'm not interested," Stephanie lied.

"But don't you wanna know what he said? He asked a lot of questions about you."

"Like what?" Stephanie asked.

"How do I know you? Are you from here? Do you have a man? Blah, blah, blah," Natalie said.

"What did you tell him?"

"I told him we met through friends. You're from California and you really like women." Natalie laughed.

"What?! Girl, don't play like that."

"Not for real," Natalie said, still chuckling. "I'm joking. He said he wanted me to give you his number so you could call him. I'm simply doing what I said I would do. I think you should call," Natalie said.

Stephanie twisted the left corner of her mouth in deep thought. She wondered why he would want to talk to her after the spectacle. Maybe he liked her. Maybe he pitied her. Or maybe he thought she'd be an easy woman to play, since she was vulnerable and all. Either way, she couldn't see herself facing him again.

"I don't want it," Stephanie said, shaking her head.

"What? Are you kidding?"

"No. Tell him I'm not interested." Stephanie bit her thumbnail.

"Didn't you say you wanted to make some contacts? But now, you're turning one down? Are you crazy?" Natalie asked.

"I don't wanna talk to him. I don't ever want to talk to him after what happened."

Natalie sighed. "Yeah, that really sucked, Stephanie, but you can't let that bother you. Let that slide off your shoulder. Besides, I really don't think Levin even cares about that."

"I don't know. He kinda looks like trouble. You saw those girls falling all over him."

"Chile, every chick wants him. Take his number and think about it." Natalie ignored Stephanie's apprehension. "If I were you, I'd be all over that. I heard he's good, if you know what I mean." Natalie burst into laughter.

Stephanie rolled her eyes. "Bye, Natalie."

CHAPTER 3

Dee

D ee sped eighty-five miles per hour down Gulf Boulevard, switching lanes in between cars. She peeped through the rearview mirror every two minutes to look for a police car. She had a radar detector on her dashboard to warn her of their presence but somehow she always managed to miss them. That is until they were behind her, blaring their sirens and flashing their red and blue lights. Dee already had five unpaid tickets buried under her car manual in the glove compartment. She didn't need any more.

Right as she was about to outrun the Ferrari ahead, her phone rang.

"Agh!" Dee jumped, nearly losing her grip on the steering wheel. She pressed the button on her Bluetooth.

"What?!"

"Hey, Dee," Monica sang into the phone. "Listen. I know you're busy but I was thinking. It would do you some good to give back."

"To who?" Dee asked.

"Me!" Monica said.

"I don't have time for this right now," Dee said.

"Why? What's your problem?"

"I'm running late for my fitting with Tasha and that's a no-no. You know how my clients are." Dee thought back to her former client who hired a new stylist, after Dee arrived five minutes late. That was the part of her job she hated the most. People with a ton of money felt like they should never have to wait for anything. Yet, they didn't mind making you wait—for a phone call, for an answer, or for a check. They were such hypocrites. The more she thought about it, the more she wanted to stop everything she was doing and get her magazine going today.

"Okay. Then say yes and I'll call you later with more details," Monica pressed.

"You know what…" Dee paused as she stretched her neck to look around the slowpoke in front of her.

"Out of all of us, you've lived in the Tampa Bay area the longest and your vendor list is much bigger than mine. You could make this process much easier for me," Monica said.

"Why don't I give you a list of people I know that could help you? Why do I have to do the work?" Dee asked.

"Because you're supposed to be my friend," Monica said.

"What does that have to do with anything?"

Monica sighed.

A truck driver honked at Dee as she dodged him.

"I really have to go," Dee rushed off the phone.

After Dee finished risking her life on the road, she arrived to Tasha's estate twenty-five minutes late and agitated. If she hadn't been arguing with Monica, she might have been at least ten minutes earlier. It's hard to dart through traffic when you're on the phone. As she pulled up the driveway, she thought about her excuse, barely noticing the blue-gray BMW beside her car. Dee usually didn't apologize but, this time, she had to make an exception. This was one of her easier clients, and she didn't want to risk losing the relationship or the money. She conceded as soon as she walked through the double doors.

"Tasha, I am so sorry. I thought I had everything I needed for you but I realized one of the outfits was missing." She turned around and spotted Roco, Tasha's younger brother, walking out of the kitchen.

Well, well. The answer to my prayers. Dee knew Roco had a thing for her. He didn't have a chance with her but she saw him as the key to retaining her client.

She laid the clothes down. "Hi, Roco. Well, don't you look handsome today? I'll bet the chicks be calling, huh, playa?" Dee asked, sticking her right hip out and placing her hand on it.

"Well, you know, I do all right with the ladies but you know I'd be even better with you." Roco shot her a crooked smile.

"Honey, everybody gets better with me. Just wait 'til you see what I brought your sister to wear to the charity event."

Tasha, a model and singer, frequented charity events and award shows to network and get her demo into somebody's—anybody's—hands. Music was not her calling, but that didn't stop her. Instead, she employed her arresting beauty to make the right connections at the right time. Occasionally, she played her tone-impaired songs for Dee and, ever the professional that she was, Dee would find something positive to say. All the while, she would tell Stephanie and Monica her true opinion. "Like listening to dogs cry, girl."

At the sound of Tasha's footsteps, Dee turned to greet her and found a tall, dark-skinned gentleman striding into the room with her.

Dee clutched her pearls. "Oh, I didn't know you had company," she said to Tasha.

The well-dressed visitor studied Dee as she returned the gesture.

"Yeah. Deidre? Let me introduce you. This is my financial manager, Dwayne Shoreshire. Dwayne, I'd like you to meet my personal stylist, Deidre Wright."

"It's a pleasure to meet you, Deidre." Dwayne's deep, articulate voice echoed through the hallway.

Financial manager. I wonder if he can help me get capital for my magazine, Dee thought. "Please, call me Dee." She reached out her hand, smiling.

Tasha's brother noticed the chemistry between the two of them and decided to interrupt it. "Is that the best he's got? I got more game than that." He cracked up laughing like a kid expecting others to join in.

"Roco, don't you have something to do?" Tasha chastised him.

Tasha pulled Roco down the hall. *Thank you. I thought*

he'd never leave, Dee thought. She returned her attention back to Dwayne. "So, financial manager? How long have you been working with Tasha?"

"She's been my client for the past year but I've been doing this for ten years," Dwayne said.

"Wow. You have a passion for numbers?"

"Among other things. I actually got into this accidentally. My brother used to play for the Houston Texans. He needed someone to handle his money. I did it. Not bad for a then-recent college graduate."

"Oh, okay. What a lucky break," Dee said.

"Eh. I don't believe in luck. Only hard work."

Interesting, Dee thought, while she nodded. "Well, my friend's husband plays for the Buccaneers and I think those guys need to always keep a financial advisor and a lawyer on speed dial."

Dwayne laughed. "You're right."

"So, how did you do?" Dee asked.

Dwayne stopped laughing and cocked his head to the side. "What do you mean?"

"With your brother? How well did you handle his money?"

She peered at Dwayne and he frowned. "Just fine. I would say."

"Yeah, but what do you mean by 'fine'? Does he own real estate? Does he own a yacht? Is he part owner in the Houston Texans?" Dee asked. She fired off questions one after the other, without paying attention to Dwayne's growing discomfort with the conversation's direction. It wasn't that she didn't care; she really wanted to figure out his level of expertise. Was he a flunky who lived off his brother? Or did he actually help his brother amass a bigger fortune?

She had to know because she didn't want to waste her time. The last man she dated, Mark, told her he was a successful businessman. He told her he owned a 15,000-square-foot vacation home in Jamaica and three cars worth $250,000. As it turned out, his vacation home was a two-bedroom apartment in a lowly part of Orlando. And those three cars were a 1998 Honda Accord, an old, rusted-out Chevy, and a Ford. Every time she thought about Mark, it surprised her that she actually believed his lies. She thought she'd seen it all, heard it all, and could smell the stench of bull from a mile away, but, for some reason, she didn't see Mark coming.

To tell the truth, that still bothered her. It changed her forever. She hated that someone could take advantage of her time and energy without offering her anything in return. She decided that would be the last time a liar would come into her life and turn it upside down. The next man must be legit, honest and stacked. For real stacked. No brand-new money. No "I just got this money yesterday in a lottery" money. More like "I've been stacking this money so long it's starting to collect dust" money. She wanted the security and the financial push to finally bring her magazine to life. That meant Dwayne had to get the third degree.

Dwayne straightened his back and scowled. "I don't

discuss my clients' financial portfolio with others. However, if you would like a consultation," he reached into his jacket pocket and pulled out a crisp business card, "You can give me a call."

Dee grabbed the card and read.

Dwayne looked out the window and inched toward the door. "I must be going now. It was good to meet you," Dwayne said, nodding his head and leaving the room before Dee could ask anything else.

Dee stood there, twirling the card between her fingers, while watching him pull out of the driveway. Something about Dwayne intrigued her. Between his expensive suits, polished manners and refined speech, Dee knew he wasn't an ordinary man. He had too much dignity and pride to be a loser, unlike Mark, and he was too educated to be anything less than professional. Even though her questions must have annoyed him, Dwayne made sure he gave her his card before he left. *Business first. I have to call this one*, Dee thought putting his card in her purse.

∞

The next night, Stephanie and Monica sorted through the food platter. Cheese, crackers, fruit, chocolate and wine—the usual spread across Dee's dining room table. The women often congregated Thursday nights to talk about their week, their plans and their problems. But, this night, excitement hung in the air. Dee had found a new man and the ladies demanded details. After Monica and Stephanie settled into the living room, Monica decided Dee should spill it.

"Uh, Ms. Thang. I need you to come on out here and start talking!" Monica yelled.

"Yeah, I feel like I'm watching a bad movie, where the trailer built me up and then let me down," Stephanie chimed in.

"I'm coming. I'm coming." Dee emerged from the kitchen. "Where do you want me to start?"

"From the top. Who is this guy? What is he like?" Stephanie said. She poured a glass of wine and sat on the couch next to Dee.

"Well, his name is Dwayne and he is absolutely delicious. He's suave and distinguished," Dee gushed.

"You don't mean he's snobbish, do you?" Stephanie asked, scrunching her face.

"No, just really smart and confident. Best of all, I think he might be the answer to my magazine dreams."

"You think he has the money?" Monica asked.

"No. Not all of it, but I found his website. It says he works with models, athletes and other business people. They might be interested in investing. I have a business plan. All I need is a couple of really good, solid investors. I think he can help me with that. There's just one problem," Dee said, taking a sip of her wine. "He hates me."

"What?" Stephanie and Monica asked in unison.

"He doesn't exactly hate me. You see, I teed him off a little bit in our first meeting."

"As usual," Monica said, picking up a strawberry from her plate.

"It's not that bad. I asked him some questions and I think he took them the wrong way but that's okay. I'm gonna call him and schedule an appointment to meet with him."

"And you're sure he'll want to talk with you after you've pissed him off?" Monica asked.

"Yes. I'm still not sure he's going to be open with me about his contacts but I'm up for the challenge."

"So, are you using him or do you really like him?" Stephanie asked Dee.

Dee paused to think back to the day she'd met him at Tasha's house. She instantly recalled his tailored black suit and tie, clean-shaven face and neatly trimmed hair. He looked like he visited the barber every week. She appreciated his impeccable style and attention to detail. She also sensed great drive and determination from him, qualities that were sorely missing in some of her previous men. Qualities that she was about to give up on—until now. In many ways, she felt like she'd met her match. Dee wasn't pining away for Dwayne but, when she stared into his face, she couldn't help feeling like he was the male version of her.

"Both," Dee said.

"Are you sure?" Monica asked.

"Yeah, 'cuz he's the perfect complement to me. He's ambitious and he takes care of himself. I do like that.

Ultimately, I want the best of both worlds," Dee said.

"I don't think that's possible. In my experience, you either get love or money, not both," Stephanie said, frowning.

"Oh, I don't know. I knew Tony and I would make a lot of money but I can still say I love him," Monica said.

"Yeah. But would you have loved him, if he didn't have any money?" Dee asked, leaning forward.

"I might have loved him but I wouldn't have wasted my time marrying him," Monica said.

"Some love," Dee said.

Stephanie laughed.

"You know why?" Monica added. "Because from the beginning Tony had everything he needed to succeed. He had scouts coming to the campus to see him. He even had me marketing him to teams and media. So, if he didn't become successful, it would have been because he wasn't trying. And I would never want a man like that."

"I've never heard of that before. How did you market him?" Stephanie asked.

"I got to know the media, sent them information on him—pictures and stats. How do you think footage of Tony in college and high school got to the media?"

Dee raised her eyebrows. She never thought about the kind of monetary effect a woman could have on a man. Getting what a man already had was more natural to her. Helping a man make something of himself seemed like too much work to Dee, but she guessed she understood why Monica might have done it. They were in college and she wanted to support him. Dee, on the other hand, was not a college kid. There was no way she planned to help carry a grown man to greatness. He should either already be there or have the drive to do it on his own. Besides, if she could rely on him, there was less chance he would use her for money or anything else.

"Well, I don't need to contribute to anyone else's success. I need someone to contribute to mine," Dee said.

"Dee, I know you say you want to date this man *and* get his help, but are you sure you don't just want some money from him?" Monica asked.

"No, I like him. I just have my priorities straight," Dee said.

"Still, you should be careful about using him," Monica said.

"So, I shouldn't meet with him?" Dee asked. Sometimes she tired of Monica's self-righteous, upstanding attitude. It was easy for her to tell somebody not to use a man. She had a husband at home to use.

"No, I'm saying be careful," Monica said firmly.

"Whatever." Dee rolled her eyes and faced Stephanie.

"You're asking about me. How was Jam Fest? Did you meet any new victims?" Dee cheesed. Stephanie grimaced.

"Very funny. No, I didn't. I *did* meet that singer Levin."

"Oh, I heard he's about to blow up," Monica said.

"Yeah, he's okay. He gave me his number but I have no intention of calling him," Stephanie blurted out.

"Calling him? He really gave you his number?" Monica asked.

"Yeah, he gave it to me through Natalie. I don't know why." Stephanie shrugged.

"Uh…'Cuz he wanted to talk to you," Dee said, looking at Monica and shrugging.

"I know that, but there was a little incident with Jimmy at the show. And he started all this drama saying that he took care of me for two years and that I'm not worth it."

"He was there? Ugh! In a minute, you're gonna need a restraining order," Dee said.

"I know. He said this in front of everybody, including Levin, and I don't know if I should call," Stephanie said, shaking her head and staring at the table.

Dee sucked her teeth. "Oh, girl. I wouldn't worry about that. Levin's an entertainer. They're used to drama. It's called publicity. Right, Monica?" Dee asked.

"That's right," Monica said.

"You said you wanted a contact for a video gig, right?" Dee asked.

Stephanie nodded.

"Well, there you go. Focus on that. Forget Jimmy! It's time for him to get over you. Just make sure Levin doesn't use you," Dee said.

"And I hope you make sure Mr. Dwayne isn't using you. Don't forget about that Mark character," Monica chimed in.

"Girl, please. You've forgotten who you're talking to. Give me a couple of weeks. I'll have Dwayne wrapped around my finger."

CHAPTER 4

Monica

Monica's Tuesday morning started off rocky. First, her six-year-old son, William, didn't want to wake up. Then, she went through his book bag and found a math quiz with a D at the top. She didn't even know he'd taken a quiz. If that wasn't enough, Angela wanted to argue with Monica about the outfit she'd chosen for school. In Monica's opinion, eleven-year-olds should not wear blouses with their tummies out. No matter how many times she told Angela this, they still argued about it every single week. It was as if the child thought she would wear her mother down. There wasn't a chance, but Monica had other issues with Angela. In addition to the typical preteen problems, Angela hadn't adjusted to life in Tampa very well. Monica initially thought things would change after they moved and her little girl would make new friends. She did make new friends; however, she still resented uprooting and leaving the old ones. Instead of overcoming her sadness about leaving friends behind, she became moodier, even though two years had passed since their move from St. Louis. Monica couldn't understand why Angela hadn't gotten over it. Tony thought it was a phase. Monica wasn't so sure. She was sure about one thing: she would not let this girl run her crazy. If push came to shove, she'd ship Angela off to boarding school.

By breakfast time, the morning seemed to return back to normal. Angela was dressed in the clothes Monica approved and sitting at the kitchen table. She appeared peaceful but time had taught Monica this was likely the calm before the storm. For that reason, she kept one eye on Angela. Marianna, the Hatchers' cook and nanny, placed a plate of hot pancakes on the table in front of Angela. The butter was melting quickly, running off the sides of the cakes. Angela picked up the syrup to finish drowning them.

Monica leaned over and grabbed Angela's hand before she could shove a bite in her mouth. "Thank you, Ms. Marianna," Monica said to Angela.

The girl sighed. "Thank you, Ms. Marianna," Angela mumbled.

Marianna patted Angela on the head and left the kitchen. Monica released her hand. She glanced at the kitchen clock and noticed William still hadn't come downstairs. *He'd better not be asleep*, Monica thought.

"William, come down here right now!" Monica shouted.

Within a few minutes, the little boy raced into the room. He stood beside his mother, breathing hard and shaking.

"What's wrong with you?" Monica asked him.

William pointed at Angela. "She took my Spiderman."

Monica turned to her daughter, who hadn't missed a bite of her pancake. "Do you have his toy?"

Angela didn't say a word.

Monica counted to five silently. In addition to giving Angela a chance to respond, she also wanted to give herself a chance to calm down and resist the urge to snatch her daughter out of her seat. "Angela, you better answer me when I'm talking to you."

"No, I don't have it," Angela said, looking at her plate.

"Yes, she does!" William yelled.

"How do you know?" Monica asked.

"'Cuz she's always taking my stuff and hiding it. She's always being mean to me." William's eyes watered and his lip quivered.

"I'm gonna ask you one more time and you'd better not be lying. Do you have his Spiderman?" Monica asked. This time she had much more force in her tone.

"Look, Mama! It's in her pocket. See?" William pointed to the girl's jacket pocket.

Angela squinted at William.

"Empty your pockets," Monica said to Angela. "Now!"

Angela threw her fork on her plate and shoved her hands in her pockets. She pulled William's Spiderman figure out of her right pocket. At the sight of his favorite toy, the little boy lunged over his mother to grab it. Angela waved it back and forth, keeping him from grasping it.

"Give it back," William whined. "Stop!"

"Hey. Hey! Cut that out," Monica scolded. "Angela, give him his Spiderman back!"

Angela finally returned the toy to her brother. When he snatched it back, she sucked her teeth and rolled her eyes.

"You keep rolling your eyes, little girl. I'mma slap 'em right out of your head, you hear me?"

"Why do you always take William's side? He stole my hair brush and he threw his truck at me," Angela said.

"Because knowing you, you probably instigated it," Monica said.

"So, it's my fault?" Angela yelled.

"You need to watch your tone with me, young lady!" Monica yelled back.

Angela fell back in her chair and poked her lip out.

"I am still your mother," Monica said. Before she could lay into Angela further, Marianna walked back into the kitchen with mail.

"This came for you yesterday. I think you missed it," she said.

"Oh, thanks, Marianna." Monica grabbed the letter but looked at Angela first. "I'm not finished with you."

Angela played with her pancakes to avoid her mother's intense gaze.

When Monica opened the envelope, she found a letter from her bank stating one of her checks had bounced and they'd covered it with overdraft services. The check was written for her scholarship dinner. She needed to place a deposit on the venue to hold it. When she finished reading the letter, her mouth dropped. She'd never had this happen before. She searched her brain for the charges she'd made all month. There were the clothes: $58,307.87 for William, $62,090.16 for Angela. She'd bought herself a couple pairs of shoes for $1,594. Then there were ordinary household expenses: $2,000 for landscaping, $4,166 for house staff and $15,000 to redecorate their home office. Nothing should have caused a check to bounce.

Monica's brow furrowed as she continued to stare at the letter in a daze. When Tony opened the back door, she snapped out of it long enough to see her husband trudge into the kitchen. The kids jumped from the table and ran toward him, talking at once, but Tony passed them without looking down. Monica frowned and rushed over to run interference. "Go back and finish your breakfast," she directed them.

Tony walked upstairs, oblivious to his family. The silent treatment was highly uncharacteristic for Tony, especially when it came to the children. He always had time for them and if he didn't have time for them, he always tried to make time for them. Never did he blatantly ignore them. After Monica sat the children back down, she decided this was something she needed to nip in the bud right away. She left the kitchen and followed Tony upstairs to talk to him. She found him in their room, peeling his clothes off to start a shower.

Monica sat down on her vanity bench. "You do know your children have feelings, right?" she asked.

"Huh?" Tony asked, raising his eyebrow.

"I said you do know your children have feelings, right? They rushed to talk to you and you pushed them aside like they weren't even there."

"Oh, I wasn't paying attention." Tony sighed. "I'll talk to them later."

Monica stared at him. "What's going on?"

Tony shrugged. "Nothing."

"Okay. Then, how's everything going with the team?" she asked.

He squinted his eyes and shot her an ice-cold look. "You know how things are going," he snapped. "They cheated me out of my money and they don't think they did anything wrong. I know I'm worth at least another two million. Now I have to train twice as hard to prove to them I can help them make it to the playoffs."

Since negotiating his latest contract the previous week, he moped around the house, sometimes complaining to anyone who listened. He had to, because after a while his own agent stopped listening to him. A person could only listen to him talk about how many passes he'd caught, how many yards he'd run and how much of a deep threat he was for so long. To hear him tell it his $8 million contract was an insult. Its provisions and bonuses were merely a smokescreen for the fact they didn't intend to pay the money he felt he deserved.

"Have you considered talking to the front office? Better yet, try inviting the decision-makers out for drinks."

Tony grimaced. "You don't invite the owner of the team out for drinks, Monica."

She blinked. "I think anyone would be open to the prospect of a good cocktail or Jack Daniel's. People let their guard down when they have a few in them."

"That's not going to work." He stared at the floor.

"Well, there must be a solution. With all you've done and all you're doing, I know something can be worked out."

He shook his head and continued to undress. "I guess we'll have to wait and see," he responded.

"In the meantime, I think we should cut back on spending in this house. Just until we see exactly where this is going," Monica suggested. The letter from the bank was still fresh on her mind. She considered asking him about it because she really did want to figure out what was happening, but changed her mind. He was already irritable. It would only add fuel to his fire.

Tony rolled his eyes when she mentioned cutting back.

"What?" she asked him.

"Monica, I work hard to get what I have. Don't tell me how to spend my money."

"I'm not telling you how. I want to be cautious for a little while. That's all. Cut back on some things."

"Things like what?"

"Like a diamond-encrusted headboard," Monica said, pointing behind her. Every time she glanced over at that thing, she swore he was crazy. "Listen. It's time you change your thinking. The unfortunate truth is your days in the NFL are numbered. You have to start plotting your next move. What are you gonna do when teams begin looking to move you out for the next young big shot?"

Tony slumped down on the bed. For the first time, he appeared to be giving his post-football future some thought, and he didn't look happy. Monica knew he preferred to postpone planning for the future, but they had to think about it so they could plan together. She had already considered the opportunities, like maybe he could take a sportscasting gig. Get people used to seeing him on TV and parlay his popularity and charisma into a show. Or they could start a business. She'd always wanted to manage her own business, with or without Tony. Monica relished the notion of using her marketing and public relations skills professionally. Maybe it would even prevent them from bouncing checks.

She looked over at her husband's slouched shoulders and long face. She hadn't revealed her wishes to him yet, but she started thinking it might be a good time to test the waters.

"I've talked to a few people who need PR help. With my skills, I could always start a business in it and do really well," Monica said.

Tony jerked his head back toward her. "Why would you do that?"

"Because I'm good at it and I can bring in money."

"I already bring in money," Tony said.

"Yeah but we could bring in more money with both of us working."

"So, what are you saying? That I can't afford to take care of you and the kids?" Tony jumped up.

Monica's eyes widened. "No! I'm saying it's time to look at what we're going to do next. The NFL doesn't last forever. It will end."

"That's not gonna happen anytime soon. They can't afford to get rid of me right now. You don't have anything to worry about it. So we don't even have to consider you starting a business. You don't need to." Tony grabbed his clothes and stomped into the bathroom.

Monica sighed. Even though she should have known he'd disapprove, she couldn't help feeling a little disappointed. She wanted their marriage to evolve into a union where they could grow together in a direction that benefited them both. After eight years of marriage, Tony still had this archaic caveman perspective on their union. He believed he was the king of the jungle and he should be the sole provider. He prided himself on bragging to others about what he did for Monica or what he bought the kids. She didn't have a problem with that. She even expected him to be the capable provider in the family, but she grew restless. Monica wanted to start realizing her own potential, like he was realizing his on the football field. She saw herself contributing much more, not only to the finances in the household, but to the world in general. She didn't know how to move them forward, but she believed that she needed to figure it out soon. It was vital to the health of their marriage.

Shaking off her concerns, Monica stood up, gave herself a once over in the mirror, and trotted downstairs in time to take the kids to school. When she thought of all the errands she had to run she picked up her pace. She also had to meet her new temporary, part-time assistant, Melissa. Since Dee and Stephanie had dodged her requests for help, she'd contacted a staffing agency for qualified candidates. She couldn't wait to unload some of this work on a new capable assistant.

"All right, kids. Let's go," Monica ordered William and Angela. They seized their backpacks and beat her to the car. Monica took the school drive time to chat with them about their classes and their friends. She even laughed at a few of their knock-knock jokes. The laughter between them made her feel better about her issues with Tony, as well as her earlier problems with them that morning. It restored her faith that everything would work out.

When she reached their school, Monica pulled up to the curb to let the kids out. "Marianna will pick you guys up from school today. Okay?" Monica asked.

"Okay," the kids said in unison.

Angela opened the car door and tumbled out. Before William followed, he leaned forward.

"Mama? Is Daddy mad at us?" William asked.

Monica frowned and faced her son. "No. Why would you ask a thing like that?"

"Because he doesn't notice me anymore," William said. Monica reached out to touch her son's face.

"Your father is very concerned about doing the right thing for you guys, but I can guarantee you he is not mad at you. Okay?" Monica asked.

William cocked his head to the side to contemplate his mother's words. He shrugged. "Okay."

Monica hugged William and he hopped out of the car. She watched him run into the school. Tonight, she planned to remind Tony to apologize to the kids for his behavior, in case he forgot. The more she thought about their situation, the more she believed she should start bringing her own money into the house. Maybe then Tony would worry less about his contract and more about the kids. Shaking her head, she switched gears and drove home to meet her new assistant.

CHAPTER 5

Stephanie

Stephanie stood on her balcony, overlooking the Atlantic Ocean. Night had set in and the soft sound of the waves beating against each other almost lulled her to sleep. But Stephanie couldn't allow it. She kept thinking about—and staring at—the piece of paper with Levin's phone number on it. She'd told Natalie she wasn't interested in Levin and didn't plan to call him, but she couldn't bring herself to throw away his number. *He must be interested in me, if he went through the trouble of sending me his number,* Stephanie told herself. Yet, she still hesitated about giving him a call.

That night, she pretended to watch TV while going back and forth on her decision to call him. Stephanie would pick up the phone, question her motives, and put the phone down. She'd pick it up again, think it was too late at night and she'd put it back down again. Each time she picked up the phone, she thought about the warm feeling that consumed her when she first saw Levin smile. Every time she placed the phone down, she thought about the Jam Fest drama and the women after him.

Once she moved to the balcony, Stephanie finally broke

down and called Levin. The phone rang five times. She was about to hang up, when Levin answered. At first she could barely hear him because there was a lot of music and talking in the background. She thought she even heard slurping.

"Hello?" Levin said, trying to elevate his voice over the noise.

"Hi, Levin. It's Stephanie from the Jam Fest."

"Who?"

Stephanie's pulse raced. She hadn't thought about the chance he wouldn't remember her. It had only been a week and a half since they'd met, but, for him, that was probably more like a year and a half. He met so many women in so many cities. How could she expect him to remember her? He only talked to her for a few minutes. *I knew I shouldn't have called*, she thought.

"It's Stephanie. Natalie gave me your number and…"

"Oh! Stephanie! Yeah, yeah. I'm glad you called. Hold on."

When Levin asked her to hold, she could hear the noise on his end slowly fade. Then she heard a door close. She couldn't help wondering what was on the other end of the door. She hoped it wasn't a woman but she had to close the door on that thought once Levin returned to the phone.

"Okay. I'm back. How's it goin'?" Levin asked in the smooth-as-silk voice she'd heard the night of Jam Fest.

"It's good. Did I catch you at a bad time?" Stephanie asked. "I can talk to you another day."

"Oh, no! I was just thinking about asking everyone to leave." He laughed. "No, I'm really glad you called me."

For a second, that warm feeling returned to the center of Stephanie's body. She'd heard many lines but something about the way he delivered his made her believe it. She felt like he was really happy to hear from her.

"Yeah, I'm sorry it took so long to call you. I have so much going on right now."

"I know. I was starting to think you didn't like me." Levin chuckled.

"No. You're cool. So, where are you now?" Stephanie asked, trying to change the subject.

"I'm in D.C. I had a performance earlier today and I'm due to make an appearance at a club tonight."

"Are you gonna sing?"

"Nah. I don't even wanna go," Levin said. "Just dropping in and dropping out. I was actually sitting here thinking about a way to get out of this appearance 'cuz I really don't feel like going nowhere tonight, but now I think I can make it."

"Why? You downed an energy drink or something?" Stephanie chuckled.

"No, but I did get an extra shot of energy. I guess you must've had something to do with that, huh?"

Stephanie covered her smile to keep him from hearing it through the phone. Then, she heard someone on his end open the door to say something to him.

"Listen, I have to go. I'm so glad you called me."

Stephanie's smile faded. *Is that it?* she thought. She

tried not to allow her disappointment to escape through the phone. "Oh, okay. Take care."

"Hey! Are you going to be in Tampa Saturday?" Levin asked.

"Yeah."

"Would it be okay if I swing by and take you out? Dinner? Maybe a movie?" Levin asked.

"Sure," Stephanie said as the smile returned to her face. This time she didn't cover it.

"Great! I'll call you when I get in town."

When Levin hung up, Stephanie leaned over the rail and sighed. She'd conquered her fears. She called him and now they were going out on a date. She was then able to give in to the waves and sleep. Stephanie walked back inside, turned off all the lights and crawled into bed, where she slept peacefully. But from the moment she woke up the next morning and throughout the rest of the week, Saturday couldn't come soon enough for Stephanie. She spent the next couple of days agonizing over the right things to say and the right outfit to wear on the date, sending her nerves into a frenzy. When Saturday night came, she stood in her full-length mirror, analyzing the short jean dress she'd chosen. She finished the outfit off with a pair of strappy silver heels. She thought about accessorizing with a long, silver necklace but decided her size Ds were the best accessory she could ever wear.

At 6:12 that evening, her doorbell rang. She ran to it but slowed down midway. He could probably hear the pace of her footsteps and she didn't want to run and seem too desperate. She reached the door and took a deep breath. Then, she opened it to reveal Levin in a pair of urban jeans, a black fitted T-shirt and a designer jacket. He looked like he was ready for the paparazzi to photograph him. She approved of his style and from the look on Levin's face, he approved of her choice as well.

"Hey!" Levin said with his eyes stretched wide to take Stephanie in.

"Hey! You made it," Stephanie said. She leaned in for a gentle hug.

"Of course, I did. Well, I would ask if you're ready but I know you are 'cuz there is nothing else you could possibly do to look any more beautiful than you already look," Levin said, holding Stephanie's arms out and looking her up and down.

Stephanie could feel herself blush. "Thank you. As a matter of fact, I am ready. Let's go."

He walked her down to the black limousine, where they rode to a restaurant for dinner. Their evening started off positive and stayed that way throughout dinner. He complimented her, telling her how shiny her hair looked, how much her skin glowed and how much her eyes sparkled. Levin stared deep into her eyes while she talked. The intensity of his stare made her feel like she was the only woman in the world. For awhile, Stephanie actually forgot about Jimmy and that travesty at Jam Fest. Levin didn't mention it and neither did she.

By 12:35, they were leaving the movie theater after

watching *300*. Levin had arranged for the limo driver to park down the street so they could have more time to walk and talk alone.

When they exited the neon-lit theater into the clear, cool night, Levin put his jacket around her shoulders without giving her a chance to shiver. Stephanie beamed.

"Did you like the movie?" Levin asked, walking beside her.

"I didn't like it that much. It was too long," Stephanie whined. "Gory."

"What? That movie was the bomb. It was ground-breaking. You ain't never seen a movie like that before," Levin said.

"I hope I never see one again either," Stephanie mumbled.

"Boooo," Levin said. They both laughed. "That's okay. I enjoyed seeing it with you anyway, even if it took you forever to call me."

Stephanie blushed. "I was going to call. I got busy with some things."

Levin raised his eyebrow. "Um-hmm."

"Really!" she said, laughing.

"Sure, I believe you," he said, staring straight forward.

"I did. But after what happened backstage at the show, I didn't know what to say." Stephanie stopped talking and hung her head. She didn't want him to see her concerned about this. Yet, she had to act like a big baby and bring it up. All she needed was a pacifier and a bib.

"Hey, don't worry about that. Some people become bitter when you have to leave 'em alone. You should never take that personally. I know I wouldn't," Levin said.

"Have you had to leave a lot of women alone?" Stephanie asked him.

"A few," Levin said with a coy expression on his face. "But I know if someone is not the person for you, then there's nothing you or they can do about it but move on."

Stephanie smiled a little. "Yeah, you're right. How can I make amends for not calling you right away? I know! How about we go to Busch Gardens next week?"

"Uh, I can't. I have to be in Virginia and Chicago next week."

"Oh, what about the week after that?"

"I have two TV appearances, two shows and a hosting job to do."

Stephanie frowned. "Well, dang. I guess I won't see you again."

"Aww, c'mon. I can't help it. I'm releasing my new CD. Promotion is always crazy," Levin said.

"So, this is your second one, huh?" Stephanie asked.

"Yeah, but I like this one better," Levin said, looking down.

"How come?"

"I have a feeling *Metamorphosis* is going to be my breakthrough CD. You know? I think this one is going to help me get more endorsements and movie roles," Levin said, gazing up at the sky with a dreamy look in his eyes.

"How do you know?" Stephanie asked.

"The feeling I had recording. The reaction people have when they hear it. It's unlike anything else I've created but people have to know it's out there. I have to promote. So one day, I'm in Los Angeles, the next day, I'm on a flight to New York." Levin held up his hands. "I know. It's murder on a relationship but I gotta do what I gotta do."

Stephanie's heart sank. She could tell she'd have difficulty keeping up with Levin. His hectic schedule overshadowed any hope of a real bond between them. If it weren't for phone calls and texts, she'd probably never hear from him. She was starting to wish she hadn't called him. What was the use of meeting up with him one time and getting her hopes up only to be let down?

Her shoulders drooped at the thought that she wouldn't get to know Levin better. Levin sensed her despondence and leaned over to whisper in her ear.

"But I have time this week. I'd like to spend more of it with you," he said. "Is that okay?"

Physically perking up, Stephanie gazed into Levin's brown eyes and handsome face. A solid relationship with Levin would be a long shot but right then, she didn't care. She felt safe, supported and accepted with him. *What the heck?* she thought.

Stephanie smiled wide. "Absolutely."

∞

"Hey! Just in time to help me with the party favors," Monica shouted to Stephanie from across the island in her kitchen. She stood, experimenting with different center-pieces, while Dee sat on a stool reading a fashion magazine.

Stephanie hadn't told Dee or Monica about her date with Levin. She wanted to make sure he came. She couldn't imagine running to her friends, all excited about their impending date, to have Levin stand her up. So, she waited for the first date to come and go before gushing about him to her friends. Now that they'd hit it off, Stephanie couldn't wait to tell them how well it went.

"Not quite. I can't stay too long. I just came by to give you the good news," Stephanie said.

"What good news?" Monica asked.

"I finally went out with Levin," she said with a mega-watt smile.

"Really? When?" Monica asked.

"Saturday."

"Well, how was Mr. Smooth?" Dee asked.

"He's actually very charming. I think I might stick around this one," Stephanie said.

Dee raised an eyebrow. "Um. I've heard that before."

"I think I mean it this time."

"Where did he take you?" Monica asked.

"Dinner and a movie."

"That's all?" Dee asked, scrunching her face.

"Dee! What do you expect? A trip to the moon?" Monica asked.

"No, but it's so common. Why not a play or opera? Something to separate her from the groupies he hangs out with," Dee asked.

"He doesn't hang out with groupies," Stephanie said.

Dee and Monica chuckled. "All entertainers do, Stephanie," Monica said, catching her breath.

Stephanie planted her hands on her hips. She'd heard a few stories about Levin's offstage antics. One story about him, a stripper and a nightclub bathroom would not go away, even though he denied it several times. Still, she wanted her friends' support, not ridicule. Instead, their laughter hurt her feelings. She knew they would do this.

"Yeah? Well, what if I said all athletes hang out with groupies?"

Dee stopped laughing and ducked behind her magazine. Monica straightened her back and addressed the comment. "I would say you are wrong. While athletes do have groupies, not all of them partake in that."

"You mean like Tony," Dee said, peeking from behind the magazine and batting her eyelashes. Monica threw a couple of orchids at her. Dee ducked and yelled.

"Uh, don't play. If thorns get in my weave, I know something," Dee said. Monica laughed.

Distracted, Stephanie plopped on a stool across from them. "We enjoy each other's company and I believe the relationship is off to a great start but there's one little problem," Stephanie said.

"What?" Monica asked.

"He has a strange schedule. It's going to be a challenge for us to spend time together," Stephanie said.

"Oh, you might as well get used to that. Music is a hard grind. They often have to be gone weeks at a time," Dee said.

"There's got to be a way to still make it work, right?" Stephanie furrowed her brow in concentration. She only half expected an answer from them.

"Well, when do you see him again?" Monica asked.

"Tonight. I'm gonna cook for him," Stephanie said, smiling.

"Whoa. You really do like him," Dee said.

"I believe he likes me, too. How do I keep him around?" Stephanie asked. She looked back and forth between Dee and Monica. This time, she did expect an answer.

Monica leaned on the kitchen island. "Try taking an interest in his hobbies, his plans, and his work. Maybe then, he'll see you as someone he can spend more time with."

About six hours later, Monica's advice echoed through Stephanie's mind as she stood in the kitchen of her condo in Pebbles Island. It was Levin's last night in town because he received a last-minute call to perform at an event. Since he had to leave early, she wanted to make sure she used this night to make a big impression. She had great food, a breathtaking view and a ton of questions written on her mental notepad. Her excitement grew as she peeked around the corner at him looking through her large, oceanfront window.

"I like your place. It's very cozy. And this view!" Levin paused staring at the water.

"Thanks. I'm glad you like it," Stephanie said, turning around. She didn't want him to see the self-satisfied look on her face. "Would you like a glass of wine or something?" Stephanie asked.

"Sure," he said.

Stephanie walked to her mini bar, grabbed some red wine and headed back to her kitchen for two glasses. As she poured, her eyes fell on the spread she'd created. She normally avoided cooking for her dates but she wanted to impress Levin and make up for not calling him sooner. So, she prepared black-eyed peas, yellow rice casserole, sweet potato casserole with a marshmallow topping, corn bread and meatloaf. Stephanie cooked like the man had to leave for war but she didn't mind. He might be worth it.

Stephanie stopped pouring the wine and searched her table for a place to put all the food. She almost feared she'd overdone it but Levin reassured her when they sat down at her dining room table. He devoured everything. Stephanie watched him tear into the meatloaf and swipe a second serving of yellow rice casserole. Amazed, she breathed a silent sigh of relief.

"How is it?" she asked.

"Umm. It's great, girl. Where did you learn to burn like this?" Levin asked between chews.

"Well," Stephanie reached for the wine and poured

more in his glass, "When I was a kid, every summer my parents would send me and my older sister to live with my grandparents for a month. Grandma Rose insisted that we learn how to cook. We had to clean greens, cut potatoes, literally mash potatoes," Stephanie described. "It sounds like a chore but I liked doing it and spending time with Grandmamma."

"Agh. You're a family woman. I like that. I'm a family man myself. I try to visit my mother once a month," Levin said.

"Yeah, I don't always visit but I talk to my mom almost every day." Stephanie put her elbows on the table and shook her head. "I owe her so much. I've put her through a lot."

"Really?" Levin asked.

She nodded. "I remember when I was twelve, I almost burned the whole kitchen down." Stephanie laughed.

"Uh-oh."

"Yeah, it was kinda bad but nobody told me you couldn't put out a fire with cooking oil."

Levin almost spit his food out. He grabbed a napkin to catch it, while muffling his laughter. Stephanie smiled. She liked his response to her simplistic brand of charm. It showed her that he was down-to-earth. She needed someone she could be real with and he seemed to be that person. She liked that about him.

He wiped his mouth. "Well, the important thing is you made it out safely." Levin gave her a gentle smile.

The dimples in his cheeks played peek-a-boo, threatening to come out and melt her heart. She smiled and looked down at the table.

That was the other thing she liked about him. He seemed to always know the right thing to say. When she was with him, it was like she could do no wrong. Like he could actually love her unconditionally. Like he'd take care of her no matter what. She hadn't felt that way in a long time.

Stephanie was starting to believe she'd hit the jackpot. She needed to keep this connection. Her mind searched her memory and found Monica's advice for taking an interest in his career. She thought this was the best time to do it. Since his work was important to him, she'd let him know she took an interest in it, too.

"So, how's everything going with your career?" Stephanie cringed, hearing herself. Her attempt at showing interest in his life came out sounding forced and insincere. *But I gotta start somewhere*, she thought, shaking it off.

"It's fine," Levin said, looking at her sideways, smiling.

"Do you have any new projects coming up?"

"Actually, I do," Levin said. "I just had a phone conference with a producer about a movie. It went pretty well. He told me about the film, when they were looking to go into production and the role I was being considered for. It was cool."

Stephanie's eyes flashed. Levin had it all. He had warmth and kindness but now he was about to become a movie star. She could see the red carpet and the mansion already. She and Levin would have two kids. She'd make sure they had the best of everything, including schools. Better yet, she'd pay to have the children homeschooled. Well, more like *Levin* would pay for home schooling.

"What's the role?" Stephanie said, smiling and pushing her daydreams to the side.

"A singer who gets hooked on drugs." Levin grimaced. "Depressing, right? I'm still not sure I'll do it. Besides, they haven't even cleared financing for the project yet."

Damn. So much for the movie thing, Stephanie thought. "Oh. Well, if they haven't financed it, you might as well call it a day."

Levin looked up at her, raising his eyebrows. "Yeah, but there's still another four months before they'll know for sure."

"But you don't want to keep hanging on without a set date and contract to get started. They'll probably never make it."

"That's not necessarily true. Some movies take years to make, like *Dreamgirls.*"

"How many *Dreamgirls* scripts do you think are out there? That was one in a million. Unless there's a big-shot producer or director behind it, you should probably forget all about it." Stephanie waved the idea away with her hand.

Levin nodded, as if in deep thought. Then, he stood up from the table and pulled on his jacket. Stephanie panicked. Her eyes followed his movements.

"I gotta go. I have to pack for tomorrow," Levin said in a flat tone.

"Really? Well, do you want something to go? There's plenty left." Stephanie stood up. Her voice betrayed her concern.

"Nah, I'm good. Thank you, baby." Levin leaned over, cupped her face and kissed her on the lips slowly. "Bye."

After he closed the door behind him, Stephanie stood motionless. *Did I say something wrong?*

CHAPTER 6

Dee

D ee stumbled through the door of her Deerwood Hills townhome with three large shopping bags. *Tasha better like these shoes or we're gonna have problems*, Dee thought. She dropped them, kicked off her own shoes and plopped on her couch. It felt good to come home after spending hours shopping for someone else. She hadn't shopped for herself in weeks, which was highly uncommon, but she knew it would become more common once she started her magazine. She almost felt overwhelmed at the work ahead of her until images of her magazine cover and high-profile celebrity parties made her smile.

With renewed optimism and determination, Dee jumped up to look for Dwayne Shoreshire's business card. She fished it out of her purse and dialed the number on it. For the past couple of days, she thought about how she would break the ice with Dwayne. She decided an apology might do the trick. Since apologies didn't come natural to her, she'd practiced it all night to make sure she got it right. Dwayne answered his phone, sounding as confident and professional as he did the day she met him.

"Hello, Dwayne. This is Dee. I mean, Deidre Wright. I met you the other day at Tasha's house," Dee said.

"Yes, I remember. How are you?" Dwayne said.

"Good. Good. I'm calling because, well, first let me apologize for my line of questioning during our previous meeting. I was a little brash and I'm sorry I wasn't more tactful. I'm so interested in your expertise that I got carried away. I hope you accept my apology," Dee said, cringing.

"Oh." Dwayne sounded surprised. "Well, thank you, Deidre. I appreciate and accept your apology. No hard feelings on this end."

"Thank you," Dee said.

"So. Uh. What can I do for you?"

"Well, I wanted to take you up on your offer for a consultation."

"Really? What do you have in mind? Money market? Stocks?" Dwayne asked.

"No. I really want your advice on an investment."

"Investment," Dwayne said.

"A business investment."

"A business investment? Okay. Well, I can schedule a meeting with you later this week," Dwayne said. She could hear him flipping through his planner.

"Actually, I think you'll want to see me sooner. This venture is bound to be a great opportunity for me and you," Dee said. She waited, listening closely to the silence on the other end of the phone. She searched for an inkling of his thoughts through sighs, mumbling or movement. For about five seconds, she heard nothing. Then, Dwayne caught her off guard.

"I tell you what. A friend of mine left his yacht for me to watch. What do you say we meet up tonight to discuss this business?" Dwayne asked.

Dee smiled. She thought he'd treat her stuffy and cold but he actually sounded warm and open. "I say what time?" she asked.

"How does five-thirty sound?" Dwayne said.

"Sounds great."

"Okay. I'll pick you up."

"I'll be ready," Dee chimed.

∞

At 5:30 sharp, Dwayne arrived at Dee's house in the same blue-gray BMW she'd seen at Tasha's house. Dee wore a white blouse and a black pencil skirt topping it off with a red belt. Dwayne came dressed but not over-dressed in off-white pants and a blazer to match. As she walked to his car and he opened the door for her, she had asked herself the same question Monica asked her a couple of weeks ago. Was she using him or did she really like him? The answer would dictate the way she conducted their meeting or date—whether she flirted or talked business. However, she came to the same con-clusion she reached before: she liked him and she wanted to use him. Either way, she needed to keep the ball rolling. As they rode, Dwayne didn't seem to have much to say. So, Dee started thinking of topics. *I see I'm going to have to break the ice*, she thought.

"So, what's the name of your friend's boat?" Dee asked.

"*Odyssey*," Dwayne said.

"That's kinda unoriginal."

Dwayne looked over at her.

Dee shrugged. "Sorry. I'm only saying if I had a yacht, I'd name it something fresh and different."

"Like what?"

"I don't know. Something with a theme. If it's going to be mysterious, you have go with something like *Midnight Connection*. Or if you want it to be stylish, you have to choose something like *High-End Diva*. You know what I mean?" Dee asked.

"Um-hmm."

"Your boat has to have personality. It has to say something about its owner. The only thing '*Odyssey*' says is he's going somewhere."

Dwayne burst into laughter at Dee's logic. He even wiped his eyes. "Are you always this opinionated?"

"Yes. What can I say? It's a gift."

He shook his head and chuckled again.

"What about you? What would you name your yacht?" Dee asked.

"I wouldn't waste money on a yacht."

"Me, neither. But if you were to buy one, what would you call it?"

Dwayne thought about it for a minute. *"Down to Business."*

Dee raised her eyebrows. *"Down to Business?"*

"Yep, if I bought one."

Um, so he's conservative, Dee thought. That could be good and bad. Good because more than likely he'll always have a lot of money stashed away somewhere. Bad because he's probably skeptical of everything he hears. She could have a challenge on her hands dealing with him.

When they reached the *Odyssey*, a host dressed in a white shirt and black pants gave them a tour of the facilities before sitting them down at a table and pouring a glass of champagne. Dee marveled again at Dwayne's taste and attention to detail. Everything looked polished and new. When the food arrived, however, her excitement changed to disbelief.

"What is this?" Dee asked.

"This is stuffed crab cakes…" the host explained but Dee interrupted.

"I can see that but why are you bringing this to me. I haven't ordered anything yet," Dee said, rolling her neck.

"Mr. Shoreshire ordered for you," the host answered.

Dee turned to Dwayne. "Why did you order for me?"

Dwayne waved the host away. "I thought you might like this and to keep the meal from taking too long to prepare, I took the liberty of ordering for both of us ahead of time."

"Then why didn't you ask me what I wanted over the phone?" She liked that he could take charge but he couldn't take charge of her. Dee kept an even tone but her blood boiled beneath the surface. She could feel heat rushing to her face.

"I guess I didn't think about it. If you don't want that, then we can always have the host write down what you really want and let the chef cook you another meal."

"Why didn't you do that before?" Dee snapped. This was typically the point where she would go off but, given that she wanted his help, she pulled herself back in. Dee took a deep breath. "That'll be fine," she said.

Dwayne waved the host back over. "Remove this plate and take another order for Ms. Wright."

"Yes, sir." The host followed his orders.

Once the confusion subsided, Dee sat in front of a Maine lobster tail with a side dish of shrimp fettuccine alfredo. Dwayne dined on lamb chops with steamed asparagus and herbed potatoes. The yacht coasted on the Atlantic Ocean, while they dined on their respective choices. The sun took on a soft orange hue as it set behind the water.

Despite the inspired scenery, Dee and Dwayne sat in relative silence again. *Okay, this isn't the way it's supposed to go*, Dee thought. She had to keep their conversation moving forward. There were so many things she needed to know about him. How did he end up in Florida? Did he know anyone with at least $80,000 to spare? She needed to get the answers to these questions fast.

"So, what brought you here? If you don't mind my asking," Dee asked him.

"That's fine." Dwayne said. "I wanted to acquire my own clients."

"I thought you said you managed your brother's finances? He was a client, right?" Dee asked.

"Not really. I didn't have a business. I was on his payroll." Dwayne's face tensed a little talking about working for his brother. "After a few years of working under my brother, I realized I could make much more money, if I went out on my own and got more clients. I tried finding clients there for about a month or two but it didn't work out. So, I packed up and moved to make a new start," Dwayne said.

"So, you created a company there but couldn't find clients?" Dee asked, chewing on a shrimp.

"No, I couldn't." Dwayne focused on his glass.

"I don't understand. Why didn't it work out in Texas? You were from there and you already knew the people," Dee said.

"Financial planners are everywhere in Texas. I wanted to find a market I could penetrate without much competition. Believe it or not, there are a lot of potential clients in this area."

Dee raised her eyebrows. More potential clients for him meant more potential investors for her. She leaned forward.

"Besides, I wanted to do it without my brother," Dwayne said.

Dee nodded at his determination to make it on his own.

He appeared to have few excuses. She admired that. On the other hand, she wondered how many contacts he'd left behind. He had an air of confidence, which was fine, but she hoped he wasn't crazy.

"I think it's great that you're so focused on being successful," Dee said.

"Yeah. What about you? Are you focused on success?" Dwayne asked.

"Absolutely."

"Really? What are you doing?" he asked.

Dee took a deep breath. Her opportunity to talk about her business had approached and she hoped to break through with him. "Well, it's the reason I wanted to talk to you."

"Um-hmm," Dwayne said, pushing his fork through a potato.

"I'm starting a fashion magazine and I want you to help me find money for it," Dee blurted out her goal. She exhaled. *That's finally over*, Dee thought.

Dwayne looked up from his plate and leaned back. "Why a fashion magazine?"

"Because fashion is what I do. I'm an expert on it," Dee said.

"Yeah, but everyone's moving toward the Internet now. People don't really buy print media anymore," Dwayne said.

Dee rolled her eyes. If she heard that one more time, she would punch somebody. "Listen. I've heard print sales are decreasing and advertising is slow, but I know women will love my magazine."

"How? Have you performed market research?" Dwayne asked.

"Yes," Dee said.

"Okay. What's your SWOT?" Dwayne asked.

"My what?"

"SWOT. Strengths, Weaknesses, Opportunities, Threats," Dwayne said.

Dee frowned. "I don't remember all that," she snapped.

Dwayne tossed his head back and laughed. "You're going to have to know those things really well, if you want to convince someone to invest in your business."

"I'll memorize it. I'm just asking for help finding an investor," Dee said. "So, what do you say?"

Dwayne sighed. "All right. I'll help you under two conditions. One, you let me, and only me, find the investor for you; and two, I get a percentage of the investment money."

"How much is a percentage?" Dee grimaced.

"Twenty percent," Dwayne said.

"Twenty?!" Dee shouted. "Don't you think that's a little high?"

"Okay. Fifteen. I can't go under fifteen," Dwayne said. "And I know you don't expect me to give you my services for free."

No, I was hoping you'd be so impressed with me you'd immediately agree to help from the kindness of your heart,

Dee thought as she tapped her fingernails on the table with furious speed. She never intended to share the money with Dwayne. She only wanted him to help her get the money. For a moment, she thought about throwing this guy back where she found him but then she caught a glimpse of his snow white teeth, meticulous haircut and clean, even fingernails. He had all the signs of a good bet. If she could keep him engaged, he'd probably help her get the money she needed for her magazine without taking a cut.

"Okay. I'll think about it," Dee said, taking a swig of her champagne.

Dwayne shrugged and turned around as he heard music playing behind him. A violinist strolled over to their table.

"Do you want to dance?" Dwayne asked, extending his hand with a confident smile.

"Sure. Why not?" Dee said.

As they stood in the middle of the floor, swaying back and forth, Dee quietly rested her chin on Dwayne's shoulder, pondering a way to get what she wanted from him without paying for it.

∞

The next day, Dee stood in the biography section of the bookstore flipping through *The Billion Dollar BET*. She was on the part where Robert Johnson basically reused someone else's business plan to create one for the network. *Genius*, she thought. Ever since she decided to create her own magazine, she spent at least three days out of the week, hanging out in the bookstore researching information on publishing, business and financing. She loved to read stories about people who made their businesses thrive.

Dee leaned her head back, closed her eyes and imagined she'd get a call on the phone from someone with money to give her for the magazine. In her dreams, they'd call in five seconds. Five, four, three, two…one. No phone call. Dee sighed and turned the page of her book. Then her cell phone rang. She scrambled to answer it.

"Hello?"

"Hey. How did the date with Dwayne go?" Monica asked on the other end of the phone.

Dee's shoulders sagged. "Oh, it's you."

"Well, excuse me. Who else would it be?" Monica asked.

"An investor. I just thought one up."

"We're dreaming up investors now?"

"Might as well."

"Aww. Something will come through. How did it go last night? Did he offer to help? Or did you spend the night in each other's arms, kissing passionately?"

"What? Girl, please. I think you've been reading too many romance novels," Dee said, grimacing.

Monica chuckled. "Hey. I only read one."

"One too many." Dee closed the BET book and walked toward the café with it. "The meeting, date or whatever it was went okay but he'll only help me if he gets to pick the investor and I give him fifteen or twenty percent of the money. Ain't that something?"

"Oh, so he wants his share?"

"Yeah. Can you believe that?" Dee asked.

"He is going to do some work for you. So, he should be compensated for it."

"On my account?"

"Who else is going to pay him, Dee?"

"I don't know. I was hoping he would be so charmed by me that he wouldn't care about getting paid," Dee said.

Monica burst into laughter. Dee followed suit.

"Aww. Monica, what am I going to do?"

"You're going to try him out and see if he comes through for you. And if he actually finds you an investor, great! Pay the man and call it a day."

Dee hated to admit it but Monica was probably right. She had no other way of getting investors. Why should she reject the only help she'd received? On the other hand, she still didn't want to share the money. She figured there must be some way to avoid it and she was determined to figure it out.

"I guess," Dee said.

"So, with all this talk about money, I take it you guys didn't exactly make a love connection?"

"He's okay."

"Just okay?" Monica asked.

"The date almost went haywire," Dee confessed.

"Why?"

"He ordered my food for me. Without me. Chile, I almost went off." Dee's temper almost flared again thinking about it.

"I'll bet. We all know you got a temper problem," Monica said.

"No, I don't!" Dee shouted a little louder than expected.

"Really?" Monica asked, noticing her friend's tone.

Dee sucked her teeth. "Whateva."

"Did he tell you why he did that?" Monica asked.

"He said he wanted to save cooking time."

"Oh. What else happened to make him just okay?"

"I think he's going to be a tough nut to crack," Dee said.

"Good," Monica said.

"What? Why?"

"Because you cannot date a pushover. You're way too strong for that."

"I guess the date wasn't too bad. I'm disappointed that I have to share my money," Dee said. "But I'm going to work on that, though. We're supposed to go out again in a couple of days. I'll see if I can get around that little agreement."

Monica sighed. "That figures."

"You know I got to do it. It's not in my nature to accept the first offer. And Monica, this is only the first offer."

CHAPTER 7

Monica

"Ooh. What's this?" Monica swooned as she stared at a picture of a cake on the wall.

"That's the Strawberry Cream Torte on a baked nut crust. It's very yummy," Linda Knight, Monica's selected caterer, said. Monica stood in her office, admiring the wall of cakes, pies, seafood, pastas, meats and everything in between. The dishes ranged from Southern to fine cuisine. Linda called it her Wall of Fame.

It was really a wall of culinary greatness. Monica especially liked that the woman had been in business for fifteen years and that her references spoke highly of her. The two women had a ball all afternoon looking through different menus. Monica even sampled some of Linda's work. She stared at the wall, making a mental note to thank Dee for looking out for her on this one.

"Oh my gosh! It looks yummy. I need to get out of here. My butt gained five pounds looking at that thing," Monica said. The women laughed.

Linda walked around to her desk, while Monica sat opposite her. After a few clicks on her computer, Linda pulled up an invoice for Monica.

"Okay, that'll be $4,000 today."

Monica reached into her purse for her checkbook. She wrote the amount in and handed it to Linda. The caterer ran the check. She squinted and twisted the left corner of her mouth. She ran the check again.

Linda turned back to Monica. "I'm sorry but I can't take this."

Monica's eyes stretched wide. "Excuse me."

"I can't take this. Do you have another form of payment?" Linda asked.

"Wait a minute. What do you mean you can't take it?" Monica didn't have a history of high blood pressure but she was certain she could feel her pressure reaching 140/90. She sat erect, bracing herself for whatever Linda was about to say.

"I can't accept your check. I'm gonna need another form of payment. My system is kicking it back out."

"Why would it do that?" Monica said, raising her voice.

Linda leaned back a little but maintained her composure and professionalism. "Well, this usually happens when someone has a series of bad checks out there."

"I don't have any bad checks anywhere," Monica said. She, then, remembered the notice from her bank a few weeks ago about the overdraft. She hadn't heard anything else about it. So, she figured everything was resolved.

Linda shrugged. "I don't know, Honey. I can only tell you what I see. Do you have a credit card?"

Monica took a deep breath to calm herself down and

nodded. "Yes. Yes, of course." Monica reached in her purse for her platinum Visa card. Linda's merchant machine accepted the card without issue but Monica barely noticed. She was still hung up on the rejected check. She had to call the bank and find out what was going on.

"Okay. Here is your receipt for your deposit of $4,000 paid by Visa. The other $4,000 is due the day of the event. Do you have any questions?" Linda asked.

Still distracted, Monica only shook her head.

"Are you okay? Honey, don't worry about it. I'm sure it's a misunderstanding. Banks do make mistakes, you know."

After Monica thanked Linda for her time, she jumped in her car and rushed home to call the bank. Somebody had some explaining to do. She'd placed the letter she received about the overdraft somewhere in her office. When she arrived home, she stormed into her house and headed straight there. Throwing her purse on the desk, she opened drawers, disturbed papers and moved desk pieces, looking for contact information for their bank. She finally found it, buried under her son's Crayola drawing.

Monica sat down in the black leather executive chair and dialed the bank's customer service number. The annoying automated voice instructed her to push option one, push option four and then push option two. She scowled when the automated voice wanted to walk her through the online process instead of giving her a live person. She dialed the number zero three times. The voice agreed to send her to a customer service representative. The rep answered the phone cheerful and pleasant, only to be greeted with Monica's irritation.

"I have some questions about my checking account. I tried to pay for services with a check and it was erroneously rejected. I want to know why," Monica said.

"Okay, ma'am. Could I have your account number and verify your contact information?" the rep asked.

Although she did not feel like doing it, Monica gave the rep her address, the answer to her security question and her social security number. She leaned back in her chair and waited for the rep to pull up her information—certain she would confirm that this was all a terrible misunderstanding. The rep would apologize profusely and offer some lame, free perk to rectify the situation. Monica closed her eyes and readied herself for the apology.

"Yes, Mrs. Hatcher. There is a notation on your account that you have bounced four checks in the past month," the rep said.

Monica opened her eyes and shot forward. "What?! I don't think so! When?"

The rep read off the dates. Monica wrote them down. She remembered one was for the venue, while two of them were for the flowers and the ice sculpture. But there was one check she didn't recognize. She didn't even think she wrote it. *I can't believe this*, she thought.

"How could this happen? The only notice I received was for the venue and you all paid for that with the overdraft service," Monica said.

"Yes, ma'am, but when the last two bounced, we stopped the overdraft services. We do not overdraft more than two checks per month. If the bounces continue, we suspend overdraft services altogether."

"Why didn't you send me a letter about this?" Monica asked.

"We're not required to notify you when we stop the service."

Monica shook her head. "Well, do you think you can tell me where the check on July 3rd was supposed to go?"

"Yes, ma'am." The rep typed for a few seconds. "The check came from Mr. Hatcher and it was made out to Mr. Fred Nelson in the amount of four thousand dollars."

Fred? Why would Tony send an extra check to his manager for that much money? Monica thought. She hoped she could resolve this herself but she saw she would have to get with Tony about his bounce. As a matter of fact, she needed to know why all of a sudden there wasn't enough money in the checking account to cover their checks. Thoughts of the worst ran through her head. Was he gambling? Was Fred stealing from Tony or blackmailing him? Was Tony hiring prostitutes? She laughed at the ridiculousness of her concerns and threw them out. More than likely, this was a one-time incident. A simple fiscal error. She was, however, disheartened with Tony's refusal to watch his spending. They would have to manage the money more effectively. Besides, time continued to wind down and the dinner was a few weeks away. She needed everything to come together and that wouldn't happen if she was bouncing checks all over the place.

Aggravated, Monica hung up with the rep and decided to go have a little talk with Tony about her request to cut back on the spending. She stood up to search the house for her husband but stopped short when her cell phone rang.

Now what? Monica thought. She answered it, allowing her irritation to creep into the greeting.

"Is that any way to answer your mother?" Corlene, Monica's mother, asked.

"Hello, Mother," she sighed. Two months had passed since the last time Monica had talked to her mother, and, quite frankly, she hadn't missed her. They had a caustic relationship; she could only take her mother in doses. Most of the time, she was grateful her mother lived in New Jersey—far away from her.

"Well, don't sound so happy," Corlene said.

"Always happy to hear from you, Mother."

"I'll take that literally. What are you doing these days?" Corlene asked.

"I'm putting the finishing touches on my scholarship dinner."

"Really? Who's on the guest list?"

"Entertainers, business owners, politicians. Representative Simpson is going to be there."

"Oh, that's marvelous. He is a dear, dear friend. Your father and he went to Brown together."

Monica rolled her eyes and looked at the clock. She hoped her mother wouldn't talk too long. "Yes, I know, Mother."

"Do put on the best dinner possible. He's a lovely man but his wife has a mouth that will not stop. If the dinner is a bust, I will surely hear about it. You may be gone but I still have a reputation to uphold here," Corlene said.

"I assure you the dinner will be of the highest caliber," Monica said.

"Is that so? Enlighten me on the logistics."

Monica proceeded to lay out all the details, including the eight-foot ice sculpture, the orchid centerpieces, and the scrumptious menu.

"Wonderful. I'm glad to see you've learned how to put on a quality event. I would come but I have other things to do. You'll have to inform me sooner next time," Corlene said.

Monica covered the phone so she could laugh. Her mother had a strange way of showing her support. Corlene preferred to avoid emotions at all costs. Instead, she used impractical demands and subtle aggression to show she wanted involvement in her daughter's life. It made for an unusual upbringing, but she grew used to her mother's ways. Nonetheless, Monica didn't have time to feel warm and fuzzy from her mother's veiled show of affection. Corlene's next question guaranteed a cloudy overcast to their conversation.

"How *is* everything going with you and Tony?"

Monica hesitated. She debated whether she should tell her mother about Tony's contract issues and she knew better than to tell her about the check that had bounced. Tony always received Colene's harshest criticism and the check fiasco would only invite a heated tirade against him. But on faith, Monica took a chance and told her mother a little about the contract.

"Everything is great. Tony's having a few issues with his contract but it'll be okay," Monica said.

"What kind of issues?"

Monica could hear her mother frown through the phone. "He is not getting the money they promised him but he and his agent are working on it," Monica said. She hoped the last part would smooth things over but Corlene started in on him right away.

"I never understood what you see in him. What a waste! Spending all these years with the equivalent of a construction worker," Corlene said.

"A construction worker?!"

"Yes. Football is a blue-collar job. Getting beaten and banged up for a check is physical labor. It's as simple as that."

Monica's blood boiled. She hated when her mother talked down about Tony.

"Why couldn't you have married an investment broker, like your father? At least you wouldn't have to wait so long to get all your money."

"Because I married a football player, Mother."

When describing Henry Patterson, Monica's father, Corlene tended to decorate him, like a Christmas tree. The elaborate ornaments and lights looked enviable in the window to passersby, but those on the inside of the house—Monica and Corlene—could see the paint peeling off Santa's beard or the row of lights that didn't blink. The truth was Henry lived a double life with another woman, complete with another house. Both mother and daughter, however, chose to hide it as one of those imperfect lights on the tree.

Henry made it easy. Charming and gracious, he spoiled his only daughter rotten. Monica loved her father. She just preferred to live a different way. She wanted to marry a man who was faithful *and* affluent. Her mother didn't see it that way.

"But look at what you're going through now. You are trying to create a spectacular benefit and you must have everything done properly for the caliber of people coming. Yet, now you'll have to become money conscious because you don't know what his employer will do next. Does that sound like an ideal situation to you?" Corlene snipped at Monica. Monica regretted telling her anything.

"It's not about ideals, Mother. And we aren't paupers. We just don't want to be unprepared."

"Well, I would have preferred you marry that nice fellow, Louis. He came from a good family and I hear he's made partner at a very prestigious law firm."

Monica met Louis at fourteen years old and Corlene had tried to match her with him ever since. To Monica, it felt like another form of control, perpetuated through years of private schools, debutante balls and social organizations.

She refused to allow Corlene to dictate her choice for a life mate. She enjoyed helping her husband build his image and she seriously considered using her own developed skills to start a marketing/public relations firm. Her efforts with Tony and dedication to the benefit dinner reinforced her strengths in handling people and solving problems, but she didn't dare explain this to her mother. She, like Tony, didn't believe Monica should work anywhere.

"I have to go, Mother. I have more calls to make for the dinner."

"Fine. But remember what I said."

"Sure," Monica said.

As soon as she hung up, Monica marched downstairs to look for Tony. She found him in the movie theater watching one of his football games on the large screen. She grabbed the remote control and paused the game.

"What's going on?" Monica said, standing in front of the large screen. Tony looked like she had poured cold water on his face.

"What are you talking about?"

"We have bounced four checks in the past month. Do you wanna tell me something?" Monica put her hand on her hip.

Tony shook his head. "That must be some mistake. I've never bounced a check in my life."

"I just called the bank. They say you wrote a check to Fred for four thousand dollars. What are you giving him that much money for?"

"Listen, Monica. I said the bank is wrong. I didn't bounce any check." Tony stood up and walked over to her. "I will personally go into the bank tomorrow and get everything worked out, okay?"

He snatched the remote from her and plopped back down in his seat.

"Why won't you answer my question?" Monica said, still standing in the way of his view.

"I did."

"No you didn't. I asked you why you gave Fred an extra four thousand dollars."

"I needed him to take care of some business for me."

"What business?" Monica asked.

"Non-ya." Tony mocked.

Monica took a deep breath and squinted her eyes. "I'm warning you, Tony. You don't want to play with me right now."

"So, what are you, my accountant?" Tony scoffed at her.

"No, I'm your wife."

"Right. And I'm your husband. As your husband, it's my responsibility to provide for this family. I do that and then some. So, what I do with the rest of my money is my business! Now, I don't know about you but I have some studying to do." He flicked the screen back on.

"I tell you what. Since you act like you can't account for your own finances, I don't wanna hear no noise when I take over the accounts. I don't have time to be embarrassed when my checks are rejected," Monica yelled and stormed toward the door.

"I don't need you to tell me what to do with my money! I'm a grown man. I know what I'm doing," he yelled.

"No, you don't," Monica yelled back and slammed the theater door.

She stomped down the hall. Angry with Tony. Angry with herself. When she first married him, she thought she'd have a partner in life. Someone she could confide in. Someone she could turn to with problems. But the longer they were married, Tony became less of a partner and more of a dictator. He believed he could do whatever he wanted because he was the breadwinner, but Monica had every intention of changing that.

CHAPTER 8

Stephanie

S tephanie frowned as she sat at her dining room table, dialing Levin's number. She hadn't talked to him since their disastrous dinner a couple of weeks ago and she missed him. After two rings, his voicemail picked up. She threw her phone on the table and dropped her head in her hands. Every time she tried calling him, his voicemail kept her from hearing his voice. She'd spent days obsessing over the things she'd said at their last dinner, trying to figure out where she went wrong and worrying she might have missed her opportunity to have the man of her dreams.

Lost in thought, the sound of her own phone ringing startled her. She sighed, preferring to ignore the call. The phone rang again. She reached over to pick it up and smiled. Levin's number appeared on the caller ID screen.

"Hello," she blurted out.

"Hey. What are you doing?" Levin asked.

"I was making some calls for my friend's scholarship dinner," Stephanie lied. She wanted him to think that she'd been busy, doing more than sitting around thinking about him.

"Oh. I thought you just called me," Levin said.

"I did. I was taking a little break to see how you were doing," Stephanie said.

"Cool. Listen. I was thinking. I'm gonna be home for a couple of days. Would you like to come visit me in Georgia?" Levin asked.

Stephanie gasped. "I would love to. I mean, sure. I think I can make it."

"Great. I'll get you a ticket and see you tomorrow."

"Okay, see you tomorrow," Stephanie said.

When they hung up, Stephanie squealed, grabbed her purse and headed to the mall. She stepped outside to a sunny day. People poured into the Heron's Walk, as if they were preparing to go out of town, too. Stephanie sifted through the racks, looking for outfits that would catch Levin's attention. She held up a pair of short, white shorts and admired their design but felt a little self conscious about the way she'd look in them. Stephanie had dimples in her thighs. The shorts would call attention to them. Maybe she should work out. She'd bought a treadmill six months ago but she hadn't used it.

That might have to change soon. The girls that followed Levin around weren't a size eight; they looked like they were a size zero. Although Levin never seemed to mind, he had to notice. If she noticed, he noticed.

Thinking about her weight, Stephanie sank into a temporary funk. Suddenly, she couldn't pick anything to wear. She needed to figure something out because it was almost time for her to go home and pack. She sighed and picked up her cell phone to call Dee.

"Dee. Help!" Stephanie said as soon as her friend answered.

"Help you do what?" Dee asked.

"I'm at the mall trying to find something to wear and it's killing me."

"Why? All that stuff you got in your closets. You mean to tell me you can't find anything to wear?"

"I can't wear the same things. I'm going to see Levin in Atlanta," Stephanie said.

"Oh, I see. Dressing to impress."

"Yeah. We hadn't talked in a couple of weeks. So, I need to look extra special."

"Why haven't you talked in the last couple of weeks?" Dee asked. "Did I miss something?"

"The last time he was here, he left mad with me," Stephanie said.

"What did you do?"

"Nothing. Well, I guess I kinda tried to tell him about his career but I didn't mean it in a bad way," Stephanie said.

Dee sighed. "Girl, we said take an interest in his career. We didn't say tell him what to do with it. You know no man wants to hear that."

"Yeah. I guess I just got caught up in the moment but anyway that seems to be behind us. He called me today and asked me to join him in Atlanta. Isn't that great?"

"That's wonderful, honey. Just don't dole out any more advice," Dee said.

"Oh, I won't but I wanna make sure I do everything right, you know what I mean?" Stephanie asked.

"Well, Stephanie, you can't worry about all that. All you can do is go up there. See ya man and have fun. That's it. Don't make this a do-or-die situation."

"You're right. But what do I buy? I see a lot of baby doll dresses. I don't like those. I'm wide enough. I don't need any help there," Stephanie said.

"If you don't like the baby doll dresses, don't buy them. Stick to what you know. And for you that's likely anything showing cleavage and a lot of skin," Dee said.

"Thanks, Dee. I'll call you later." Stephanie hung up and decided to try the shorts on anyway. Maybe she could find a way to make them work.

The next day, Stephanie caught an early morning flight to Atlanta. The flight went smoothly, unlike the ride to Levin's house. Police cars and ambulance trucks flew past her cab responding to a three-car pileup. As a result, Stephanie's cab ride stretched to two hours but Stephanie looked straight ahead, unfazed. She had other things on her mind. She'd thought a lot about Dee's advice and she'd decided her Georgia trip should be fun. However, she still intended to make the most of it. Levin needed a little help seeing how good she was for him. While in Georgia, Stephanie planned to make sure he realized her value to him. She would clean his house, wash his clothes and cook his food. She already placed the number in her phone to a nearby flower shop to arrange for fresh flowers at his house every morning.

The cab driver pulled into Levin's driveway and Stephanie could smell freshly cut grass and newly laid pavement. She noticed a carpenter's truck parked on the side of the street. A man in a beige cap trimmed the bushes along the side of Levin's five-acre mansion. Levin wasn't home yet, but his housekeeper stepped outside to introduce herself and show Stephanie the European-inspired home. It had five large bedrooms, a bar, a music studio and a ground pool. Levin's master bedroom hosted a large circular bed and a walk-in closet big enough for another bed. As Stephanie unpacked her suitcase and gawked at his room, Levin walked through the door.

"Hey, baby."

"Hey!" Stephanie ran and jumped on him at the door, giving him a hug and kiss.

"How was your flight?"

"Good. I'm so glad to see you."

"Yeah? Well, I have reservations at Morton's for six o'clock. Go ahead and get ready. I'll meet you downstairs in an hour."

"Okay. Great!"

"Oh, and before I forget…" Levin pulled a box out of his pocket. "I'd like you to wear this."

She opened the box to see a stunning diamond-links

platinum necklace. Stephanie gasped. She gave him another hug and kiss.

"Thank you. I love it." She looked at the necklace and smiled all over again.

He gave her a kiss on the cheek. "I'll see you when you're ready," he whispered.

When Stephanie finally walked downstairs, she'd pinned her long curls back and put on a long, blue, spaghetti strap dress with a split up the side. She wore Levin's gift prominently around her neck. He escorted her to a limo waiting outside to take them to a candlelit dinner. They wrapped the night up over a bottle of brandy and pillow talk. As Stephanie lay next to Levin, she breathed a silent sigh of relief. He hadn't mentioned their last dinner at her house. They carried on as if it had never happened. *To think, I spent hours worrying for nothing*, Stephanie thought.

She turned and placed her arms around him. "I'm so happy to be here with you. I know it's hard for you to find time to see me," Stephanie said.

"Sometimes." Levin nodded.

"Is that what happened in your last relationship?" Stephanie asked.

Levin paused. "No. She didn't trust me," he said. "She thought I wasn't ready to settle down."

"Are you ready to settle down?" Stephanie asked. She turned to look into his face for clues that confirmed or dispelled his next response.

He looked down at her. "Yes. I want someone to come home to. I want a permanent woman by my side, but most women can't handle my job. And those that can only want me for my money."

"Maybe you haven't been looking in the right places," Stephanie said.

"Maybe. What about you? Do you want to get married?" Levin asked.

"Yeah, sure," Stephanie said, smiling wide as her previous daydreams danced around in her head.

"Have you ever thought about marrying someone like me? Career and all?" Those words caused her heart to pound like a drum.

"Of course. You're wonderful. Any woman can see that. Forget that other chick. It's not your fault she couldn't handle a successful man."

Levin grinned at Stephanie. "Thank you, baby. Can you handle me?"

"Yes!"

Levin laughed and hugged her. "That's good to know. That's real good to know 'cuz I like having you around. I'd like to have you in my life for awhile. And maybe one day, that marriage thing can happen for us, you know?"

"Well," Stephanie said, tightening her grip on him. "I would like that very much." She knew right then he was the man for her.

∞

Stephanie pressed her hands to her stomach to calm it down. For the past couple of days, she'd had continuous butterflies for Levin. Sadly, she'd reached her last night in Georgia with him but she commended herself on implementing her plan to the letter. As she promised, he came home each day to the airy scent of lilac flowers on the dining room table and something baking in the oven. She even collected his messages and handed them to him at the end of the day—except for the ones from women. He'd noticed her efforts and rewarded her with affection and gifts. Last night, he'd bought her a Gucci purse and a pair of five-carat earrings.

Stephanie picked up the phone, thinking if she talked to Dee or Monica her butterflies would subside. She called Monica but no one answered. She then called Dee and her voicemail came on. She picked up the phone one last time and called Natalie. Her friend answered on the second ring.

"Hey, Natalie! It's Stephanie."

"What's up, girl?"

"Oh, I'm hanging out at Levin's house," Stephanie said, trying unsuccessfully to sound nonchalant.

"Really? How long have you been there?" Natalie asked.

"A couple of days." Stephanie chuckled. "The time we've spent together has been truly amazing. I think we're getting serious."

"Already!" Natalie said. "How do you know?"

"We've already talked about marriage, girl. I think he's ready to settle down with me."

"Levin? Settle down? Now that's something nobody would see coming. What..." Natalie cut her own words short. "Stephanie, I have to go. We have a problem with our next venue. I'll call you back later."

Disappointed she couldn't brag a little longer, Stephanie ended the call and turned her attention back to the evening she had planned. She walked into the kitchen and flopped down on a stool, anxiously awaiting Levin's return from a business meeting. She wrapped her curly, dark brown hair around her index finger and mulled over the details for the night. First, she would sit him down at the dining room table. Then she would place a napkin on his lap, bring out dinner and feed him. After dinner, she would bring out the cake she'd baked and feed him that, too. Once dinner was over, she planned to blindfold him and lead him upstairs.

The sound of a key wiggling in the front door interrupted her thoughts. *Great! He's home*, Stephanie thought. She leaped off the stool and trotted toward the door.

"Hold on, man. I'll be right back," Levin said to someone waiting outside.

"Hey. What's up, baby?"

Stephanie rushed him like a linebacker. "Oh, I've been making the best dinner for the best man ever. I even baked you a cake."

"Sounds great."

"Yeah. Well, that's only the beginning." Stephanie giggled.

Levin raised his eyebrow. "Ohhh. Baby, that's hot. Really.

But I need to go back out tonight. My boy is waiting outside and I already told him I'd be going with him. I'd love it if you could wrap everything up nice for me and I could eat it when I get home. Thanks." Levin patted her on the butt and ran upstairs. Stephanie stood stunned for exactly one second before screaming as loud as she could.

"Are you kidding me?!"

Levin stopped at the stairs. He slowly turned around, while Stephanie walked up behind him. "What?"

"You're gonna leave me alone on my last night here?" Stephanie asked.

"Listen, baby. I understand you wanted me to be with you tonight but I have to go. I didn't know you were doing all this for me. Why didn't you call me first?" Levin asked.

"Because it was supposed to be a surprise! How could you plan something else to do?" Stephanie said.

"I know, but I'm gonna be in Orlando next week. We can do all this then."

"Why don't you want to be here with me now?" Tears welled in her eyes. She felt like this was a bad sign. One minute, he'd dote on her; the next minute, he'd leave her behind. Was he playing a game?

"Don't do this to me now, Stephanie. I told you I'll be back later and we can get together in a week. Everything's been great. Why you gotta make this so complicated?"

"Why do you have to be such an inconsiderate jack-ass?"

"Oh. After all I've done for you this week, I'm inconsiderate? You know what? I'm glad I'm going out 'cuz I'm not dealing with you tonight." Levin switched jackets and jogged back downstairs.

"Fine. Take your ass on then, since you got somewhere else to be. I won't be here when you get back."

"Fine. Make sure you lock the door when you leave." Levin slammed the front door shut.

"Aghhhhhhh!"

Stephanie ran over to the china cabinet, opened the doors and hurled his $1,300 china and wineglasses to the floor. Her anger not satisfied, she took the food she'd cooked for him and smeared it all over the table, refrigerator and floor. When she felt better, she walked upstairs, called a cab and packed her clothes.

∞

A week and a half after the kitchen incident, Stephanie woke up at seven o'clock in the morning to the sound of her phone ringing. She maneuvered to the edge of the bed and saw it was Monica.

"Stephanie! How are you today, sweetie?" Monica chirped after hearing Stephanie's groggy voice.

"Sleepy," Stephanie said.

"Agh. Wake up, girl. You have a life to live." Monica chuckled.

Stephanie groaned. She knew her friend's reason for calling. After hearing her whine about the trip with Levin, she wanted to try and cheer her up. Unfortunately, she wasn't in the mood. Even though a few days had passed, she still felt bitter about their blow up. She believed they had something special and hated to have it end this way.

"I have to go talk to a few people today about the scholarship dinner. Do you wanna ride?" Monica asked.

"Not really."

"We'll have lunch. My treat."

Stephanie shook her head. "I'm really not up to it. I'll talk to you later. Okay?"

Monica sighed. "Okay. I'll call you later."

Stephanie hung up the phone and rolled over, intending to fall back to sleep. Following fifteen minutes of failing to sleep, she moved from her bed to her couch. She turned on the TV and the stereo, a habit she'd developed as a teenager. For some strange reason, it made her feel better to play both.

After an hour of switching TV channels and ignoring radio commercials, she turned the TV volume down. As she rolled over for a second attempt at falling sleep, gossip maven Jackie O'Donnell opened the next segment on *The Huey Martin Morning Show*.

"Jackie! What's up, girl?" Huey burst through her stereo speakers with his usual morning gusto.

"Oh, I have a lot to tell you this morning," Jackie said.

"Uh, oh. Well, let's get started," Leslie, Huey's sidekick, chimed.

"All right. First off, I want to talk about our darling, Levin," Jackie said.

"Ooh. He's here?" Leslie asked, excited. Everyone on the show burst into laughter. Stephanie turned back over and reached for her stereo remote to turn the volume up. She sat up on the couch to listen.

"No, honey. He's not here but soon you might be disappointed for another reason. Rumor has it your boy is on the verge of popping the question," Jackie said.

"To who?!" Leslie yelled.

"No one famous but I think she's a video chick. It's a woman he's been dating for a little while and sources say they're pretty serious. She recently spent some time with him in Georgia," Jackie said.

Stephanie clasped her mouth. *Oh, my gosh. They're talking about me*, she thought. Who could have told people she was in Georgia? *Of course. Natalie.* She wondered if Levin had told others, too. Unfortunately, the nature of their relationship prevented her from saying for sure. Dating Levin was like riding a roller coaster—one day up; the next day down. Her emotions ranged between anger and curiosity.

"So, it looks like he may be off the market soon," Jackie concluded.

"Aww, man," Leslie said.

Jackie laughed.

"Well, don't get too upset, Leslie. We'll have to see," Huey said.

"You don't think he's serious about anyone?" Jackie asked.

Huey paused before answering. "Let's say you might

not wanna place any bets." Everyone exploded in response.

Stephanie turned the volume back down. She sat there, thinking about Jackie's entertainment report and Levin. Butterflies fluttered around her stomach again. Even though she still had doubts about their relationship, she couldn't help the excitement she felt about their relationship ending up on the radio.

Suddenly, her doorbell rang. She jerked her head toward the door. After fishing for her robe, she tied it on and looked through the peephole. She saw a delivery guy and opened the door to a large bouquet of red roses.

"Ms. Robinson?" the gentleman asked.

She nodded and he handed her the flowers along with a card. She took them and closed the door. On the front of the card was the name of a hotel and a room number. Inside the card, it read, "I'll be waiting, baby." As much as Levin's actions frustrated her, Stephanie felt a pull toward him. Her heart soared to know he still wanted to see her, even though she'd trashed his kitchen. The engagement rumors excited her even more. So, she went to her closet to pick out a dress and get back on the roller coaster.

CHAPTER 9

Dee

D ee smiled in the mirror as she combed her hair and waited for Dwayne to take her to Christopher Coles' exclusive party. A tinge of excitement climbed up Dee's spine. She'd prepared long and hard for this moment and looked forward to checking out Dwayne's business connections. Since they'd started seeing each other regularly, he'd told her several times he planned to help her find a generous investor for her magazine but, so far, nothing had materialized. She couldn't tell if he'd been trying. This party gave her an opportunity to observe his tactics firsthand and scrutinize his efforts. She hoped he wasn't leading her on.

She peered out of the window as Dwayne pulled up her two-car driveway. His black Versace suit complemented Dee's deep purple, satin dress. He rang the doorbell. She adjusted her dress in a nearby mirror.

"Hey!" Dee gave him a kiss on the cheek. "I'm glad you're a little early but I still need a couple of minutes."

"Why? You look ready to me," Dwayne said.

"Thanks, but I haven't even put my lashes on."

"Uh, please don't put those on. You really can do without them," Dwayne said.

"What do you mean? I always wear my lashes when I go out somewhere," Dee said. She eyed him, wondering if he really had the nerve to criticize her.

"Yeah, but I think you look even better without them," Dwayne said, hesitating and choosing his words carefully.

"It's a little soon for you to be telling me how to dress, isn't it?" Dee asked.

"I don't think I'm telling you how to dress. I'm making a suggestion. A strong suggestion," Dwayne answered.

Dee opened her mouth to say something smart but changed her mind. *He's about to hook me up with an entrée of contacts. I need to be quiet. One of them could be the jackpot*, Dee thought. If he wanted her to leave the lashes home, she could oblige him for one night.

Dee raised her arms in surrender. "Okay. Fine. I won't wear them but don't get used to this." She pointed at Dwayne. "They will be on and in full effect tomorrow." She turned to leave the room.

"Good, I won't see them," Dwayne mumbled.

Dee leaped backward, picked up her couch pillow and hurled it at him. He ducked and laughed.

About an hour and a half later, they approached Coles Manor, a sprawling four-acre estate. The mansion belonged to Christopher Coles, TV personality and owner of The Connection. The popular restaurateur reveled in showing people how good food had been to him. So, he threw an annual soiree to display his extensive knowledge of important people and exotic dishes.

A line of luxury cars followed the circular driveway. Three young, male valets helped the women out of the cars, and then disappeared. When Dee and Dwayne reached the French doors, two men in tuxedos opened them, revealing an elegantly decorated foyer that provided an immediate view of the open-armed staircase. A young woman dressed in a French maid uniform took their coats, while music greeted them from all directions. Local celebrities waved and motioned across the room. The mix of voices, music, and clinking glasses engulfed the mansion.

After they stepped over the threshold, Dee leaned toward Dwayne. "So, where the money-makers at?"

Dwayne shook his head. "It doesn't work like that."

"Then, how does it work?" Dee said.

"We have to pinpoint a target and woo them. You don't go up to people and ask them for money. We aren't the Girl Scouts," Dwayne said.

"Well, okay. Let's get to pinpointin'." Dee scanned the room, searching for tell-tale signs of wealth. Nice watches, good shoes, the faint air of entitlement. She spotted a man standing near the sofa, intent on making a point to his audience of two.

"What about him?" Dee asked.

"Him? That's Pete Jenningson. He owns a few retail

chains in Tampa but he's not a good choice. The man is as stingy as they come," Dwayne said.

Dee nodded to their left. "Okay. What about him?"

Dwayne followed her motion. "Oh, Alex Mariotti." Dwayne chuckled. "He's supposed to be a big-time real estate guy down here but he's really broke."

Dee sighed. This was harder than she thought. Why couldn't she find a bunch of people with money and ask them if they wanted to invest in her magazine? All this scoping the scene wasn't her thing. She preferred to be more direct. She appreciated honesty and liked being around people that appreciated it, too. Nevertheless, Dwayne was calling the shots. Dee said she would cooperate with him and she needed to do that. Looking around the room, she found someone else to bring to his attention.

"Now, I know Ms. Thing over there has some money," Dee said, eyeing a lady wearing pearls and her hair in a tight bun. To Dee, the woman's appearance oozed old money.

"Agh. Ms. Angela Dunst. You're right, she does have a lot of money. Unfortunately, she's one of the nastiest people you'll ever meet," Dwayne said.

"Wait a minute!" Dee raised her voice.

"Shhh," Dwayne said. He looked like Dee's tone had mortified him. A few people nearby stopped talking and glanced her way, shooting her odd expressions.

"Sorry," Dee said. "Do you mean to tell me, out of all these people, there isn't one resource we can tap?"

"No. I'm telling you we need to search more. Listen. Have fun. Don't worry about all this stuff tonight. Go get a drink, okay?"

Maybe I will have a drink, she thought. Dee didn't like the way this was going but a few drinks later she succeeded in relaxing in spite of it. She ended up listening to the live band and making small-talk with other guests. Even though Dwayne told her not to worry, she still took note of who was who. One of the guests was a television executive, Albert Koster. She saw him standing next to the fruit tray and strolled over.

"Whew!" Dee said once she reached him.

He turned around and looked at her. "What?"

"I'm relieved. I was afraid you were going to grab all the nuts. If I don't get something in my stomach fast, this alcohol is going to take me down for the count. I'm serious. Somebody's going to have to carry me out of here," Dee said.

Albert smiled. "Not a drinker, eh?"

"Don't get me wrong. I hold my own with the big boys but there are so many different types of wines and champagnes here, I can barely keep up."

"Oh, then maybe you should slow down."

"No, I'll manage," Dee said, coyly holding her glass close to her lips.

Albert laughed and placed his plate on the table. He reached out his hand. "I'm Albert Koster."

"Deidre Wright." Dee shook his hand.

"So, how do you know Christopher?"

"I don't know him per se. I was invited by a friend. You?"

"I'm the producer of his show," Albert said. "Yeah. Every time he hosts one of these, I'm that much more blown away. His knowledge of food and beverage is really extensive."

"I can see that."

"What do you do?"

"I'm a fashion stylist," Dee said.

"Really? Who do you work with?" Albert asked.

"Models, singers, actors."

"That sounds fascinating."

"Right now, I'm working on a fashion magazine."

"Oh, you're not concerned about the market?" Albert said.

Dee could feel her ears burn. Perhaps they were trying to block the words that came out of Albert's mouth. Dwayne had warned her she needed to prepare for these types of responses. Even though those comments still stung, she was happy she did practice her answer to the doubters.

"No, because all markets and industries go through change but few of them collapse. The magazine industry will pick up again and I intend to make sure my magazine is ready when the market revitalizes," Dee said.

Albert nodded. Across the room someone waved to him. "Listen. I enjoyed talking with you and your work sounds very interesting. Do you have a card?"

"Sure." Dee reached into her little bag and pulled out one of her business cards. Albert reached for one of his.

"Thanks. Here is mine. We may need a stylist for the set soon. I'll call you," Albert said, walking away.

"Great! Good talking with you," Dee said. She sighed. It was cool that her stylist experience interested him but she really needed someone to be excited about her magazine. This "feeling people out" thing wasn't working for her. She believed she would've gotten better results, if she had asked straight out. Do you have money to invest in a magazine? Do you know anyone else that has money to invest in a magazine?

Dee felt restless, so she decided to locate Dwayne. After searching the house, she spotted him outside, near the pool enjoying a cocktail and the company of a tall, blonde woman. Dee didn't waste time approaching him and the mystery lady.

"Hey! There you are. Thought I'd have to send out an APB on ya," Dee said, leaning in. Without missing a beat, Dwayne introduced Dee to his new friend.

"Deidre, I want you to meet Rachel Parker. She's the VP of Marketing at Walt Disney World."

"Oh, hello," Dee said.

"Rachel, this is my girlfriend, Deidre Wright." Dee did a double-take. They'd been dating for about four months but this made the first time Dwayne ever referred to her as his girlfriend. She smiled to keep from drawing attention to her surprise.

"It's a pleasure to meet you, Deidre," Rachel said, extending her hand.

"Please, call me Dee. All my friends do." She shook Rachel's hand. "So, what brought you to this party?"

"The host did some work for us and he invited the execs to the party. No one else could come. I decided to drop by. It's been a great party," Rachel said.

"Yes, it has. I guess it's a nice little break from the hustle and bustle of marketing. You know," Dee leaned forward, "I may need some marketing services soon for my magazine."

Dwayne shot Dee an aggravated look. Dee knew he preferred she take the magazine process slower but she felt like she had to take advantage of this opportunity.

"Really? What kind of magazine?" Rachel said.

"Oh, it's great. It's a fashion magazine for the working woman. Something that'll make it easy for the average woman to look fabulous." Dee rolled out her ideas, summarized her business plan and described her expertise in glowing terms.

"You know what? I think that's wonderful. As a matter of fact, take my card. Give me a call. We should chat."

Rachel left to catch one of her friends but she insisted Dee keep in touch. After Rachel departed, Dee braced herself for a verbal spanking.

"I thought we agreed you would relax and let me handle this," Dwayne said.

"I know, but, technically, I didn't ask her for money.

I just told her about the idea. That can't hurt, right?" Dee tried her best to look sorry.

"We still need to keep our cards closer to us. Let's not tell everyone the plans yet."

Dee sucked her teeth. "Fine," she said.

Dwayne looked toward the pool. "Oh, no," he groaned.

"What?" Dee turned around and saw a short, dark-skinned man with a lot of bounce in his step approaching them. He looked out of place with his wide grin and tight Italian suit.

"Hey, Dwayne! What's up?" the man called.

"Nothing, man. What's up with you?" Dwayne said.

"Oh, you know. Making my rounds, surrounding myself with good company," he said. "Speaking of good company, who is this fine specimen you done brought to this here shindig?" the stranger asked, eyeballing Dee and giving his best impression of a sexy Southern accent.

Put off by his antics, Dee quietly but firmly introduced herself. "My name is Deidre. Deidre Wright."

He put out his hand to shake hers. "Bobbie Mitchell. But most people call me 'Sunny' 'cuz I brighten up everybody's day," Bobbie said, cackling so loud people standing close to them stared at him.

"It's a pleasure to meet you. So, how do you two know each other?" Dee asked. She glanced at Dwayne, then Bobbie, curious to find out how these two men ever shared the same air, let alone shared any acquaintance.

"Oh, we go way back. Way back. Our bond is thicker than water. Ain't it, Dwayne?"

"Right," Dwayne said between clenched teeth.

"I remember this one time…"

"You know what? We have to go. Catch you later, Bobbie," Dwayne interrupted. He grabbed Dee's arm and pushed her toward the house.

"It was good seeing y'all. Hey, 'til next time, man!" Bobbie's shouts caused more people to look his way. Some glared at him; others moved away from him. "What are y'all looking at?" Bobbie asked them.

"Dwayne, what's going on?" Dee asked. "Who is that?"

Dwayne didn't answer. He grabbed their coats and stormed out the door. Dee trailed behind him, continuing to ask him about Bobbie. As she stepped inside the car, she looked at him. Dee expected him to answer but Dwayne only cranked the car and sped off without explaining his hurry.

They rode three miles while Dwayne maintained his brooding silence. Dee glanced over at him, periodically, but she remained cautious about asking any more questions. She could see him turning the events at the party around in his head. After fifteen minutes passed, Dee felt brave enough to ask a question.

"Do you want to talk about it?"

Dwayne shot her an ice cold stare under his hooded eyes. She fell silent. *What is going on here?* Dee thought.

Two minutes later, she tried again. "Who was that dude?

He seemed to think you all are friends," Dee noted.

Dwayne scowled and broke his silence. "No, he doesn't. He's being an ass," Dwayne said. "Trust me. He's no good. Let me know if you see him again."

Dee snapped her head toward Dwayne. "Why would I see him again? Who is he?"

"He's somebody I knew from Texas."

Dee's mind raced. She wanted to ask if he was someone with money but decided against it. Knowing Dwayne, he would probably call Bobbie stingy or mean. However, something about this situation didn't sit right with Dee. She'd never seen Dwayne react to anything or anyone that way. He was always cool and calm. Very little upset him. Not even her—and she knew how to try anybody's nerves.

"How did you meet?"

"Listen. I don't want to talk about it. It doesn't matter. Just make sure you tell me, if you see him again," Dwayne said.

"But why?"

"Because you should let me know. That's why," he barked.

"Wait a minute. I know you're not trying to boss me." Dee frowned at Dwayne. "I'm trying to find out what the hell is going on here."

Dwayne faced Dee. "This isn't about bossing you. Bobbie's no good. Don't acknowledge him. Don't talk to him and definitely don't do business with him. I want you to tell me if you see him again. Do you understand?"

Dee continued to stare at Dwayne, expecting more details but it became clear he wasn't going to budge.

"Do you understand?!" Dwayne shouted.

"I understand. Fine." Much to her discontent, Dee gave in. She thought about going off on Dwayne but she felt like there was more to this story and she needed to figure it out. She also thought about the progress she'd made with him. She didn't want to risk everything over a silly argument. They rode the rest of the way in silence. They both had a lot to think about.

CHAPTER 10

Monica

O n August 15th, one hundred and twenty politi-
    cians, business owners, executives, entertainers
    and news professionals hobnobbed at the
Pavilion, waiting for the Hatcher Scholarship Foundation
dinner to start. The media lined the red carpet, snapping
pictures of the famous and infamous, while ignoring the
attendees they found boring and unimportant. There
weren't many losers around, since Monica took great
care in choosing her guest list.

Initially, Monica envisioned walking the red carpet
with Tony, smiling and chatting with the media about
the foundation. She should have been mingling with her
high-profile guests squeezing the last dollar out of their
designer pockets. Instead, Monica stood in her bedroom
trying to figure out which dress to put on her size-four
body. After an hour passed and she still hadn't decided,
she called Dee.

"Hey! Come over here and help me pick a dress,"
Monica said once Dee answered her phone.

"What? I thought you already had one," Dee said.

"I do. I have three and I've been standing here for an
hour trying to figure out which one to wear."

"Monica, please tell me you're joking."

"I'm afraid not. It shouldn't take long," Monica said.

"Why not? It's already taken you an hour."

"Well, then. It shouldn't take much longer."

"Monica, I don't feel like coming over there. Why don't you close your eyes, point to one and wear that one?" Dee asked.

"I got an even better idea. Why don't I keep your ticket to the dinner?" Monica asked.

Dee sighed. "You know what? I hate you sometimes."

"Yeah, yeah, yeah. Come over here," Monica said. "And bring Stephanie with you."

Monica hung up the phone satisfied. *I told them they would end up helping me one way or the other*, she thought.

About forty-five minutes later, Monica heard footsteps down the hall, following Dee's big mouth.

"Monica! We're here. Where are you?" Dee yelled.

"Hi, Auntie Dee. Hi, Auntie Stephanie," Monica's daughter, Angela, greeted them. They both gave her a hug.

"Where's your mother?" Dee asked.

"Down the hall on the left."

When Dee and Stephanie entered her room, Monica felt compelled to give them a hard time. "Whew! It's about time," Monica said, smoothing the back of her head. She'd spent the past forty-five minutes making sure her signature haircut laid right.

"Whateva. This is cruel and unusual punishment. Making

me show up to the dinner with you guys. Depriving me of my grand entrance. You know I have a job to do. I got haters to entertain," Dee said, swiping a glass of Dom Perignon, vintage 1998 from a tray nearby.

"Girl, please. Help me pick out this dress." Monica pointed toward the three dresses hanging from a rack. "Now, there's the green, blue and the black. Which one do you think is more appropriate?" Dee and Stephanie sat on the edge of the bed and offered their opinions of the choices Monica presented.

"I like the blue," Stephanie said.

"I like it okay but there's quite a bit of cleavage going on. Remember this is a benefit for the kids. I want their minds on the cause, not on my 'girls,'" Monica said.

"I don't see anything wrong with showing the 'girls.'"

"We know," Dee said, eyeing Stephanie's cleavage-baring Versace dress. "You know black always looks good."

"Yeah, but it's such a common color; other women there will be wearing it. I need to stand out. I guess I'll go with the green," Monica said, holding the green dress in front of the mirror.

"See, Stephanie. She chose for herself. I knew we didn't need to come here," Dee stood up. "If you were going to wear what you wanted to wear, why did you ask us to be here?"

"It doesn't matter. You didn't have anything else to do," Monica said. Dee rolled her eyes.

At 10:00 p.m., they departed from Monica's home in

a black limo to go to the Pavilion. By the time they backed out of the driveway, Dee had downed her second glass of champagne.

"You might wanna slow up. I hear they got food there," Monica said.

Stephanie laughed.

"I'll drink more if I want to," Dee said.

"Umm. I'm scared of you," Monica said.

"Speaking of scared, that is one serious necklace, you're wearing," Stephanie said, checking out Monica's neck.

"I know, isn't it amazing? Three hundred fifty thousand dollars. It's the last piece we'll be auctioning off tonight." Dee and Stephanie raised their eyebrows at the diamond-encrusted masterpiece. "That's why I only invited the ballers for this charity. It is not a game."

The ladies nodded and Dee turned to Stephanie.

"What about your little baller? Everything going better?" Dee asked.

"Yeah, it's okay. I asked him to come here but he's really busy with promotion," Stephanie said.

"That's okay. We can share Dwayne during the party," Dee said.

Monica laughed. "Why?"

"Because he's getting on my nerves."

"I thought you guys were getting along well," Monica said.

"We were until Coles' party," Dee said.

"Oooh. How was it? I've always wanted to check it out," Stephanie said.

"Chile, you didn't miss nothing. I could have stayed home and watched the *Law & Order* marathon," Dee said, chugging down another drink.

"So, what did you guys fall out about?" Monica asked.

"He wants me to hang back and let him find the investor, but he's not moving. He's not talking to anybody. All he's doing is telling me what's wrong with everybody," Dee said.

"You think he's doing it on purpose?" Stephanie asked.

"I don't know," Dee said. "We also ran into some guy he knew in Texas. Dwayne almost broke his neck trying to get away from him."

"Maybe the guy is a pest," Monica offered.

"Whatever he is, Dwayne can't stand him," Dee said.

The limo stopped and the three women stepped out in front of the Pavilion. The venue buzzed with excitement from the outside. On the inside, the party moved along like a well-oiled machine. The microphone checked out; the people mingled and schmoozed and the rest of the jewelry up for auctioning sat in a secure glass case. As they entered the massive hall, pyramid-folded napkins, sparkling glasses and shiny silverware lined the dinner tables, along with Monica's handpicked orchard center-pieces. She rushed into the kitchen area to check on the food. The sight and smell of grilled salmon, angel hair pasta, broccoli and a side of key lime pie with raspberry sauce calmed her nerves and put her stomach on notice. While they were waiting for dinner, Monica instructed the servers to keep the alcohol coming before and during dinner. Everybody's drinks needed to stay full. The drunker they became, the more money they would spend.

Between mingling with guests and checking on the logistics, Monica ran into Tony for the first time since he'd left the house. He looked quite good in his tuxedo. It's not that she was surprised; she already knew she had an attractive husband but he looked especially handsome in his black pants and white jacket. She cocked her head to the side, as she watched him approach her.

"Hey. When did you get here?" Tony asked, giving her a gentle kiss on the cheek.

"About fifteen minutes ago," Monica said.

Tony raised his eyebrows. "What took you so long?"

"I couldn't figure out what to wear."

Tony sighed and shook his head. "Women."

"Oh, please. Don't even go there."

"I was ready," Tony said.

"I would have been ready, too, if I had my personal stylist to help me beforehand."

"You could have used my stylist. I would have recommended it, if I had known it would take you so long."

"Well, that's fine. I ended up calling Dee and Stephanie over. Not that they were much help."

"Of course not. Your friends never are."

"Okay. That's enough." Monica shook her head. She could not understand why her husband refused to get along with her friends. They hadn't done anything to him. He rarely ever saw them but she decided the dinner was more important than his petty feelings about Dee and Stephanie.

"The dinner is about to start. I'll talk to you later," Monica said.

At the start of the dinner, Monica addressed the room with a welcome speech. She talked about her and Tony's vision for the foundation and the reason they started it. Monica looked out over the crowd and found herself overcome with emotion. This was her dream come true. Standing in front of an audience of important people who came because she invited them made her feel relevant. She didn't want the feeling to end. Despite the emotion, she managed to make it through the mini speech, without crying at the podium. She introduced the two recipients of the scholarship and the audience erupted in applause, offering the two kids a standing ovation. Then, everyone ate and circulated. Guests visited their friends' tables to catch up until the auction began. After the speech, the food and the auction, the guests moved to the banquet room where they grooved to the sounds of Mint Condition. Unfortunately, Monica couldn't groove anything. Her dogs were woofing. She had to sit at a separate table to the side for at least two seconds and rest her aching feet. *The cost of beauty*, she thought.

When she scanned the room, she noticed Stephanie sulking in the corner. So, she stood back up—wincing—and maneuvered over to her friend's side of the room.

"Hey! Enjoying the party?" Monica asked.

Stephanie shrugged.

"Miss him, huh?" Monica elbowed Stephanie.

"I've left him voicemails and text messages. Whether they're nice and sweet or angry and vicious, he's only replied twice with one- or two-word messages. I haven't heard from him in a few days, which makes me nervous."

"Okay. Well, then maybe it's time for you to give him a break. Give him time to call you."

Stephanie frowned. "When you've invested so much energy into the relationship, it's easier said than done."

"That's why it's time to give it a break. Come on. Let's take a walk for a minute."

Stephanie sighed. They walked to the ladies room. When they opened the door, two women were standing at the mirror. Monica sat on a plush chair to rest her feet, while Stephanie entered a stall.

"Girl, my feet are killing me," the first woman at the mirror said.

"You, too?" Monica asked her. The three of them laughed.

"I told her 'bout buying shoes too small just 'cuz they're cute," the second woman said.

"They fit in the store!" the first woman said.

"Riiiight." They all laughed.

"Well, I know the feeling. I guess I should have tried to break them in before tonight. I don't know what I was thinking," Monica said.

"Yeah, but I look at the bright side. At least they'll be broken in for the concert coming in a few weeks," the first woman said.

"Oooh. Levin's coming here, right?" the second woman asked.

"Yep," the first woman said.

"He's fine. I wouldn't mind a sample of that." The two women chuckled. Monica took in a deep breath and sat up straight. If Stephanie had heard them, she could only imagine what she was feeling. Stephanie wasn't the most secure person in the world, especially when it came to Levin.

"Well, honey, get in line. Many have tried that out. Have you heard there's a girl in his hometown that's supposed to be pregnant by him?" the first woman asked.

"I think I did hear about that. She's about three months along now," the second woman said, fixing her loose curls.

Monica's eyes grew wide. She rushed to think of a way to clean up the mess about to be made. "Oh. I'm sure that's a rumor," Monica said.

"Uh uh." The first woman shook her head. "I heard it on the radio yesterday and I got a friend that works at his label. They all say he's gonna be a daddy."

"I wonder if they'll marry," the second woman said.

"The woman seems to think they will," the first woman said.

"I think this is all premature. Nothing has been confirmed. I won't believe it until then," Monica said, glancing at Stephanie's stall.

The two women raised their eyebrows. "Well, I believe my sources. It has to be true if everybody's saying it," the first woman said.

Her friend nodded. "Um-hmm. C'mon, girl. We gotta go," the second woman said, as she led her friend out of the door.

Monica sighed. *What a disaster*, she thought. How could those women spread gossip about something they couldn't even prove? It always boggled her when people acted like they would swear before ten priests the rumor they heard was the truth. Didn't they know radio hosts didn't necessarily verify everything they said? The women were making people feel bad.

Monica leaned back in her chair. Then, she remembered Stephanie was still in the stall. She hadn't made a sound since the women started talking. Monica stood up to check on her friend. "Stephanie?"

She didn't respond.

Monica knocked on the stall door. "Stephanie? Open the door."

Monica heard Stephanie slide the latch back. She pushed the door and saw Stephanie sitting on the closed stool.

"Honey, don't believe what they said. It's got to be a rumor," Monica told her but she knew Stephanie would believe it anyway.

Stephanie nodded and burst into tears.

∞

It must have taken twenty-five minutes for Monica to calm Stephanie down, but, after she did, she realized it was about time to wrap everything up. She sent Stephanie home in her limo and returned to the event to break it down. When Monica saw Dee, she motioned to her.

"Hey. Have you seen Stephanie lately?" Dee asked, scanning the room.

"Yeah, she had to leave early. I'll tell you later," Monica said as Dwayne approached them.

"Well, I'm getting ready to follow her 'cuz I need to get home," Dee said.

"Okay. Dwayne, make sure she doesn't drive. Okay?" Monica tossed back an imaginary glass of alcohol. Dee waved her away and kept walking.

Monica smiled to herself. She felt like she'd accomplished a lot but she also felt her energy draining away from her. She saw Tony standing in a circle of people—his usual post—telling jokes to his loyal subjects. Life wasn't worth living, unless he could impress somebody. She paused to get a drink from a passing server, hoping to rejuvenate herself with some bubbly. A tall, slender man leaned over her from behind.

"Hey, there."

Monica spun around at the sound of the voice and almost dropped her glass. Robert Alexander, her college sweetheart, smiled down at her.

"Oh my gosh! Hey!" Monica said. It was like seeing a ghost. She reached out to give him a big hug. "What are you doing here?"

"I'm in town on business."

"Wow! How did you end up at my dinner?"

"I was invited to come with a friend. By the way, did you really put all this together?"

Monica placed her hand on her hip. "Yes. Who else would it be?"

Robert threw up his hands in surrender. "I guess you did always know how to do it big. It's great. So, this is where you live now?"

"Yeah, Tony and I moved here about a year ago."

"That's right. He's playing for Tampa Bay."

Monica nodded. While he talked, she flashed back to her time with him in college. They had an intense on-again, off-again relationship. When it was good, it was great; when it was bad, it was worse. She used to think that they would work it out. When they had parted permanently, it took her months to come to terms with her broken heart.

Monica and Robert exchanged a few more niceties and awkward glances before he told her he needed to go. "Well, I must find my friend. She'll have my head, if I try to leave without her."

Monica understood they couldn't talk forever but she wished they could talk longer. It was so surreal. Looking at him, she couldn't believe how much time had passed.

"Oh, okay. It was good seeing you. Take care," Monica said.

"You do the same." Robert turned to walk away, and then turned right back around. "I hope this doesn't sound strange but what would you say to meeting me for lunch Tuesday?"

Pleasantly surprised, Monica tried not to seem too eager and happy. "Okay. That would be nice."

"Great." After agreeing to meet at noon, they waved goodbye to each other. Monica watched him walk away, then, allowed her eyes to fall back on her husband's circle. She found Tony standing there with a scowl on his face. She knew exactly what to expect next.

Tony broke from the group and bolted over to Monica. "What was all that about?" he said when he reached her.

Monica sighed. "What was what about?"

"This little love fest going on over here," Tony said.

"I don't know what you're talking about," Monica said, refusing to even look his way.

"What did Robert want?"

"To say hello," Monica said with sarcasm.

"Yeah, right.

"Don't go there with me tonight. I have a dinner to wrap up." She turned to leave the growing argument. Tony grabbed her arm and pulled her toward him.

"Don't you walk away from me," he said in a low voice.

"Don't you put your hands on me!" Monica shouted,

a little louder than she intended. A few people looked their way. He loosened his grip.

"This isn't over," he whispered. Monica shook her arm loose and walked away.

She looked at the servers clearing the tables and the janitors cleaning the floors. At that moment, she would have stared at anything to keep from looking guests in the eye after her and Tony's blow up. She'd considered canceling her lunch with Robert, thinking maybe it wasn't appropriate. She briefly wondered if it was the right thing to do. But as she walked away from Tony, she knew she was going. *I don't know who Tony thinks he is, but I will not be bossed around*, Monica thought.

CHAPTER 11

Stephanie

At two in the morning, Stephanie stared at the ceiling from the center of her queen-sized bed. She stopped crying for the tenth time but expected to start back any minute. After she arrived home from the scholarship dinner, she tried calling Levin eight more times. He still hadn't answered his phone. So, Stephanie lay in bed with her eyes open and her mind racing. *Is he avoiding me? Is he with someone else? Is he with the girl that's supposed to be pregnant?* Stephanie asked herself. The only thing worse than asking herself these questions was longing for the answers she hadn't received. She knew Levin was busy but she still felt he could have returned her call, especially when he knew the streets were talking.

Of course, it crossed her mind that Monica was right: the baby rumor could be an awful lie meant to cause trouble, but Stephanie couldn't help feeling unnerved. The rumor shed flood lights on her biggest fear—Levin's fidelity. She always suspected he saw other women but she didn't have any proof. The truth was she wanted him so bad she didn't want to see any proof. Evidence of his cheating would be like sticking a pin in the fragile bubble that was her dream. But the baby rumor changed the situation altogether. If it was true and he'd made a child with someone else, she'd have to let him go. She took a deep breath, as she felt another sob coming.

Stephanie leaned over and reached for a tissue and her phone. She dialed her father's number. It was around midnight where her father lived but she needed to talk to someone warm and supportive. She could always count on her father to give her unconditional love. He picked up on the third ring.

"Hey, Daddy."

"Princess? What are you doing up so late?" her father asked.

"Oh, I was up watching TV."

"At two o'clock in the morning?" he said, yawning. "What's really going on? Are you okay?"

Stephanie wanted to start the conversation off light to avoid worrying her father, but she should have known he'd suspect a problem. He always knew when something was wrong.

"I'm fine. A little sad, that's all," Stephanie said. Her voice dropped at the end.

"Does it have anything to do with that guy you're dating? What's his name? Kevin?"

"Levin," Stephanie said. "Yes, Daddy."

"Well, what's wrong?" he asked.

"I've been hearing some rumors about him and I don't

know if they're true but I'm afraid they are," Stephanie's voice cracked.

"Oh, Stephanie. You worry too much, honey. If it's just a rumor, you need to talk to him first. Who knows? Maybe it's not true."

"I know, Dad, but women fall all over him and I keep thinking I'd be a fool not to be concerned," Stephanie said.

"It sounds to me like you and he have some trust issues. And you know, a relationship can only go so far without trust," her father said. "You have to remember, Princess. You chose to date this man, even though you knew the circumstances. If it's too much to handle, you can always let him go. Don't lose yourself in this man."

She thought about how much stress she would lose if she let Levin go. No more wondering where he was. No more wondering if he had another girl in another city. No more waiting days for him to call. As she went down the list, it seemed like her life would be a whole lot easier without him. Then, she thought of what she would lose. Gifts. Money. A big house. Not to mention, the man she loved. Before she could say "I'm out of here," someone else would come right along and swoop up her man and her life. *Why should I give my blessings to someone else?* Stephanie asked herself.

As she processed her father's advice, Stephanie decided she couldn't let Levin go. There were some really good things about their relationship. She simply had to talk to him to find out the truth. Since he avoided her call, it was difficult to discover the truth but she still felt like she needed to keep trying. "Yeah, you're right. I'm probably overrreacting," Stephanie said.

Her father sighed. "Okay. Think about what I said."

"Okay. I think I'll go to sleep now. Good night, Daddy."

"'Night, Princess. I hope I made you feel better."

"You always do."

∞

The next morning, Stephanie sat in a booth at Henrietta's Bistro across from Dee and Monica. While they recapped the dinner's highlights, she stared at her cup of hot tea. She didn't expect it to perform any tricks for her but she figured focusing on it would prevent her from ruining her friends' morning with her self-pity. Though she woke up positive, her mood changed once she checked her phone and saw Levin still hadn't called her back. Her friends, however, barely noticed her attitude. Dee drank her water, while Monica shared the dinner's reviews and pictures from the newspaper.

All of a sudden, Dee turned to Stephanie. "Where did you disappear to last night?"

Stephanie continued to stare at her cup. Dee looked at Monica with a question in her eyes. Monica chewed on her lip.

"Hey! Hellooo!" Dee yelled.

Stephanie jerked her head up at Dee. "Huh?"

"What happened to you last night?" Dee asked again.

"Oh, I left to go home," Stephanie said.

"Why?" Dee asked. "I looked for you for half an hour."

"I didn't feel like the crowd," Stephanie said.

Dee sighed. "I know you were missing Levin. Maybe he can make it to another event or something."

"I don't know," Stephanie mumbled.

"Sure, he will. I know he's busy but you can try letting him know things ahead of time," Dee said.

"It doesn't matter," Stephanie said.

"Why?" Dee asked.

Stephanie sat silent, looking back at the tea as if it would speak for her. Monica placed her paper down and leaned forward. "Stephanie? It's gonna be okay," Monica said.

Stephanie shook her head and sniffled. Monica, then, put her hands over Stephanie's hand. "Have you talked to him yet?"

Stephanie shook her head.

Dee looked back and forth between Stephanie and Monica. "What? What is it?" she asked.

"He's going to have a kid," Stephanie whispered.

"What?" Dee said.

"Some girl is going to have Levin's baby," Stephanie said louder. "While I was at the dinner last night, I overheard two girls saying another woman is three months' pregnant from him. I've been seeing him for five months. How could I not know there was somebody else?"

Dee cut her eyes at Stephanie.

"Are you sure that's true? Have you talked to Levin yet?" Dee asked.

"No. I tried calling him fifteen times between last night and this morning and I haven't been able to reach him yet. I keep getting his stupid voicemail," Stephanie said, dropping her head into her hands.

"How could this happen? We were doing so well. I mean, we've had our ups and downs but I thought we were special," Stephanie said. Her voice started to quiver.

"Yeah. I've heard the rumor mill. Everybody seems to think you guys are heading for the altar," Dee said, rolling her eyes.

"Maybe it's a rumor. I really think you need to suspend your anger until after you talk to him. This may be nothing," Monica offered. Stephanie reconsidered Monica's logic. She really missed Levin and wanted to hear his side of the story. After thinking about the time she'd invested in the relationship and the feelings she'd developed for him, she reached the same conclusion she had the night before: she had to talk to Levin.

"You're right. I'm gonna talk to him. As a matter of fact, I'm going to Georgia to see him," Stephanie said.

"No. No. No," Dee said.

"Now, wait a minute, Stephanie," Monica interrupted. "Yes, you should talk to him but you're really upset right now and I think you should try to chill out a little bit. If he doesn't call you back right away, don't sweat it. Give it some time."

"Time? I need to know what's going on!" Stephanie shouted.

"Yeah, but you don't want him to think you're a stalker, do you?" Dee said.

"No, but I can't tell if he's lying over the phone. I need to see his face and his eyes to make sure he's telling the truth. And since he won't call me back anyway, that gives me all the more reason to go see him. It'll be fine. We'll work everything out," Stephanie said, as she leaned back in her chair and dipped her spoon in her cup.

When she returned home from her breakfast with Dee and Monica, Stephanie tried to call Levin one last time. As she expected, he did not answer. So, she allowed her emotions to take over and booked a flight to Georgia. The whole time she typed her credit card number into the online order form, she told herself an unannounced visit would be fine. Number one, he was her man and, number two, she tried calling him first. It wasn't her fault he never answered.

After much hustle, Stephanie arrived in Atlanta within thirty hours. She sped to Levin's house only to find out he had headed to the studio a couple of hours beforehand. Undeterred and unwilling to wait for him to get home, she drove her rented Mercedes-Benz to the rehearsal studio, parking a block away. She sat in the car watching the building's activity. Three dancers strolled into the building followed by a big, burly guy. She saw Levin's Maserati but she didn't see him get in it or come out of the vehicle. Forty-five minutes into scoping out the place, she cranked up the car and pulled up to the big brown, unmarked building.

Evening had settled in since she touched down in Georgia, which made her nervous. She scanned the neighborhood, jittery about its safety. Then, she thought about Levin's gentle voice and heart-shaped lips and decided it was safe enough. She couldn't wait to hear his soothing words and stare into his clear, brown eyes. Stephanie checked her makeup and hair in the rearview mirror and stepped out of the car. She walked through the studio doors and headed toward the front, round desk, where the guard played solitaire on his cell phone. He looked up briefly, then looked down.

"Sign in, please," he said.

He can't even do his job right. What if I was a serial killer or lunatic? she thought. Stephanie picked up the pen to sign. She heard a woman's laughter and stopped writing. When she heard a man's voice, she dropped the pen and turned to follow the voices.

"Ma'am, you have to sign in. Ma'am!" The guard stood up to follow her.

Stephanie continued to walk down the hall, heading for the exit. She pushed the door open, paying no attention to the guard. All her attention fell on the scene in front of her.

"What the hell are you doing?!" Stephanie screamed.

Levin stopped in the middle of planting one on a five-foot-eight, model-looking tramp. He shook his head for a minute as if to clear his vision.

"Stephanie? What are you doing here?"

"Never mind that. What are you doing here? I must've left you thirty messages. You don't even have the decency to call me and let me know you got them?"

"Ma'am, I need you to come back and sign in." The guard finally caught up. He stopped beside them, bending over and breathing hard.

"James, it's all right. I got it," Levin said.

"Ah. It's you." Sucking his teeth, James looked at the two unsuspecting women. "I should have known."

"C'mon, man," Levin said. James turned away, shaking his head.

Levin turned to the leggy girl. "I'll talk to you later, okay?" She nodded and walked off. Stephanie watched the other woman saunter away.

"Later?! Who is she?"

"She was auditioning for background vocals on my tour," Levin said.

"Oh, really?"

"Yes, really," Levin said, allowing irritation to creep into his voice.

"So, what is this? Her callback?" Stephanie asked.

Levin dropped his head back.

"What song did she sing?" Stephanie asked.

Levin didn't answer, which infuriated Stephanie. He'd been caught red-handed and he had nothing to say.

"What song did she sing, Levin?"

"None of your business."

"Oh, it's none of my business. So, I guess your baby

on the way is none of my business either, huh?" Stephanie asked.

"What?"

"Tell me something, Levin. When were you gonna tell me about it? When the child started preschool?"

"What are you talking about?!"

"I'm talking about the girl in Virginia that's pregnant with your baby!"

"Aww, Stephanie. That's a rumor! I don't have no baby."

"Yeah, right. And I guess you weren't hooking up with the girl that just left, either." Stephanie fought the tears welling in her eyes. She covered her face.

"Are you finished?" Levin asked.

"No! I think it's pretty clear you're playing games. Why are you telling me that you're ready for a real relationship when you're still doing the groupie thing? If you're not serious about me, just say so!" Unable to hold it together any longer, Stephanie burst into tears. It had never been this hard for her to keep a man interested in her but then again, Levin wasn't any man. He was rich, talented, kind-hearted and warm. He was beautiful. She had to find a way to make him want her and only her.

"Listen. I'm not with other women. I've been busy. I would've called you but I couldn't talk to you that long and that would've been hard for both of us. I want you but you gotta trust me," Levin said in a gentle, yet stern voice. "I wanna marry you someday but all this sneaking up on me stuff ain't cool. Come here."

Levin stretched out his arms and pulled Stephanie closer to him. She slipped in for one of his trademark bear hugs. When he squeezed her tight, she sobbed. His hugs felt so good. In her heart, Stephanie felt he'd lied to her about seeing other women but, right then—in his arms—she didn't care.

∞

Stephanie spent the night with Levin. They had a long talk about their relationship. He admitted he was wrong for not calling her and said he would treat her better. She left for the airport the following afternoon as happy as a kid with a chocolate sundae. She had to wait for her plane to board at the terminal, so she decided to give Monica a call for an update.

"I'm in love," Stephanie exclaimed to Monica over the phone.

"Again?" Monica asked.

"I always was. I was concerned but that's over now," Stephanie said, smiling.

"I take it he doesn't have a child on the way?" Monica asked.

"Nope."

"Good. What did he say when you turned up at his house?"

"He wasn't there. I had to go to the studio."

"You mean you interrupted him while he was working?" Monica asked.

"No. I was going to meet him upstairs but I didn't make it there. I found him outside with some girl," Stephanie said.

"What girl?!" Monica asked.

"Just a girl performing background for his songs."

"Oh. What were they doing outside?" Monica asked.

Stephanie took a few seconds to respond. Her mind returned to the moment she found him outside with the leggy girl and she felt a brief touch of jealousy. She refused to give in, though. She forced herself to push it back down. Levin belonged to her and she wasn't going to allow anything to stop their happiness. "They were taking a break," Stephanie said.

"Well, I hope it turns out well for you. I want you to be careful," Monica said.

"Why?"

"Because I see you're really in to him, and I'd hate to see you lose yourself trying to hold on to him," Monica said.

"Hold on to him? He's holding on to me," Stephanie said. "Really. Levin is so kind, sweet, caring and attentive. And he loves me. I know that, for sure."

"I'm saying, Stephanie. You know how you can get fixated on a man sometimes. Take some time with this guy. Make sure he's really going to treat you right."

"I don't understand. He's not having a baby with anyone else. That's a good thing. Why are you still warning me?"

Monica paused. "Because, usually, when there's smoke, there's fire."

"So, what does that mean?" Stephanie asked, a little defensive.

"If there are rumors about him and other women, there may be other women," Monica said.

"I don't believe that," Stephanie whined into the phone.

"All I'm saying is be careful."

When she and Monica hung up, Stephanie crossed her arms and frowned. She didn't understand why Monica wouldn't share in her bliss. Levin wasn't going anywhere. She'd never let him.

CHAPTER 12

Dee

On a humid afternoon, Dee, Monica and Stephanie rode to Heron's Place. Dee initially wanted to pass but Monica insisted they have a girl's day out. Dee was still recuperating from her tiring day at Tasha's house. As she did every month, she went over her house to discuss the model's schedule. They liked to plan her wardrobe for upcoming engagements ahead of time, except this time, Tasha's hairstylist, Candice, was there. The minute Dee began tossing out ideas to Tasha, Candice felt the need to intervene with her opinions. Candice had a problem with every suggestion Dee made. When did hair stylists become fashion stylists?

By the time Dee left Tasha's house, she had a headache. It was days like that when she felt ready to drop the stylist job and work on her magazine full-time. Unfortunately, she needed more time. She hadn't located the money to launch the magazine yet, and Dwayne was taking his own sweet time finding an investor. She may have been tired of dealing with Tasha, but she was even more tired of waiting for someone else to help launch her dream. Thinking about it made her frown. At the mall, Monica picked up on her sour mood.

"When are you going to cheer up, chick?" Monica said to Dee.

"When I'm finally able to move on my magazine," Dee said.

"How's that going?" Monica asked.

"Nowhere," Dee said.

"Why?" Stephanie asked.

"Because Dwayne still hasn't found an investor for me. You know for a while I was asking him every day if he'd found someone. After hearing 'no' so much, I stopped asking," Dee said. "It's either that or I curse him out."

"What's his excuse for not at least having prospects?" Monica asked.

"He says the ones he's met are not a good match. Their goals are different and they won't want to invest in such a risky business," Dee said. "Is it me or does that sound like bull?"

"I'm not sure, but if you haven't heard anything within a month, it may be time to have a little talk with Mr. Dwayne," Monica said.

"Otherwise, how's the relationship?" Stephanie asked.

"It's okay but if he doesn't come through with this money, he can forget about a relationship," Dee said.

"Just like that, huh?" Monica asked.

"Yes. He said he'd do something for me. He has to deliver or there's no room for a relationship," Dee said.

Stephanie waved her hand. "He'll come through. Like Levin came through for me." She pulled her hair back to reveal new diamond drop earrings. "Look at what he bought me," Stephanie said, cheesing.

"Those are nice. I guess everything is roses now that he's not having a baby," Dee said.

"Yep." Stephanie nodded.

Monica rolled her eyes. "Anyway, gifts are not signs a relationship is going well."

Dee stretched her eyes. "What's this about?"

"Monica is hating," Stephanie whined.

Monica looked at Stephanie. "What reason do I have to hate on you? Girl, please."

Stephanie frowned and stuck her lip out.

"Well, at least she's getting something out of it," Dee said. "What could Dwayne be doing?"

"Maybe he really hasn't found anybody yet," Stephanie said.

"I don't believe that. I'm gonna have to find another way to get what I want," Dee pondered. She felt a gnawing feeling in her stomach. Anxiety had overtaken her optimism. Her past confidence gave way to an uncomfortable sense of urgency and frustration about the magazine. She expected to have a cover for the magazine already and it discouraged her to think she had to start all over again to find another way to pay for it.

"From another man?" Stephanie asked.

"Maybe," Dee said.

"Watch out now," Monica said.

Dee sighed. "Yes, Mother."

Monica sucked her teeth.

"I'm gonna go to the Gucci store and take a look around. Anyone coming with me?" Dee asked.

"I'm gonna stay here and look around some more. Let me know if they have something I haven't already seen," Monica said.

"What about you?" Dee asked Stephanie.

"I'll stay here, too. I don't plan to buy anything today anyway," Stephanie said.

After her friends decided to stay put, Dee left them for the Gucci store, with her mind on her friends' advice. Maybe she should find another man. It wouldn't be hard. Still, part of her wanted to believe Dwayne would come through. He knew people. He was a professional. She needed someone like that on her team. The more she thought about it, she felt like she needed someone like that in her life.

How could she throw him away so quickly? Even if he didn't come through on the magazine money, he was a good man. He seemed honest and, from her experiences, that was a rarity. Dee walked down the aisles, unimpressed with the current collection of clothes in Gucci. She passed on all the merchandise and headed for the next store. Dee stepped across the store threshold and bumped into Bobbie Mitchell, the guy from the party a couple of weeks ago.

"Hello, there. I didn't expect to see you here," Bobbie said, smiling.

"Yeah. Well, here I am," Dee said. Dwayne's words of warning about Bobbie echoed through her mind. A chill ran down her spine and she stepped forward. Bobbie stepped in her way.

"So, how's your shopping experience been? Good, I hope. If not, I know the manager of the mall. I could let him know the standards aren't up to par," Bobbie babbled.

"No, that won't be necessary. The mall is fine. Well, I'd better be…" Dee moved to the side to walk away.

"How's Dwayne? I haven't seen him since the party," he asked, stepping in front of Dee again. Her nerves stood on edge.

"He's fine. He's on a business trip."

"Is he looking for investors outside of Tampa?" Bobbie asked.

Dee's mouth dropped open. "What?"

"Is he traveling to look for your investors?"

"I don't know," Dee said, frowning.

"You know, it's gonna be hard for him to find you an investor," Bobbie said.

Dee stared at Bobbie in disbelief. "Why?"

"His reputation isn't what it was," Bobbie said.

"I don't know what you're talking about," Dee said. She felt uneasy and wished she had run the moment she laid eyes on Bobbie.

"People aren't lining up to work with him like they did in Texas. Even his old clients are steering clear of him."

"Old clients? You mean his brother. He only worked with his brother," Dee said.

"Yeah, he worked for his brother but he had a thriving business in Texas, too," Bobbie said. "Wait a minute. Didn't he tell you that?"

Confusion and anger threatened to take root in Dee's mind. Flashbacks of the nightmare she'd endured with her last boyfriend resurfaced and she could feel steam coming out of her ears. She could not imagine Dwayne lying to her; as a matter of fact, she thought she knew Dwayne pretty well. But if she found out he did deceive her, he would pay. Then, she thought about Dwayne's words. Bobbie shouldn't be trusted. She needed to get away from him as quickly as possible.

"I don't believe you," Dee said. "Move." Dee tried to push past him but he stepped in her way.

"Okay. I'll tell you what. The next time you talk to him, ask him if he's ever tried asking Maximus to invest in your magazine. See what he says," Bobbie said.

Dee squinted. "Who is Maximus? A cartoon character?"

"Ask Dwayne."

Dee scowled at the smug look on Bobbie's face. "Listen. I don't know you and you don't know me. So, let's cut the crap, okay? I don't have time to stand here and play games with you. If you're so interested in what Dwayne's up to, you need to find Dwayne yourself. Otherwise, stay out of my business and out of my face."

"Umph. There is no reason for the attitude. You are not all that," Bobbie said, smirking.

"Well, step the hell off then," Dee said, pushing past Bobbie.

"Sure thing. Tell Monica and Stephanie I said hi!" Bobbie called to Dee.

She stopped dead in her tracks and turned back around. She never told him her friends' names.

"What did you say?"

"I said tell your friends I said hello." Bobbie smiled.

"Stay away from me or I'll make you stay away from me," Dee said. Then, she faced the escalators and stomped off, refusing to turn around and look his way. Who was this guy? Why did he bump into her here? And how did he know her friends' names? Her pulse raced. Before stepping off the escalator upstairs, she stole one last look at the Gucci store. She saw no trace of Bobbie.

When she reconnected with Monica and Stephanie, they stood in the china section of Nordstrom.

"Are these the ones you broke?" Monica asked Stephanie between laughs.

"Yep. I even stepped on them," Stephanie said, grinning.

"Girl, you're lucky. Anybody else woulda still been kicking your tail." They laughed.

"That's okay. Things are going better now. I told you he loves me."

"I hope so. If it doesn't get better, he might want some money for his dishes."

"Are you guys ready to eat yet?" Dee asked, fidgeting.

"Sure," Monica said.

After they entered a nearby restaurant, the waiter took

their orders and disappeared. Monica and Stephanie stayed lost in conversation about the dishes incident at Levin's house but Dee had a hard time concentrating. She couldn't even laugh at their jokes. She kept looking around to see if Bobbie was posted in the corner or at a table. When Dee felt like she couldn't hold it in anymore, she shocked the table.

"I'm thinking about buying a piece," Dee blurted out.

Monica and Stephanie stopped laughing and stared at Dee.

"A piece of what?" Monica asked.

"A piece! A gun."

"Oh, no!" Stephanie laughed.

"You not gonna buy no gun, girl. You'd shoot yourself," Monica said.

"Well, I have to do something. I don't like feeling like I'm not safe," Dee said.

"Wait a minute! Back up. Why don't you feel safe?" Monica asked.

"Remember when I told you about Bobbie, that guy Dwayne warned me about? Well, I ran into him. At the Gucci store."

"What did he say to you?" Stephanie asked.

"He asked how Dwayne was doing. But that's not the worst part. He told me Dwayne owned a company in Texas," Dee said.

"So?" Monica asked.

"Dwayne said he didn't start his company 'til he got here," Dee said.

"Maybe Dwayne meant to say he started his company there but slipped up," Stephanie said.

"How do you slip up and leave out that you had a company elsewhere?" Dee asked.

"I don't know, Dee. Are you sure this guy is telling the truth? He may be stalking Dwayne. Didn't Dwayne tell you to let him know if you see this guy? You may need to let him know Bobbie was at the mall talking crazy," Stephanie said.

"It was so odd. I mean, he knew you guys' names! I never told him that. He's got to be casing me or something."

"Well, to be fair, I'm not exactly anonymous. Maybe he saw me on TV or something. Did Dwayne say Bobbie was a danger to you?" Monica asked.

"No," Dee admitted. Leave it to her friends to make it sound so harmless. Spoken out loud, everything seemed fine but Dee sensed more going on. She didn't like being out of the loop. She definitely needed to talk to Dwayne.

"It doesn't sound like you're the issue. I think he really wants to get at Dwayne. The question is why," Stephanie said.

"But most of all, Dee, if this guy really bothers you, you should tell Dwayne that you saw him. That means no gun. Okay?" Monica asked.

"Okay," Dee conceded.

"Great. That's settled. Now, did Stephanie tell you what she did to Levin's kitchen?" Monica asked.

∞

Later that week, Dee had dinner at Dwayne's two-story home located in an exclusive country club. He prepared lasagna, salad, and breadsticks. Dee sat at Dwayne's dining room table, amazed at how well he'd put everything together. *Most guys I've dated can't even boil water*, Dee thought. She smiled to herself.

"What are you smiling about?" Dwayne asked.

"You," Dee said. "You continue to amaze me. And you know that's hard to do."

Dwayne nodded. "Well, the feeling is mutual." He held up his glass to clink hers. Once they clinked, they both took a sip of their white wine.

Dee calmed down a lot since her encounter with Bobbie. She'd dismissed the idea of purchasing a gun but she still felt like she needed to get to the bottom of this Bobbie situation. His claims, if true, would raise a lot of red flags about Dwayne. Flags that might be deal breakers. Though she wanted to push it aside and continue with their deal and their relationship, she had to find out what was going on.

She considered coming straight out and telling Dwayne she'd talked to Bobbie but that would've left her at his mercy for the truth. If she asked him straight out about his company, and his relationship to Bobbie, he could refuse to answer or worse, spazz out like he did at the Coles' party. Then, she thought about Bobbie's

suggestion: ask about Maximus. That seemed risky. She
didn't even know who this guy was or what relevance he
would have to Dwayne but, at this point, she was willing
to try anything to move their situation forward. So, she
transitioned the conversation to Maximus in the most
obvious manner.

"How's the search coming?" Dee asked.

Dwayne looked up from his glass.

"My magazine investors?" Dee asked.

"Oh, it's coming. I have a few ideas in mind but haven't
found any solid prospects yet," Dwayne said.

"Where are you looking?" Dee asked.

Dwayne raised an eyebrow.

"I'm only asking," Dee said.

He sighed. "I've approached a couple business owners
but, right now, I'm trying to focus on wealthy, retired
business people. They usually have a lot of money to spend
and are willing to share it for the right opportunity."

Dee nodded. "Is Maximus a retired businessman?"

In that moment, Dee swore she could hear a plane
take off in China. The room went dead silent. Not to
mention, the look on Dwayne's face. All of his muscles
tightened and locked. She would have feared for her
life, if she didn't know him but then again, maybe she
didn't know him as well as she thought. Looking at his
expression, Dee panicked a little.

"Dwayne?" Dee asked.

"Yes," he said.

"Is everything okay?" Dee asked.

After a pause, he turned to her. "Why are you asking me about Maximus?"

Dee opened her mouth but nothing came out.

"Where did you hear that name from?" Dwayne asked.

"I don't know. Somewhere. His name came up when I was talking with someone about people with investment money. Why?" Dee asked.

He leaned forward. "Who were you talking to?" Dwayne asked.

"No one you know. What's the problem?" Dee asked.

"Don't play with me, Dee. Who told you about Maximus?" Dwayne asked.

"I'm not playing with you. I just wanted to know if he's someone you talked to about the magazine," Dee said.

"Stop lying to me!"

"I'm not lying! What's your problem?" Dee stood up.

"I told you to let me handle this but you refuse to do that. I'm telling you, Dee. You're asking stuff you don't know anything about," Dwayne said, pointing his finger at her.

"Enlighten me!"

"No!" Dwayne yelled. "You either let me handle this or nothing at all." He stormed out of the dining room.

"Dwayne?" Dee called him. "Dwayne!"

She could hear Dwayne stomp upstairs and slam the door behind him. *What just happened here?* Dee asked herself. She headed to the living room to grab her purse and leave. This turned out to be far more than she had expected. Something must be wrong. No one would respond that way unless they had something to hide. As she cranked up her car, she thought about her magazine but decided there was more at stake now. It was time to find out if Dwayne had been honest with her. And if he wasn't honest, then what was he hiding?

CHAPTER 13

Monica

Monica turned giddy as she glanced across the table at her college boyfriend, Dr. Robert Alexander. He'd come a long way since his days as a lanky junior, unable to commit to a major. Now, he'd become a dentist. She found herself beaming as she watched him tear into a thick, juicy steak. In between staring at him, she, occasionally, manipulated the little pieces of peppers and onions hidden in her soup. As she scooped some of the soup juice into the spoon, she glanced up and saw Robert staring at her. They both broke into laughter.

"What?" Monica asked a little embarrassed.

"Watching you play with your food," Robert said. "Looks like fun."

"Well, I don't want these little peppered things they put in here. It's too much."

"I remember there was a time when you would've torn that plate up and asked, 'What else you got?'"

"Well, people change."

"You?! The bottomless pit?" Robert laughed.

"Aw, man. Shut up."

She tried to keep a straight face but he spoke the truth. Monica could always put it away. Her public life, however, changed that. Now, she had to eat right and exercise. She needed to maintain a certain image; her figure had to stay svelte. She didn't have any excuses, not even childbirth justified permanent weight gain. The public had no mercy for a sloppy appearance. She simply had to preserve her looks.

Monica smiled and sighed. She hadn't realized how much she missed talking to Robert until then. He always accepted her without question. Still laughing over the food joke, Robert shook his head, leaning down to take in another fork full of steak.

"So, what's been going on in your life? Are you married? Have any kids?" Monica asked.

"Yes, I was married but I'm now divorced. I have one son, Robert, Jr. He's five years old," Robert said.

"Really? Aww, do you have a picture of him?"

"Yeah," Robert pulled out his wallet and showed her a little boy posing with a baseball bat.

"Oh my gosh! He's adorable," Monica said. "He looks just like you."

"Yeah, that's what my mom says."

"How is Ms. Agnes?"

"She's great. She still remembers you. You're the one I let get away, she says."

Monica laughed. She always loved Robert's mother. A very sassy and fun lady. "I miss her."

"She'd love to hear from you. Maybe I can take you to see her some time," Robert said.

Monica shifted her weight. How in the world did he think that would go over with Tony? She shook her head and kept the conversation moving.

"I don't know about that," she said. "I'm sorry to hear about your marriage, though. How long were you together, if you don't mind me asking?"

Robert shrugged. "It's cool. We were married for four years. Felt like forty years," Robert said.

"Oh. That bad, huh?"

"I think she and I married for the wrong reasons. We had a child and thought that meant we were supposed to get married and be a family but it didn't work out that way. We constantly argued. One time, she called the police on me."

Monica gasped. "What happened?"

"It was around the time we knew things weren't working out. I had moved out and I came by to see my son. I wanted to take him to the park and stuff. Well, she didn't want me to take him. She told me to leave. I told her, 'Not without my son,' and she called the police on me." Robert shook his head. "It was a bad situation."

"Dang. Are you guys able to be friends now?"

"Yeah, we're okay. As a matter of fact, we're better now than we were when we were married," Robert said.

"I've heard a lot of people say that!"

"It's definitely the case for us. It eliminated a lot of

unnecessary stress. I think we're better parents, too," Robert said. "So, look at me, going on and on about me and my dysfunctional family. What about you?"

"Oh, my family's good. Tony's in his second season with the Buccaneers. William is a very active kid. I think he wants to play football like his dad and Angela makes A's and B's in school. They're really great. I'm so proud of them." Monica beamed for a second, then looked out the window wistfully.

"What?" Robert asked.

Monica redirected her eyes back to Robert. "Huh?"

"What's with the look?" Robert asked, leaning forward.

"What look?" Monica frowned.

"That look that says 'I'm happy but…'" Robert said, mimicking her facial expression.

"Nothing." Monica laughed. "I just…" She hesitated.

"Hey." Robert placed his hands over hers. "It's me you're talking to. What is it?"

Monica sighed. "I really feel like I want to do my own thing, you know? I mean, don't get me wrong. I love my family but I would love to run my own PR firm. I know I'd be good at it," she said.

"You would. Why don't you?" Robert asked.

"Well, Tony doesn't really want me to work," Monica said, gazing down at the table.

"What do you want?" Robert asked.

"I want my professional independence *and* my family, but he makes me feel like I can't have both," Monica declared.

Robert shook his head. "You should do it."

"But I don't need the headache at home," Monica said.

"Then you'll have heartache from not following your dreams," Robert answered.

Monica took a deep breath. She knew Robert was right. She'd never stop wanting to pursue a career in public relations. She'd always remember how she felt on that stage at the scholarship dinner. If she waited for Tony to understand that, she'd be waiting a long time. He believed that she should stay home and raise the kids since she didn't have to work, but it wasn't about the money for her. It was about personal fulfillment. Besides, Angela was getting to the age where she was very impressionable. Monica wanted her daughter to see a woman going after what she wanted. Not taking the path of least resistance because a man was footing the bill.

As she mulled over Robert's words, he offered her a surprise.

"You should do what you want to do, Monica. That's what life is about. I'm confident your business will grow quickly. As a matter of fact, I already know your first client," Robert said, taking a sip of his drink.

"Who?"

"Me," he said with a big smile.

"What are you talking about?" Monica asked.

"It's the reason I'm in Tampa. I'm thinking of starting a practice here and I could use your PR skills to get it off the ground," Robert said.

"Wow! That's great. How close are you to making a decision?

"I'm pretty close. We have a few details to secure but things are looking good."

"Cool."

"So, are you game?"

Monica cocked her head to the side. This was exactly what she needed to get the ball rolling. Tony's words bounced around in her head but she shut them out. She wanted to create her own business and her opportunity had arrived. She had to snatch it up.

"Yes, I'll do it."

Robert clapped his hands once. "Great! I should have more details within the next couple of weeks and I'll keep you abreast of what's going on."

"Okay. It should be fun working together. It'd be like old times." Monica chuckled.

"I hope so," Robert said.

When their lunch ended, Monica drove home, thinking about what she was about to do. She looked forward to working with Robert. Even more so, she looked forward to developing a business. Tony, however, would not look forward to the news. It would likely cause an argument. Therefore, she decided not to tell him about it. At least not right away. Eventually, she would have to tell him what she was doing but, for now, she'd keep him in the dark about the business. She also needed to keep him in the dark about lunch with Robert. Although

Robert never did anything to him, Tony harbored a lot of distrust for him. He knew Robert was her first love and he seemed to resent him for that.

Monica pulled into her driveway and walked into the kitchen, vowing to keep her mouth shut. Once she saw Tony sitting at the kitchen table, she jumped.

"Oh my gosh!" Monica said.

Tony looked at her. "What?"

"I didn't expect you to be here," Monica said. "What happened to practice?"

"They sent me home early. I have a little injury."

"What?" Monica asked, walking quickly over to him.

Tony held up his hand. "Don't worry. It's not serious. Just a sprain," he said.

Monica breathed a sigh of relief.

"Where have you been?" Tony asked.

She straightened her back and tried to think fast. "Uh, I went shopping."

"Where are your bags?" Tony asked.

"I didn't buy anything. I didn't see anything I liked."

"Did you really not see anything you liked? Or did you hold back on buying because of the bounced checks?" Tony asked.

Monica temporarily had forgotten about the checks but she was grateful for the reminder. It was the very topic she needed to keep the conversation from drifting toward her lunch with Robert. "Well, I don't want another bounced check. Or an insufficient funds notice."

"Monica, that's not gonna happen again. I had my accountant get that all straightened out."

"Your accountant? Don't you think you should have checked up on that yourself?" Monica said.

"What is that supposed to mean?"

"It means I thought you said you would visit the bank yourself to check on it."

"Why would I need to do that?" Tony asked, standing up. He wobbled a little bit. "That's what I pay my accountant for."

"All I'm saying, Tony, is it doesn't hurt to check after the accountant to make sure he's not stealing money."

"He's not stealing money," Tony said.

"Then, what was that extra check for?"

"I don't remember," Tony said, scowling.

"Then don't you think you should figure it out?" Monica asked.

"I don't have to explain to you every single thing I do with my money. The important thing is I wrote it."

Tony moved away from the table and hobbled upstairs. Monica sighed. This is what she was tired of hearing. Every time an issue with money came up, Tony liked to make her feel as though she had no say. She planned to change that. It would start with this new business. If she could keep it to herself until the business was all the way running, there would be little Tony could say or do about it. He'd have to respect her decision to contribute to the household and the world.

∞

The next day, Monica went to visit Stephanie before she left town. Stephanie was supposed to go to Las Vegas with Levin. The two women took a long walk on the beach behind Stephanie's condo. The waves crashed over the rocks near the pier, creating the only sound for miles. Monica broke the silence talking about her lunch with Robert. Stephanie didn't waste time sorting through the implications.

"So, what are you doing?" Stephanie asked. "I mean why did you even want to meet with Robert?"

"I wanted to find out how his life was going but that's not all. He wants to be my first client." Monica smiled.

"Is that all?"

"Yes." Monica tried not to sound defensive but she failed. She opted to keep talking. "He's planning to start a practice here and he wants me to help him market it when the office is all set. Isn't that something? I already have my first client and I haven't even opened my doors yet." Monica laughed.

"I'm happy for you but..." Stephanie trailed her sentence. Monica cut her eyes down at her friend. "You don't think this is going to start something?"

"Something like what?" Monica asked.

"Uh, like an affair?"

"No! Out of the eight years Tony and I have been married, I've never cheated on him. Not even once."

"I'm just asking because I'm picking up signals that you have some leftover feelings for him," Stephanie said, backing up a little. "Am I wrong?"

"Well, yeah. I still care about him. He and I used to sometimes talk about getting married. I really did love him."

"What happened?"

"I think we were too much alike. We're both very stubborn and our fights became like WWF Smackdowns. The more intense it got, the harder the relationship got." Monica hadn't thought about their relationship in years. For a minute, nostalgia took over. She remembered the dates, the picnics, the talks and their plans. If she couldn't get a job at a public relations firm, Monica was thinking about getting a job as an account executive at a television station after graduation. Robert had planned to start his own business. He didn't know what type of business but he was certain he would start one. Robert believed he had to do it so he could give Monica the kind of life she was used to having. The one she'd had with her parents. It was funny how all those dreams disappeared when her life with Tony began. It was like she suddenly became a whole other person.

After spending years with Tony, she couldn't tell if the change was good or bad. Perhaps it was a combination of the two but one thing was for sure: she was ready for another change. She found it funny Robert would be a part of that change.

"It sounds like Robert is trying to see if there's an opportunity for you guys to get together now," Stephanie said.

"Oh, girl. Please. He has a good business opportunity, that's all. Besides, I wouldn't up and leave my family for anybody. He knows me well enough to know that."

"But if he wants to rekindle the flame, what would you do?" Stephanie asked.

Monica was certain she'd never leave her family because they made her happy. Yet, she could find herself tempted having Robert around. Then, the thought occurred to her. *If I'd married Robert, how would my life be different?*

CHAPTER 14

Stephanie

S tephanie opened her eyes to the bright rays of sunshine coming through the window. They blinded her until her eyes adjusted to the daylight. For a moment, she forgot she'd flown to Las Vegas. When the memories of the previous night swept over her, she smiled to herself. Not only did Levin fly her there to stay at the Wynn Hotel with him, he also surprised her with an invitation to attend the MTV Video Music Awards with him. The excitement hit her all over again and she jumped up to call home. She reached Monica first.

"Monica, I'm going to the awards with my baby," Stephanie gloated.

"Oh! That's nice. I forgot it was going on out there this year. I take it the trip is going well," Monica said.

"It's great! He takes me out. He takes me shopping. I'm so happy; we are finally on the right track. That's why we're getting married."

"Excuse me? I thought those were rumors. When did he propose?" Monica said, shocked.

Stephanie envisioned the last time she was in Georgia.

He'd told her he wanted to marry her and she believed they were well on their way to making it down the aisle. So, what if he hadn't exactly proposed yet? It was as good as done.

"A couple of weeks ago when we were in Atlanta. Oh, Monica. It was so beautiful. He says he wants to be together forever and ever."

"Why didn't you mention this the other day at the beach? Or the day at the mall?" Monica asked.

"Levin swore me to secrecy. You know the rumors were getting way too loud." Stephanie pretended to know the intricacies of the entertainment rumor mill.

"Well, what kind of ring did he give you? I never saw it. Is it Winston or Tiffany? Wait a minute. He looks more like a Jacobs kinda guy," Monica said.

"I don't know yet. He'll be surprising me with the ring soon."

Before Monica could pry into the situation, her phone beeped. "Well, honey, I gotta go. Have fun and tell Lev I said, hi."

"Sure thing. Kisses."

As Stephanie hung up the phone, she turned her attention to the night ahead of her. She expected to have a blast at her first red carpet appearance. Levin's invitation validated their relationship—putting it on a whole new plane. Since they were going to marry soon, people would start to look at them differently. Treat them with a little more respect. Stephanie stretched back in the bed and pictured Levin walking her around to meet his colleagues, introducing her as his fiancée and posing for the photographers with her. They'd appear in all the magazines with a caption that read, "Singer Levin and his girlfriend, Stephanie." Since rumors of their engagement picked up steam, the captions may even call her the "fiancée." She couldn't wait. She smiled at the thought that things had gotten serious. Her dreams had become a reality.

The more Stephanie thought about the evening ahead, the more her euphoria gave way to panic. She only had a few hours to prepare for the awards show and she didn't have an outfit or shoes to wear. Stephanie snapped up out of bed and dressed to go shopping.

Fortunately, Levin had left her his credit card before he left to meet with his producer but even though she had the money, Stephanie had difficulties picking an outfit. Since she didn't have Dee's help, she decided to stick with her usual formula: anything that showed plenty of cleavage. While in a boutique at the Wynn, she settled on a canary yellow, low-cut mini dress with shoes and a purse to match. When she saw that there was more time to spare, she continued to browse around and find extra ways to spend Levin's money.

With one more hour to spare, she rode down the strip to Caesar's Palace and purchased more shoes and purses. She bought gifts for Monica and Dee. She even bought a scarf for Levin, which she tried to avoid because he had picky taste in clothes. He was the only man she knew that could identify fabrics better than her. By the time she finished shopping, she needed help loading the black limo with all of her bags.

Stephanie waited on the curb for the store clerk to bring and load her bags into the car. Out of the corner of her eye, she caught a glimpse of a couple walking across the street. Their little girl walked between them, holding on to each parent's hand. The child must have been about four years old. At one point, the father swooped the girl up. She giggled as he placed a gentle kiss on her cheek. Stephanie watched the family in a daze. All of a sudden, it made sense to her. That's what she and Levin needed: a family to bond them together, despite the circumstances. That way even if other women approached him, she would still hold court as his "wifey" and the mother of his child.

After her epiphany, Stephanie rushed to the hotel to get ready. She returned to a hairstylist and makeup artist waiting for her, courtesy of Levin. She grinned as she watched them transform her into a red carpet diva. The best part was seeing Levin's smile when she walked into the living room. He whistled.

"You're gonna get me in so much trouble tonight, girl," he said. He walked toward her and placed an arm around her waist.

Stephanie looked down and covered her smile. "Thank you, Levin."

He escorted her to the black limo, waiting outside the hotel. When Stephanie stepped inside, Levin's publicist, Kelly, greeted her. Stephanie responded cordially, but she felt surprised and disappointed. She'd hoped to spend this time alone with Levin. He'd been on the run all morning. Instead, she had to share it with Kelly and her speed updates for Levin on which media to avoid.

The ride, interrupted with frequent traffic jams and a slow trek through the sea of limos and SUVs, ended at the Palms Casino Resort. Levin turned to Stephanie.

"Are you ready?"

"Suddenly, I'm very nervous," she admitted.

"Don't be. You look great." He gave her a soft kiss on the lips. "Just remember to smile. Come on. Let's go."

Levin and Stephanie walked onto the red carpet with Levin's publicist, trailing behind them. They waded through the mass of bodies in their path. In between getting daps from his music associates, Levin stopped to talk to a couple of media outlets. One of his stops included Tweet, a radio personality for a Miami hip-hop radio station. She stepped to the edge of the red carpet and called out to him.

"Hey, Levin! How you doing?" Tweet asked, pointing her microphone in Levin's face. He stepped closer to her to answer her questions.

"Aww, I'm good, baby. How you feeling?" he answered.

"Great! Now that I get to talk to you." Tweet giggled. "You're having a phenomenal year, right?"

"Yeah, definitely. My single and my CD debuted at number one on the charts and have been there for four weeks. Thanks to stations like yours. I'm out there performing and reaching out to my fans. The reception is great. Everything is falling into place exactly as I wanted," Levin said.

"So, what can we expect from you next?" Tweet asked.

"Actually, I'm looking at getting into movies pretty soon. Some things are in the works and it's looking good."

"Anything you can tell us about?" she asked, leaning in closer.

"No. We're still working on it but when there's a green light, you'll be the first to know," Levin said, giving Tweet a wink and a smile. She smiled back and he began to move away from her. She noticed him inching toward Stephanie and stepped right over, not missing a beat.

"Levin, who's your date?" she asked.

"Oh, this is Stephanie," he answered, pulling her closer to him. Stephanie shot the woman a coy smile.

"Nice to meet you. What's it like being here with one of the most eligible bachelors in the world?" Tweet asked.

"It's a lot of fun." Stephanie laughed.

"So, how long have you two been together?" Tweet asked Stephanie. Levin shifted his weight. He began moving Stephanie toward the building.

"For a little while," Levin said, standing between Stephanie and the woman. His publicist motioned for them to end the interview. Levin nodded. Oblivious, Stephanie continued to talk into the microphone.

"We've been together for about a year now but this is my first event with him. There'll be more. We're inseparable," Stephanie said, hugging Levin.

"Oh, okay." Tweet raised her eyebrows. Levin immediately grabbed Stephanie and nudged her down the red carpet. She stumbled but regained her footing, looking back at him with a puzzled expression. Visibly flustered with the interview, Levin tried to head inside the venue but the media called his name every few steps.

He posed for a couple more pictures taking most of them alone and one with Stephanie. Flash bulbs popped off so fast Stephanie couldn't even see where they came from. Happy that she made it through the flash jungle, Stephanie said a secret thank you when they stepped inside the venue.

As they sat down, Stephanie noticed Levin clenching his jaw and leaning away from her.

"Is something wrong?" Stephanie asked.

"No," Levin said, looking straight ahead.

Stephanie's heart sank. She thought the red carpet experience had gone so well. She didn't want this to be her last time. "I don't believe you," she said. "If there's a problem, say it."

Levin sighed. "There's no problem. It's just that…" He trailed off.

"What?" Stephanie pressed him for an answer.

He faced her. "In the future, could you avoid making statements in the media about our relationship?" Levin said, grimacing.

"What do you mean?"

"Don't tell people stuff like 'we're inseparable and we've been together for a year,'" Levin said.

"Why? I was trying to answer the question. Don't you want people to know we're happy together?" Stephanie asked wide-eyed.

Levin took a deep breath. He held it for a minute, as if to make sure it and his words came out easy so it wouldn't allude to his hidden frustration and growing anger. "Look, Stephanie. I try really hard to keep my personal life out of the media. When you say things like that, I'll always have to answer those questions later."

"But if they know that we're happy, what difference does it make?" Stephanie answered. His motivation puzzled her. It didn't make sense to her that someone would deny their relationship. She'd always heard the stories of artists that do it but she knew Levin wouldn't do something like that. He respected her too much.

"No matter what I say, the media will always turn it into what they want it to be. I need you to do this for me. No more talking to the media." Levin stared at her with a stern look in his eyes.

"Fine," Stephanie said, throwing her hands up in the air. "I won't talk to the media. I'll pretend I don't exist."

Levin rolled his eyes.

The show began with anticipation as Britney Spears opened with her new single. Stephanie and Levin said very few words to each other. They were even quiet during the commercial breaks. That is, until Felicia, Levin's label mate, approached them around mid show. She wore a slinky spaghetti strap dress that turned heads whereever she walked. Felicia's looks and stage presence drew an equal amount of attention but most people wanted to know more about her personal life. Many male artists had already been on record saying that they wanted to date her. Levin played coy on that subject. As Felicia inched closer, Stephanie cut her eyes at Levin.

"Hello, Levin," Felicia said.

"Hey, Felicia. What's up, girl?" he asked. He stood up to hug her.

"Oh, I just came back from Europe. Have you talked to Victor yet? He's looking for you," she said. Felicia scanned the room and rested her eyes on a man with his hair slicked back. "He's over there." She pointed.

Felicia talked to Levin for about four minutes. Stephanie waited for the songstress to say something to her but it looked like she didn't even see her. When Felicia didn't look like she was going to acknowledge her, Stephanie finally cleared her throat. Levin looked down at his date.

"Oh, Felicia. I want you to meet my date, Stephanie. Stephanie, this is my label mate, Felicia," Levin said.

"Pleasure to meet you," she said, barely glancing Stephanie's way. Instead, she focused her attention to the left, where Victor stood motioning to her and Levin. "Let's go talk to Victor."

"I'll be right back," Levin said over his shoulder to Stephanie.

This is great. It's my first night out with Levin at an indus-

try function and they're treating me like a piece of scrap meat, Stephanie thought. The night wasn't turning out at all how she envisioned. First, she messed up with the media on the red carpet. Then, Felicia ignored her. She felt like steam would come out of her ears any minute.

Stephanie's eyes followed Levin and Felicia. When they approached Victor, the older man hugged Felicia and patted Levin on the back. He kept his hand on Levin's back the whole time he talked to him. At one point, he shifted his eyes over to Stephanie. Victor finished his point and patted Levin on the back one last time. Levin nodded and shook his hand. Stephanie sat there watching the scene unfold, wondering what they were talking about. After Levin returned to his seat, Stephanie pounced.

"Who is that?"

"Who? Victor? Oh, that's my manager. He's good people," Levin said.

"What did he wanna talk about?" Stephanie asked.

"Label stuff." Levin shrugged. Everyone returned to their seats for the rest of the show, including Felicia. She sauntered her way across the room back to her seat, making sure she threw a glance backward to watch the men watch her walk. *What a troublemaker*, Stephanie thought.

It wouldn't have surprised her if she found out Felicia was after Levin. That's probably the real reason she had pulled him away. Stephanie made a mental note to Google the singer and find out more about her reputation. But not only did Felicia's presence bother her, the image of Victor's face when he pointed at her still haunted her. She wondered if he'd heard about the red carpet incident and scolded Levin for it. Stephanie frowned. The thought of harming her man's career concerned her. She turned to Levin and scrutinized his face for a clue to their conversation. She saw nothing. Just in case the situation hurt him later, Stephanie planned to apologize to Levin at the hotel. In the meantime, she tried to push Felicia, Victor and the red carpet faux pas out of her mind and enjoy the rest of the show. After the awards show, Stephanie and Levin ate at Tao in The Venetian, one of several after-party spots. Stephanie didn't really feel like going but she didn't want to go back to the hotel without Levin. They sat down at a table with a couple of other singers and their dates. Stephanie ordered Alaskan Salmon and Avocado with Yuzu Sesame Dressing; Levin ordered the omakase.

Stephanie frowned. "You eat sushi?" she asked.

"Yeah," Levin said, giving the waitress their menus.

"But it's raw. You could get sick."

Levin smiled. "Thank you for your concern." He leaned over and kissed her on the forehead.

In that moment, Stephanie's anger melted and her heart warmed again. She remembered why she'd come in the first place and how she felt about it. She had looked forward to this moment since they started dating. So, Stephanie pushed her sulking aside and they'd interacted with each other much easier. It also helped that they sat with a lively, yet friendly, crowd.

All was going well until Felicia and Victor walked through the door. As soon as she saw them, Stephanie felt like someone had thrown cold water in her face. She spotted them before Levin and hoped she could keep him from seeing them. Her attempts didn't work. When Felicia saw Levin, she yelled to get his attention.

"Levin! I knew you would come to this party. Isn't it a blast?" Felicia asked.

"Yeah, it's pretty cool," Levin answered.

"Hello, everyone. Is there any room at this table?" Felicia asked the group. The women exchanged uneasy glances and rolled their eyes as if they really wanted to say no. The men, however, swiftly squeezed together so the seductive singer could sit down with them.

Stephanie wanted to believe herself above feeling intimidated but she couldn't deny her feelings. She looked at Felicia's long, slender arms and size two frame and questioned whether Levin found her appealing. After all, Stephanie was no size two or size six for that matter. She looked at him to check his reaction. He squirmed a little in his seat.

"I see you found a table," Victor said, walking up. "How's the night been treating you, Lev?"

"Good. This year was an interesting show," Levin said. Everybody at the table chuckled. "But man, I'm glad they had it here this year." Levin said.

"Yes, there is something about Las Vegas," Victor said.

"Hey! Have you met Stephanie yet?" Levin reached for Stephanie.

"No, I haven't. Good to meet you," Victor said, looking at Stephanie. "I've heard quite a bit about you."

I knew it. He heard about the red carpet situation, Stephanie thought. Levin avoided her eyes.

"All good I hope," Stephanie said with an apologetic smile. Victor nodded.

Then, their side of the table lapsed into an awkward silence. Stephanie decided to try to break it. "How long have you been a manager?" Stephanie asked Victor.

Victor raised his eyebrows. "For about six years."

"Is it a lot of fun?" Stephanie asked.

"I suppose. And what do you do?" Victor asked.

"Oh, I'm a video dancer. Well, I don't really dance. More like a video model."

"Really?" Victor asked. Stephanie scanned around the table to see the reactions to her response. She sensed some disapproval. So, she tried to clean it up.

"Yeah, but I'm not gonna do that forever. No. I plan to become an actress," Stephanie said. She thought she heard a short laugh from the end table.

"Oh, okay. Good luck," Victor said. Victor glanced at Levin but he focused on the rest of the table.

"Okay. I'd like to make a toast. To a fun party and a great night," Levin said. Everyone clinked glasses. Stephanie's nerves jittered. Her efforts to make small talk made her feel like she didn't belong. She felt like a little kid trying to fit in with the in crowd. Unfortunately, Levin, the man that she wanted, was a part of that in crowd.

∞

When Stephanie opened her eyes the next morning, the rush of excitement she felt the day before had vanished. She felt indifferent to the day ahead. She tried to make peace with the events from the night before, but she was having a hard time. On the way back to the hotel, Levin must have asked her what was wrong a thousand times but she would not respond. Her somber demeanor made it difficult to talk to her and she refused to explain her feelings.

Stephanie lay in the hotel bed motionless, when Levin entered the room the following morning.

"Hey, Stephanie. Breakfast is here," Levin said, leaning over her. Stephanie did not move or respond. She kept her head buried under the pillow.

"C'mon, baby. There's eggs, toast, biscuits, waffles with blueberry topping smothered in syrup. It's really good," Levin said. Stephanie still didn't move or say anything.

"I know you're hungry." Levin tickled Stephanie. Despite her sour mood, she laughed.

"Stop! That's not funny!" Stephanie laughed until she maneuvered away from Levin. "I'm not hungry." Just as she said those words her stomach growled.

Levin chuckled. "You're not hungry? Girl, get up and come eat something."

When she went to the dining room, Stephanie ate breakfast without any complaints, but, afterward, she returned back to bed. When she was still in her night-clothes at seven in the evening, Levin marched into the bedroom suite and bugged her again.

"Stephanie, I'm going to the studio to record some music. Are you coming?"

"No," Stephanie said.

"Stephanie, I don't know what's wrong but I think you'll feel better if you come to the studio with me. At least, you'll go out and get some fresh air," Levin said. He frowned when Stephanie didn't move.

"This ain't cool. You mean to tell me you're gonna act like this the whole trip?" Levin raised his voice.

"What do you want from me?" Stephanie whined.

"I want you to get up, wash up, cheer up and come to the studio with me," Levin said.

Stephanie turned over, sat up and glared at Levin. "Are Felicia and Victor going to be there?" She rolled her eyes.

Levin sighed and sat on the side of the bed. "Listen. I'm sorry if you didn't have a good time last night but today is a new day. Let's try to make this one better. Okay?"

Stephanie glanced at the clock. "Fine. I'll get dressed." Her feelings hadn't changed but she realized she had to get over it around Levin. So, she changed clothes and left for the studio with him.

Levin needed to record a song for his deluxe edition of *Metamorphosis*. Stephanie showed up at the studio in jeans, a white fitted T-shirt and big sunglasses. She returned to her muted demeanor and sat on the studio couch to pout. Levin went to work, pouring his heart out on the song he and his producer had written. When the producer gave him a cue, he was off.

Dedicated to you/After all I put you through/It was the least that I could do/'Cuz they don't make em like you no more/I was not prepared/For what was standing there/A love so pure and sweet/I never thought I'd meet

There he stood, singing the song. His eyes peered deep into her soul. As she sat mesmerized, Stephanie knew she loved him, and despite everything that had happened the day before, she believed he loved her, too.

CHAPTER 15

Dee

When the alarm clock buzzed, Dee slapped it quiet. After getting into bed at 2:50 in the morning, she wanted to sleep hard. The day before, Dee spent four hours running back and forth at Tasha's photo shoot, laying out the mounds of clothes, shoes and jewelry the model needed. The shoot ended around one o'clock a.m., leaving her exhausted.

Dee moaned and reluctantly sat up in her bed. She maneuvered into the kitchen to cook herself breakfast— grits and cheese eggs. As soon as she finished scrambling her eggs, the doorbell rang.

Dee wiped her hands and looked through the peephole. She saw Dwayne. She sucked her teeth. This was the first time she'd seen him since their argument at his house. She didn't understand his reaction then and, even though a week had passed, she still didn't understand his reaction. There was something major going on but she couldn't put her finger on it. The thing that bothered her the most was he wouldn't tell her why he was so upset. Dee looked through the peephole again and sighed. She hated to go through all the drama this time of morning; she hadn't even drunk her orange juice yet.

She steamed all over again when she thought about the way he'd talked to her, but she decided to push her anger aside and listen to what he had to say. When she opened the door, Dwayne was leaning against the frame. Dee noted he looked nice in his beige khakis and oxford shirt. It almost made her forget their argument. Almost.

"Hey," Dee said with no particular enthusiasm. She kept her hand on the door.

"Hey. What are you doing?" Dwayne asked.

"Cooking eggs."

Dwayne nodded. "Can I come in?"

Dee shrugged and moved out of his way. He walked into her house toward the kitchen. Dee headed for the refrigerator.

"Do you want some eggs?" she asked.

"No. Thank you." Dwayne leaned his waist against the counter. "Look, I came over this morning because I wanted to say I'm sorry for the way I acted a week ago. I was very out of line."

Dee stared at Dwayne.

"I hope you can accept my apology," he said.

Dee stood still.

"Well?" he asked.

"Sure. I'll accept your apology. On one condition," Dee said.

Dwayne frowned. "What?"

"You tell me why you got angry in the first place," Dee said. She sat down on one of her stools to listen to his excuse. *He'd better make it good because if I'm not convinced that he had a breakdown or something, I'm gonna let him have it*, she thought.

Dwayne threw his head back.

"I became angry because…" he paused. "Because I had a hard time with one of the people that I thought would be a good investor for you. He told me he might be interested, but once I tried to schedule a meeting with him, he reneged and I was frustrated."

Dee crossed her arms.

"I should have never taken that out on you. It's not your fault this man didn't come through. It's the normal process of finding an investor," Dwayne said.

"Was it Maximus?" Dee asked.

Dwayne tensed at the mere sound of the man's name, but he recovered quickly. "No, it wasn't."

"So, what does he have to do with this?"

"Nothing. I was upset about the failed attempt but I promise it won't happen again," Dwayne said.

Dee stared into his eyes.

"Fine. Consider the situation squashed," Dee said.

Dwayne nodded. "Well, I have to meet up with a friend. I'll call you later." He walked over to where she sat and kissed her goodbye.

After Dwayne closed the door behind him, Dee shook her head. She didn't believe him. There was still something going on between him, Bobbie and Maximus, but it was obvious he had no intentions of telling her. She knew what she had to do. She had to find the truth elsewhere.

Dee grabbed her cell phone and turned it on. She found she'd missed a call from Stephanie. *Oh, well. I'll call her back later*, Dee thought. She had other things on her mind.

In times like these, Dee had learned to rely heavily on gossip—to heed the word on the street. There must be someone who knew the deal on these guys and she was determined to find out. Since Dwayne wouldn't divulge any information, she decided it was time to do some investigating of her own. She called the one person she knew with the scoop on everything—Antony, her interior decorator. Antony traveled in high-class circles. His client list ranged from celebrities to mistresses. He had family everywhere, even in the ghetto. He'd definitely have information about what was going on.

Dee waited for Antony to answer his phone, but his voicemail picked up. She left a message. "Hello, Antony. This is Dee. Listen. I'm looking to redecorate my bedroom and you know I need you. So, give me a call back at your earliest convenience. I'll be home all day today. Bye."

Dee finished her breakfast, showered and dressed. When she checked her phone, Antony still hadn't called her back. Dis-appointed, she plopped on her couch and turned on the TV. About fifteen minutes into a show she liked, her doorbell rang. She opened it to find Antony.

"Hellooo," Antony sang.

"How are you? You're looking fierce, my dear," Dee said, leaning over to give him an air kiss on each cheek.

"Oh, honey. It's a full-time job but it's very necessary. I like what you're doing with your hair. It makes you look twenty," Antony referred to Dee's new, short hairstyle.

"Thank you. Saundra did it but you know I had to watch her. She likes to go crazy with the scissors."

"Yeah, that's why I don't trust her with these tresses." Antony flipped his long, black weave. "I got your call earlier and since I was in the neighborhood, I decided to stop by. Let's see what you want to do now, Ms. Thang."

For about forty-five minutes, Dee pointed out the things she wanted to change, which was really nothing. She only invited him over to pump him for information, but Antony wasn't the type of person who would spend this much time with you for free. It had to cost you something—money, time, business contacts, whatever. But Dee went along with him as he recommended different colors and fabrics. In between his suggestions, she saw an opportunity to introduce her real reason for inviting him. She dropped down on her bed and slid in some inconspicuous small talk.

"Oh, Antony. Did I tell you? I've met this wonderful man. His name is Dwayne and he's an investment manager. He works with the rich and famous."

"That's fabulous. How long have you been seeing each other?"

"About five-and-a-half months."

"Oh. It's getting serious?" Antony asked.

"I don't know."

"What? It's not working out?"

"Oh, it's fine. I just don't know if I'm ready to walk down the aisle with him or anything like that," Dee said.

"Chile, I know what you mean. I've been with Rick for two years and I still don't know if it's serious," Antony said. "But hey, look on the bright side. You won't have to worry about your money."

Dee laughed. "That's what I thought."

"Actually, I probably need to talk to him 'cuz I could sure use some help with my money. The stockmarket today is so fickle. I don't wanna lose what I've worked so hard for to a bad stock, you know what I mean?" Antony asked.

Bingo, Dee thought. "Honey, you should've stopped by earlier. He was here."

"Here? Well, I wouldn't wanna interrupt anything," Antony said, placing his hand on his chest.

"Ha-ha. Very funny. Seriously, I'd be happy to introduce you to him. He's very good with finances. Name the day and I'll set it up."

Antony hesitated. "Wednesday or Thursday of next week should work fine."

"Great. I'll set up a lunch time for the three of us to meet."

As Antony explained his ideas, Dee couldn't stop herself from smiling. The plan had worked out even better than she had imagined. Besides the fact that Antony was the King (or Queen) of gossip in this town, he also had great radar. He knew how to detect a problem. She could use his help. He would help her get the answers she needed. Antony finished consulting Dee. They walked down the hallway and he gave her an estimate for the changes he planned to implement.

"Whew! Every time I see you, you're hittin' up my pockets." Dee laughed.

"If you want the best, you have to pay for the best, right?" Antony asked.

"I guess," Dee said. "Too bad I can't get the best on layaway."

"Girl, you betta hush your mouth."

Dee laughed. "Would you like a glass of wine?"

"I'm always in the mood for some alcohol," Antony said. He sat down at the stool next to Dee. "So, tell me more about this Dwayne. Does he have a brother?"

∞

Dee could hardly hear over the constant chatter at Sharlow's, an upscale, five-star restaurant. People filed into the place like the owner was giving away free dinner. In reality, the opposite was the case, but that didn't stop the traffic. Dee and Dwayne sat beside each other at a table, waiting for Antony to show up. He had to show up after all Dee had gone through to arrange the meeting.

Dwayne's skepticism almost prevented it from taking

place. He acted like Dee didn't know a potential client when she saw one. He gave her excuse after excuse in attempt to avoid the meeting. Once Dee made a comment about his inability to spot a business opportunity, his ego stepped in and he agreed to meet Antony. All Antony had to do was prance through the door. She watched Dwayne drum the table with his fingers.

"He should be here any minute," Dee said.

Dwayne nodded. "This is a really good sign. Late for a meeting."

"I'm sure he has a good reason," Dee said.

"I'm never late to a meeting."

"C'mon. I know you've been late to a meeting before."

Dwayne shook his head. "Not when there's money at stake."

"Well, like I said, I'm sure there's a good reason," Dee said.

"I don't want to waste my time," Dwayne said, scowling.

"You're not wasting your time. I told you he really needs your help, but since he's not here yet, I would like to brief you on something."

"What?"

"Antony is gay. I'm telling you this because I don't know how you feel about that and I don't want you to be uncomfortable once he gets here."

"As long as he don't try me, we'll be fine. Besides, I've done business with gay people before."

"You mean Bobbie?"

Dwayne laughed for the first time that day. They chatted a few minutes while they continued to wait. Antony sauntered into the restaurant thirty minutes late.

"Hello, everyone. I apologize for my tardiness. I had an appointment run over," Antony said.

"Hey, Antony! No bother." Dee stood up and gave him an air kiss on each cheek. "Antony, this is Dwayne Shoreshire. Dwayne, this is Antony Waters, the extremely talented specimen I was telling you about," Dee said.

"Hello, Antony. Nice to meet you." Dwayne stood up to shake Antony's hand. Afterward, everyone sat down.

"Well, Dee. You told me so many good things about Dwayne but you never told me how handsome he is." Dee noticed Dwayne squirm in his seat. She gave his thigh a gentle squeeze under the table.

"But do I know you from somewhere?" Antony asked Dwayne.

"No, I don't think so." Dwayne's chest swelled as if he'd taken a huge gulp of air.

"It's probably someone who resembled you. I've seen so many faces. Sometimes the faces run all together."

Dee's eyes darted back and forth between Dwayne and Antony. Her interest was piqued. If Antony said he'd seen someone before, he had. It was only a matter of time before he knew where. She added a mental note to inquire about this later.

"That must be it," Dwayne said.

When silence began to hang in the air too long, Dee intervened.

"Dwayne, Antony wanted to know about investing in

stocks and bonds. I told him you'd be able to help him with that."

"Yeah? Have you tried investing before?" Dwayne asked Antony.

"No! I'm scared of the stockmarket," Antony said.

They all laughed. It took a couple of minutes but, as Dee expected, the atmosphere lightened. Antony had the type of personality that compelled people to overlook any differences. Some might call it charisma. Even Dwayne laughed at some of his jokes.

For the next thirty minutes, Dwayne talked about his company and explained his services. He even made recommendations for Antony to consider. "Well, Antony, I hope I've been helpful to you," Dwayne said, after he'd delivered his spiel.

"Oh, very. You know, I've tried looking at the Dow and the Joes and I can't tell one from the other. It's all Greek to me," Antony said.

"Jones," Dwayne said.

"Who?" Antony asked.

"Jones. Dow Jones," Dwayne corrected.

Antony burst into laughter. "See what I mean?" The whole table erupted in laughter.

"Don't worry about it. You shouldn't have to. That's what financial managers are for," Dwayne said.

"Dee is very lucky to have you on her side for her new magazine," Antony said. "You can probably even help her pay for the first three issues." *Oh, how I wish that were true*, Dee thought. She cleared her throat. Then, she took a deep breath and braced herself for Dwayne's response.

"Well, we're working on it for her," Dwayne said. He looked over at her and patted her on the lap.

You'd better be, she thought.

Antony shrugged and rose from his chair. "Good people, I must be going. It was a pleasure to meet you, Dwayne." Antony extended his hand. Dwayne took it and reached for his business card.

"When you're ready to begin working on your financial future, let me know," Dwayne said.

"Thank you. I should be calling you next week," Antony said.

Dee stood up to walk Antony outside. She couldn't wait to talk to him alone. She felt like a kid opening up a present on Christmas Day.

"What did you think of the meeting? Was he helpful or what?" Dee asked.

"Oh, yeah. He made me think of options I hadn't thought about before," Antony said.

"I know. See, I told you he was good. Maybe that's how you recognized him. You'd seen him in an advertisement or something?"

"Well, no. Not exactly. I thought I'd seen his face somewhere but I can't remember. Don't worry. It'll come to me soon. It always does."

That's what Dee was counting on. Maybe he could shed some light on Dwayne and the secrets he'd been keeping from her.

CHAPTER 16

Monica

Monica sat at the desk in her and Tony's office, searching the Internet for information on the number of doctors in Tampa. Robert still had to iron out the details for his new practice before he could move, but Monica figured it was better to start researching now. This way if he did get it started, she'd have a better idea of how to advise him. As it turned out, there were many practices all over the city, but not as many dentists. *Robert might have something here*, Monica thought. The sound of Tony's rhythmic footsteps broke Monica's concentration. She swiftly closed the search engine window and opened up a shopping website.

Tony jogged into the room with a little more pep in his step than usual. "Hey! What 'cha doin'?"

"Nothing. Looking on the Neiman Marcus website," Monica said.

"Oh." Tony barely looked at Monica while she answered his question. "Guess what? I got a call from my agent on an endorsement."

"Who's offering?"

"Express Gym." Tony sat down in front of the desk.

"Really? How much do they want to pay you?"

"One-and-a-half million for a two-year contract."

Monica shrugged. "It's okay. Can they afford it? Those are the types of numbers Coca-Cola shells out to athletes."

"Cola pays more than that," Tony said, tooting his lips to the side.

"To a select few." Monica sighed. "I say pass."

"Why?"

"I don't know. I kinda have a bad feeling about this one. They seem like a fad to me."

"You're the one that was ranting and raving about money and bounced checks a few weeks ago. Now you want me to turn down money." Tony shook his head. "I don't get you sometimes, Monica."

"There's nothing to get, Tony. I'm trying to look out for your best interests. All you have is your good name, and you can't get mixed up with something that's not the best quality."

Tony sucked his teeth and stood up. "Why did I ever come to you?"

"Because you know I'm right."

He shook his head. "I gotta get to my personal trainer," Tony said, walking toward the door. "I won't be coming home before practice."

"Okay. You gonna do what I said, right?" Monica shouted.

Tony closed the door behind him without a response. Monica flopped back in her chair. Contrary to his belief, she always looked forward to Tony's endorsement opportunities, but she wanted the right opportunities. She hadn't ruled out a television show for him, but, for that type of endeavor, he needed to keep his popularity high and his newfound excitement in perspective.

Tired of thinking about Tony and his business, Monica shut down the computer and left the office. She found herself wondering what Robert was doing. They'd had lunch almost every week since they'd reconnected at the foundation dinner. During these meetings, they sometimes chatted about their lives; other times they chatted about their dreams. It had dawned on Monica associates might see her out with Robert and wonder what was going on. As a precaution, she chose restaurants out of the way to reduce the likelihood of a collision between her past and her present. If Monica somehow still ran into someone she knew, she would have to tell them Robert was a businessman thinking about donating to her foundation. But so far, no one had found them, and she didn't have to answer any questions.

Nonetheless, Monica's conscience liked to nag her about it. Even though she wasn't officially having an affair, a little voice in the back of her head would tell her she was wrong for sneaking around to see Robert. She didn't want to listen to it, though. Her relationship with Robert liberated her. She could finally be herself and know someone supported her, unconditionally. That meant a lot as she transitioned into the business world.

When she reached for her purse and her phone, she decided to call on that support. Instead of inviting Robert to a restaurant for lunch, she asked him to meet her at The Nail Palace for a pedicure. He agreed and they met there. To her surprise, he fit right in to the atmosphere. They sat in black leather chairs, allowing the chairs to massage their backs as two young women gave them paraffin pedicures. Monica picked up a magazine and glanced over at Robert. He had leaned his head back, closed his eyes and smiled.

"Ahh," he said.

Monica chuckled.

"What?" Robert asked, opening his eyes.

"You." She smiled. "You are really enjoying this."

"Yeah. I missed this. I haven't had one in a while." Robert leaned back and closed his eyes again.

Monica laughed.

"You gonna stop laughing at me, woman!" Robert playfully threatened. Monica couldn't help it. She never expected to see Robert getting his feet scraped but there he sat lapping it up.

"I'm sorry, Robert. I don't mean to make fun of you. I'm actually proud of you for being confident enough in your masculinity to do this," Monica said.

"You act like this is new to me. I get these all the time. Yeah!" Robert said.

"What are you? One of those metrosexuals?" Monica asked.

Robert glared at her with a raised eyebrow. She burst into laughter.

"No, it's that you've always been a man's man," Monica said.

"I'm still a man's man. But I also know how to take care of myself." They exchanged glances, and then burst into laughter again.

"Well, since you're doing this you might as well go all the way." Monica turned to the young girl scraping Robert's feet. "He'll try a nice powder pink polish to set his whole outfit off."

"Lady, you better not put no pink on my feet," Robert said. Everyone within earshot laughed.

When the laughter subsided, Monica turned to Robert. "If I tell you something, do you promise not to tell anyone?"

"Who am I gonna tell?" Robert asked.

"Okay. Tony and I are having some problems," Monica said.

Robert raised his eyebrows. "What kind of problems?"

"Well, he's having problems with his team. The contract they gave him is not what he expected. The money is not what he expected."

"Oh, that's not good."

"No. I'm trying to get him to refocus his energy into other opportunities. Tony lives for the thrill of the field and the game. So, even though his contract is less than what he wants, he loves having a chance to do what he loves to do."

"That's a good thing."

"Yeah, but I'm trying to get him to think of the other variables. Tony is a very hardheaded man. He doesn't like me to tell him anything or give him too many ideas."

"Most men don't," Robert said, laughing.

"But this is our future. He needs to put his ego aside so we can make our lives better," Monica said.

"I don't know. Give him a chance to do that. Sometimes you, I mean women, have a habit of jumping in to fix things, instead of letting us do what we need to do. Maybe if you step back, he will work things out," Robert said.

"Are you taking Tony's side?"

"No. I'm saying I think you should give some thought to letting him handle it," Robert said.

Monica thought about it for a second. He might have had a point. Sometimes she did feel the need to be Ms. Fix-It. Maybe Tony did need time to get it together. "So what? I should give it a few more weeks and see how it goes?"

Robert nodded.

Monica decided she should give Tony some more time. Maybe he would surprise her with a new team contract and a new endorsement. "Okay, I'll try it."

"Good," Robert said. "Other than that, is your marriage going pretty well?"

"Yeah. We have our moments but it's nothing we can't handle," Monica said. In the midst of answering his question, it suddenly occurred to her Robert might think she and Tony were on the rocks. She never meant to tease Robert or give him the idea she was on the verge of divorce. Though they had a past, she wanted them to confide in each other as friends. Besides, she figured she could use his male point of view. Looking at him, she hoped confiding in him wouldn't backfire on her.

Robert nodded. "Okay. Well, if it goes south, you know where to find me." He winked and laughed. Although his words were presented as a joke, Monica sensed he was only half kidding. She shifted her weight and returned her attention back to the young woman rubbing her feet.

By the time they finished their pedicures, the awkwardness between Robert and Monica lifted. They walked back to the front counter and stood in line to pay for the service. Monica dug into her Louis Vuitton purse, fishing for her wallet.

"Uh-uh. I know you're not trying me like that," Robert said, eyeing Monica in disbelief.

"What? Oh, Robert. Come on. You've paid for the last two lunches and parking. At least let me take care of this," Monica said.

Robert shook his head. "You know your money is no good with me."

Monica sighed. The woman in front of them turned around. "You sound like a keeper to me," the lady said.

"Janet! Girl, when did you sneak in here?" Robert said, reaching over to give the woman a hug.

"I've been here for a little minute. How've you been

doing? I've been meaning to call you," Janet said, tugging at her ethnic necklace. She looked like she'd stepped off an island with her yellow, ruffled blouse and a white peasant skirt.

"Yeah, I'm sure that's what you tell all the young men," Robert said. "Hey, Janet. I want you to meet my friend, Monica Hatcher. Monica, this is Janet Lowery. She's the one I went to your dinner with."

"Oh! You're Tony T. Hatcher's wife! It's a pleasure to finally talk to you. I knew you were so busy with everything I didn't want to bother you at the dinner. It was absolutely beautiful. I'm so happy to see two people as blessed as you and Tony give back to the community. I think it's awesome." Janet's words tumbled out. Monica backed up two steps from the woman's exuberance.

"Thank you," Monica said.

"Janet is going to open an upscale seafood restaurant in October. She's been a chef for twelve years. She's award-winning," Robert said, turning to Monica.

"Well, congratulations!" Monica said. "You have a lot of competition down here."

"Yeah, but they don't have my love for food and ambiance. When people dine with you, everyone should feel special. Like they're important, you know?" Janet said. Monica nodded her head but she didn't quite understand Janet's point.

"Maybe you can help her with that," Robert said, wiggling his arm around Monica.

"What?" Monica asked, looking back and forth between Robert and Janet.

"Your new public relations and marketing firm?" Robert said. "Maybe you can help drum up publicity for her restaurant opening. Kinda like you're going to do for me?" He smiled wide.

Janet gasped. "Oh, my gosh! That would be great! Do you have a card? Better yet, let me give you my card. When can we meet to discuss the details?" Janet rummaged through her purse, before pulling the business card out. "Is Thursday good?"

"No," Monica hesitated.

"Why?" Robert asked.

"I have to take care of some business with Tony."

"Can't you reschedule?" Robert asked.

Monica furrowed her eyebrows. "No, I'm afraid not."

"Sure, you can," Robert urged.

Why would he put me on the spot like this? Monica thought. Robert knew Monica hated it when people pushed her. If she remembered correctly, that's what started most of their arguments. It's also what led to their final break-up. She stared him straight in the eye. "No, I cannot."

"It's okay. I'm open any day you can meet. Please give me a call when you're available and we can meet up," Janet said.

"I'll call you with a time," Monica said, reaching for Janet's business card.

"That would be awesome. Well, I look forward to

seeing you." Janet extended her hand to Monica. She shook Janet's hand.

"Bye, Robbie." Janet leaned in to kiss Robert on the cheek.

"Later, Janet," Robert said.

Janet pranced through the front door, each step confirming her optimism over the interaction. Monica's body language told a different story. She faced Robert. "What was that about?"

"What?" Robert asked.

"I told you Tony doesn't even want me to do this. It's one thing for me to work with you. It's a whole other issue to go around collecting clients. And you want me to cancel an appointment with him to meet with someone. Tony would have a fit," Monica said. "Are you trying to piss my husband off?"

"You were only going to work with one person?" Robert frowned.

"For now," Monica answered. "I have to see how this goes. How I'm going to manage this and my family. I don't even know how I'm going to break this to him." As Monica spoke, her tone turned frantic. How could Robert treat this so carelessly? She took a major step, deciding to pursue her business. This could put her marriage on the rocks and he acted like it didn't even matter.

Robert sighed. "Monica, he has to find out someday, right?"

"Listen, I want to do this. I will do this but I'm gonna do this my way. I know Tony better than anyone and suddenly changing routines is not the way to get him to accept my decision."

Robert nodded. "I want you to give it your best, Monica."

"Don't worry. I will."

∞

As she promised, Monica sat in front of Janet Friday afternoon—determined to give the culinary professional her best. Monica had called Janet the day after they'd met at The Nail Palace and recommended they have lunch, but Janet was so eager to share information with Monica, she insisted they meet somewhere she could present her full plan. The very thought of sitting through a long presentation made Monica yawn. However, Janet assured her the presentation would take no more than twenty to twenty-five minutes. Monica agreed to meet with her.

When Monica first saw Janet, she almost didn't recognize her. The peasant look she had before disappeared; Janet replaced it with a conservative black pants suit. She even pulled her wild hair back into a bun. At first glance, Janet looked mellow but when she opened her mouth, she greeted Monica with the same force she'd displayed at the spa.

"Hey, Monica. Thank you so much for meeting with me. I know it must be a bit unusual to meet in a conference center, but I wanted to make sure I was able to give you a full perspective on what I plan to do with the restaurant."

"No problem, Janet. Happy to be here."

Janet nodded and placed detailed graphs and her marketing plan on the table. She pushed a button on her remote and the curtains to a large screen opened. As she started the presentation, Janet channeled some of her boundless energy.

Janet's PowerPoint presentation began and, over the next twenty minutes, Janet covered everything from general information about the building and design for the restaurant to her plans for marketing it. Monica had to admit Janet did her homework. Her concerns about Janet and the venture melted away as the eager woman spoke.

She did wonder about Janet's marketing strategies. Monica thought Janet needed to spread the money around, instead of focusing exclusively on advertising. Once she finished her presentation, Monica found a way to break her suggestions down to her.

"Well, what do you think?" Janet said.

"Wow! I think you've really put all your energy into this and, despite the saturation from other restaurants, you have a real chance at taking this town by surprise," Monica said.

"I told ya." Janet winked and jumped up and down. "So, what do you see in the way of PR?"

"Well, I see the usual. A thorough press kit, which should be created immediately. A photo shoot of the restaurant and you. A bio. Television and radio appearances. Magazine articles. Blogs and of course, all of this would lead up to the biggest opening this town has ever seen. I'm talking red carpet, media, music. The works," Monica said.

As she spoke, Janet's eyes got bigger. She set her remote down and dashed over to sit next to Monica like an excited schoolgirl.

"Do you think it would be possible to have some of your famous friends show up?" Janet asked, drawing circles on the wooden table.

Monica smiled. "Why, it wouldn't be an opening without them."

Janet squealed loud enough to break nearby windows. "Will you work with me?"

Monica pretended to think on it but she already knew the answer. "Absolutely."

CHAPTER 17

Stephanie

S tephanie set her bags down on the steps and rang the doorbell to Monica's Upper Greenland estate. Waiting for someone to answer the door, Stephanie wandered toward the edge of the steps. The neighborhood's distinguished lush, green landscape always amazed her. On this particular day, the clear, blue sky and sharp sun rays made the grass look even greener than usual.

Monica opened the front door and smiled. "Hey! You're back." She hugged Stephanie.

"Yes, I am. I bought something for you guys," Stephanie said, returning the hug. She reached down for the bags and stepped into Monica's foyer. "Where's Marianna?"

"I woke up in such a great mood today, I gave her the day off." Monica smiled.

"Wow. What you so happy about?" Stephanie asked. The two women walked into Monica's kitchen.

"Remember how I've always talked about having my own public relations and marketing company? Well, it's happening. I'm gonna do it!" Monica shouted.

"That's great! What made you decide to do it now?" Stephanie asked.

"I have a client," Monica said.

"Who?" Stephanie sat down on one of the stools near the kitchen island.

"Janet Lowery. She's a chef who just moved to the Tampa area. She's opening a new restaurant called The Open Table and wants me to do PR for her." Monica smiled.

"Cool. I'm so happy for you, Monica," Stephanie said. "I feel like all of our dreams are starting to come true."

Monica nodded, still cheesing. She moved behind the island to finish stirring her chocolate chip cookie dough.

"I saw the VMAs. They looked like they were a little rowdy this year. It must have been pretty interesting behind the scenes."

"Girl, I was on the other side of the room. I could not be mixed up in that foolishness. But you know what? There's nothing like the experience of walking down the red carpet and having the media call out your name. It's wonderful." Stephanie giggled.

"The media knew your name?" Monica asked.

"Well, yeah. They even interviewed me." So, what Stephanie's first media experience was a bust? There would be more interviews. It would get better. She planned to practice. Monica didn't even have to know about the argument she'd had with Levin. Stephanie saw nothing wrong with embellishing the facts a little. If the media didn't know her name before, they would soon, especially after she and Levin married.

Monica raised her eyebrows. "Hmm. What did they ask?"

"Girl, they wanted to know all the goods on our relationship but I had to tell 'em, 'no comment.' They were being too nosy," Stephanie said.

"I'm glad you were able to handle yourself," Monica said. "What's in the bags?"

Stephanie jumped up and reached into the bags. She pulled out a crème-colored sweater. "I bought this for Marianna."

"Ooooh. She's gonna love that," Monica said.

"And this is for you." Stephanie pulled out a purple Hèrmes purse.

"That's beautiful! Something I can add to my collection." Monica stopped stirring. After wiping her hands, she felt the fabric on the purse.

"You really like it?" Stephanie asked.

"Yes, I do." Monica hugged Stephanie again. She placed the purse back in the bag and moved it to the side.

"That should fit nicely in the room with your other two-thousand purses," Stephanie said.

"Uh, excuse me. It's fifteen-hundred purses," Monica said.

Stephanie laughed. "Well, whateva."

"So, what did you buy Dee?" Monica asked.

"I saw the Fendi Silver bag and thought about getting that for her but I figured that was more my style."

Monica nodded.

"I settled on some Prada sunglasses," Stephanie said. She reached in the bag and pulled them out to show Monica.

"Those are nice," Monica said.

"I think so. It's kinda hard shopping for her being that she's a stylist and all."

"I'm sure she'll love it," Monica said. "You know what? I think we all should go out to dinner next week. Everybody. Us and the men. What do you think?"

"That's a great idea. Levin has to go to Miami early next week. I can get him to stop over."

"Yeah. How's everything going on that front?" Monica asked.

"Oh. It's awesome."

Monica glanced down at Stephanie's left hand. "Has he bought you the ring yet?"

Stephanie eyes widened. "No. We didn't have time to look."

"Well, when is he going to get you a ring, girl?" Monica asked, frowning.

"Soon. Why are you harping on it?" Stephanie glared at Monica. She'd forgotten about telling Monica they were getting married. It was kind of a spur of the moment thing she hadn't thought all the way through but one thing was for sure; she never expected Monica to give her such a hard time about it. Stephanie figured the ring wouldn't matter, but, apparently, it did.

"I'm not harping. It's your business. I thought it was strange for a man to propose and not give you a ring, if not right then at least within a couple of days," Monica said. "Don't you think that's strange?"

"No, because he and I already know we're going to get married. So, it's not a big deal for us," Stephanie said.

"As long as you're not being gullible."

"I'm not being gullible. You'll see," Stephanie said. "For all you know, Levin might have the ring for me the night of the dinner."

"That would be great. Then, we'll have two reasons to celebrate. Your engagement and my first, unofficial client."

"Unofficial?" Stephanie asked.

"Yeah. I haven't exactly told Tony yet."

"Oh, this is gonna be interesting," Stephanie said.

"Tell me about it."

∞

Levin's album had caught fire and he spent most of his time meeting appearance demands. He was also trying to set up another meeting with the producer for his movie. As a result, Stephanie had a harder time convincing Levin to attend the dinner with her friends. He stopped in Tampa but he only intended to stay for an hour or two. She understood his situation but she refused to give up.

Stephanie stood in front of Levin, arms crossed and bottom lip to the floor. "I don't see any reason why you can't spend two hours with me and my friends."

"I told you. I wasn't planning to stay here for long. My manager wants me in Miami ASAP," Levin said.

"So what? Tell him you can't get there until tomorrow. He works for you. You don't work for him."

"Stephanie, it's not that simple."

"Why not?!" she shouted.

"Hey! Don't start that, okay? I'm really not in the mood for it." Levin glared at Stephanie.

She sighed. Stephanie needed to keep him happy. Angering him was a sure-fire way to make him flee. She had this bad feeling that every time she teed him off, he ran into the arms of another woman. She didn't have hard proof, other than the night outside of the studio, but she felt it was true. "My friends are really looking forward to meeting you. I already told them you would be there."

"Why did you do that?"

"Because I was excited and knew you would want to be there." Stephanie walked closer to him and ran her fingers up his arm.

Levin rolled his eyes.

"Come for one hour. That's all I'm asking for. One hour and then, if you need to leave, you can go."

"Okay. Fine," Levin said. "One hour and then, I have to go."

"Yay," Stephanie said, hugging him and jumping up and down. She knew he'd come around. Levin loved her and really wanted to be with her, no matter what else he had to do. He needed that extra push to stay focused.

∞

Once they settled at the table with her friends, Stephanie looked over at him and felt all the whining and yelling was worth it. She watched Levin laugh and converse with the group. Everyone responded to his innate charm and warmth. She beamed while he joked around with Tony.

Right before dessert, Dee, Stephanie and Monica excused themselves to the ladies room, where they freshened up and briefed over the night.

"Okay. So far everything is going well," Stephanie said.

"I'm actually surprised. How did you manage to get Levin here?" Monica asked.

"Well, you know. He's busy but he'll do anything for his lady," Stephanie said, grinning.

"Don't you mean fiancée?" Dee asked. "By the way, where's your engagement ring? I thought he would've bought that in Vegas."

Stephanie's stomach turned queasy. She felt like Dee and Monica were teaming up on her about the engagement. As they waited for her to answer, she regretted telling anyone she and Levin were getting married. The original purpose of her claim was to make sure her friends understood Levin loved her. Now that some time had passed, Stephanie felt trapped—as if she couldn't take the lie back. She couldn't say they'd changed their minds because it would look like they weren't working out. Then again, she couldn't admit Levin hadn't officially proposed to her because she'd look like a liar.

"Oh, he did get me a ring but it was too small. So, he's taking it back to be resized," she said, manipulating her long curls in the mirror. She figured she could lie better if she concentrated on the mirror and avoided their eyes.

"As long as you guys are still on track," Dee said.

"Of course. As a matter of fact, I think he's ready to start a family."

"Already? He said that?" Monica asked, looking at her through the mirror.

"Not exactly, but I think we're ready. I don't think he would have a problem if I got pregnant."

"Now I think that's a bad idea," Monica said.

Stephanie turned around to face Monica. "Why? We *are* getting married."

"Yeah, but you're not married yet. What if things change? Do you really wanna have to take him to court for child support?" Dee chimed.

"That won't happen because we're happy!" Stephanie frowned.

"Having children with someone is nothing to take lightly, Stephanie. All I'm saying is think about it. Please," Monica said.

Stephanie nodded in an effort to end the uncomfortable conversation. The lie couldn't even convince her friends she and Levin were serious. If she didn't have the support of her own friends, how was she supposed to gain anybody else's support? Dejected, Stephanie walked ahead of Dee and Monica with her head down. They made their way back to the table where the men laughed heartily.

"Hey! Break it up. Too much male bonding here," Dee said, sitting down next to Dwayne.

"We were sharing stories about meeting you guys. It's very telling," Dwayne said.

"Really? What kinda lies did you tell each other?" Dee asked.

"Ooooooooh," Dwayne said. All the men at the table booed her comment. Monica chuckled but Stephanie was still thinking about her restroom conversation with Dee and Monica. She barely heard the joke.

"That's okay. I'll save the stories for later," Dwayne said. "When you're not here."

Tony turned to Levin. "So, when is the big day?

Levin frowned in confusion. "What do you mean?"

"The wedding?"

Levin shook his head and scanned the table for answers. "What wedding?"

Stephanie snapped out of her haze. *Is Tony asking what I think he's asking?* she thought. She crossed her fingers under the table and prayed an act of God would strike Tony and prevent him from talking. As a matter of fact, she'd never wished harm to Tony before but right then, she wouldn't have minded, if he somehow started choking. Instead, he continued, oblivious to the train wreck coming.

"You know, you and Stephanie's wedding? You guys haven't set a date?" Tony asked.

Monica winced. She placed her hand on Tony's arm. "Uh, Tony? Let's not pry. I'm sure Stephanie and Levin would tell us if they had any wedding plans."

Stephanie covered her face, red in embarrassment. She looked like someone had slapped her across it. Levin didn't look much better.

"I was just making conversation," Tony said, irritation seeping into his voice.

Levin raised his eyebrows and looked at Stephanie for a minute. "What is this about? There's no wedding."

Before Stephanie could say anything, Tony kept digging a hole for her. "Of course, there is. Stephanie said you proposed during her last trip to Georgia. Remember?"

This time, Monica firmly intervened. "Tony. Let it go."

"Why? I wasn't even talking to you," Tony said to Monica.

"'Cuz I'm talking to you," Monica said.

"Excuse me," Levin said. He stood up from the table. "I have a flight to catch. It was great meeting all of you. I hope you enjoy the rest of your evening." With those words, he exited the restaurant without even glancing Stephanie's way. When Stephanie glanced Monica's way, her friend mouthed *"I'm sorry"* to her. She nodded, knowing she had some serious explaining to do.

To Stephanie's surprise, the ride to her condo was quiet, which scared her. She sat thinking about the months she and Levin had spent together. He hadn't said anything about marriage since her first visit to Atlanta. No ring, no nothing, and, though she had faith in their relationship, she had grown frustrated. They seemed to always take three steps forward and five steps back. She also sensed he still messed around with other women but she made a conscious effort not to think or talk about it until now.

She imagined Levin disappearing into the night, never to be seen again. She saw herself calling him only to have her calls screened. He'd probably even show up at future red carpet events without her. Or worse he would show up to events with someone else. The thought of another woman in her place sent her into a panic. She kept trying to get Levin to talk during the car ride but he wouldn't. Before she knew it, tears started to flow down her face.

"I didn't tell people we were getting married," Stephanie said.

Levin kept his eyes on the road.

"You believe me, don't you?"

Although Stephanie asked the question, Levin remained still as a board.

"Levin? Say something." Her quiet sobs took over her voice.

Unmoved, Levin stared straight ahead. His silent treatment continued until they reached her condo. When she and Levin stepped inside, the tide turned and he let her have it.

"What the hell were you thinking, Stephanie?"

Stephanie took a deep breath. "I told you. I didn't say we were getting married. They assumed it because we've been together for awhile," she lied.

"That's not what Tony said. He specifically said that you told people that we were getting married," Levin said.

"Then he was mistaken."

Levin threw his hands in the air.

"They thought that we were getting married because we've spent so much time together. I'm sure of it."

"We've been off and on for seven months. I hardly qualify us as marriage material."

"Then what are we doing?" Stephanie shouted. "People usually date with the intent of marrying. I'm not with you just for kicks. I'm with you to have something—to see this thing go somewhere."

"Where's it going?" Levin asked. "We don't even get along all the time, baby."

"Every relationship has problems. You don't give up."

"I'm not giving up. I think we need to take it slow. We need more time."

"Time for what? What are you gonna do? Sing forever so women can throw their raggedy drawers at you on stage? That doesn't mean anything. One day, years from now, you're gonna wake up and be alone. And wonder how you got there. Well, this is how, Levin! You're gonna wish you had done everything in your power to keep me."

Levin looked at her like she was crazy. He then picked up the luggage he'd left at her place earlier, and walked toward the door.

"You need me!" Stephanie shouted at his back.

Levin turned back around at the sound of her rant. "Girl, let's get one thing straight. I don't need you! I can find somebody else like I found you and you know it."

Levin stomped back toward the door and opened it. "I don't know who the hell you think you are."

He walked out, slamming the door behind him.

It looked like the first part of her nightmare was coming true. Levin had disappeared into the night. Stephanie wiped her face. *What do I do now?*

CHAPTER 18

Dee

When Dee entered the Enterprise Center, a chipper receptionist greeted her at the front desk. She signed in and followed the arrows pointing toward the conference room. The noise from incessant chatter leaked through the door before Dee could turn the knob. After she opened the door, the noise accompanied the sixty-five guests mingling about the room. A few held court at the food table; many others circulated and gathered into groups. One of the volunteers at the door handed her a name tag. Dee accepted it without fuss but walked off, refusing to wear it. She thought it looked cheesy.

Instead, Dee found an empty spot and sat down. She tapped her fingers on the table, wondering if the meeting would start soon. Ordinarily, she reveled in collecting the names and numbers of everyone in the room within a half-hour, but, today anxiety got the best of her.

Rachel, the Walt Disney executive from Coles' party, had invited Dee to this meeting. She felt The National Entrepreneurs Club, would be a good match for Dee. It targeted new business owners seeking to help them get their ventures off the ground with resources and support. They facilitated a monthly nomination and voting process to determine membership. Rachel had arranged for Dee to attend and present an ice breaker to the group. She instructed Dee to prepare a speech about her background and her business aspirations. Initially, she'd balked at the idea, failing to see how the club could help her. She hadn't delivered a speech in five years but she finally broke down and decided to go through with it. Dee hoped her speech served her well because she hated speaking in front of people.

While Dee ran over her speech in her head, she felt a tap on her shoulder.

"Hi, Dee. I'm so glad you could make it," Rachel said, extending her hand.

"Hello, Rachel. I'm glad to be here," Dee said, shaking Rachel's hand.

"Are you ready?" Rachel asked.

"About as ready as I'll ever be."

Sensing Dee's speaking anxiety, Rachel offered words of encouragement. "Well, I'm sure you'll do a great job. Relax. Tell them about your business plan and the rest will fall into place. You'll do fine. In the meantime, feel free to get up and network or eat some food. We don't need any leftovers." Rachel laughed.

"Thank you. Oh, Rachel? At what point will I speak?" Dee asked.

"We should be starting the meeting within the next five

minutes. You're in the second portion of the meeting. Good luck," Rachel said.

Dee pushed her shoulders back. On the surface, she looked confident but, on the inside, she was jittery. When the meeting finally started, she listened to the host tell dry jokes, while praying for her time to speak to arrive. It felt like hours had passed before Rachel introduced her and called her to the podium. When she stood in front of the audience, Dee felt beads of sweat gathering under her armpits. She took a deep breath and started her speech with a story about her hometown. She talked about the struggles her single mother had faced raising three children. Dee then recounted the day she'd come up with the idea to create a magazine and the plan she developed to make it work. She ended using examples of her work ethic to drive home her entrepreneurial spirit and determination. After her last sentence, the audience gave her a standing ovation. *I thought I'd done well but I didn't think I did that well*, Dee thought.

After the meeting, people approached her with congratulations on her new business. Each person gave her their business card and encouraged her to call. Their positivity made Dee feel like she had made the right choice in attending the meeting. Maybe these people would have the resources to help her start the magazine, after all. Maybe some of them had the money to invest in it. She smiled on her way back to her seat, thinking about ways to use this network to find funding. She didn't notice everyone had filed out of the conference center. Everyone, except one person.

Dee picked up her purse and glanced up to see Bobbie a couple of tables away. He sat back in his chair with his legs crossed, smiling. Her smile faded and her pulse raced. *What does he want now?* Dee thought. Furious, she grabbed her bag and marched over to him.

"You have exactly two minutes to explain why you're following me or I'm calling the police."

"Oooooh. The hostility and coming off such a touching speech. I almost had tears in my eyes," Bobbie said, wiping his eyes.

"What do you want?"

"I'm here congregating amongst my fellow business men and women. Supporting a businesswoman on her road to The American Dream."

"We'll see how much congregating you do behind bars with a big, burly guy named Bubba tapping you on the shoulder at night," Dee pulled out her BlackBerry and unlocked her keypad to call the police.

"Umm. It'd be a shame for me to spend time behind bars, especially when I can help you make your business dreams come true."

"What are you talking about?" She dropped the hand holding her cell phone to her side.

"Well, I know creating a magazine requires a lot of capital. There are writers, graphic artists and printers."

"Yeah. So?"

"What if I told you I could give you the money for that?"

As Dee pondered Bobbie's words, she couldn't help but think about Dwayne and his warning to stay far away from Bobbie. On the other hand, what if Bobbie could help her? She could really use the money. Besides, Dwayne hadn't offered her a dime and he still hadn't introduced her to any investors.

Bobbie smiled as he watched Dee consider her options. "Well?"

"I would say how much are we talking about?"

"We can start with one hundred-thousand dollars but there's always more where that comes from," Bobbie said.

"How can you give me that kind of money?"

"I'm a businessman. I always make money. It would do my heart great good to use it to help another person reach their professional dreams."

Dee sat down in front of him. She swallowed her fear back. There was something slimy about Bobbie but she owed it to herself to inquire more about his offer. "What's the catch?"

"So cynical! There's no catch. Think of it as angel money." He smiled.

His smile unnerved Dee. "What about Dwayne?" Dee asked.

"What about him?"

"He tells me to stay away from you and you're no good," Dee said.

Bobbie chuckled. "He's not offering you money. I am." He made a valid point. Dwayne had been working on funding for her magazine for months and she had nothing to show for it. It was getting more and more difficult to believe he would come through. The fact he hadn't delivered disappointed her. The more she thought about it, the angrier she became. He'd misled her. Memories of her lying, last boyfriend resurfaced and she committed herself to doing something about her anger. Although Dee couldn't say she completely trusted Bobbie, she planned to at least consider his proposal.

"I need to think about it," Dee said.

Bobbie sighed. "You know, Dwayne is not gonna come through for you. You're wasting your time."

"If I am interested in your offer, I will let you know," Dee said.

"That's fine but my offer is only good for exactly forty-eight hours. Here's my card." Bobbie placed his business card on the table and slid it in front of Dee. She looked down and read it. *Mitchell Financial Services, LLC.* "If you're interested, call me. If you don't, it's your loss."

∞

The next morning, Dee woke up buzzing. She tried to keep busy. She called a fashion designer to arrange clothes pick-up and worked on looks for her next photo shoot. She thought focusing on the logistics of her next shoot would keep her mind off of Bobbie's offer but it didn't. One hundred-thousand dollars was the best offer she'd had all year but she realized Dwayne would fight her over this.

On the other hand, she could try telling him. Maybe Bobbie's generosity would change his opinion about the man. But that was hard to determine since she still didn't know anything about him and Bobbie's past. Since Antony never came through with information, she had no other leads to find out what was going on. Dee finally picked up her phone to call Dwayne.

"Hey. What's up?" Dee asked.

"The usual. What are you up to?" Dwayne asked.

"Just hanging around."

"Hanging around? You don't have any work to do?" Dwayne asked.

"Well, I don't meet with another client until tomorrow," Dee said. "So, have you found any investors yet?"

Dwayne sighed. "Not yet."

Dee bit her lip to keep from berating him. *This truly makes no sense*, she thought. "Why don't you try networking though associations? Isn't there one for your field?"

"Yes, but they're full of financial advisors like me. Most of them are not gonna have the type of money we're looking for."

"Then, maybe they'll know someone who does have that kind of money," Dee said.

"Even if they did, they wouldn't give that type of information to me. If anything, they would reserve those types of resources for their own clients," Dwayne said.

"Okay. So, what are you doing next?"

"What is this? An inquisition?"

"No, it's a checkup. I've been waiting almost seven months for you to find someone to invest in my magazine. And every time I ask you how it's going, you tell me nothing," Dee said.

"That's because I have nothing to tell you."

As Dee listened to Dwayne, she was convinced her lack of funding was Dwayne's fault. What kind of professional would make his client wait this long for results? And the worst part was he didn't see a reason to update her, give her a progress report or anything. He seemed to think he didn't have to keep her abreast of his progress, which really burned her. She thought he might be taking for granted the fact they were dating but business was business.

"That's why I think we should look for the funding together. Like I was thinking about following up with a few people I met at the NEC meeting."

"The what?"

"You know the meeting I told you about?"

"Oh, yeah."

"I met some really good people that may be able to help. I think I may have found some investors for the magazine," Dee said. She avoided mentioning Bobbie. After a few seconds of silence, Dwayne's response sounded tense. "When we first talked about my helping you find investors, you agreed to let me handle it. Now, I understand you would like it to move faster. So would I but it's not going to happen. It's going to take time," Dwayne said.

"You don't want to at least get the contact information for the people I talked to?" Dee asked.

"No! Did you tell them you were looking for funding?"

"Not exactly," Dee said.

"Good 'cuz if you had, you'd see all that good energy they were giving you disappear. The print publishing industry has been taking a hit lately. People aren't lining up to lose money, Dee," Dwayne said bluntly.

Dee looked at the phone, as if another language had come through the wires. "I'm not trying to lose money either. Are you trying to tell me no one is going to invest in my magazine?"

"Basically."

"Just because you can't find the investors, doesn't mean they aren't out there," Dee snapped.

"I doubt it. It's a poor investment."

How dare he tell her that her dream was a poor investment? If he thought so, then why did he offer to help her find funding? Dee had enough. "Well, Bobbie didn't think it was a poor investment."

"Bobbie?" Dwayne asked.

"Yes. As a matter of fact, he offered me money to get started."

"You saw him? Where?!" Dwayne demanded.

"He showed up at the meeting," Dee said. "He's offering me money to get started and I'm thinking about taking it."

"Dee, you don't want to do that. You don't know anything about this man. Bobbie's not trying to help you. He's trying to hurt you," Dwayne said.

"That doesn't even make sense," Dee said. "What's the problem? Mad because I found someone to do what you couldn't do?"

"He's not what you think he is. Don't take his money. The next time you see him, call me right away. I need to know when he's around you." Dwayne's frustration took over his voice. Dee could hear Dwayne breathing hard. He sounded like he was losing control.

"If you don't tell me why it's a problem, I will take it."

"Dee, I insist you not take Bobbie's money!" Dwayne shouted.

"Who are you yelling at?" Anger shot up Dee's spine.

"It's for your own good."

Dee hung up on him. She didn't care to hear any more. She resented Dwayne's opposition. The more he tried to convince her she couldn't trust Bobbie, the more she felt she shouldn't trust him. His words seemed pompous and chauvinistic. Dee had every intention of proving him wrong. She decided to take the money Bobbie had offered whether Dwayne liked it or not.

She marched over to her desk and opened her top drawer. After rummaging through papers and stamps, she found Bobbie's business card. When Dee dialed the number, his voicemail picked up. She left a message.

"Hey, Bobbie. It's Deidre Wright. I'm calling about your offer from yesterday...I'll take it."

∞

After Dee hung up on Dwayne, he dialed her number back right away. However, he received a busy signal. He beat his fist on the desk. Dwayne tried so hard to keep his past separated from his present but his attempts failed over and over again. Dwayne picked the phone back up and dialed a number.

"Hello?"

"It's Dwayne."

"Well, Dwayne! It's good to finally hear from you," Bobbie said.

"Cut the crap, Bobbie. Why are you bothering Deidre?"

"Now, who says I'm bothering her? Did she say that?"

"That's what it sounds like to me."

"I'm offering her an opportunity you can't. Funny, huh? I'm the one that got shafted but I can make more things happen than you."

"Listen to me and listen real good. I want you to stay away from her. You hear me? And quit offering her money."

"What are you gonna do about it?"

"Whatever I need to do about it," Dwayne said.

"Oh. Now is that supposed to be a threat? Aww, man, I'm disappointed in you."

"Bobbie. I'm serious."

"Well, I would be willing to do just about anything for the right price."

Dwayne sat silent. He knew what that meant. It had been years since they'd parted ways as business partners. Yet, Bobbie still hunted him like a lion searching for prey. He never ceased to find ways to take advantage of their past and make money from Dwayne. Everywhere he went, Bobbie followed. Sometimes, Dwayne wanted to let it all go and allow Bobbie to do what he wanted to do, but he couldn't risk Bobbie putting his personal and professional future in jeopardy again. So, he continued to pay him off to keep him quiet. Dwayne had paid Bobbie sixty five-thousand dollars, not including the money he'd paid to buy him out of their business.

"How much?" Dwayne asked.

"I think forty-thousand dollars ought to cover it—for awhile anyway."

"Forty-thousand dollars?! I'm not paying you nothing." That was twice what he'd paid him last time.

"Okay, I can call Deidre up and tell her some stories about the good old days. I wonder where I should start first? I know. I'll send her a copy of some newspaper articles from Texas."

"Fine," Dwayne said through clenched teeth.

"Great. I do thank you. It's always a pleasure doing

business with you. You can send my money to the same spot."

"Bobbie, I'm not going to take this forever."

"I got news for you, buddy. You'll take it as long as I give it." Bobbie laughed and hung up.

As Dwayne replaced the phone on the receiver, he leaned back in his chair and rubbed his temples, thinking he had to end this. Unfortunately, the only idea Dwayne had meant killing Bobbie. And more and more, that looked like the only permanent solution.

CHAPTER 19

Monica

Monica sat at her kitchen island, waiting for Tony to get ready for dinner. They made reservations at Ruth's Chris to celebrate Little William's birthday. As usual, Tony took forever to get dressed. He kept switching outfits—trying one on, deciding he didn't like the shoes to match and then searching for something to wear all over again. Monica gave him at least one extra hour to primp in front of the mirror, hoping he would move faster. She also hoped he would move faster because it was his son's day. Apparently, that made no difference to him. Daddy still had to look good.

To keep herself from bolting upstairs and yelling at him, she pulled out her phone and started checking emails. As she sifted through her messages, she realized Tony's delay created the perfect opportunity for her to check on progress with Janet's opening without his knowledge. Yesterday, she'd called a local reporter about writing a story on the new restaurant. Monica sent him Janet's bio and press kit via email. The reporter seemed interested but said he needed to get with his editor about it. Although she thought he was giving her the runaround, she thanked him for his time and expressed her confidence in the story. So far, she hadn't heard back from him yet. In the meantime, she'd contacted five other reporters. Two of them were already scheduled to interview Janet next week.

Overall, Monica's strategy worked out the way she planned because she already knew a lot of people in and outside of Tampa. People that could make things happen. Most of the time a couple of phone calls got results. However, the same thing that had advanced her new business quickly caused her the most concern. She knew them and they knew her, and they already knew her husband, which meant they could tell Tony about her covert activities. To prevent any outside suspicions, Monica often told them she was helping a friend with her restaurant. Yet, every day she was reminded that the balancing act had to end sometime.

Monica closed her emails, set her cell phone down and walked over to the house speaker phone. "C'mon, Tony. Hurry up!" she yelled into the speaker.

Her cell phone rang and she sucked her teeth. Irritated, she dashed back over to pick it up.

"Hello."

"Hey, lady! How's everything going?" Robert's voice boomed through the receiver.

Monica's mood shifted from irritation to elation. "Hey! It's going good." Her excitement spilled over.

"Yeah, I hear. I talked to Janet yesterday. She's very excited."

"She's always excited." Monica laughed.

"True but something tells me she has a reason to be. She especially liked the photo shoot you guys did for the press kit," Robert said.

"I thought that went well, too. Wait 'til you see the photos. She looks classy, yet modern in her black Bottega Veneta dress."

"So, what's next?" Robert asked.

"I need to prep her for the interview with *South Shore Magazine*. Then, we need to finalize details for the October eighth opening," Monica said.

"Uh-oh. Look at you. I knew you would be great at this. I'm proud of you, Monica," Robert said.

Monica swallowed the lump in her throat. She hadn't heard anyone tell her that in a long time. Hearing it from her first love brought back a ton of memories and a renewed belief in her abilities and her future. Her tone softened.

"Thank you. I owe this to you. If you hadn't…" Monica heard Tony stomping into the kitchen and cut herself short. She straightened her back and turned around.

"Yeah, I'll call you later with the rest of the details, Dee," Monica said, seeking to camouflage her caller's identity.

Robert caught on quick. "I take it Tony walked into the room. I'll call you tomorrow. Bye." Robert hung up.

Monica slowly placed her phone back inside her purse.

"Who was that?" Tony asked, pulling his black blazer over his white T-shirt. It casually complemented his snow white tennis shoes and loose-fitting, light blue jeans.

"Oh, that was Dee," Monica lied. She eyed him from head to toe. "You gonna wear that?"

"Don't start, okay?" Tony warned, scowling.

Monica smirked at him.

"What were you and Dee talking about?"

"Her magazine," Monica said.

"What do you have to give her details about?" Tony asked, puzzled.

"She wants advice on how to get it started and people to talk to. You know she needs money," Monica said, annoyed with the third-degree treatment.

"Calm down. I was just asking," Tony said.

"Well, what are you so interested for? You got some money you wanna give her?" Monica asked.

"Nooo. I need more money," Tony said. "I'm asking 'cuz you seem to be pretty busy all of a sudden. I wanna know what you're up to."

"I'm helping out a friend," Monica said. She hated lying to Tony but he would've pitched a fit if she told him about her new client. She didn't need that on her son's birthday. Instead, she searched for a different subject.

"Speaking of a friend, when are you going to apologize to Stephanie?" Monica asked.

"For what?"

"For being rude at The Red Door. Why did you repeat what I said to you?" Monica asked.

"I didn't know it was a secret. If she was lying, that was her problem," Tony said. He opened the refrigerator and reached for a bottle of water. "I don't have time to be concerned with your friends' emotions, especially if they're playing games."

"Whether she's playing games or not is none of your business. That's why you shouldn't have said anything," Monica said.

Tony stopped and stood in front of her for a minute. "Are you finished?" Tony asked.

"Are you ready to go to dinner?" Monica said, taking a nearby dishtowel and playfully snapping him on the behind with it.

"Don't start nothing you can't finish," Tony said, raising his eyebrow.

Monica and Tony walked from the kitchen to the end of the stairs.

"William! Angela! Let's go!" Monica yelled up the stairs. The kids came rumbling down with jackets in hand ready to eat. They all piled into the car, with Angela and William arguing over whom should ride shotgun. Monica expected the commotion to last for a minute or two, but when the kids were still arguing a mile away from home, she intervened.

Monica turned around in her seat to face the kids. "What's the problem?"

"Angela wouldn't let me ride shotgun. It's my birthday. I'm supposed to get what I want," William said.

His sister rolled her eyes. "You're such a baby," she said.

"Am not!" William said.

"Of course, you are," Angela said.

"No, I'm not." William stuck out his lip and crossed his

arms so tight he could have cut off his own circulation.

"Stop it!" Monica shouted. "Now, Angela, I know for some reason you find it difficult to be nice to your brother, but the least you can do is be nice to him on his birthday. Right?"

Angela didn't respond.

"Right?!" Monica asked again. *This girl is gonna make me come back there*, Monica thought.

"Yes, ma'am," Angela mumbled.

"So, I want you to turn to your brother and apologize," Monica said.

"I'm sorry," Angela said, glancing over at him.

Monica turned back around in her seat and sighed. "You need to do something about your child," she said to Tony.

"What do I need to do?" Tony asked.

"Talk to her, punish her. Or restrict her privileges."

"Don't you do that already?"

"Yes, but I think it would mean a lot more coming from you," Monica said.

"No, I'll tell you what I think. I think you're too hard on her."

"Are you serious?"

"Yes. Monica, you are always giving her a hard time. According to you, she can't do anything right."

"That's not true. And you know that's not true."

"You harp on her about everything, especially when it comes to William."

"She bullies him," Monica said.

Tony waved her claim away. "He's not being bullied. It's normal sibling rivalry. It's not like this is going to scar him for life or anything. He has to learn how to defend himself. You know, toughen up."

"Well, maybe if you were around more to show him, he'd know without becoming target practice for his sister."

Tony stopped at the red light and faced Monica with a serious look in his eyes. "I try, Monica. I know I travel a lot but I really am trying to do what's best for you guys. Don't you think I'd like to be home more often?"

Monica sighed. They'd had this discussion before. It was the grand catch twenty-two. On one hand, Tony's career allowed them to live in a large mansion, drive expensive cars and send their kids to exclusive, private schools. Yet, the same career kept Tony away from them a lot during game season. When he wasn't playing games, he practiced almost daily and watched video on the team and their opponents. That didn't leave much time for his son, who idolized him.

Deep down, Monica believed Tony was doing the best he could; they all were. For a moment, she felt guilty, thinking she'd been too hard on him.

"Yes, Tony. I know you would like to be home more," Monica said. "But I want the family to be more cohesive. And I want William to have his father when he needs him."

Tony pulled away from the red light. "What do you suggest I do?"

"I don't know." Monica peered out of her window. "We have to figure something out."

After their talk, the mood in the car turned heavy but it didn't stay that way long. The kids saw the bright red sign for Ruth's Chris and perked up. Little William hopped out of the car first and reached the restaurant door first. He opened it for his family.

Despite the evening hour, the restaurant looked sparse. A twenty-something server seated them and quickly took their orders. Monica started her meal with Lettuce Wedge. Tony ordered a Steakhouse Salad. The kids happily picked apart the fried outer shell of their Tempura Onion Rings. Though the mood had lifted somewhat, Monica and Tony were still quiet at dinner until Tony broke the silence with an announcement.

"I talked to my agent today," Tony said between bites.

Monica sipped her water. "Yeah? What did he say?"

"That things are looking better. Since we won our last game against the Saints, they're starting to open up a little on the negotiations," Tony said.

"How do you mean?" Monica asked.

"Well, they're more willing to listen to our ideas about the contract. Of course, it's too late for this season but I'm hopeful I'll get a better deal next season," Tony said, grinning a little.

"I'm glad your agent is on your side," Monica said.

"Me, too! I know he thought a five million-dollar sign-ing bonus was pretty good, especially for the Buccaneers, but I think it could be better," Tony said.

"Maybe we should look at better endorsements," Monica said.

"They should be paying me more," Tony said, shaking his head.

"What if they refuse?" Monica asked. She hated playing the pessimist but she sometimes felt like he never asked himself the hard questions. So, she always had to do it or suffer uncomfortable consequences. Once, Tony's optimism caused them to lose a lucrative endorsement for watches.

"Then I look for another team," Tony said.

"Whatever happened to the endorsement you told me about a few days ago? The one with the gym?"

"Um. I think I'll be passing on that one."

"Okay. Taking my advice, huh?" Monica asked, cocking her head to the side.

Tony sucked his teeth. "Not necessarily. I went over the agreement and thought it would be a good idea to look for better opportunities. That's all."

"Um-hum." Monica raised one eyebrow at Tony. He waved her obvious suspicion away.

"Well, whatever you decide to do, I'll support you," she said, sipping more water.

Tony grinned. "Thank you, baby. I may need you to garner more media attention for me in the coming weeks."

"I knew there was another reason you were treating me tonight," Monica said, eyeing Tony.

He laughed.

After they finished their meal, the waiters brought out a surprise candlelit Spiderman birthday cake for William. The whole table, as well as the waiters, sang "Happy

Birthday" to him. The little boy jumped up and down before blowing out his candles. Everyone clapped for him. Another staff member rolled out a table full of presents for William. His eyes grew big as he tore through his birthday gifts. Once the festivities ended, they all piled back into the car to head home. "The Quiet Storm" played slow, soft songs on the radio, lulling the kids to sleep. Monica nodded off, too, until Tony interrupted her sleep.

"Hey, Monica?"

"Yes," Monica said, opening her mind but keeping her eyes closed.

"I enjoyed being with you guys tonight," Tony said.

"Good," Monica answered.

"Really. I know it's been rough for the last six months. Well, I know I've been rough for the last six months but I promise, from now on, things will get better."

Is it me or do I feel an apology coming on? Monica thought. She ran through all the attitudes and temper tantrums Tony had thrown since he'd signed his contract. He was right; he'd acted like a real jerk toward his family and friends. Whenever she thought he'd let up, he only seemed to act worse. It was hard to believe he was ready to apologize for his behavior. Monica opened her eyes and peered at Tony. She placed her palm over his forehead. "Are you okay?" she asked.

Tony moved his head. "I'm serious. I wanna work on becoming a better husband and father. I heard what you said earlier and you're absolutely right. I wanna be with you guys more. As a matter of fact, I want you and the kids to be with me as much as you can."

"Really?" Monica asked.

"Yeah." He snapped his fingers. "I know! Why don't you guys come see me in Indianapolis? The kids have never been there."

"What is there to see?" Monica asked.

"Me. When was the last time we took them to one of my away games?"

"I don't know. A couple of years, I guess."

"I think it would be good. It doesn't matter where. As long as they are able to see what their daddy does for a living."

"Wait a minute. When is the game?" Monica asked.

"Four-oh-five in the afternoon," Tony answered.

"No. The date. When is the date?"

"October Seventh. Why?" Tony asked.

Monica took a deep breath and looked straight ahead. She had to help Janet open her restaurant that same weekend. She couldn't leave Janet. Monica needed to manage the press, the VIP guest list and all the other issues that were bound to crop up. *How am I going to tell him I can't go?* Monica thought.

"No reason." She slouched down into her seat and stared out of her window.

CHAPTER 20

Stephanie

It had been a few days since Levin had left Tampa and he was back to avoiding Stephanie's calls. His only preference of contact was sending the occasional text messages. She felt uneasy about their argument but she had no outlet since he wouldn't speak to her. She didn't know what to do. Stephanie called Monica to vent her frustration.

"Hey. Why do you sound so down?" Monica asked.

"I still haven't heard from Levin."

"We're on that tip again, huh?"

"I don't know if this is his way of punishing me or what. I've never quite seen him this angry before," Stephanie said. "What's the big deal? We're probably going to get married anyway, right?"

"Yeah, but men still don't like to be pushed into these types of decisions," Monica said.

"What's the push? If he doesn't know he wants me by now, then he doesn't. And I know he does."

"How do you know?"

"Because he said it."

"He actually said, 'Stephanie, I want to marry you'?"

"Yes," Stephanie said.

"Then, why haven't the gossip rags and Internet message boards talked more about the engagement?" Monica asked.

Stephanie scowled. This is why she hated defending herself to her friends, especially Monica. They questioned everything she said. Worst of all, Monica knew how the entertainment and media machine worked, making it hard to tell her a lie. For the most part, she was right; Levin was becoming a popular singer and certified heartthrob. If the media thought Stephanie was taking Levin off the market, they would break their necks to find out every little detail about her. Every word printed and published about them would be devoted to assessing whether she was good enough for darling Levin. Instead, Stephanie had only reached blurb status—mentioned in a few blogs and magazines. Stephanie hated that and desperately wanted to change it.

Unfortunately, she didn't know how. Levin's resistance to change made it hard for Stephanie to hold a solid position in his life or convince anyone else she belonged there either. Even after several months together, he'd continued to do his own thing. No one viewing their relationship would classify her as the leading lady in Levin's life. Still, acknowledging she'd lied about the "proposal" was like accepting failure. That was unthinkable. Regardless of the situation or Levin's sporadic wandering, he belonged to Stephanie. She needed to keep up the charade, which meant finding creative ways to explain no wedding date and no engagement ring.

"Because Levin is trying to keep it private. You know how he is," Stephanie said, trying to offer an excuse.

"Or maybe he changed his mind."

"No!" Stephanie yelled.

"Okay, okay. Then, maybe he's playing coy about it because he doesn't want to lose his popularity. You know how these male singers are about that."

"Maybe," Stephanie said, reducing her volume. "I wish he would answer my calls."

"Do you think he's with someone else?" Monica asked.

"No. I think he's trying to give me a hard time because I told him he needs me," Stephanie said.

"What? Why did you say that?"

"Because I was angry," Stephanie said.

"Girl, I don't know about you sometimes."

"He does. He just doesn't know it yet," Stephanie said. "Let me go. I have to call him in a few to see if he's finally come to his senses."

"I'll say a prayer for you," Monica said.

After they hung up, Stephanie opened her laptop and logged on to her usual entertainment websites. Since Levin liked to extend partial answers about his life, she figured the Internet would help her fill in the blanks and stay in the loop. It also helped her feel connected to him when she couldn't hear his voice.

She clicked on the first message board thread and read

Levin and his label mate, Felicia, had been spotted at a party a couple of days ago. She considered that common since they appeared on the same record label but a link to the article claimed they stuck together all night, whispering and canoodling. When Stephanie scrolled down and saw the pictures, she stopped clicking. In the first photo, Felicia danced to music playing, while Levin whispered in her ear with his hands around her waist. The second photo he leaned over her shoulder from behind. They really did look cozy. Stephanie covered her face with her hands, hoping blocking the sight of them together would block her thoughts about them together. She tried not to worry about Internet rumors but pictures like this made it difficult. Some of the posts were too convincing. It was as if someone from their camps were typing on the message boards, posting pictures of Levin in the act.

Looking for reassurance, she dialed Levin's number. He picked up on the third ring.

"Hey, Levin! What's up?"

"Same ole, same ole. What's up with you?" he asked, sounding disinterested in her response.

"Just glad I got to talk to you. I haven't heard from you in a few days. I was starting to get worried," she said.

"Umph," he said.

"So, what are you up to today? Are you in the studio?"

"No, I'm trying to relax today. No stress, no drama." Levin sighed.

"Are you trying to say I give you drama?" Stephanie asked.

Levin sucked his teeth.

"Levin, I'm only trying to be with you but you make it so hard," Stephanie said.

"Maybe you're trying too hard. Telling people we're getting married. I was wondering where those rumors were coming from."

"You mean like I'm wondering where those rumors about you and Felicia are coming from?" Stephanie asked.

"I've told you about listening to rumors all the time."

"But this one has pictures attached. They're all over the Internet. You gonna tell me you weren't at a party with her recently?" Stephanie asked. She pressed her ear to the phone. She wanted to hear him try to lie this time.

"No. We were at a party but that was an industry party. It's not like we were on a date."

"You were acting like it. Leaning all up on her. Whispering sweet nothings in her ear."

Levin laughed. "Sweet nothings? What is this, poetry night? How you know I was doing all that?"

"It's in the picture!" Stephanie shouted.

"If I was whispering to her, it's because the music was too loud," Levin said.

"Then why did you have to have your hands all over her?"

"Stephanie, I'm not gonna sit here and let you laundry list everything you saw in the photo so I can justify it.

Now, I told you I'm not with Felicia. I'm telling the truth, unlike you telling people we're getting married," Levin said. "Why would you do that anyway?"

"The only thing I did was talk good about us. Is that so wrong?"

"No, but I can tell you one thing. You might wanna be careful about putting so much stuff out there. I'm certain you don't wanna play with the rumor mill," Levin warned.

"Oh, yeah. Why do you play?" Stephanie asked.

"Because it's part of my job. Listen, I have to go."

"Where are you going?" Stephanie asked, unable to conceal the desperation in her voice.

"I got an interview with Huey Martin and *The Morning Show* tomorrow and I need to be briefed on it. I'll call you later, okay?" Levin said.

No, Stephanie thought, gripping the phone. She wanted to talk longer. "Do you promise you'll call me?"

"Yes," Levin said.

"For sure?"

Levin sighed. "Yes, Stephanie. I'll call you."

"Okay," she said. "I love you."

He paused. "I love you, too, baby."

∞

The next morning, Stephanie popped out of bed like a pop tart jumping out of a toaster. She hadn't set her clock but somehow she remembered to wake up in time for Levin's interview with Huey Martin. She looked forward to hearing it, especially when she heard the teaser. Levin planned to finally respond to the "girlfriend" question. *Aww, he's finally gonna talk about me*, she thought. Even though they'd had problems, Levin had chosen to do the right thing. She knew he'd come around.

Stephanie shuffled into her kitchen and ran water into her favorite mug. She placed it in the microwave, setting two minutes on the timer. While the water heated, she stared out of the window at her ocean view, daydreaming about Levin's interview and their life together. She imagined him confidently professing his undying love for her. He'd call her up and tell her he was ready to marry her. She'd set the date. Their wedding would rival Prince Charles and Princess Diana with at least fourteen-hundred guests, including his celebrity friends and other important people. They would honeymoon in St. Tropez.

Before she could ponder what their house would look like, the microwave's *beep, beep, beep* interrupted her thoughts. Startled, Stephanie grabbed the mug and glanced at the clock. She dunked a tea bag in the water and dashed over to the couch to retrieve the stereo remote control.

When she turned the stereo on, she heard commercials and then, the show began with its usual fanfare and jokes. Waiting for Levin's interview, Stephanie wandered back into the kitchen, sipping her tea. She suddenly heard Levin's warm voice come across the speakers. Her heart fluttered as she raced over to the stereo to turn the volume up. She proceeded to lie on her couch and hug her pillow. The interview started out standard. Huey and his morning crew asked questions about Levin's latest album and the great reception it had received. They asked him about his stalled plans to get into movies; then, came the personal part of the interview. Stephanie leaned toward the radio.

"So. Uh, Levin? Are you single?" Leslie, Huey's sidekick, asked.

"Yes," Levin said.

"Wasn't there some woman you were supposed to be engaged to?" Leslie asked.

"No, I was never engaged," Levin said. Stephanie shrugged. Maybe he wanted to keep the engagement a secret a little longer. She hoped he wasn't holding a grudge about the lie.

"So, that was a rumor, right?" Leslie asked.

"Right," Levin said.

"Umph. I know some women are breathing a sigh of relief right now," Huey said. Everyone in the studio broke into laughter.

"Well, let me ask you this. Are you dating?" Leslie asked.

"Weeeell." Levin dragged his response out.

"Aww, c'mon man. You were almost there. You were doing good," Huey said. Levin laughed.

"Yeah. Yeah, I'm dating," he finally said. Stephanie

could feel herself perk up. This was the moment she'd waited so long for. The world would know they loved each other and were happy about their relationship.

"So, who are you dating?" Huey asked.

"I heard you're with Felicia. Is that true?" Leslie asked.

"I'm kinda seeing her. Yeah," Levin said.

The crew whooped and hollered. Stephanie, however, had a different reaction. Stunned, her body lay frozen on her couch. So many questions and emotions ran through her head and she couldn't sort through them. Stephanie searched for an explanation for what she'd heard but she couldn't find one. The thought of him playing her angered her to no end. She jumped up, grabbed the magazines on her coffee table and threw them against the wall. Breathing hard, Stephanie stood motionless. She thought things had gotten better. How could he deny her? Did this mean they were over?

CHAPTER 21

Dee

D ee and Bobbie's meeting almost didn't happen. She called Bobbie three times. Each time, his voicemail picked up. At first she was irritated, but then she calmed down. Waiting to talk to Bobbie gave her time to think about her real reason for accepting his money. Yeah, she did need it for the magazine, but was she primarily doing this to get back at Dwayne. Dee hadn't talked to him since the argument because he'd made her so mad. She had a serious problem with his disregard for her professional goals. He didn't believe in her magazine. Yet he said he wanted to help her find an investor? *No wonder he hadn't found one*, Dee thought. His presentation was probably underwhelming at best and lousy at worst. How can you sell an idea you don't believe in? One thing was for sure: if he wanted to reconcile, he would have to make the first move.

As far as Bobbie, she was about to give up on him until he finally answered her call on her fourth try. He apologized, telling her he had accidentally left his cell phone on vibrate. They arranged a meeting at a nearby restaurant. When they arrived, Dee made sure to sit toward the back of the establishment, facing the kitchen.

She wanted to eliminate the chances of someone spotting her. To her surprise, she could feel her palms sweating and her nerves rattling as she sat down. She even felt a sinking feeling in the bottom of her stomach. She began to have second thoughts about their meeting. On one hand, she still wanted the money to start her magazine, but she couldn't shake her bad feelings about Bobbie. She looked up at his aviator shades and black jacket. He appeared so jovial, almost as if he was laughing on the inside. She didn't even know this man and she was going to take his money.

Dee glanced at the crowded café. They fit into the atmosphere well enough. Yet, she took extra precautions, hiding behind a black baseball cap and Fendi B Buckle Square shades, in case someone thought they knew her.

Bobbie sat across from her, smiling. "I love your get-up," he said, commenting on her semi-disguise.

Dee smirked. "Same here."

"Have you told Dwayne about our little arrangement?" Bobbie asked.

"As a matter of fact, I have." Dee straightened in her seat.

"What did he say?"

"It wasn't his favorite news of the day," Dee admitted.

Bobbie laughed and grabbed his cappuccino. "I'll bet."

"What's up with you and Dwayne anyway?" Dee leaned forward. Since Dwayne wouldn't give her a straight answer, she thought Bobbie could shed some light on their relationship.

"How much time you got?" Bobbie asked.

"Enough time to get an answer."

"Well, basically, I think Dwayne's a stand-up guy. We don't see eye-to-eye on some things. That's all," he said.

"How did you meet?"

"About seven years ago, we worked together as partners in the financial company he's now running."

Dee flopped back in her seat. "Wait a minute. You guys worked together?"

"Yeah. We were doing great. Dwayne had the financial experience and a lot of NFL connections. I had a lot of street and practical knowledge." Bobbie stirred his drink. "Unfortunately, two years into the partnership, we started to disagree on how the company should be run. He bought me out and kept the company. I went and created my own."

"He told me he worked for his brother for several years and didn't start a company until he moved here," Dee said.

Bobbie chuckled. "I'm sure that's how he'd prefer to remember it." He continued to stir.

"Why would he lie to me about something like that?"

"Because he's embarrassed by me. He doesn't want to be reminded of the partnership because..." Bobbie trailed off. He looked up from his coffee at Dee. "Because we have a complicated history."

Chills ran up Dee's spine when Bobbie looked at her.

"What is that supposed to mean?"

"Oh, you'll find out soon enough," Bobbie smiled at her slowly and tasted his cappuccino. "Any other questions?"

"Yeah, how did you know so much about my venture and my friends? Do you have a friend working for the FBI or something?"

Bobbie laughed. "No, but that's next on the list of things to do. Actually, it really isn't that hard to find information on someone."

"That's comforting." She was growing tired of the game playing. Why couldn't anybody give her a straight answer? Before she allowed herself to huff about it, she imagined holding a photo shoot for her own magazine cover. *I will get down to the bottom of this, but not before I get my money,* Dee thought with renewed determination.

She swallowed her fears and switched the subject back to the reason she'd come. "Do you have my money?" Dee asked, attempting to regain control of her anxiety.

"Now that's what I like to hear. A woman getting down to business. I thought you'd never ask," Bobbie said. He then reached into his jacket pocket and pulled out a business check for one hundred and twenty-thousand dollars. Dee seized the check, stunned.

"I added another twenty-thousand dollars. Just 'cuz I like you." Bobbie laughed.

She put the check in her purse to keep someone from snatching it. Hiding the check also kept her from gawking at it.

"That should be enough to get you started, right?" he asked.

Regaining her composure, Dee nodded. "I'll be depositing this check as soon as possible. That won't be a problem, will it?"

"None at all."

"Well, then. Thank you. It was a pleasure doing business with you," Dee said.

Bobbie nodded, extended his hand to Dee. When her hand closed on his, he pulled her forward. "I look forward to doing business with you again." He released her hand, grabbed his jacket and left the table without saying another word.

Dee exhaled. *Well, that wasn't so bad*, she thought. Once Bobbie disappeared out the door, Dee snuck her hand back into her purse for the check. She opened it up as if to make sure her eyes hadn't deceived her. She smiled when she saw they hadn't. All of her anxieties disappeared as she thought about the things she would do with it. Suddenly, doing business with a man she barely knew didn't seem like such a bad idea. In fact, it was paying off—big time. To think, Bobbie offered her more money if she needed it.

Satisfied with the amount, she finally placed the check in her purse and slid out of the booth. She walked out of the front door with her head down, deep in thought about where she'd spend the money first. Paying no attention to anything but her own thoughts, she bumped into a larger frame and looked up to see Dwayne.

"Hey! What are you doing here?" Dwayne asked, surprised.

"Oh, I was meeting a potential client here," Dee answered. Many thoughts seemed to hit her at once. She wondered if Dwayne had seen Bobbie. She hoped not. She wondered if he was going to apologize for his behavior. He'd better. Dee also wondered if this would take long. She really wanted to rush the money to her bank account before Bobbie changed his mind.

"Really? Who?" Dwayne said. Dee wracked her brain to find a good story to tell him.

"Well, I don't wanna say. I'm still trying to woo her into working with me. So, I don't wanna put her out there yet. But she's very popular, really famous."

"I didn't see anybody famous come out." Dwayne looked around.

Dee shook her head. "That's because really famous people often leave out the back door to keep from getting hassled. It's okay. You'll get it one day." Dee laughed.

Dwayne shrugged. "So, I take it you're not hungry? I was about to get a sub. Do you want to join me?"

"No, I did eat something and I need to get going. I'll call you tonight," she said.

"Well, why don't you come in anyway? I could still get you a cappuccino or something."

"No, I got some more errands to run today. I'll talk to you later," Dee said. When she turned to leave, Dwayne caught her arm and pulled her closer. Dee stopped. She winced, bracing herself for an interrogation.

"Hey."

Dee looked up to him. "What?"

"We need to talk about the other day," Dwayne said.

"I can't go back in there right now. I really need to run," Dee said, looking toward her car.

"Well, would you at least listen to what I have to say?" Dwayne stared into Dee's eyes.

Perfect timing, Dee thought. She wanted to dash to her bank, which was only two blocks away. Instead, she had to stand there and have a big, ugly argument with Dwayne. On one hand, she was relieved he didn't run into Bobbie on his way in; on the other hand, she wasn't in the mood for any emotional scene outside of the restaurant.

Dee maneuvered her arm away from Dwayne. She crossed her arms across her chest and sighed. "Okay. What do you have to say?"

"The other day, I know things got a little out of hand and I wanted to say...well, what I really wanted to say is I'm sorry."

Dee rolled her eyes and shook her head.

"I should have been more supportive of your goals."

"Then why weren't you?" Dee interrupted.

"I guess I was a little jealous other people were helping you. I wanted to be the one to help you. So I got angry, and I apologize for doing that," Dwayne said.

Dee sucked her teeth and looked toward the parking lot. "What took you so long to apologize?"

Dwayne looked down and shook his head. "I knew you weren't going to make this easy."

"Why haven't you called me to say all this? Would you have apologized if you hadn't run into me today?"

"Yeah," Dwayne said. "Dee, come on. Are you going to give me a hard time?"

"No, Dwayne. Thank you for reaching out to me. I appreciate that," Dee said. She could have continued to give him a hard way to go but she realized it must've taken him a lot to apologize. She also wanted to get away from him before he pried further about her afternoon meeting.

Dwayne nodded and continued. "I don't want you to deal with Bobbie. He's not a good guy. I'm going to do whatever I can to support you from now on, but I need you to steer clear of him. Can you promise me that?"

Dee felt the acid in her stomach bubble over. His sincerity touched her but she couldn't bring herself to tell him she'd just accepted one hundred and twenty-thousand dollars from Bobbie. She couldn't tell him, and she didn't want to tell him. Sure, he said he would support her and help her find the money, but that's what he said months ago. She had a check in her purse, ready to be deposited into her bank account. It didn't get any better than that. Dee preferred to evade the truth. Besides, he wasn't telling her the truth, either. She said the only thing she could think to say.

"Sure, I promise." Dee nodded.

Dwayne winked and leaned over to hug her.

"I'm glad we were able to have this talk," he said.

"Me too," Dee agreed.

"Are you sure you don't wanna come in with me and get something?" Dwayne motioned toward the café.

"Oh, no. I'm gonna go now."

"Then I'll see you later?" Dwayne asked.

"Yeah. Later."

Dwayne kissed her on the forehead and walked into the café. Dee turned and sprinted to her car. *Whew, that was close*, she thought. She sped off. If she hurried, she could still catch the bank open.

∞

When Sunday came, Dee had to drag herself out of bed. She didn't really feel like attending church. But since Stephanie wouldn't answer her phone and Tony had an away game, she figured she'd go to church with Monica this time. Once Dee told Monica she and Dwayne were on better terms, she invited him, too. She said she figured he could help Dee stay awake during the service. *She's probably right*, Dee thought.

Dee and Dwayne followed Monica to First Metropolitan Baptist Church. When they arrived, they pulled into one of the three parking lot levels. Dee stared out of the window at all the cars in the parking spaces next to them. Lexus, Benz, Maserati. She wondered how many business owners belonged to Monica's church. They then took an elevator down to the first floor and walked over to the "Dome," a nickname given to the church due to its size and shape.

Dee expected the worst from the service, but it surprised her in several ways. For one, she stayed awake, a fact Monica noted as well. But the most surprising part of the service was Dwayne's interest in it. The sermon seemed to captivate him. He recited all the scriptures and sang along to each hymn. Even Monica looked surprised. After service, the three of them lunched at Soul Food Cuisine, a popular restaurant that served Southern cooking.

Once their plates hit the table, Monica groaned.

"Great. I'm gonna have to exercise for an extra two hours behind this food."

"Yeah right," Dee said.

"As fit as you are, you probably never gain weight no matter what you eat," Dwayne said.

"I wish." Monica laughed. She picked up her fork and dug into her macaroni and cheese, savoring the rich blend of cheddar and butter before she spoke again. "Dwayne, where did you learn all those hymns?" she asked.

"Well, my mother is pretty religious. When I was a kid, I was in church every day for something. I even had to go to summer camp. If there was nothing going on at church, my mother would say, 'Go anyway. I'm sure there've got something for you to do." They all laughed.

"At least my mother wasn't that bad. She had some limits," Dee said.

"Then why don't you and your mother get along?" Monica asked.

"Chile, she always wanted to tell me how to live. She's fond of the simple life and I'm not. I want to do a lot with my life but she thought I should get married, stay home and make babies."

"Are you saying you don't want children?" Dwayne asked.

Dee hesitated. "Let's just say I won't feel unfulfilled as a woman if I never have children."

Dwayne raised his eyebrows.

"What about you, Dwayne? Do you want children?" Monica asked.

"Yeah, I don't mind having a few crumb-snatchers." He smiled.

"Oh, okay," Monica said. She nodded and eyed her friend. Dee rolled her eyes. "Did you know that, Dee?" Monica asked her.

"No, Monica. I didn't know that," Dee said.

"What? You mean to tell me you guys haven't had this conversation before?" Monica asked. "Shame on you." Monica raised an eyebrow at Dee.

Dee peered at Monica in return. "The topic hasn't come up. That's all."

"Why not? You guys have been together for a little while," Monica said.

Dee stole a glance at Dwayne for help but he preferred to play with his collard greens instead. "We're taking the relationship slooooow." Dee dragged the last word out. Dwayne laughed.

"Is that true, Dwayne?" Monica asked.

"Yeah, I'm sure we'll talk about those things more, but so far we've been concentrating on getting investors for Dee's magazine," Dwayne said.

Monica gasped. "Oh. And how's that going?"

"It's coming. Not as fast as we'd like but it's coming," Dwayne said.

"Any prospects in mind?" Monica asked.

"A couple. Nothing confirmed yet," Dwayne said. He glanced down at his watch to avoid eye contact with Monica. When he read the time, he suddenly sat upright. "I'm gonna have to cut lunch a little short, ladies."

"Really? Why?" Dee asked.

"I have some last-minute business I have to take care of." Dwayne stood up from his chair.

"On a Sunday?" Dee frowned.

"When you have your own business, you work whenever duty calls, right?"

"I guess. Well, I'll walk you out." Dee tried to stand up but Dwayne raised his hand to stop her.

"No need. I'm running late," Dwayne said. "I'll call you later." He nodded at Monica and rushed out of the door.

Dee and Monica looked at each other.

"See what you did?" Dee said.

"What?" Monica asked, wide-eyed.

"Asking all those questions."

"I thought they were good questions, especially the children and investor ones. I can't believe you guys never talked about having children," Monica said, biting her roll.

"Why would we? It's not like we're getting married."

"So, you know he's not the one, huh?"

"Nope. Not even close," Dee said. "Look at the way he hopscotched around the investors question. The one for me would've found one already. I can't believe I misjudged him." Dee shook her head.

"Well, don't give up on him so soon. Maybe he'll come through," Monica said.

"Oh, girl, it doesn't even matter anymore. I got the money on my own," Dee said.

"How?"

Dee leaned in. "Remember when I told you about Bobbie, that weird guy Dwayne doesn't like?" Dee asked.

Monica nodded. "Yeah?"

"He offered me the money and I took it."

Monica's eyes widened. "Whoa! How much money did he give you?"

"One hundred and twenty-thousand dollars."

"One hundred and twenty-thousand dollars?!" Monica shouted.

Dee shushed her. "Dang, Monica. Say it louder. I don't think they heard you in Jamaica."

Monica covered her mouth for a second. "I'm sorry.

I'm just…one hundred and twenty-thousand dollars?" Monica frowned.

Dee nodded.

"What are the stipulations?" Monica asked.

"What do you mean?"

"The terms? When do you pay him back? Is there interest on it?"

"No. I don't think so," Dee said, looking up at the ceiling to think.

"Wait a minute. What do you mean 'you don't think so'?"

"He said it was angel money. And he offered to give me more if I need it," Dee said, smiling.

"Dee, something doesn't sound right. Did you sign a contract?" Monica asked.

Dee waved Monica away. "No."

Monica gasped. "I think you need to give this money back."

"What?! Why?" Dee yelled.

"Because I smell something fishy and it's not the catfish at the next table." They both glanced over at the dish served to the elderly lady at a nearby table. "I take it you haven't told Dwayne about this money yet?" Monica asked, raising her eyebrow.

"Chile, please. Let him keep thinking he's looking for me." She chuckled. "I even promised him I wouldn't deal with Bobbie. Oh, well."

"That's wrong. You should tell him," Monica said.

"I don't have to tell him anything." Dee scowled. "I wouldn't have had to go behind his back if he'd done what he said he would do. He doesn't even believe in the magazine."

"I think he said that in the heat of an argument, Dee. I'm sure he didn't mean it."

"Oh well. Too bad. I have my money now." Dee crossed her arms.

"Please return this money. I really don't think this is right," Monica said. "Tell me what type of man—excuse me—*businessman* gives you one hundred and twenty-thousand dollars with no contract?"

Dee shrugged. "I don't know. One with more money than he can spend?"

Monica looked down and shook her head.

"Let me handle it. I got this," Dee said.

"Then why do I feel like you don't 'got this'?" Monica asked.

"'Cuz you're a worrywart," Dee said. "Have you talked to Stephanie today?" Dee asked, attempting to change the subject.

"No. She's not returning any of my messages. I'm gonna have to go over to her house and talk to her," Monica said.

"Well, you know how she is sometimes. Moody," Dee said.

"You'd be moody, too, if your man was playing you like an eight-track," Monica said.

"That's nothing new. What did he do this time?" Dee rolled her eyes.

"Do you mean you haven't heard about what Levin said?"

Dee leaned forward. "No. What?"

"He went on *The Huey Martin Show* and told them he's dating Felicia," Monica said.

"Oh my gosh! That is crazy. See, I knew something was going on. That man don't wanna marry her."

"Yeah, well. It's out there now. I plan to go see her between today and tomorrow. Are you coming with me?"

"Sure, I'll be there," Dee said. "I'll bring a box of tissues 'cuz I know the tears are gonna be flowing like crazy."

∞

Down the street, Dwayne pushed his gas pedal a little closer to the floor, hoping to arrive at his meeting before the other guy. Even though he only had to drive a couple of blocks, he drove down the street at seventy-five miles per hour in a thirty-five miles-per-hour zone. He stopped his car midway to park, opting to walk the other block to take extra precautions. He didn't want this guy to write down his license plate and track him down. Dwayne just wanted the whole thing to be over.

He walked down the alley on the side of a corner store. His associate had already beat him there. *Not bad. At least he's prompt*, Dwayne thought. The young man waited, leaning on a white Ford that looked like it used to be a police car. He had on black, baggy jeans, a black shirt and a wave cap. Dwayne frowned when he saw his attire. *Does this fool know it's ninety degrees?* Dwayne asked himself. Dwayne hated dealing with these kinds of characters, but someone he trusted had referred him to this guy as a go-to person. He hoped he was good at what he did.

"What's up, man?" the stranger said. "You got my money?"

"Let's go over some details first. Number one, you get half now, half when it's finished. Number two, don't call me. Ever. I'll call you. And number three, don't ever tell anyone you met me. Got it?" Dwayne asked.

"What did you say your name was again?" the stranger said, smirking.

Dwayne sucked his teeth. He reached into his jacket pocket and pulled out fifteen thousand dollars cash in a brown envelope. He placed it in the man's hand. Before letting go of the money, he pulled it back. Dwayne stared him in the eyes.

"Make it happen," Dwayne said.

"Don't worry. Bobbie won't even know what hit him."

CHAPTER 22

Stephanie

It was two o'clock in the afternoon and Stephanie lay on her couch, moping. She stared at the blank TV as if it was on, but her mind was really somewhere else. To say Levin's radio interview had devastated her was like calling the temperature of the sun lukewarm. Since his interview had aired, Stephanie hid in her condo under a dingy bathrobe and pink bunny slippers, avoiding all phone calls and emails. It seemed like the whole world had heard the interview and her many friends and family wanted to talk to her about it. Some wanted to reach out to her in a sincere spirit of concern; others wanted more juicy details. All they really had to do was look at the entertainment shows, blogs and message boards. They all buzzed about Levin and Felicia, the new "It Couple." The media even showed more photos of the two together since Levin's interview. Levin and Felicia posed at after-parties and shows. Stephanie also found a photo of Levin sneaking away from Felicia's hotel. It made her want to throw up, but she insisted on keeping her dignity. She didn't want to make her humiliation a public event, not even for her friends. Levin had already done a bang-up job of making her look like a fool.

But she was still trying to understand how she'd become so insignificant to him. She had to be insignificant if he was willing to throw her away so carelessly. Over the past two days and nights, she'd wracked her brain, breaking down their conversations before the interview, but no matter how hard she tried she couldn't find any hint he was ready to let her go. Maybe she only saw what she wanted to see. Yet every time she thought about their time together—the way he talked to her, the way he held her—she knew their relationship was real. They were in love. *Then why did he make me look like a fool in front of the world?* Stephanie asked herself.

She felt a tear sliding down her face. She was about to release the wave of tears struggling to fall when her stomach growled. Reminded that she hadn't eaten all day, she wiped her cheek and stumbled over to the kitchen. Opening up the refrigerator, she noticed it was almost completely empty. She had eggs but no cheese. Cereal but no milk. Hot dogs but no mustard. She cringed as she thought about going to the grocery store. She imagined people pointing and laughing at her.

Stephanie closed the refrigerator door and walked toward her phone to call for a pizza, but remembered that the pizza places didn't deliver to her neighborhood. Then a thought struck her. It had been a while since people had seen her in public with Levin—the MTV Awards to be exact. And only a few media outlets had published pictures of her with him. At the time it irked her but now it could work in her favor. It decreased the chances that people would recognize her. Stephanie smiled slightly. Maybe she could go outside without people making fun of her. As each second passed, she found herself more open to the prospect of going to the store, and like that, she picked up her pace toward her room. She reached into her closet and pulled out a pair of blue jeans and a purple blouse. She finished her look with matching purple shoes and makeup. After primping in the mirror for forty-five minutes, Stephanie smiled at her reflection. It was the first sincere smile she'd had in the past couple of days. Seeing it gave her renewed confidence and optimism. Suddenly, the situation didn't seem so bad. She and Levin were going to work things out, and the public was going to be nice to her.

After battling ninety-eight-degree heat, Stephanie arrived at the grocery store. She pulled into the parking space closest to the entrance.

Just get it over with, Stephanie, she told herself. She took a deep breath and opened her car door. As she made her way into the store, Stephanie glanced around to see if anyone was staring at her. Nothing. People pushed their shopping carts along as if she were nobody. She was relieved they weren't bothering her; on the other hand, she was a little miffed they didn't recognize her. Deciding to finish shopping before someone did recognize her as Levin's fool, she grabbed a cart and flew down the frozen food section.

By the time she reached the checkout line, her cart was

almost full. Chips, cookies and ice cream accompanied the milk, cheese and mustard she needed. Surprisingly, she managed to shop the whole time without anyone noticing her. Since she was more comfortable, she leisurely picked up a magazine on the stands next to her, waiting for the checkout line to move along. She flipped page to page until something caught her eye on a previous page. Stephanie turned back to the page and her mouth dropped open. To the bottom left-hand side, she saw the picture of her and Levin at the MTV Awards, as well as one of him with Felicia. The small article highlighted Levin's relationships and the women in his life.

Upon scanning the article, Stephanie found the journalist called her "an unidentified video chick." She gasped. Unidentified? She'd been working in the industry for at least five years. She knew a lot of people and a lot of people knew her. She closed the magazine and shoved it back inside the rack. *Well, I guess that's why no one recognized me. I'm unidentified,* Stephanie thought. Tears welled in her eyes again. She shook her head and her shoulders, as if to shake her emotions off.

As Stephanie neared the conveyor belt, she placed her items on it for scanning. The cashier scanned everything without looking up at Stephanie. Once she reached the last item, the cashier looked into Stephanie's face.

"Your total is forty-five dollars and thirteen cents," said the cashier.

When Stephanie reached in her purse for a debit card,

the young girl behind the cash register cocked her head to the side. "Have I seen you somewhere?" she asked.

Stephanie's eyes widened. "No, I don't think so." She swiped her card in the machine.

"Yes, I have. Do you sing or something?" the cashier asked.

"No." Stephanie knew what she meant but hoped the girl would give up and stop trying to guess where she'd seen her. *Please, oh please, don't call me out. I'm almost out of here*, Stephanie thought.

"You don't sing?"

"No," Stephanie said, waiting for the girl to press the button to accept her card.

The cashier finally pressed it. "But I know I know you." She waged her finger and tucked it under her chin, while she examined Stephanie's face for recognition. Just then a young man walked up to the end of the cash register to bag Stephanie's food and place it in the cart for her. When he put the last bag in the cart, Stephanie thanked him and pushed it forward, grateful she was getting away before the cashier could figure out who she was. Unfortunately, she wasn't quick enough. Right after Stephanie took a few steps, the cashier snapped her fingers.

"I know now! Levin dumped you for Felicia," the cashier shouted.

Stephanie looked at the people walking around her. They were stopping to check out the cause of the commotion.

"It's you, isn't it?" the cashier yelled. Horrified, Stephanie shook her head and pushed her cart out of the door. She reached her car and threw the bags in as fast as she could. She sped off without looking back. When she reached her condo, it took all the strength she could muster to bring her groceries inside. She ended up putting away the frozen foods and leaving the rest in bags on her kitchen counter. Stephanie trudged into her bedroom, kicked off her shoes, peeled off her clothes and flopped back into her robe and slippers.

Once she'd changed, she looked in the mirror. The smile she had earlier had disappeared. It was replaced with a somber expression. She should have known someone would recognize her. She turned away from the mirror and walked back to the kitchen. Stephanie bypassed the rest of the food left in the bags. Instead, she reached for a large spoon and the half-gallon of ice cream she'd placed in the freezer a few minutes earlier. Sitting down in front of her plasma TV, she turned it on and popped open the carton top. She spent the next fourteen minutes savoring the rich taste of vanilla fudge ripple.

Stephanie had reached the center of the carton when she heard her doorbell ring. *What now?* she thought. She wiped her mouth with the back of her hand, put the top back on the carton, and tipped over to the door peephole. She saw Dee and Monica.

Stephanie wanted to run in the room and bury herself under her covers, but she knew they would stay at the door as long as it took for her to open it. She put the ice cream back in the freezer, tightened her bathrobe and opened the door.

"Hey, girl. What's up?" Dee greeted Stephanie.

"Oh, nothing. What's up with y'all?"

Monica scanned Stephanie's unkempt attire, stopping at her mouth. She reached over and wiped ice cream from the corner of Stephanie's mouth. Stephanie stepped back and wiped her mouth with her sleeve.

"We were thinking about going shopping? Wanna come?" Monica asked.

Stephanie scowled and glanced down at her robe. She tugged it together. "Not really."

"I hear Prada has some great deals. There's a new dress in there that screams Stephanie. It shows cleavage and everything," Dee offered.

Monica glared at her.

"What?" Dee asked.

"No, I think I'll stay home for now." Stephanie plopped down on her couch. She thought about the horror she'd faced earlier at the grocery store. She couldn't imagine facing that again.

"You can't stay home forever," Dee said.

"I really wanna be home for awhile." Stephanie stared at the TV.

Monica sat down next to her and sighed. "Look. I know you must be absolutely livid and hurt by what Levin did. There's no excuse for his behavior, but you can't allow this to change your life. There'll be other men who'll treat you so much better. And one day, you're going to look back on this and think, 'what did I see in that guy?'" Monica told her.

Stephanie shook her head. "I can't believe he lied to me for so long about Felicia." She looked out of her window at the diamond reflections coming off the ocean waves.

"Why? You lied about being engaged to him," Dee blurted out.

Angry, Stephanie snapped out of her daze and faced Dee. "I did not lie! He really does want to marry me."

"Does?" Dee asked, raising her eyebrows.

"Yes," Stephanie said.

Monica placed her hand over Stephanie's hand.

"Okay, okay. Maybe he got scared and needs some time to think the commitment over. After all, marriage is a big commitment," Monica said.

"Maybe." Stephanie pouted.

"Come shopping with us. I really think it'll make you feel better," Monica said.

Stephanie shook her head.

"If we leave now, you have to promise me we'll go out later," Monica said.

"Monica, I don't want people staring at me. People read and watch shows, you know," Stephanie said.

"Nobody's going to stare at you," Monica said.

"I'm sure there are still people who don't know who

you are. Now, if you were Felicia, then, people would be staring. As it stands, I don't think anybody cares about you," Dee said.

Stephanie and Monica stared at Dee.

"What?" Dee asked.

"Why don't you let me handle this from here, okay?" Monica asked.

Dee rolled her eyes.

Monica turned back to Stephanie. "Come to dinner with us. I insist."

Stephanie thought about it for a second and frowned at the memories of the store cashier shouting at her. "Okay."

Monica hugged her. "Good. I promise nothing will happen to you. We won't let it," Monica said. "Right, Dee?"

Dee gave the thumbs-up sign.

"We'll see you around nine. You'd better be ready," Monica said.

Stephanie walked Monica and Dee to the door. As they left, Stephanie closed the door behind them and overheard them talking in the hall.

"I think it's gonna be okay," Monica said.

"It'll be okay when she pulls her head out of the clouds and sees Levin for what he really is—a self-serving jerk who's stringing her along," Dee said.

Stephanie sighed and pulled away from the door. She sat back down on her couch, thinking about all the ways

Levin had wronged her, as if she hadn't already scratched her emotional skin raw. Like a tape recorder, her mind replayed the interview over and over again, looking for a rainbow in the middle of this storm. She wanted to prove Dee wrong, but so far, she came up with nothing to support her belief in her and Levin's relationship.

Suddenly, her phone rang. Although she'd been avoiding people's calls, Stephanie opted to answer her phone this time. On the other end, she heard her friend, Natalie.

"Stephanie! I've been trying to reach you for the past three days. Where have you been?" Natalie exploded over the phone. She almost sounded breathless.

"Oh, I haven't felt much like talking," Stephanie said.

"Aww. Girl, I know. I am so sorry about everything that's happening. It's a real shame," Natalie said.

Stephanie felt a lump form in her throat but she refused to cry. She thought about all the times she and Natalie had talked trash about other people. She hated being the subject of the gossip. She hated pity. Her pride couldn't take it.

"Oh, it's no big deal. It'll be fine," Stephanie said.

"No, it's awful. You guys aren't even getting a chance to make it work," Natalie said.

"Well, Levin always said the media was ruthless," Stephanie said. She didn't realize he had the same quality.

"Media? Who said anything about the media? They're the puppets. Victor's pulling the strings!" Natalie snorted.

"Victor?" Stephanie asked.

"Yes. Levin's manager. He's controlling the whole thing. He's the one who put Levin and Felicia together. I thought you knew that."

"How would I know something like that?"

"You've dated music guys before. How do you think the media got all those photos of the two of them together? That was staged," Natalie said.

"I don't understand, Natalie. What's it to him? Why does he care who Levin dates?"

"The same reason anyone else cares. Money. He has a lot riding on Levin. Victor thinks he's going to make it big, but only if he keeps a playboy image, you know? He couldn't let him look like he was tied down already," Natalie said.

"So he tied him to Felicia? That doesn't make any sense," Stephanie wondered out loud.

"That's a temporary fix," Natalie answered. "In a couple of months, they'll quietly 'go their separate ways.' You know what I mean?"

"But what is he trying to fix?" Stephanie asked.

"You," Natalie said.

Overwhelmed, Stephanie dropped her head in her hand. She had devoted so much time to landing the man of her dreams. She feared other women taking him away or his busy schedule keeping them apart. She never expected Levin's manager to become the problem in their relationship.

"So, what are you gonna do?" Natalie asked.

"I don't know but I have to go. I'll call you later," Stephanie said.

"Well, okay. Make sure you call me."

Stephanie put the phone down and stretched out on her couch. She couldn't believe Victor would try to ruin her relationship with Levin, but she should have known there had to be something up. She and Levin had genuine feelings for each other—feelings that did not justify his radio interview. Everything was starting to make sense now. She didn't care what Victor had up his sleeve. She and Levin deserved to be happy together and Stephanie intended to make that happen. Instead of giving in, she decided to regroup and move forward full throttle.

Stephanie hopped up with a spurt of energy. She bolted over to her desk, opened the drawer, and pulled out an orange notebook and a blue pen. She opened the notebook to the first page and wrote down the first part of her plan. With each sentence, she became more and more confident in the next step she would take. It took five pages for her to create an outline of dates and tactics to implement. She finally stopped writing and sat back satisfied. *Let's see what Victor does when word spreads that Levin and I have a baby on the way*, Stephanie thought.

CHAPTER 23

Monica

"Marianna, I'm going to the gym. If Tony calls, let him know I'll be back later and don't let him intimidate you into telling where I am," Monica shouted, jogging downstairs in her Pacific blue criss-cross back cami and black yoga pants with hoodie.

She, Dee and Stephanie had had a great dinner the night before, but Monica knew the food would stick with her if she didn't work it off. She also hadn't exercised much since she'd started working with Janet on her restaurant opening. She missed beating her feet against the walking belt of a treadmill while listening to Jill Scott on her iPod. If she wasn't careful, the neglect of her body would start to show.

She rushed to take advantage of the opportunity to get back into her routine before Tony could call and stop her. He loved to call her several times a day to keep tabs. Even on her trips to the supermarket, he still called every five minutes. She wanted to stop it before it started, but exercising wasn't the only reason why.

The truth was she didn't know how to tell him she couldn't go to Indianapolis. Since William's birthday dinner, he chirped around the house like a brand-new bird.

He'd even made an extra effort to talk to the children more. It made a real difference. William was controlling his outbursts and Angela became a lot easier to handle. She really wanted to keep the peace. "Yes, Senora," Marianna said. "You have mail on kitchen counter. I think Butch left it," Marianna said, interrupting Monica's sprint.

"Oh, okay!" Monica strolled over and picked up the envelope addressed to her in handwriting. She walked out of the kitchen door. *Jessica Alexander. I don't know her*, Monica thought.

"Where you going, Mama?" William ran up to Monica and hugged her leg.

"Oh. I'll be right back, sweetheart. I'm going for a run. Be good and I'll see about bringing you guys a treat back, okay?"

"Okay." William nodded and ran back into the house.

She pulled the letter out of the envelope and read.

Dear Mrs. Monica Hatcher:

You don't know who I am, but I'm very aware of who you are. I've seen you in magazines over the years. I've seen you on many shows, talking candidly about your life and your husband. You always look like you've got it together. I especially liked the green number you were sporting at the benefit dinner. What was it? Eli Saab?

Anyway, my name is Jessica. I haven't met you but I've met your husband, Tony. We have a five-year-old son together named Tony, Jr.

Monica stopped reading and fell against her car. She stared at the letter before shaking her head as if that would make the words in the letter disappear, but it didn't work. The words were so strong she felt like they were burning her eyes. She looked around to see if anyone could see her reading the letter or even knew about it. Nobody else was around.

Monica jumped at a noise only to realize it was her cell phone ringing. She frisked her waist for it.

"Hello, this is Vivian Harrell. I'm a reporter from *Sights and Sounds Magazine*."

"Yes," Monica answered.

"I recently emailed you about Janet Lowery's new restaurant opening and getting press credentials. Just calling to follow up on the progress."

"Oh, yes," Monica said, blinking to focus. "You are on the list. We'll send you an email with all the details shortly."

The reporter thanked her and hung up. Monica sat down in her car and tried to refocus on the letter. She read it again but the words made no more sense than they did before. She couldn't believe Tony would do anything like this.

For years, people called Monica naïve because she refused to consider the possibility that Tony could have an affair, but she always believed in marriage, especially her own. She and Tony had a partnership as much as they had a marriage. They built everything they had together. She had a hard time seeing him risk his family and his money for some groupie.

On the other hand, some things made sense, such as the unexplained bounced check. It was unusual for them to write bad checks. It was even more unusual Tony didn't want to explain them. *This has got to be a joke*, Monica thought. However, if by chance this wasn't a joke, she wondered whether she had what it took to stick the situation out. She couldn't see herself enduring the same foolishness her mother had. Her breathing quickened as she imagined women calling the house. Showing up at important functions. Monica wouldn't be able to take that; she'd have to hurt somebody.

As Monica's disbelief turned into anger, all thoughts of exercising disappeared. She needed to talk to someone. So, Monica picked up her phone and dialed Stephanie's number but she didn't get an answer. She then called Dee but she didn't pick up either. Out of desperation, she called Robert. Within thirty minutes, she and Robert sat in her parked Jaguar. Monica didn't explain the situation over the phone but the moment Robert saw her, he knew something was up.

"You sounded bad over the phone. What's wrong?" Robert asked.

Monica took a deep breath and pulled out the letter. She read it to him. The words from the letter tumbled out of her. For a minute, Robert sat stunned.

"Wow. She really sent you this letter, huh?" He grabbed it from Monica and looked at it for himself.

"Yeah."

"Oh, Monica. I'm sorry. This is awful."

"Why would she do this? Now? After five years?"

"Got to be the money," Robert said.

"I think she's already gotten that."

"What do you mean?"

"A few months ago, I found out some of our checks were bouncing, even some of mine for the scholarship dinner. When I inquired further about it, the bank told me Tony wrote a bounced check to his financial manager. It wasn't even regular payroll. It was a separate personal check," Monica said.

"Oh. Did you ask Tony about it?" Robert asked.

"Yes. He pitched a fit and told me he didn't remember."

"You think he tried to give the money to his manager so he could give it to Jessica without you or anybody else asking questions?" Robert asked.

Monica nodded her head. "It makes perfect sense." She shook her head. "But you know what's really bothering me?"

"He let it go five years without telling you?" Robert said on cue.

"Yes! He didn't once think, 'Gee, I should really tell her.' What if the media had found out? Our families would have been humiliated. If it's true, this is so unforgivable."

"I get it. It wasn't the smartest thing in the world to do. I guess he thought he was doing the right thing," Robert said.

"What? By lying to me?!"

Robert shook his head. "By lying in the bed he made. By trying to keep a happy home for the family he already had. I'm sure he was also fearful you would walk out. I think you would have contemplated leaving. You may have even left temporarily but, knowing you, you would have stayed."

Monica rolled her eyes. "How do you know that?"

"Because I know you love your family and you're not a quitter. You're very tough. Looking back, I think that's why we didn't make it. I didn't know how to handle your kind of strength back then, but I know this is what will get you through everything."

"Agghh. I was really looking forward to working with Janet," Monica said.

Robert raised his eyebrow. "You still are, right?"

Monica kept quiet.

"Right?" Robert asked.

"Well, Robert, I don't think it's appropriate for me to work with a client now. My home life is going haywire. I know you don't think I should continue?"

"Yes!" Robert yelled. "Monica, you have to do it. You have to gather that strength you have and pull through."

"No, I need to get down to the bottom of all this."

"But you made a commitment."

"My marriage is a commitment. I don't wanna leave the woman hanging but this is important. I have to take care of my family," Monica said.

Robert stared straight ahead in silence.

"You don't agree?" Monica said, frowning at Robert.

He shrugged. "It's up to you. You have to do what you feel is best for you and your family," Robert said.

"Don't give me that, Robert. Are you trying to say you really think I should forget about my family and work with Janet?"

Robert turned and pointed at Monica. "You told me you wanted to do your own thing. To be independent. I supported you because the Monica I know could conquer the world if she wanted to. Now you have the opportunity to make your dreams come true. To come out from under Tony's shadow and you're throwing it away," Robert said.

"I'm not throwing it away! I'm postponing it until tomorrow," Monica said.

"You've been postponing for eight years! There is no tomorrow, Monica. There's only today. And as far as this letter, whether it's true or not, won't you feel better about it if you take the time to take care of yourself first? Go after what you want instead of catering to Tony's wants. Isn't that the model you want your children, especially your own daughter, to see?" Robert asked. "If you really want this, you have to do what it takes now because that's the only way you'll truly be independent."

Monica looked across the street at two kids playing Cops and Robbers. She watched the little girl fasten imaginary handcuffs on her big brother, asserting her play-play authority. Monica remembered when she was that sure of herself. What was she waiting for?

She was waiting for the guilt to subside. Before Jessica's letter, she felt wrong for wanting to create a part of her life separate from Tony, even though she'd experienced great fulfillment working on the scholarship dinner and Janet's restaurant. On some level, she believed her children needed her home on a permanent basis. Tony had convinced her something bad would happen if she started working regularly. Since she'd found out about his indiscretions, his words felt more like manipulation used to keep her dependent on him.

Monica turned back to Robert.

"You're right. The opening is a big opportunity for me, but I don't know how I'll stay focused through all of this," Monica said. She really wanted to maintain her enthusiasm and be the soldier Robert thought she was, but it still didn't feel logical to continue working given her situation.

"Well, when you feel like you won't be able to make it, call me. Just like you did today and I'll help you pull through it in any way I can."

Monica hesitated. "I'll tell you what. I'll think about it."

Robert sighed. "Okay. Fine, Monica. I understand."

"I'm not saying I'm quitting. I'm saying I need to figure out how I'm going to do this."

"Okay."

"Really?" Monica asked, searching for the truth in his eyes. "You're not just saying that, are you?"

"No, no. This is a tough decision, and whatever you decide, I'm behind you one hundred percent."

Monica smiled. "Thank you."

She leaned over and hugged Robert. After he returned the hug, they loosened their embrace, catching a gaze in each other's eyes. For a second, she almost forgot where she was. Flashbacks of their years together in college engulfed her mind, causing an overload. Monica pulled away and moved back to her side of the car, staring ahead. *God, I don't need any more complications,* she thought.

∞

When Monica pulled into her circular driveway, she sat in the car for about five minutes. She wanted to mentally prepare herself to go inside. She felt the need to pretend nothing had happened because she didn't want to upset the kids. Before she went inside, she said a little prayer to keep herself focused. She exited the car and walked through the front door. The sound of William playing upstairs drifted down the stairs to greet her. She walked into the kitchen and immediately smelled the aroma of lasagna and garlic bread. It was dinnertime.

"Hello, Marianna." The family nanny and cook stood at the stove uncovering one of her best dishes.

"*Hola*, Mrs. Hatcher. Did you enjoy your run?"

"What? Oh yeah. It was good. Is Tony here yet?" Monica asked.

"Yes. He is upstairs and so are the kids. They've already finished their homework. Do you want me to call them down?"

"Oh only when you're finished. Thanks, Marianna. I forgot to ask. How did the sweater Stephanie bought you fit?" Monica asked, happy to have found a distraction.

"It fits perfectly. I've never had cashmere before."

"No? You should try it more often. I guess I know what I'll be buying you for Christmas," Monica said.

The two women laughed.

William and Angela came tumbling down the stairs. William ran to Monica.

"Mama, did you bring me anything?"

"I'm afraid not. I didn't really go anywhere to bring you anything. Were you a good boy while I was gone?"

"Yes." William nodded.

"Then I'll tell you what. Tomorrow we'll go out for some ice cream. How does that sound?"

"Cool!" William dashed over to the table and sat down, swinging his legs happily.

Tony dragged into the kitchen. "What's cool?"

Monica took a deep breath. She wasn't as prepared to see him as she thought. The mere sight of him made her want to hurl a utensil at him. She closed her eyes and counted to ten, while her son answered his father's question.

"Mama gonna take me to get ice cream tomorrow," William said.

"Really? I wanna go." Tony chuckled.

"Dinner's ready!" Marianna said.

Throughout dinner, Monica kept her attention on the kids to maintain her composure. When Tony asked her a question, she made her response as brief as possible. By the time dinner ended, she had to give herself an imaginary pat on the back for staying calm. It's not easy to keep your cool when you want to take your fork and drive it right into the eye of the person sitting across from you. After dinner was over, Monica put the kids to bed and walked into her bedroom, thinking about how she was going to approach Tony. She could start in on him as soon as he jumped in the bed but then she thought that was far too late. Besides, she really didn't want him in the same bed with her. She decided she would grill him as soon as she could get him alone.

As it turned out, she didn't have long to wait; Tony entered the bedroom shortly after she did. He flopped down on the bed and took his slippers off. Then Monica realized she couldn't hold her anger in any longer. "So," Monica started. "How's Jessica?"

He jerked his head up and turned to face her. "What?"

"I said how is Jessica?" she repeated.

"What are you talking about?"

"Jessica? You know, the mother of your five year-old son?" Monica stood up and placed her hands on her hips.

Tony scowled and returned his attention back to his slippers. "I don't know what you're talking about."

"Oh. Of course you do."

"No, Monica. I don't. Where are you getting this?"

"From the letter I got in the mail today. She says you've been taking care of her and her child for the past five years," Monica said, beginning to raise her voice. "Now are you sure there's nothing you wanna tell me, Tony?"

Tony stared off in silence before responding. "No, I don't have anything to tell you."

"Are you sure?!" Monica yelled.

Tony jumped up. "Monica, I don't know nothing about that. She must be a stalker or something."

"Tony, don't lie to me."

"I'm not lying."

"You know what? This is real sad. To think you wasted all that hot air telling me about how you wanted to be there for our kids, for our family. And you're out there doing whatever you want to do."

"Monica, it's not like that."

"Then what is it like?"

"I don't have a child with that woman."

"So, you do know her?"

"Not like that." Tony looked at the floor to avoid Monica's glare.

"Antonio Terrell Hatcher. You have ten seconds to start spilling your guts or I will pick up that phone, call Fred, and see what he knows about this woman," Monica said.

Tony's eyes widened. "No! My manager don't have anything to do with this."

"Then, you better start talking," Monica said.

"Okay, okay," Tony said, frowning. "Jessica is a groupie. She used to show up to some of the practices and bat her eyes at everybody. She knew everything about all the guys, including their stats and the money in their bank accounts. She also knew which of us were married but it didn't matter to her." Tony paused, reluctant to go on, but Monica crossed her arms, waiting for him to continue.

"Our thing only lasted about five months." Tony said, lowering his head.

"Your thing?"

"C'mon, Monica. Don't make me say it."

Monica sat down on her vanity chair.

"Early on I told her I won't be leaving my family for nobody. I guess she thought she could change my mind because she spent time and money following me from game to game and calling me. I got a little worried about it sometimes but I felt like I could handle her. She told me she was pregnant after I called it off. I never believed it was really mine, Monica."

"How do you explain all the money you gave her?"

"I gave her a few pity dollars."

"Or you were trying to keep her quiet so she wouldn't talk," Monica said.

"I don't believe she had my child. I don't care what she wrote you in that letter," Tony said.

"And you expect me to believe you weren't paying her child support?"

"There is no child support because that's not my child!"

"How am I supposed to believe that?!" Monica shouted. She covered her mouth after she remembered her children were down the hall.

Tony's forehead wrinkled and his shoulders slumped. For the first time in a long time, she saw no trace of his usual grandeur. "Monica, I'm really sorry. You know she meant nothing to me."

"Save it! Save all of it! I will not listen to your excuses, and furthermore, I will not be going to Indianapolis with you. My children and I will stay right here," Monica said, tapping her pointer finger on her vanity table.

"C'mon, Monica. I said I was sorry," Tony pleaded.

"You need to stay in one of the other rooms tonight," Monica said, pointing toward the door.

Tony started to say something else but Monica shot him a look that would melt icebergs. He stood up and walked out the bedroom door.

CHAPTER 24

Dee

Dee laid the usual spread out on the dining room table for Monica and Stephanie. It was time for their Thursday night get-together. A time to catch up, relax and release around friends. It was a night they always looked forward to and rarely broke. Dee, in particular, couldn't wait. She wanted to surprise the ladies with the samples of her first magazine cover. She hoped they would give her enough feedback so she could make a decision on one of them. For the time being, she kept it in a drawer nearby.

After arranging everything for the ladies, Dee sat down to check her emails, only to hear the doorbell ring before she could read the first one. She opened the door to Monica and Stephanie. They filed in without saying a word.

"Hey, ladies! What's crackin'?" Dee asked with booming enthusiasm. She stopped short when she looked into their faces. Their typical verve for their night of sisterhood was gone. Instead, Monica and Stephanie looked like someone had killed their puppies.

"What's going on?" Dee asked. She looked from one to the other and back again, expecting an answer.

Monica and Stephanie walked past Dee into the dining room. Stephanie grabbed a bottle of champagne and poured a glass for Monica and handed it to her. She then poured another glass and placed it in Dee's hands. She finally poured a glass for herself. Monica took her glass over to the couch and sat down.

"Hello? Is anybody going to tell me what's going on?" Dee asked.

"We'd better sit down," Stephanie said, looping her arm with Dee's to pull her toward the couch.

Dee followed suit and sat down next to Monica, staring at them. Finally, Monica turned to Dee and spoke.

"Tony cheated on me," she said.

Dee stared at Monica as if she'd landed from Mars. "What are you talking about?"

"I received a letter." Monica pulled the letter out of her purse and handed it to Dee. She fixated on the letter, shocked at what she was reading.

"Whoa! Some chick actually sent you this?" Dee asked. Monica nodded.

"This is crazy. How are you holding up?" Dee asked.

"I kicked Tony out of the bedroom." Monica shrugged.

"You need to kick him out of the house!" Dee said.

"Well, I can't believe Tony would cheat like this," Stephanie said.

"Aww, man. Grow up! You know how those athletes do. You'd be hard pressed to find one that hasn't cheated," Dee said. "It's this baby business I can't believe. You mean your husband is really stupid enough to make a baby with a groupie?" Dee asked.

"Apparently. According to Ms. Thing, he's been taking care of her and her child financially for five years. I knew it was a mistake to let him and his manager handle all the finances. If I had been paying attention, I would've noticed ten-thousand dollars leaving his account each month," Monica said. "She even sent a picture of the child." Monica handed the photo to Dee.

Stephanie leaned over to peek at the picture. "Ooh. He kinda looks like Tony. That skank. What kinda woman sends you a picture of the child she made with your husband?" She shook her head.

"One that wants more," Dee answered. "The money she's been getting must not be enough now or at least she doesn't think so. Now she wants more," Dee said, giving Monica the picture back.

"Well, I'm not giving her anything," Monica said.

"Yeah, but maybe she was trying to get Tony to grease the palm a little more. He probably told her no. She got mad and tried to blackmail him. He refused to give in. So she decided to let the truth come out," Dee said.

"What are you going to do now?" Stephanie asked. "If she went through all this trouble, I doubt she's going away."

"It's too soon to tell. I have a lot to think about."

"One thing is for sure. You're about to be in for a very bumpy ride. Women like this don't just go away," Dee said.

"I can't believe this is happening." Monica leaned her head back on Dee's couch. Stephanie reached out and patted her on the shoulder.

"So much for the opening, huh?" Stephanie asked.

"No. I think I'm still going to do the opening. I just won't be going to his Indianapolis game," Monica said.

"That a girl. Don't let this crap get you down," Dee said. "When is it?"

"The same weekend as the opening," Monica said.

"Hey. That gives you an out then," Dee said.

"I don't know. I think you should take some time out," Stephanie said.

"For what? So, she can mope around the house, like you did with Levin," Dee said.

"Hey," Stephanie said.

Monica held up a hand. "All right. You have a point, Dee. I think I need to keep busy doing something positive and I think the opening will be what I need to keep my mind occupied. Even Robert thinks I should continue working with Janet."

"Oh. You told him. What did he have to say about it?" Dee asked.

"He said he thinks I should work it out."

"What? You mean he took the high road? I thought for sure he'd take advantage of your vulnerability," Dee said, gesturing air quotation marks on the word *vulnerability*.

"We're friends. Nothing else," Monica said.

"Yeah. We'll see how long that lasts," Dee said.

Monica sighed and turned to Stephanie. "You believe me. Don't you?"

Stephanie scrunched her face. "I think you're walking a tightrope."

"You guys are tripping. Nothing's going to happen between me and Robert. That's a closed chapter." Monica folded her arms.

Boy, is she in denial, Dee thought. She was walking into the danger zone with Robert and she didn't even know it, but Monica had the type of personality where if she didn't know, nobody could tell her. Dee decided to drop the topic and focus on something she'd been waiting to talk about for days. As if she'd just remembered something, Dee snapped her fingers and darted over to her desk to grab the samples. She spread them on the coffee table for Stephanie and Monica to see.

"Switching gears, I have something I want to show you guys." Dee laid out three covers: one had a model in the outdoors, the other had a model in a studio and the last cover had three models in a studio. "These are the ideas for my first cover and I wanted you guys' opinion. Which one is better?" Dee said.

Both women studied it for a few seconds. "I like the one with the woman outside," Monica said.

"What about you, Steph?" Dee asked.

"I like the one with the three women on it," Stephanie said. Dee looked at the samples in deep thought.

"I was looking at the single-model studio shot," Dee said.

"What about the title? Have you come up with a name for the magazine yet?" Monica asked.

"Yes and it is perfect," Dee said. She turned around to face Monica. "Maven."

"Maven? What does that have to do with fashion?" Stephanie asked. She frowned as she looked at one of the other sample covers.

"My magazine is going to make all women fashion mavens. It'll take the guess work out of fashion for busy women. Think of it as a style for dummies magazine," Dee said.

"So, you're teaching fashion now, huh?" Monica asked.

"Yeah. I thought now would be a good time to give back." Dee giggled. "That reminds me. Given your situation, this might be a bad time but I wanted to ask you something," Dee said to Monica.

"That's okay. What is it?" Monica said.

"Would you be able to help me manage my magazine?" Dee asked.

"Aww, honey, I'm honored you're asking me to participate in your dream. However, I don't know if I'll be able to find the time to manage it. I need to concentrate on my family issues. I already feel funny about working on the opening. I don't want to spend too much extra time away from home," Monica said. Dee nodded. She'd figured Monica would say that.

Dee really did understand Monica's situation, but she

felt like she needed her friend's help. Monica could advise her on the media side, as well as the publicity side. It was a win all the way around. Dee planned to give Monica some time to sort out her family issues and then try asking her to help out more with the magazine. *I wonder how much work I can get from her before she starts to charge me,* Dee thought. "I understand. How about helping me build my staff?" Dee asked.

"I may be able to give you some pointers on that," Monica said.

"I'll take that," Dee said.

"How far are you now?" Stephanie asked.

"Well, I've found a printer that's giving me a really good deal. I've purchased a domain and web hosting plan and my next step is to hire someone to design my website. I'm also thinking about looking for office space later. I wonder if I should rent or buy?" Dee thought aloud.

"Have you told Dwayne about the money yet?" Monica asked.

Dee rolled her eyes. "No, Mother. I haven't."

"He hasn't said anything about all these moves you're making? He hasn't asked where all the money is coming from?" Monica asked.

"No, he doesn't even know what I'm doing. He still thinks I'm waiting for him to get it together." Dee chuckled.

"Dee, you're gonna have to tell him at some point. You don't want the news to come out without you being the one to break it," Monica said.

"Oh my God. For the last time, I can handle it," Dee said.

This was the problem with Monica. Because she was the only one of the group married with children, she felt like she was the most responsible. She always knew better than Dee and Stephanie and she didn't mind letting them know she thought so. It really irritated Dee sometimes.

The way Dee lived her life didn't necessarily equal irresponsible. As a matter of fact, she considered herself quite responsible. She'd built her fashion stylist business. She'd taken care of herself. Dee preferred to stay away from the stereotypical life, which included the husband, the 2.5 children and a dog. Those things didn't appeal to her, but that didn't make her an untrustworthy imbecile.

"Well, I guess that money from Bobbie really came through, huh?" Stephanie asked, leaning back on the couch.

"Eh," Dee shrugged.

"What does that mean?" Monica asked.

"The money is not stretching as far as I thought. I think I might have to go back for another one hundred thousand dollars," Dee said, taking a swig of her champagne while avoiding Monica's gaze.

Monica's eyes widened. "Dee? Are you crazy?'

"No. I want to give Maven every opportunity to succeed. To do that, I need more money," Dee said. She stood up to get some meat, cheese and crackers.

"I really don't think this is a good idea. No, I'm sure this isn't a good idea." Monica's glare followed Dee to the dining room table.

Suddenly, Dee felt like she was back at Henrietta's Bistro several months ago. Nothing had changed. She still had to convince her friends she was capable of making her dreams real. Even after she'd secured money to start the magazine, they searched for cold water to throw on her. Dee's blood boiled. *They are never going to be happy for me*, she thought.

"You don't even know that!" Dee yelled.

"I know one thing. If you go back for more, you'll be digging a hole for yourself. You still don't know what this man's intentions are. I think you should talk to Dwayne about this man," Monica said.

"Well, I don't think I need him," Dee said, walking back to the living room. "This is what I want. You need to support me. That's what friends are supposed to do."

"I do support you, Dee, but friends are also supposed to let you know when you're about to do something that could hurt you. This is one of those times," Monica said.

"Well, let me figure that out," Dee said.

The women lapsed into a tense silence. Monica crossed her arms while Dee furiously munched on her snack. Neither woman looked at the other. This was not the evening Dee had in mind and she had second thoughts about it. Maybe she should have waited to meet up with them. Or maybe she shouldn't have even mentioned the money, but she didn't think it would become this big of a deal. Monica made it sound like Bobbie was going to do some real damage to her.

In truth, out of everyone—including her own friends—he seemed to be the most supportive and the most enthusiastic about her magazine plans. Everyone else was either stalling or telling her what she was doing wrong. She was getting tired of it.

Stephanie stood up and looked through Dee's entertainment center for DVDs.

"Anybody in the mood for *There's Something About Mary?*" Stephanie asked.

The three women watched the movie and munched on the snacks without much talk. As they laughed at the movie, the tension lifted without completely disappearing. When Monica and Stephanie left, Dee cleared her tables and reviewed the night's events. Anger consumed her. Despite Monica's warnings, she wanted to use all her resources to push her magazine forward. That included Bobbie's money.

Then a thought occurred to her. What if asking Bobbie for more money really was a mistake? She didn't know where it was coming from, and she didn't know much about Bobbie's past. Maybe Monica was right. But Dee had waited so long to put the magazine together. She wanted to assume the best of circumstances. It had felt good to drop that check off to the printer. So good that she couldn't allow anything to get in the way. Not even pesky formalities.

Dee set her plates in the dishwasher and walked over to her phone. She dialed Bobbie's number. She was relieved when he answered right away.

"Hey, Bobbie. It's Dee."

"Well, hello there. How are you?"

"Great!"

"And the magazine?" Bobbie asked.

"It's going really well. I'm looking at the sample covers right now."

"Excellent! I couldn't be happier for you."

"There's one thing," Dee said. "I could use more capital."

"Really?"

"Yeah. I'm in the process of working with a company on a top notch website and…"

Bobbie cut her short. "There's no need to explain. Tell me what you need," Bobbie said.

"Another one hundred thousand would be good."

"How about two hundred thousand?" Bobbie asked.

Dee swallowed her excitement. *Now this is more like it*, she thought. She didn't want to sound too eager but inside she jumped up and down. "That would be excellent," Dee said.

"Would you like me to deposit it into your business account, or do you want another check?"

"Deposit," Dee said. She gave him her bank name and routing number.

"It's on the way," Bobbie said with a smile in his voice.

∞

Bobbie had just pulled into the Grand Hyatt Hotel parking garage when Dee called him. After hanging up with her, he typed a note in his BlackBerry to make money arrangements for her when he returned to his room. He ran his hand over his face and looked in the rearview mirror at his crow's feet. Once everything settled, maybe he would locate a first-rate plastic surgeon to fix that.

Before he could open his car door, his BlackBerry rang. Looking at it, he sighed.

"Hello, Maximus," Bobbie answered.

"Sup, Bobbie? How's e'rything?"

"Never been better."

"Is the situation handled?' Maximus asked.

"Oh, yeah. The last amount is going out right now. I have a lady starting a business…"

"Whateva. Just make e'rything happen. Aight?" Maximus asked.

"Sure thing," Bobbie said. Maximus hung up without a goodbye.

Bobbie hung up the phone, breathing a sigh of relief. He knew what that call meant. He had to move this money before Maximus called again. Anxious to get started, Bobbie popped out of the car and entered the hotel lobby.

"I want to add five more days on to my bill." Bobbie said to the front desk clerk.

"Sure, sir." The clerk found his name on the computer to make the adjustment to the bill, "Nice night."

"Yes, it's lovely."

"Are you here on business?"

"You can say that." Bobbie wondered why it took so long to add a few more days. He really wasn't in the mood to chitchat. He had so many things to do before the night ended. He also thought he saw a car trailing him on his way to the hotel. He peered out of the glass door to look for the car but didn't see anyone. He returned to the desk. Antsy and tired, he really wanted to go to his room.

"Where are you from?"

"Texas. Is this going to be much longer? I have an early morning tomorrow."

"Not at all. As a matter of fact, you're all set."

"Thank you." He smiled.

Bobbie dashed out of the door toward his room and remembered he had forgotten his checkbook in the car. He turned around and headed back toward his rental Cadillac. Bobbie sifted through papers in the front seat, unaware that a stranger disguised in a ski mask lurked in the bushes nearby. Bobbie grabbed his checkbook and as he emerged from the car, the assailant rushed up behind him and poked a gun in his side.

"Don't move," the masked man whispered. Bobbie obeyed temporarily but, within a few seconds, he spun around and grabbed the man's wrist. The two men struggled with the gun. Bobbie had almost maneuvered the gun from him when the stranger kneed him in the groin.

When Bobbie bent over in pain, the attacker pistol-whipped him in the head. Bobbie fell to the ground, groaning while blood oozed off his forehead. The assailant stood over Bobbie and shot him twice in the stomach. His body jerked from the impact of the bullets, then lay as stiff as a board.

Looking around, the attacker patted Bobbie down and reached into his pockets. He removed his wallet without checking for money. As the attacker disappeared into the night, Bobbie lay in the hotel parking lot barely breathing, clinging to his life.

CHAPTER 25

Stephanie

Well after Stephanie had arrived home from the Thursday night get-together, she felt uneasy. Her heart was still heavy for Monica and what she was going through. Stephanie could not believe that Tony would jeopardize his family this way. He had so much to lose.

Lately it seemed like all of them were having problems with their men. Monica was dealing with Tony's baby drama. Dee didn't have full support from Dwayne. And, of course, Stephanie had to ward off detractors in her relationship with Levin. All of this drama was depressing. So much so Stephanie went looking through her cabinets and refrigerator for distractions. Comfort food distractions. Upon opening her freezer, she spotted a tube of Pillsbury Chocolate Chip Cookie dough. *That's what I need*, she thought. She reached for the cookie dough and set it on the counter. She went into her room and changed into a big, white T-shirt and a pair of gray sweatpants before putting the cookies in the oven.

The directions said to bake them from ten to fourteen minutes, but after twelve minutes, Stephanie decided they were done and pulled the golden brown cookies from the oven. She could barely wait until they cooled before biting into the melted chocolate morsels and warm, soft center. She closed her eyes as she savored the taste. For a minute Levin, Felicia and all of her other problems drifted away. She almost choked when the phone interrupted her solace.

Stephanie scrambled over to the phone to pick up. She then heard that all too familiar voice.

"Hey, baby. How's it goin'?" Levin asked, sounding as warm and loving as ever.

At first Stephanie's heart fluttered at the sound of Levin's voice. Her initial excitement was so strong, she placed her cookie back on the plate and prepped herself as if he were standing right in front of her. Then the memory of Levin's interview brought her back to reality. If she hadn't formed a plan for dealing with him she might have screamed and cried into the phone. Instead she remained calm, despite the fact he had made her look like a fool.

"Great. Considering," Stephanie said, rolling her eyes.

"Oh." Levin paused. "So, what 'cha been up to?"

Stephanie stared at the phone. *No he is not calling me trying to act like nothing happened*, she thought. "Oh, I don't know. Fielding questions about you and Felicia. What about you?" Stephanie asked.

Levin fell silent.

"Wow. You can't be quiet now. About a week ago you had so much to say," Stephanie said.

He sighed. "Listen. I know you must be upset about everything but I want you to know it wasn't my fault."

"Oh? So somebody else was up there speaking for you?" Stephanie asked.

"No. It was me but it wasn't my idea. My record label wanted me to say I was with Felicia for publicity," Levin explained. "We both have albums out. I'm almost double platinum. They wanted that extra push. You understand, right, baby?"

"I understand. You're trying to play me."

"No! The label is trying to play the media. I told you it's all a game. It's over now."

Stephanie restrained herself, but she really wanted to scream his head off. She still had a plan to implement and she needed to be calm when she tried to apply it. "What about all those pictures?" she said.

"Those were times we were instructed to pose together. Everything is not as it seems, Stephanie. I hope you trust me."

He must think I'm stupid, she thought. Stephanie trusted him all right. She trusted him to disappoint her and break her heart. She didn't care how much he sweet talked her. He would not make a fool out of her again.

"I don't like this, Levin."

"I know what's wrong. You're just tense because we haven't been able to spend much time together. Why don't you come to New York to see me? We can spend a few days here. Sightsee," Levin said.

"Aren't you afraid of blowing your cover?"

"No, Stephanie. I told you it's over now."

Stephanie pretended to hesitate but she'd already decided this was the perfect opportunity for her to start her plan to get back at Victor. She couldn't wait to teach them all a lesson. "Okay. I'll come."

"Great! I promise we'll have so much fun," Levin said.

Yeah, yeah, yeah, Stephanie thought. "Where are you right now?" Stephanie asked, ignoring his last statement.

"In my hotel room, trying to rest. I'm shooting my next video and auditioning for a movie role. The audition is for that role I told you about months ago. The project is now on schedule and it looks like I might get the part." Levin's voice rose with contagious enthusiasm. "It'll be another three weeks before I go home."

"In that case, I guess I'd better meet you in New York. I have some shopping to do anyway," Stephanie said.

"Cool. Go to the airport. I'll have a ticket waiting for you. I can't wait to see you," Levin said in a voice as smooth as butter.

"Me neither, Levin. Me neither."

After she hung up with him, Stephanie gave herself an imaginary pat on the back for her composure. His excuses were nonsense and she knew it. Nobody disrespects their girlfriend to the world. Not when they love them. Yet she was willing to maintain her composure for the chance to teach Victor and Levin a lesson. Happy with herself, Stephanie smiled and returned to her plate of cookies.

∞

When Stephanie arrived in New York, she went to the hotel to change and dump her belongings. While she was there, she searched through her luggage to find an outfit that would stop Levin in his tracks. Her choice was a short, black Versace dress with high heels. Once she was happy with her look, Stephanie went to Levin's video set on the pretense of congratulating him on his movie role and album success. She really wanted him to see how good she looked. She showed up in her "look at me, I'm hot" dress at the high-rise apartment building where they were shooting the video. When Levin saw her walk into the room, he lit up like a Christmas tree, breaking into the biggest smile. His smile almost melted Stephanie's heart and made her reconsider her devious plan, but the key word was *almost*.

"Hey, baby!" Levin stretched out his arms.

"Hey. How you been?" Stephanie said, falling into his body and pressing her chest forward.

"I'm good. You look great. When did you get in?" He gave her another big hug.

"About four hours ago. How's the shoot going?"

"It's more of the same. We're probably going to have another day and a half of this."

"You should be happy. Your album has sold almost two million units."

"Yeah. I'm happy about that. I don't care for the long,

drawn out process of making a video," Levin said. "But I'm glad to see you."

"Really?" Stephanie read his face.

"Yeah. I missed you these past couple of weeks. I hope we can work everything out," he said, looking deep into her eyes without blinking.

Levin always had a way of looking so sincere. His ability to emote on the spot made him a great performer, but it also made him difficult to read. Stephanie couldn't tell a lie from the truth when he talked to her. Either way, she still felt the need to wait for his defenses to come down before hitting him with her plan.

"I know we can," she said, looking as deeply into his eyes.

He then leaned over to whisper into her right ear, "Everybody's going to dinner tonight. You coming?"

"Sure. I'd love to."

"All right, Levin. You ready for the shot on the roof?" Victor shouted.

Levin turned to face Victor approaching them. The manager slowed his pace when he laid eyes on Stephanie. The look on his face said it all. He didn't want her there.

Well, well. If it isn't Dr. Evil, Stephanie thought. She refused to allow him to intimidate her into leaving. She had a right to be there. Her man was there and he wanted her there. She squinted at Victor as he approached. Levin seemed oblivious to the tension.

"Yeah, man. I'm ready," Levin said. "Victor, do you remember Stephanie?"

"Yes, I do," Victor said. "Hello, Stephanie. It's good to see you again."

"Same here," Stephanie said.

"If I had thought about it, I would've suggested Stephanie for this video," Victor said, slapping his forehead.

"Yeah, man. That would've been a great idea," Levin said, smiling.

"It would've been good practice for your, um, budding acting career," Victor said. He smiled at Stephanie, but it looked more like a sarcastic smirk than an authentic gesture of kindness. It sickened Stephanie to her stomach. Levin, however, smiled and agreed.

"Yeah, that's true," Levin said.

"Anyway, the director is waiting, Lev," Victor said.

As Victor walked away, Levin leaned back over and whispered in Stephanie's ear, "I love you."

"I love you, too."

"Come on up and watch," Levin said. Stephanie followed behind him and the crew to the rooftop. She stood to the side as they set up the scene. While Levin and the crew worked, a photographer shot pictures of them. When Levin broke from shooting to talk to Stephanie, the photographer took pictures of them together. Displeased, Victor placed his big hand on the photographer's camera from behind and firmly led him back to the main area of the set.

After the shoot wrapped, the whole crew headed to a Chinese restaurant for dinner. The friendly bunch joked and laughed. Even though Stephanie enjoyed their company, she could feel Victor sitting to the side of the long table, watching her every move. She'd sometimes place her hand over Levin's hand or nuzzle against his neck to see Victor squirm. In response, he'd shoot her a dirty look. When Levin leaned over to whisper something in her ear, Victor appeared to lean in to hear the conversation. It really irritated her.

"So, Stephanie? Where are you from?" Helena, one of the video dancers, asked.

"I'm from California but I've lived all over," Stephanie said.

"Really? Why?" Helena asked.

"I was an army brat," Stephanie said.

"Oh. How did you end up in this industry?" Helena asked.

"A friend put me on," Stephanie said.

"I'll bet," Victor muttered before taking a sip of his Heineken.

Stephanie shot daggers at Victor. *How dare he try to clown me around everybody*, she thought. The rest of the crew looked at each other. Some of them frowned; others stared straight at the table as if they were afraid to question Victor's comment. Levin frowned and looked back and forth between Stephanie and Victor.

"What do you mean by that, man?" Levin asked.

Victor shrugged and sipped his Heineken.

"What *I* meant was that one of my high school female friends got in and told me about auditions for a video shoot. I auditioned. They chose me and the rest is history,"

Stephanie said, staring at Victor the whole time. While the rest of the table nodded, Victor rolled his eyes at her explanation.

Levin seemed to sense the tension and responded right away. "You ready to go?" Levin asked Stephanie.

"Um-hmm," Stephanie said. Levin stood up and pulled Stephanie's chair out for her.

"It was fun, ya'll, but we're out," Levin said to the table.

"Hey, don't you have another phone interview in the morning?" Victor said.

"What interview?" Levin asked, puzzled.

"The one with *Urban Magazine*," Victor said.

"Oh, that was canceled."

"Umm. I'm not sure. I'll have to call you about it."

Levin sighed and shook his head. Although he claimed the games were over, it looked to Stephanie like they had just begun. This time she was more prepared. Her eyes were wide open and she could see Victor's desperate attempts to keep her and Levin apart. She couldn't wait to see his face once her plans were underway. He had no idea what she was about to spring on them, and Stephanie had every intention of winning this battle and the war.

"Well, I'll tell you what. I'll make sure he wakes up nice and early tomorrow morning," Stephanie said, leaning over and wrapping her arms around Levin's waist.

Victor frowned and turned to Levin. "I'll call you tomorrow."

"That's cool, man," Levin said, as the two shook hands.

The next morning the drama from the previous night had faded into the background. Stephanie woke up to Levin's handsome face and soft embrace. She opened her eyes to see Levin had already awakened. The timing was perfect. She saw a chance to take her plan into over-drive.

"How long have you been awake?" she asked him.

"For a little minute."

"What are you thinking about?" Stephanie's mind raced with questions.

"Us."

"What about us?" Stephanie stared into his face.

"I was thinking about where we're going to go from here."

"What do you mean?" Stephanie asked.

"I heard you over the phone and I know the Huey interview was hurtful. I'm sorry for that. I want to make sure no matter what else happens from here, you can tough it out with me," he said, his voice soft-spoken and introspective.

"What do you mean? You said the games were over, right?" Stephanie asked.

"Yes, but there's more at stake than that."

"Like what?" Stephanie sat up in bed.

"Like my tour. My movie..." Levin trailed off.

"But what does that have to do with us?"

"Nothing. I want to make sure we understand this is separate from that," Levin said, pointing to the two of them, "Like whatever happens in that part of my life has nothing to do with us."

Stephanie didn't like the way this conversation was going. "Levin, are you trying to tell me something? What's going on?"

He sighed. "My album is really heating up. I'm scheduling dates for my tour and the movie producers are really interested in casting me for this role. Things are going good and they've gotten better since…" Levin trailed off again.

"Since what?" Stephanie probed.

"Since the Huey interview. I mean, I've moved over three hundred-thousand units since then alone."

Stephanie's mouth dropped open and she stared at the open space in front of her. Levin turned to her and placed his hand over hers.

"Baby, my label and Victor think I should keep the public thinking Felicia and I are a couple. Only for a little while. You know, until the tour is over and I've signed on with the movie. Again, that doesn't change us. We'll be the same. I need you to, you know, play along."

Is he kidding? Stephanie thought. Was he really asking her permission to date another woman out in the open? Heat rushed to her neck and face, turning them both red. This was embarrassing on several levels. She came all this way to swindle him and he beat her to the punch. She had to react quickly or this ship would sink faster than the Titanic. Stephanie took a deep breath and released it before making tears fall down her face. "I don't think I'll be able to do that," she said between sobs.

"Aww. Baby, I promise it won't be like this for long."

"No. You're asking me to hide our relationship and I'm not gonna be able to do that. People are gonna know."

"Well, yeah. Our friends will know, but if anyone else asks tell 'em it's none of their business," Levin suggested.

Stephanie shook her head. "They're gonna know. They'll see it because I'm pregnant."

Levin jerked his back like Stephanie had delivered him a blow to the head. She watched all the color drain from Levin's face, as he dropped his head in his hands. "Oh my gosh. Oh my gosh. Are you sure?"

"Yes," she said, watching him closely. She couldn't tell whether he was angry or simply surprised. "Levin, what are you thinking?"

He shook his head, refusing to say a word. She was afraid he would stay that way until the phone rang. As if in a trance, Levin snapped out of it and picked up the phone. He frowned when he heard the voice on the other end.

"Hey, Victor. What's going on?"

Stephanie rolled her eyes.

"I'm all right, cool. I just got some news. That's all," Levin said, glancing over at Stephanie.

She leaned toward him and listened in.

"Yeah, umm, Stephanie's pregnant," Levin said.

Levin pulled the phone away from his ear as Victor began to yell on the phone.

"Wait a minute, Victor. Calm down," Levin said. "Victor, what do you mean it's not mine?"

On that note, Stephanie snatched the phone out of Levin's hand to confront Victor.

"Hello?" Stephanie said.

"Who is this? Is this Stephanie?" Victor yelled.

"Yes."

"Put Levin back on the damn phone."

"No, he's heard enough of you. Who the hell do you think you are?"

"The last time I checked I was Levin's manager. And it's my job to protect him from sharks and skanks like you," Victor said.

"I got your skank. You must be confusing me with Felicia or maybe your wife. Oh, I'm sorry. Nobody would ever put up with your ass. That's the problem. You're jealous because Levin has somebody who loves him and the only thing you have is that jacked-up ponytail of yours."

Levin reached for the phone but Stephanie kept maneuvering it away from him.

"You know what? You are crazy if you think you're the only one. Before long, he'll be on to the next one. And all your little games will mean nothing. By next year, I guarantee you I'll still be his manager and he will barely remember you."

Before Stephanie could respond, Levin finally grabbed the phone from her.

"Victor? Victor?" Levin said. "He hung up."

Stephanie sat there in silence. Victor's last words echoed through her mind. So far, she'd barely managed to stay in this sick game of theirs, but she had to stay on top of the situation. Whatever needed to be done, she'd do it. She had to prove Victor wrong. She had to keep Levin. No matter what. Hopefully, this fake pregnancy would help her to do that.

CHAPTER 26

Monica

Monica stepped out of the bathroom, draped in a towel. She reached for her clothes, but stopped short when she noticed a black box on the bed. She sat down next to it and opened it to find a diamond-encrusted necklace. At first, she smiled at the brilliant piece of jewelry. Then, just as quickly, her smile faded. Monica remembered she still had personal issues to resolve and one of them was eating cereal downstairs while waiting for football practice.

It didn't matter how many pieces of jewelry Tony bought her. Monica still grappled with the surprise letter from Jessica. She wore a confident mask for everyone— their friends, their neighbors, and the public in general, but inside her insecurities dominated her thoughts. A big part of her didn't believe for a second Tony would ever leave her for Jessica or any other woman for that matter. Yet the knowledge Tony fooled around and may have an outside child caused her great distraction. She decided to confront Tony with a solution.

Monica finished dressing, pushed her shoulders back and headed downstairs into the kitchen. She picked up a cereal bar and sat across from Tony at their kitchen table. He glanced at her, and then returned to the sports section of his newspaper. She took his behavior as confirmation that progress on their marital woes depended on her.

"I think we should go to counseling," she blurted out. Tony looked up from his cereal.

"Why?"

"You know why."

He sighed and shook his head as if to shake the idea off. "I think we're handling everything well."

"How are we handling it, Tony? You think because you're buying me a new piece of jewelry every other day that we're doing good? This is really serious. Some people divorce because of this, and you act like everything is A-okay."

Tony's eyes shot up when she mentioned the "D" word.

"Do you want a divorce? Do you want to find somebody else?"

Divorce was such a sobering word. She tried thinking about her life without Tony. The truth was she couldn't imagine it, but Monica sought to keep the conversation focused, especially since she hadn't told Tony about her phone calls and lunches with Robert. To avoid his jealous streak, she contemplated her next words.

"No. No, I don't, but I also don't want us to pretend nothing ever happened. I'm not one of those NFL wives that can look the other way. We have to deal with it."

He sighed. "I don't wanna go to some stranger and give up the personal details of our marriage." Tony squirmed in his chair. "I told you I was sorry. I'm doing everything I can to make things better, but I don't know what else you want me to do. I would much rather you tell me what you want than have us pay two hundred dollars an hour for some quack to tell you to tell me what you want."

"Oh, now you're money-conscious."

Monica didn't understand him. His sense of logic appeared when it suited him, but never when it suited them both. As usual, he didn't like the money crack and she saw his anger rising. He stood up from his chair.

"Okay. So what is this about? Is it about the affair, the child or the money?" he asked, irritated.

"All of it is an issue. But we can start with the affair."

"Okay." Tony leaned against the kitchen sink. "What?"

"Why did you have an affair?"

"I don't know."

"See? That's not good enough. This is why we need counseling," Monica said.

Tony walked back to the table to grab his bowl and poured the contents down the sink. He turned toward the kitchen doorway. "I have to get ready for practice. Are you coming to watch?" Tony asked.

"No, I have some errands to run. Oh, and Tony?" He turned around right before he exited the kitchen. "I will be scheduling an appointment with a marriage counselor," she said.

He remained silent as he turned back around to leave

the kitchen. Monica could see he didn't understand the importance of keeping the marriage strong. He thought everything was fine, which confused and angered her. She didn't want a divorce, but she couldn't deny they had reached a crossroad. Whether Tony realized it or not, they couldn't continue the way they were going. She needed to change and so did he.

Working with Janet and The Hatcher Foundation showed Monica she had a lot to offer the world. When she didn't make use of her talents, she was cheating herself and everyone else. Well, she wasn't willing to cheat anymore. She had to step out from Tony's shadow and live her own life. Sure, it would be an adjustment but she was ready for it. The question was, did Tony feel like he was ready for it?

Monica wanted to believe he was ready, but behavior like she'd witnessed that morning gave her doubts. Even in the midst of their marital crisis, his concern for his own comfort superseded everything else. She was tired of taking a backseat to his ego. He needed to change his focus or they were going to develop more problems.

Monica picked up her cell phone and called their pastor, Dr. Ian Smith. When the receptionist answered, she asked to be transferred to his desk. While she waited, Monica thought about Dr. Smith's busy schedule and began preparing a message for his voicemail. He surprised her when he picked up and interrupted her thoughts.

"Hello, Pastor Smith. This is Monica Hatcher."

"Hello, Sister Monica. I was talking about you the other day. My wife still compliments that lovely dinner you put on a few months ago," he said.

"Oh. Thank you. I enjoyed putting it together for everyone. It was a lot of hard work but it was so worth it."

"Yes, yes. Anything to help the children succeed," the pastor said. "Well, what can I help you with?"

Monica sighed. "Pastor, I have a favor to ask. My husband, Tony, and I have run into some issues, and we could use your guidance."

"Okay. What kind of issues?"

She paused and took a deep breath. This would make the first time, outside of talking to her friends, that Monica admitted to someone Tony had cheated. Her mouth felt dry as she struggled to get the words out. "Marital issues. I would really like to schedule a time for us to come in and talk with you…"

Even as the words tumbled out, Monica still had trouble with them.

"Oh. Say no more, honey. Let me know when y'all can come in, and I'd be more than happy to help you in any way I can."

"How is Wednesday afternoon?"

"That's perfect."

"Thanks, Pastor."

When she was transferred to his receptionist, she scheduled the appointment. Monica ended the call feeling a little more hopeful about her situation. But before she had the chance to think any further about it, the house phone rang. She got up from the table and grabbed the cordless off of the wall.

"Hello?" she asked. No answer. The person hung up. She looked at the phone and placed it back on its receiver. She walked back toward the table. The phone rang again. Since she wasn't far from it, she turned around to pick it back up.

"Hello?" Same thing. The person remained silent and hung the phone up. Monica's concern increased. *This hasn't happened before. Something is very wrong*, Monica thought. She looked on the caller ID. The number was restricted. Monica considered her friends' warnings about Jessica. She hoped this woman wasn't playing games. If she was, she didn't know who she was messing with.

∞

Despite Monica's demanding hidden schedule, on Wednesday afternoon she managed to show up on time for the appointment with her pastor, Dr. Ian Smith. Unfortunately, the same wasn't true for Tony. Since he'd made such a big stink about talking to a complete stranger, she figured talking to their pastor would be much more comfortable for him. Maybe he wouldn't feel afraid of judgment. She told him that morning he could do whatever he wanted before the appointment, but he'd better find a way to show up that afternoon.

She even recommended he skip practice. To her, their marriage was that important. He scowled, huffed and puffed, but she insisted.

Monica waited for Tony in her pastor's office. In fairness, she didn't want to discuss their issues with Pastor Smith until Tony arrived, but after twenty-five minutes had passed, it became harder to avoid answering the pastor's questions.

"Do you want some water?" Pastor Smith asked.

"No, Pastor, I'm fine. Tony should be here any minute." About fifteen more minutes passed. Still no Tony. Monica shook her head.

"I'm so sorry. I don't know what happened," she said.

"It's okay. If you need to reschedule, we can do that for you," the pastor said. "But while you're here, do you want to start to tell me what's going on with you two?"

Despite Monica's attempts at fairness, she figured she might as well tell him the truth. She felt bad that he'd wasted his time. She thought she'd make some use of the appointment to keep it from being a total loss. Maybe he had some suggestions for getting Tony to come to the counseling sessions. "Tony had an affair," she said.

The pastor raised his eyebrows. "I'm sorry to hear that."

"Not nearly as sorry as I am because that's not the worst part: The woman he cheated with sent me a letter saying her five-year-old belongs to Tony."

The pastor shook his head.

"I'm kinda at my wits' end here. I don't know what to

do about this but, at the same time, I know something must be done," Monica said.

"My heart and my prayers go out to you. What did Brother Tony say about the child in question?"

"He says he doesn't believe it's his."

"Has anyone considered a paternity test?" the pastor asked.

"No, but that was going to be my next recommendation once he and I can talk about this like civilized adults," Monica said.

"Well, hold off on asking for that right now. See if you can get him to commit to coming in here to see me. This is a complicated situation you all are in, and you need to seek proper counseling so things don't get any farther off track than they are."

"That's exactly what I'm telling him, Pastor. He's not listening," Monica said. "I'm gonna step outside for a minute. I wanna try to reach him again."

"Sure. Go right ahead."

Monica stepped out of the pastor's office to call Tony on her cell phone. Actually she stepped out of the church because she didn't want to say something awful in a holy place. Monica called him six times but he didn't answer his phone. *He's gonna get it when I get home*, she thought. The last time his voicemail came on she left a scathing message.

"Well, Mr. Hatcher. Since you saw fit to have me looking crazy in front of our pastor today, let's see how you feel about sleeping outside of our house tonight. You better be glad I'm standing outside of a church. Or I would call you names that would make Satan blush. Wait 'til I get home, mutha…"

"Monica, is everything all right?" She turned around to see her pastor standing behind her.

"Everything's fine, Pastor Smith. Something came up and Tony won't be able to make it. We'll reschedule for another time, possibly next week."

"Sure thing, honey. Call me when you guys need me." He hugged her and departed.

"Thanks. Take care." She ended her call and headed toward her car, determined to really lay into Tony when she got home.

To her dismay, she ended up waiting for several hours. Tony didn't get home until 11:30 that night. As she sat on her bed lying against the headboard, she began to simmer down. She still planned to let him have it, but for the moment, she'd stopped seeing red. However, her determination to tell him off increased when he walked into their bedroom. He smelled like liquor and cheap perfume.

After she saw he wasn't going to say anything, she started in on him. "Did you have fun tonight?" Monica asked. Tony stopped walking and looked at her.

"I don't know what you're talking about."

"Of course you do. You don't smell the way you do right now unless you had a ball."

"Listen. I don't feel like arguing with you, okay?"

Monica leaned forward. "You know what? It's funny 'cuz I don't really care what you feel like. Just like you didn't care about letting me sit there in front of our pastor looking like a fool today. You didn't even have the decency to answer your phone when I called you several times. What was that about?"

"Monica, you know what that was about. I heard your crazy messages. I don't deserve all that. You didn't ask me to go to the counseling. You demanded I go. That's an insult."

"Would you be insulted if I left?"

"Is that a threat?" Tony asked.

"Maybe."

He shook his head. "You know what? I don't even feel supported in this marriage anymore."

Monica stood up. "Supported? I've always supported everything you've done! Don't try to blame everything that's going on right now on me!"

"So it's all my fault?" Tony asked.

"Yes! You're the one who has a child outside this house. And I'm the one who scheduled a counseling appointment you didn't even make!"

"Yeah? Well, what about all this sneaking around you've been doing lately? I know you, Monica. You're up to something. Every time I call you, you're too busy. Every time I ask you to do something with me, you're too busy. It's like you got a job or something." Monica gasped. In the midst of all their fighting, she still hadn't told him about her client. She was hoping she could wait to tell him at the counseling session with Pastor Smith, but since that wasn't happening the way she'd like, she wondered if she needed to tell him already. Because he was so against her working, she'd never feel good about telling him anyway. So, she blurted it out.

"That's because I do."

"What?" Tony asked.

"I do have a job. I have a client and I'm helping her open her restaurant," Monica said.

"Why are you just now telling me this?" Tony asked.

"Because you're not exactly supportive of me," Monica said, crossing her arms.

"I never meant to be unsupportive of you. I only wanted to keep our family together." Tony sighed. "If it's something you really want to do, I don't see a problem with you having one client." Tony rolled his eyes as if it pained him to say it.

Monica grimaced at his contrived show of support. "Gee, thanks, Tony," Monica said with obvious sarcasm.

Tony sat down on the bed. "No. Really. I think it's good. How did you get the client?"

"She attended the scholarship dinner. She liked what I did and asked me to help her with the restaurant." Monica conveniently left out the part about Robert introducing them at the spa. It would have only given Tony ammunition for another argument.

He nodded. "That's good. When does the restaurant open?" Tony asked.

"October eighth," Monica said.

"Oh." He dismissed the date but after he thought about it, his eyes widened. "Oooooh. I see now. That's why you don't want to go to Indianapolis with me. You wanna do your little PR thing, right?" Tony laughed.

"No. No."

"This Jessica thing gave you an excuse to leave me behind and do what you wanted to do. See, I knew it. I knew it, Monica!" Tony shouted.

"You know what, Tony? You think whatever you wanna think. But let me tell you something, buster. You can't do me dirty and have your way, too. I spent eight years putting my dreams on hold to support you, and now I've started to move in the direction I want, it's a major problem. I think you need to get over it," Monica said.

"And I think you need to come to Indianapolis!" Tony pushed his fist in the air.

"I'm NOT going!" Monica shouted. "And that's that."

Tony stormed out of the bedroom door. Monica let him go but she wasn't through with him. This situation was getting worse and worse by the minute. Between the silent calls and his perfume- stained shirts, Monica now knew she needed to investigate.

CHAPTER 27

Stephanie

The fake "pregnancy" stunned Levin, just as Stephanie thought it would. Once he accepted the news, he hugged her, stroked her hand and told her he loved her. He swore he would be there for her no matter what happened, and he would take care of her and the baby. Those were the exact words she wanted to hear. Who cares if it was based on a lie? The important thing was he said it, and Stephanie knew deep down, he meant it.

She could tell Levin was scared to pieces underneath his caring façade, but it didn't matter. Stephanie knew he would come around. By the time she finished her plan, he'd know they belonged together. He might even want to start a family, for real. It was a shame she had to tell such a big lie to get their relationship back on track, but Victor left her no other choice. If he'd left them alone, she and Levin would have probably already been engaged. Since Victor wanted to play games, she would show him how to play her game.

Now that she'd implemented the first step of her plan, it was time for the second step: promotion. It wasn't enough to tell Levin about her "pregnancy"; she needed to promote it to the world because frankly, she needed the world's help in reinforcing her message to Levin and Victor. The message was she and Levin were a committed couple and planned to stay that way. At this stage, all she had to do was tell everybody and get them on her side.

The mission sounded simple, but it was quite delicate. She had to be very careful in how she "told" people about the new "baby." She couldn't come right out and say, "Hey, I'm having Levin's baby." Besides, the venom she'd encounter from his female fans, Levin wouldn't appreciate it. She had to be more circumspect. People had to find out in a roundabout way and she knew who to go to for that.

Putting on a big smile, Stephanie strutted into Henrietta's Bistro. She saw Dee and Monica telling the waiter they weren't ready to order yet. She walked up to the table and flopped down.

"Hello, ladies," Stephanie sang, sitting across from her friends.

"There you are. I was about to call you and find out where you were," Monica said.

"Yeah, I'm hungry. Monica could do it but I couldn't wait on you. I had to order my food," Dee said.

"That's okay." Stephanie laughed. "I'll have a Sprite. Thanks," Stephanie said to the waiter.

"So what's the good news?" Monica asked Stephanie.

"What?" Stephanie asked.

"You came in here looking like you won the lottery. I wanted to know what's good," Monica asked.

Stephanie took a deep breath. "I'm pregnant."

Dee was sipping on her tea and almost choked on the news. "You're what?"

"I'm pregnant," Stephanie repeated with the same smile on her face.

"Since when?" Dee cleared her throat.

"What?" Stephanie asked.

"Since when are you pregnant?" Dee asked.

"I'm about a month and a half along," Stephanie said.

"Are you sure this isn't a false alarm?" Monica asked.

"Yes. Levin and I are going to have a baby," she said. "Isn't it great?"

Monica and Dee exchanged glances. Stephanie looked at them with an expectant expression on her face.

"Well?" she asked Monica.

"Yes, it is. Congratulations," Monica finally said.

Stephanie frowned. *This is ridiculous*, she thought. They should have been giggling and hugging her. She huffed out of frustration.

"Aren't you guys happy for me?" Stephanie asked.

"Yes. Very happy, aren't we, Dee?"

"Absolutely. You're about to get stretched out of place for nine months, puked on daily, and you don't even have a wedding ring yet. I'm ecstatic for you," Dee said.

Stephanie squinted at Dee.

"Come on now. There's no need to be negative. We're happy for you, Stephanie. Really," Monica said.

"Thank you. Oh. I wanted to ask you something. Do you have the media list you're working with for Janet's opening?" Stephanie asked Monica.

"Yeah. On my email. Why?" Monica asked.

"Is it possible for you to give me a copy of that list?"

"I guess. Why do you need it?" Monica asked, turning the corner of her mouth up.

"Oh, Natalie's working on a project and I promised her I would try to get her some media contacts," Stephanie lied.

"But I thought she worked in production. Why would she need media contacts?" Monica asked.

"The guy paying for the project is really cheap. He doesn't want to spend the money on promotion and publicity, even though Natalie told him it was important," Stephanie said.

"Sounds like a loser to me," Dee said.

Stephanie shrugged. "She doesn't want to see it fail so she's trying to save money and do as much as she can."

"Well, sure. I can email it to you now," Monica pulled out her BlackBerry and accessed her email.

"While you're at it, you can send it to me, too," Dee said.

"Now why do you need it?" Monica asked Dee.

"You know I'm doing big things now. I need to have people on hand to share the information about my magazine," Dee said. "I'm gonna need publicity." Dee batted her fake eyelashes.

"You better stop that before you start a windstorm," Monica said.

Dee sucked her teeth. "Hater."

∞

Stephanie turned the doorknob to her condo and fell in the door. She leaned against the back of the door, breathing a sigh of relief that Monica didn't press her harder about the media list. She'd had a hard enough time coming up with a believable lie about Natalie. She hated lying to Monica, but knew she would never support her plan.

Stephanie sat down at her dining room table and pulled out her laptop. She searched the day's blogs and messages on the message boards. The latest entries still linked Levin with Felicia. Only a couple acknowledged Stephanie's presence. She furrowed her eyebrows in frustration. She had to do something about this.

Stephanie clicked over to her mailbox and opened her email from Monica. She looked through the list. Many of them were reporters, editors and photographers. Stephanie wanted to find someone that handled entertainment news and gossip. Right before she was about to click away from the list, she found Pamela Waters' number. Pamela was the most sought-after gossip columnist in the Southeast region. She seemed to always know what was going on, and if she didn't, her insights into what might be happening were bankable.

Suddenly, Stephanie began shaking. This was the moment she was waiting for. She knew this woman could help push her plans into overdrive, but she was nervous. She had her story together, but what if Pamela saw straight through her? What if she figured out who Stephanie was and put her on blast? Stephanie would die from embarrassment. On the other hand, she had to do this. Her plan depended on it. She was only a phone call away from the whole world knowing the truth...Levin was in love with her.

Stephanie closed her eyes and took a deep breath. She then opened her eyes and reached for her cell phone to call the entertainment columnist. In the middle of the second ring, Pamela answered the phone. Stephanie opened her mouth to talk but closed it. Her mind went blank. She hadn't expected Pamela to answer the phone so quickly. Stephanie scrambled to pull herself together.

"Hello, Ms. Waters?" Stephanie asked, stuttering.

"Yes?" Pamela asked, sounding rushed and annoyed.

"My name is Susan Perry. I'm an entertainment publicist. I'm calling because I wanted to tell you about one of my clients. She's an up-and-coming actress. She's been photographed everywhere," Stephanie started.

"So?" Pamela barked.

"Well, I thought you should know about her." Stephanie

frowned at Pamela's rudeness. She'd always heard the columnist spoke quick and to the point. She often rubbed people the wrong way. Yet, the industry relied on her to break the gossip.

"What's her name?"

"Stephanie Robinson," Stephanie said.

"Never heard of her. What's so great about her?" Pamela said.

Pamela's words stung Stephanie's fragile ego, like a bee. She looked down at her computer where the pictures of Levin and Felicia stared back at her. She instantly felt tears welling in her eyes. She needed Pamela to hear her. She had to work past her fear. She and Levin's future depended on it.

She lifted her head and continued. "She's an entertainer and all, but you might be more interested in whose baby she's having."

"Who?" Pamela's tone changed.

"Levin, the R&B singer. Yeah, he and Stephanie have been together for months now."

In that moment, all of the columnist's indifference disappeared. "What happened to Felicia?" she asked.

"Well, I hear she and Levin were more of a fling. Nothing serious came of it. I believe you guys already have photos of Stephanie." She smiled on her end of the phone.

"I hadn't noticed any pictures concerning Levin and another woman." Pamela raised her voice to speak over the noise. Stephanie could hear the columnist rummaging through her desk trying to find the photo.

"Oh. Well, it's a good thing I called you then. I can email you a photo right now." Stephanie smiled, smug. She emailed Pamela a jpeg of herself with Levin at the MTV Awards a few months ago.

"Okay. I see it," Pamela exclaimed, after opening her email. The columnist's excitement burst through the phone wires.

"So, when will you be running the story?" Stephanie said.

"Tomorrow."

"Okay. I'll let you know about any new developments. Is this the best number to reach you?" Stephanie asked.

"Most of the time, but let me give you my cell phone number." Pamela rattled off her cell number, and Stephanie wrote it down in her planner.

"Got it. I'll keep you posted," Stephanie said. Stephanie squealed and jumped up and down around her dining room after the two hung up. She couldn't believe how well that had gone. She had one of the most powerful gossip columnists' cell phone numbers. This would open so many doors for her. She finished her happy dance and picked up her phone to program Pamela's numbers into it. Once that was secured, she went back to one of her favorite message boards. Instead of logging on as herself, she registered as a new user with a different user name. She chose "321Loxy" as her new name. She logged onto the site and started a new thread titled: "Levin having baby." In the subject section, the message read:

Reports claim hot R&B singer Levin is dating his label mate Felicia. However, I know for a fact that's not true. You see, I know the real woman he's seeing and she is almost two months' pregnant. They've been seeing each other for almost a year and they are in love. As a matter of fact, they went to the MTV Awards together. The picture is below.

I know a lot of you believe he's with Felicia but that's what the media wants you to believe. He's with someone else.

Stephanie hit the POST button and moved on to the next board. She posted a similar neat little story about her and Levin using other varying names. After she finished posting on four message boards, she sat back in her chair, satisfied with her work. So far she'd told friends, a gossip columnist and key message boards. *Now I need to find a real blabbermouth to spread the word*, Stephanie thought.

Before she could fully finish that thought, her phone rang. It was Natalie. *Just in time*, Stephanie thought. She answered the phone.

"Hey, girl. What's up?" Stephanie said.

"Chile, the usual. These shows running me raggedy. What's up with you?" Natalie asked.

"I just came back from New York with Levin," Stephanie said.

"Really? So you guys are working everything out?"

"Yeah, you know we will." Stephanie giggled.

"That's good. I'm trying to tell people he and Felicia ain't all that but you know how people like to talk," Natalie said.

"Well, soon people will have something else to talk about,' Stephanie said.

"What?"

"I'm pregnant," Stephanie said.

"Oh my gosh! You're lying," Natalie shouted.

Of course, I am, Stephanie thought. "No, I'm afraid not."

"When did you find out?"

"A couple of days before I went to New York."

"Did you tell Levin while you were in New York?" Natalie asked.

"Yes, I did. And he was ecstatic. Now Victor? Not so much."

"Oooh. You told Victor? I'll bet he was pissed."

"Yep, he was pissed but you know what? I don't care. Levin is my man. We are happy together, and now we're going to be a happy family." Stephanie smiled.

"I can't wait to tell people you two are going to have a baby. Wait a minute. Is it okay to tell?" Natalie asked.

"I guess so. Levin told Victor," Stephanie said.

Stephanie had to still herself from laughing. It was funny Natalie asked her if she could talk about the "baby" news. Everyone knew this girl couldn't hold water in a pot, let alone keep a secret, but that's exactly what Stephanie was counting on. It was time everyone knew Levin was coming off the market and she knew Natalie was the right person to spread the word.

CHAPTER 28

Dee

A t 6:45 in the evening, Dee set four bags of Chinese takeout on her kitchen counter. She really wanted to visit a restaurant to eat, but Dwayne had said he preferred to come over to her house. She didn't understand why. It's not like she was going to cook. So she still ordered out. Looking down at the bags, Dee felt like she'd done her part with transporting the food to the kitchen and that was all the work she planned to do. He would have to get his own food and put it on a plate. She wasn't a chef or a waitress.

Dee was certain he knew that about her after almost a year of dating, but maybe he didn't. They hadn't talked about the direction of their relationship. As a result, Dee wasn't sure what he knew about her. There were still many things she didn't know about him. She thought back to the day that she, Dwayne and Monica had had lunch after church. Monica asked all those questions about their plans for the relationship. She was sad to say they hadn't talked much about the relationship since that day. Dee accepted some of the blame for that; she'd primarily been consumed with finding an investor. Now that she'd found one, she was starting to pay more attention to their relationship. To her, it was like a car sitting on the side of the road; it had stalled and no one had come along to jumpstart it. She decided she would make tonight the night they talked about where their relationship was going.

Dwayne said he would be at her house no later than 7:30, but when that time came, he wasn't there. *I'm not waiting for him*, Dee thought. She opened the first bag and removed one of the boxes. She reached into her cabinet and pulled out a plate. Before she could reach for silverware, her doorbell rang. When she opened the door, Dwayne fell in with immediate apologies.

"Hey. I'm sorry I'm late, Dee. Something came up," he said, sounding out of breath. As Dwayne hunched forward to take his jacket off, Dee noticed the perspiration gathering along his hairline.

"The food's already here. Is everything okay?" Dee asked, raising one eyebrow.

"Yeah, it's fine. I need to use your bathroom for a minute." Dwayne scurried into her bathroom. Dee glanced around the corner. Dwayne always stayed calm. She wondered what made him so flustered.

When Dwayne stepped out of the bathroom a few minutes later, he had returned to his usual calm self. His shoulders were back. His breathing was relaxed and he smiled confidently.

"Is there a masseuse in there or something?" Dee asked.

Dwayne laughed. "No. I rushed so hard to get over

here because I know how you are that I ran out of breath, but I'm cool now." He smiled again.

Dee didn't quite believe him, but the rumbling in her stomach made her change her mind about inquiring more about it. "Whateva," she said.

They finally sat down to eat. Besides the low noise from the TV, they remained pretty silent. Dee thought about how to inject her "where is this relationship going" questions. Once she figured it out, she directed her attention to Dwayne.

"What are you thinking about?" Dee asked.

Dwayne looked up from his plate at her. "Nothing much." He diverted his eyes back to his plate.

Dee squinted at him. "You know, I was thinking about that day we went to church with Monica. Remember?"

"Yeah. I remember. That was a nice day. I wouldn't mind visiting her church again."

"Really? I thought about our lunch after the service when Monica was asking different questions about us."

"Um-hmm," Dwayne nodded.

"Where do you think our relationship is going?" Dee asked.

Dwayne almost choked on his vegetable fried rice. He coughed profusely, attempting to clear his throat. Dee stood up and walked over to his side of the table and patted him on the back hard.

"Do you need some water?" she asked.

He continued to cough and shook his head.

She nodded and walked back over to her seat. Dee gave him a minute to finish clearing his throat before she started talking again.

"Are you okay?" she asked.

"Yeah. Something went down the wrong pipe. That's all," he said.

Dee sighed. "Look. I'm not saying you need to propose marriage to me or anything crazy like that. I only want to know if I'm someone you take seriously. It's hard to tell. I don't know a whole lot about you."

"Well, what do you feel like you don't know?" he asked.

"I don't know anything about your past. You haven't introduced me to any of your friends. You know all my friends," Dee said.

"That's because I don't have close friends. I moved here from Texas. Remember? Any close friend I had would have been there."

"Was Bobbie a close friend?"

Dwayne took in a chest full of air and closed his eyes briefly. "No." He then stared down at his plate and pushed some of his food around.

"See what I mean?" Dee asked.

"Dee, I'm not trying to be difficult or shut you out, but there are things from my past I would rather put behind me and move on," he said. "And if you're wondering about our future together, I think we definitely have one."

Dee sat up straight. That was the first time she'd ever heard Dwayne say anything about their future. For a moment, his words flattered her. She was happy to be with a man that had a plan and saw her in it. However, the fact that there was so much he felt unwilling to tell her kept her from getting too happy. She needed to know more about the man in her life.

"Don't worry about it. As we go along we'll learn more about each other. But for now, I think we're on a good track. As a matter of fact, I had a little surprise for you tonight," Dwayne said.

"What?" Dee asked.

"I have a feeling I've found a couple of people to invest in your magazine," he said.

Oh, that's great. After all the trouble I went through, doing business with someone he doesn't trust and hiding it, now he finds an investor, Dee thought, before responding.

"Really? Who?" Dee asked.

"The CEO of a non-profit organization and a tele-marketing tycoon. I've opened the lines of communication. Now we can start explaining to them what you bring to the table," Dwayne said.

"Cool." Dee nodded. She initially thought that she was going to get really tired of pretending she still needed his help, but since Dee had started plowing through the money Bobbie had given her, she figured the more money, the merrier. She could always use more money.

"Can you get me a business plan by the end of the week?" Dwayne asked, taking a bite out of his eggroll.

"I can give it to you tonight," Dee said.

"All right. Great! We're in business." Dwayne smiled. He stopped chewing and placed his hand over Dee's hand.

"I'm glad I'm able to get you what you want. I think we got it this time," Dwayne said.

Dee smiled but she found it hard to maintain that warm and fuzzy feeling inside. She needed to see the investor with her own eyes. Dwayne had been working on this for about nine months. She had a hard time believing Dwayne was doing all he could to find her an investor. Furthermore, Dwayne continued to hide his past from her. She decided to give him one more chance to come clean about his past.

"Great. So, Dwayne? Have you talked to your brother lately?" Dee asked, pouring sauce on her Egg Foo Yung.

"About a month ago."

"Have any of your old clients called to see how you're doing?" Dee asked.

Dwayne raised his eyebrow. "I didn't have any clients. I told you I worked with my brother in Texas."

"Oh, yeah. That's right," Dee said, hitting her forehead. She had given him an opportunity to tell the truth and he refused it. *Okay. I see how this is gonna play out*, Dee thought.

Dwayne finished his plate, stood up and scraped the crumbs in the trash.

"Oh boy. That was good. I think I'm gonna go take a little nap now," Dwayne said, stretching his arms.

"Okay," Dee said, still distracted with his lies.

After Dwayne walked upstairs, she put the leftovers in the refrigerator. She walked over to her computer and logged on to the Internet. Dee started browsing for magazine marketing ideas, when her phone rang. She looked at the caller ID to find Antony's number.

"Hey, Antony!" Dee chirped in the phone.

"What's up, darling? How are you?"

"Oh, I'm perfect, my dear. What's going on?"

"Well, I'm calling because I'm afraid I'll have to reschedule my appointment with you next week. The fabrics you requested did come in but I have an emergency. My cousin, Ronnie, died and I'll be out of town all week."

"Oh. I'm sorry to hear that."

"Thank you honey. We told him so many times to stay off those drugs but he would not listen. Oh, well. He's in God's hands now."

"Tell your family you have my condolences. The bedroom can wait. Dwayne doesn't seem to mind anyway."

"Is he over there now?"

"Yep. Snoring away. You know I forgot to ask you, whatever happened with the investment thing? Did Dwayne ever hook you up?"

"Oh no, chile. I changed my mind about that."

"Really? Why?"

"I finally figured out where I knew him from."

With those words Dee sat up straight in her chair and pressed the phone closer to her ear.

"Where do you know him from?" Dee asked.

"A friend of mine that used to live in Texas had a brother who was heavy into selling drugs. He became one of those kingpin-type guys. All gunned down and had a posse as dangerous as he was. Anyway, my friend said his brother used to give his money to Shoreshire-Mitchell Financials," Antony said.

"So? Dwayne probably didn't know your friend's brother was into drugs."

"Uh-uh, honey. You don't understand. My friend's brother went to your man's company strictly to get his money cleaned!"

"Wait a minute!" Dee caught herself raising her voice. She remembered Dwayne slept a few feet away upstairs. She stepped outside on the lanai and closed the French doors to finish her conversation out of earshot. "Antony, are you telling me my man is into money laundering?"

"That's what I'm saying."

"But at the restaurant, you said you recognized him. You said you'd seen him before."

"When they were charged, a picture of Dwayne and some guy they said was his partner was in the paper. I saw the picture. That's how I recognized him."

Dee's heart dropped to her stomach, like a sack of potatoes. "Charged?"

"Girl, it sounds like you and Mr. Man have a lot of talking to do. I gotta go book my flight home. I'll call you when I get back," Antony said.

"Sure. Bye," Dee said, as she hung up her phone.

Okay. Breathe. Breathe. Maybe this isn't as bad as it seems, Dee thought. She hung up and called Monica but no one answered. She then tried Stephanie but her voicemail picked up. Then, out of complete frustration, she called Bobbie's number. Even his voicemail was full. Dee paced the lanai, backward and forward.

Desperate for answers, she dashed inside and took to the Internet again. She looked through the Chamber of Commerce, city records and old newspaper articles. After ten minutes, she had her confirmation. A picture of Dwayne and Bobbie together accompanied an article of their legal woes. According to the article, the authorities had investigated the two for money laundering. Reports had them working with Maximus, a drug dealer on the run for eight years. As a result of the trial, Bobbie served two years of his four-year sentence in Texas. Dwayne, on the other hand, served no prison time in exchange for his testimony against Bobbie.

Dee cupped her mouth. She thought about the large sum of money Bobbie had given her and wondered if she would go to prison for accepting it. She also thought about the extra two hundred-thousand dollars Bobbie had promised to send her.

"Oh my gosh. What am I gonna do now?"

CHAPTER 29

Monica

M onica received Dee's nervous phone messages, but she couldn't answer. She didn't have time to gossip, shoot the breeze or hypothesize about Dwayne and his past. She only had twenty-four hours to pull all the last-minute details together for Janet's restaurant opening, and there were many last-minute details to iron out. Media and guests were calling to RSVP at the last minute. She had trouble finding some of the decorations, and she didn't seem to have enough men to put the tables and stage together. Monica wanted to spaz out, but with Janet doing all the spazzing, she couldn't; one of them had to stay sane. By default that person had to be Monica.

When Dee called Monica twelve times in a row, she didn't even look at the phone. She couldn't allow Dee to unload on her—not if she wanted to get everything together in time for the opening. Monica did, however, call Dee the next day about picking her up to go look for tablecloths. Her assistant had bought orange and green cloths that she found absolutely atrocious. This was not a Halloween party. Monica desperately needed to buy better ones.

When Dee picked Monica up, she stepped into her car and put her purse on the backseat. She braced herself because she knew Dee would pay her back for avoiding her calls the night before.

"So, where have you been?" Dee asked as she closed the car door.

Monica faced her and frowned. "Well, hello to you, too."

"Girl, while you're dodging a sista, I got issues," Dee said.

"Tell me about it," Monica said, raising her eyebrow.

"No, seriously. I think I'm in deep doo-doo here," Dee said.

"What now?"

"Remember when I was trying to find out who Bobbie is and why Dwayne doesn't like him?"

"Yeah," Monica said.

"I figured it out."

"And?" Monica asked.

"Bobbie and Dwayne used to be business partners who fell out when they were brought up on money laundering charges," Dee said, wincing at her own words.

Monica threw her hands up in the air. "I knew it. I knew it was a mistake for you to take that man's money. Between you and Stephanie, I don't know who's worse. Why don't you listen to me *sometimes?*"

"How was I supposed to know this went on?" Dee asked. "I needed the money."

"Okay. So, you got it. Now look where it's gotten you," Monica said, shaking her head. "How did you find out?"

"Antony and the internet," Dee said.

"And they were both in cahoots?" Monica asked.

"Not exactly. Bobbie is the one who went to prison. Dwayne testified against him."

"Have you talked to Dwayne yet?" Monica asked.

"No."

"I think you should go to the police. You might even want to take Dwayne with you," Monica suggested.

Dee shook her head. "I don't know."

"What do you mean? You need to let them know what's going on," Monica said.

"What if I get convicted of laundering? Monica, I can't go to jail," Dee said staring out in the distance.

"Dee, you're not going to jail. Okay? You need to go to the police station and be honest," Monica said.

Dee shook her head. "I can't talk about this anymore. Enough about me. How's everything at home?"

Monica sighed. "Tony left for Indianapolis without even saying bye."

"Well, dang! It's like that?" Dee asked.

"Apparently. But I don't care. I've stood by him long enough. Now it's time for him to stand by me," Monica said.

"Other than the jacked-up tablecloths, how is the opening going?" Dee asked.

"If I can keep Janet from spazzing out, it'll be great. I know she's excited but the closer we get to the event, the more frantic she gets," Monica said. "She's already called me ten times today."

"Can you blame her? She's opening a restaurant. That's crazy pressure," Dee said.

"Are you going?" Monica asked.

"No, I won't be able to make it," Dee said.

"Are you sure? It might get your mind off of going to jail."

"No. I'd rather not. There's no sense in me mean-mugging people all night."

Monica shrugged. "That's okay. I'll have Stephanie to complain to."

"Janet whines that much?" Dee asked.

Monica nodded. "I guess I would be more empathetic if I didn't have so much going on in my own life." She paused. "I think Tony is still seeing Jessica."

"What? How do you know?"

"He's doing all this stupid stuff. I'm telling you something's going on. He even had the nerve to come home smelling like alcohol and perfume."

"When?"

"A few days ago. And he stood me up at the pastor's office."

"For what?"

"Since he wasn't making much of an effort to improve our problems, I recommended we talk to our pastor. For marriage counseling. I set the day and time, told him when to be there and he went partying instead."

"Ooph. If I were him, I wouldn't have even come home."

"I gotta find out what's up. I need to investigate this

371 The Golddigger's Club

situation with Jessica. As arrogant as Tony is, I'd like to believe he knows better than to bring this woman to Tampa where our family is," Monica said.

Monica shook her head. As long as she was working on the opening, she could immerse herself in all its details, keeping her from thinking about her problems at home. But the minute she actually took a minute to think or talk about it, she felt a weight lie over her. She could only use the opening to escape for so long. After awhile, she would have to deal with everything.

"Maybe he didn't invite her up here. Maybe she came on her own."

"Great. She's a baby mama and a stalker."

"The best way to put a stop to this is to investigate," Dee said. "Too bad you can't get a camera to follow him around." She snapped her fingers. "Now that's what you should do!"

"What? Get a camera to follow him?" Monica frowned.

"No, plant a hidden camera in his car, maybe even a GPS system," Dee said, getting excited. "If he's been with her, you're bound to find out using one of those device thingys."

"Yeah, but I don't know how to use those things."

"I'm sure the people at the store will teach you how to use them. That's their job."

Monica thought it over for a second. She didn't want to have to learn anything too hard. Ordinarily she would oppose snooping on a spouse, but since Tony had given her serious reasons to mistrust him, she had to consider the pros and cons. The pros were she'd get her questions about his whereabouts answered, she'd have proof if he was still cheating, and she could have some closure. The cons were he could discover the camera and fly into a rage, she would have to face the facts if he was cheating, and she'd have to fight the urge to go find the woman and beat the DNA off of her. Weighing her options, Monica knew what she had to do: she needed to know the truth.

"Do you know of a tech shop I can check out?" Monica asked.

"Yeah. There's Spy Tech in the mall," Dee said. "We can go there now."

"Uh, Dee. I have so many things to do. I think I should get the tablecloths and come back to look for that."

"Oh no. It shouldn't take that long. The sales people will have all the information. I'll bet it only takes fifteen minutes, tops."

Monica looked at her watch. "I don't know, Dee."

"Please. I've always wanted to go in that store. It'll be the most fun you've had in fifteen minutes."

Monica sighed. "Okay."

"Yay!" Dee shouted. Monica laughed.

After they located the store, Dee parked and they walked into the small shop. It had gray walls and glass counters in the center of the store. The walls were adorned with self-defense gadgets, such as mace, stun guns and tasers but two fifty-two-inch plasma screens hung from the main wall. The sets switched between four different pictures, one of which was Dee and Monica.

"Oh my gosh. This place is off the Richter scale," Dee said, leaning over one of the glass counters.

Meanwhile, Monica inched closer to the large television screens to read the information below it. The screens were promoting a DVR program and camera dome. The DVR allowed access to the surveillance system anywhere one could reach the Internet. The dome provided the clearest picture ever created, perfect for making out a home invader or an unwanted visitor. *We need one of these at home*, Monica thought.

"May I help you with something?" a sales associate said to Dee and Monica. They both jumped. Neither of them heard her approach because they were so engrossed in the store's safety products.

"Yes. I'm looking for a camera that is small enough to fit in a car, perhaps in between the seats," Monica said.

"Okay. Let me show you these." The associate walked down another aisle as Dee and Monica followed. Along the way, she pointed to all the new merchandise shipped in that week. Dee and Monica continued to gawk at the clock cameras and stun guns. They stopped in front of a glass counter with various objects in it: pens, hats, purses, sunglasses, stereos, clocks and ties.

"What is this?" Dee asked.

"These are all cameras. They range in price from sixty to three hundred dollars. Also, we can put a camera in anything. So, if you have something you would like us to place a camera in, we'd be happy to do it for you," the sales associate said.

"Hey. That's what I'm talking about," Dee said.

"I'll pass on putting a camera in something but tell me about this pen," Monica said.

"The pen is very common. Many people choose it. The video will record in color. Once you record whatever you would like, you plug it into your computer to play it back. And you can re-use it again," the sales associate said.

"I think that would work for you," Dee said.

"That's what I was thinking," Monica said.

"It's an excellent choice. Very easy to use," the sales associate said.

Monica couldn't pass this up. The camera was small enough to hide in between the seats of Tony's favorite new car, the Lamborghini. It was a decent price and it was easy to use. She couldn't beat it. Monica glanced at her watch and noticed they'd been in the shop for thirty minutes instead of fifteen. She jumped.

"I'll take the pen," she said to the sales associate.

Dee and Monica left the store and rushed to visit another store for the tablecloths. When Dee dropped Monica off at her house, she was buzzing with a lot of energy. Not only was she rushing to take care of things for the opening, she couldn't wait to put her new toy to work. She snuck into the garage, opened Tony's car door and slid the pen between the backseat. Now that she had the camera set, she could worry about other things, like how she was going to be ready and at Janet's restaurant in an hour.

∞

"Okay. When the media comes in, they are going to check in at your table. Make sure they sign in on the registration sheet. If their name isn't on the sheet, they don't get in. Those that get in, hand them the media packet and give them their press credentials," Monica ordered two young college girls. She loved the idea of allowing students to experience working a large-scale event but she feared they would make a costly mistake. Nevertheless, they nodded to her directions.

"I'll send Melissa back here to see if you need anything," Monica said. *More like to see you're not messing anything up*, Monica thought.

Monica barely made it there before the help started arriving. It seemed like the moment she set foot on that pebble walkway she'd been running nonstop. Monica trotted past the front window but stopped short to admire the location. The Open Table Restaurant sat perched on top of a hill, overlooking St. Newark's River. The sun set behind the river, which reminded her she needed to make sure the flood lights worked. As she pushed through the door, she bumped into Robert.

"Oh!" Monica said, holding her forehead.

"I'm sorry." Robert laughed. "I didn't mean to knock you out."

Monica laughed. She hugged Robert. "Whatever! I'm glad you're here but what are you doing here so early?"

"I thought I'd see if you guys needed any help."

"Aww. That's really sweet, Robert. You didn't have to do that," Monica said.

"Yeah, but I think it's great what you guys are doing and I wanted to be here for you and Janet," Robert said.

"Well, if you're sure, I could always use an extra hand," Monica said. Robert made himself useful as the liaison between her and the helpers.

Shortly after Monica set the lights and tested the food, limos and SUVs pulled up to the curb. Public figures stepped out of the vehicles, onto the long red carpet and into the bright lights. The media aimed cameras and pointed microphones their way, as if on cue. Monica dashed off to find Janet and tell her she needed to mingle with the guests. She found Janet in the kitchen area, pacing the floor.

"They're here already?" Janet asked, her hands shaking.

"Yes. Listen. Just relax. It's gonna take a few minutes for them to make their way into the building because they're walking the carpet and talking to the media. Take a deep breath and remember they're here because they want to see your restaurant. They want to meet you," Monica said.

"Okay," Janet said.

"Have you memorized your three-minute speech?" Monica asked.

"No, I'm going to forget it," Janet said.

"No you won't," Monica said.

Robert stepped into the room and clasped his hands. "You ready, girl?" he said, looking at Janet. She shook her head. Confused, he frowned and looked at Monica.

"She's a little nervous but she'll be fine," Monica said, turning back to Janet.

"Of course you will. It's a great turnout. Everybody looks great. You look great. The place is awesome. You did it, Janet. You really did it," Robert said, putting his hands on both of her shoulders.

"You're right. I'll be fine," Janet said and smiled.

Monica gave Janet about ten minutes, then told her it was time to emerge. The crowd stood around a stage. They talked and waited for the festivities to begin. Monica approached the stage first to introduce Janet. Once Monica said her name, Janet walked onto the stage to thunderous applause. The woman who'd fretted over her speech earlier delivered it with passion and confidence, as Monica thought she would. When she stepped down from the stage, the guests clamored for Janet's attention. They congratulated her and snapped her picture.

Monica mingled with the guests as well, telling them about her part in the opening. Many people asked for her business card. In between talking to guests, she spotted Stephanie at the food table, piling her plate.

"Uh, are we binging?" Monica asked over Stephanie's shoulder.

"What do you mean?" Stephanie tried her best to look innocent.

"I mean you got a lot of food on your plate."

"Well, you know I'm eating for two now." Stephanie giggled.

Monica rolled her eyes and changed the subject. "Nice dress. What made you pick it?" Stephanie glanced down at her Matthew Williamson silk, multicolored dress.

"Nothing. What's wrong with what I'm wearing?" Stephanie asked, frowning.

"It's a peculiar choice for you."

Monica had grown used to seeing her friend in anything revealing. This dress was much more modest, but then she remembered her friend's pregnancy announcement. Still, Monica didn't notice Stephanie showing. The dress truly puzzled her.

"I felt like trying something different," she said.

"Have you seen Pamela?" Monica asked Stephanie.

"Pamela Waters? No, where is she?" Stephanie searched the crowd for the gossip columnist.

"I don't know, but I hope she has enough material." Just then a photographer approached them and asked to take a picture. When the photographer snapped the picture, Stephanie covered her stomach with her hand.

"Thanks, Brian," Monica said to the photographer. She leaned over to whisper in Stephanie's ear. "You don't have to cover your stomach. You'll draw attention to it."

"Oh. My bad." Stephanie giggled.

"All right. Stop eating everything on the table." Monica walked away from Stephanie toward the French glass doors. She stepped outside to breathe in the crisp, cool air and look at the view of the lake. A few minutes later, she heard the door open behind her and saw Robert tipping outside with a glass of wine in his hand.

"Hey! Are you enjoying the night?" she asked.

"Yeah, you guys really outdid yourselves," Robert said.

"Thanks for all your help earlier."

"Oh, don't mention it," Robert said. They lapsed into a strangely uncomfortable silence, which Monica decided to break with more casual talk.

"So, when do you go back home?" Monica asked.

"Ready to get rid of me already?" Robert asked, raising an eyebrow.

"No. I wanted to know how much more time I have with you," Monica said.

"Oh. I go home in two days."

Monica's mind raced. She pondered living without Robert again. To her surprise, it was a gloomy prospect. She hadn't expected to be so sad when he left.

"Are you any closer to an opening date for your practice?" Monica asked.

"We're still working out the details; whether we really want to open the practice here or not."

"Of course you do. This is an affluent area. It would be a great place to practice. Wealthy people like to look good. And taking care of your teeth is part of it," Monica said. Her excitement took on a life of its own.

"Yeah, but I don't know if we'll do it," Robert said, looking down.

"I don't understand. Why?"

Robert sipped his wine, paused, and put the glass on the stone balcony. "Level with me, Monica. What are we going to do if I move here?"

"What do you mean?" Monica asked, shifting her weight.

"What are you going to tell your husband about me? Are you going to hide your phone calls to me forever?"

Monica stared at the ground.

Robert sighed. "Monica, I adore you. There's nothing I wouldn't do for you. I think you know that but this has become more complicated than I expected. I'm having second thoughts about moving here."

Monica straightened her back and raised her head. She wanted to look confident but his words hurt her feelings. "What are you saying? That you don't want to be here because of me?"

"No! I don't want any trouble," Robert said.

"Trouble! You think I'm trying to get you in trouble?"

"Monica, I don't think you're listening to me," Robert said.

"No, I'm listening. You know what, Robert? I'm going through a lot right now. My husband has cheated on me. He might have an outside child. He doesn't want me to pursue my passion, even though I'm great at it. The few things that keep me positive are my kids, my friends and you. If that's a burden…"

Robert interrupted Monica. "Honey, that's not what I'm saying."

"I don't want to get in the way of your business. So,

if you need me to keep my distance, I'll do that," Monica said. She turned away from him to face the river. Despite her strong stance and her stubborn will, tears ran down her cheek. She hadn't realized how much she wanted Robert in Tampa. She knew it could eventually become a problem, but she couldn't help wanting his support.

Robert reached out to Monica and wrapped his arms around her. He hugged her before turning her around and lifting her chin. Cupping her face, he planted a soft kiss on her lips. The door opened and the two college students from the media table stepped out.

"Oops!" one of the girls said.

Robert and Monica turned to see the girls there with wide eyes and shocked faces. Monica pressed her hand to her face.

"Sorry, Mrs. Hatcher. I came out to ask if it was okay for us to eat dinner now."

"Sure. Absolutely," Monica said.

The two girls scrambled back inside, whispering and giggling.

"Oh." Monica moaned. "This isn't good."

"Well, don't worry about it. They're kids. They probably won't even mention it," Robert said.

Monica scowled at Robert. "They're girls, Robert. Of course they're going to talk about it."

Robert sucked his teeth. "Nobody'll believe them. What's the worst that could happen?"

CHAPTER 30

Dee

W hen Dee woke up Monday morning, she reached over to check her phone. Still no messages from Bobbie. She found it strange all her calls to him had reached his voicemail, which was full. She hadn't heard from him in a few days. He hadn't even deposited the additional two hundred thousand dollars into her account. *Should I take Monica's advice and call the police?* she thought. But then she realized she didn't know what to tell them. Dee really didn't know how the whole money laundering thing worked. She decided to go to the bank and withdraw the remaining money—seventy thousand dollars. This way, as soon as she could find Bobbie, she would give him the money back, in hopes of staying out of trouble.

At 10:00 a.m., Dee pulled on the bank doors. A staff member unlocked it for her and she rushed through the door toward the nearest teller.

"Good morning. How are you?" the teller asked.

"Great," Dee lied.

She slid her ID and a withdrawal slip for the seventy thousand dollars under the glass pane. The teller pulled up her account and suddenly, his friendly demeanor disappeared. His eyes widened. His face stiffened.

"Hold on one second. I'll be right back," he said.

She watched him walk away and wondered if there was a problem. Dee stood at the glass, calm on the outside, nervous on the inside. She slowly turned around to scan the bank. Something about it seemed different. The atmosphere was unusually electric for this time of morning. A couple of staff members hustled through the lobby. The security guard walked around instead of standing at his usual post. Dee turned back to the glass pane. She wondered where the teller had gone and most importantly, what was taking him so long. Did he know what she was doing and why? *Please, hurry up. If you come back, I promise I will never do anything like this again,* Dee thought. As she silently begged for mercy, a gentleman wearing a brown suit with a badge around his neck walked up behind her.

"Ms. Wright, I'm FBI Agent Monroe. Would you follow me?"

Dee's pulse raced. She wanted to run but knew if she did, the situation would only worsen. Mustering all her strength, Dee nodded and walked behind the FBI agent.

Agent Monroe led her to his car where his partner, Special Agent Stokley, waited. Once they placed her in the backseat, they proceeded to drive Dee to the police station without a word about why they had approached her in the bank. Even after they had driven for ten minutes, they still hadn't bothered to explain what was happening. Dee couldn't hold back her questions anymore. She began to pound away at the situation.

"Excuse me? Where are you taking me?" Dee asked.

The two agents glanced at each other. "We're taking you to the police station," Special Agent Stokley said.

"Am I under arrest?"

"No, ma'am. We want to ask you a few questions is all," Agent Monroe said.

"Why couldn't you ask me at the bank?" Dee asked.

"We didn't want to cause a stir. It's no big deal really. We only want to ask you some questions," Agent Stokley said.

Part of Dee was relieved that they weren't arresting her, but the other part of her was quite concerned. It's not normal for FBI agents to pick you up at your bank. Something else had to be wrong. Of course her first thought was they were there about the money laundering, but was it really serious enough for the federal government to get involved? It couldn't be. She thought about the questions they would ask her. She wanted to have predetermined answers.

There were two main questions she thought might stump her. The first was where she had gotten the money. She could tell them she'd received it through an investor, but then they would want to know the name of the investor. If they had followed her to the bank, they likely knew a lot about the money, and if so, then they already knew quite a bit about Bobbie. One mention of his name would set their ears on fire. On the other hand, if she lied and was caught lying, she could look like she had something to hide. She didn't really have anything to hide; she only wanted to stay jail free. She decided to avoid saying Bobbie's name, unless they mentioned him first. Then maybe they would figure that she didn't know him well. She really didn't know Bobbie very well. That shouldn't be hard.

The second question that came was why she trying to withdraw seventy-thousand dollars. She winced. It would be hard to come up with a good explanation for that. Nothing she did required that much money. Dee thought about telling them that she wanted to switch banks. The more she thought about it, the better that idea seemed.

"Are you from here?" Special Agent Stokley asked, interrupting Dee's thoughts.

"No." Dee furrowed her brow. She wasn't in the mood for small talk. She couldn't even focus on the dialogue. She was trying to focus more on keeping her hands from shaking.

"Do you like it here?" Special Agent Stokley asked.

"It's okay," Dee answered.

"Yeah. I kinda like it here. I'm thinking about moving down here," Stokley said. She faced Agent Monroe. "What about you? Do you think this is a good place to live?"

"I think it's an excellent place to live," Agent Monroe answered.

Dee rolled her eyes. *What is the point?* Dee thought.

All this small talk was making her nerves bad. She wanted them to tell her the problem so she could tell them she had nothing to do with it, and move on with her life.

When they arrived at the station, the agents directed her to a small room with three chairs. Dee frowned at the sight of the bare, dingy gray walls. Agent Monroe motioned for her to have a seat in the chair facing a one-way mirror. Out of habit and sheer anxiety, Dee fixed her hair in the reflection. Then, she set her hands back on the table out of self-consciousness. The agents looked at each other, then back at Dee.

Stokley, the fenale agent, sat down across from Dee. "I love your hair. Who does it?" she asked.

"A stylist here," Dee said, leaning back in her chair and crossing her arms. She figured that would keep her from appearing too nervous.

"Really? That's amazing. Your hair looks so upscale. Like no one here would ever be able to do that."

"My stylist does hair for NFL wives, cheerleaders, personalities, entertainers." Dee shrugged.

"Wow! That's pretty high class," Stokley said.

Dee scanned the female special agent in her basic blue suit and shoulder-length red hair.

"I guess," Dee said.

"How did you meet her?" Stokley asked.

Dee sighed and shifted in her seat. "Through a mutual friend." She was getting really tired of the small talk. Why couldn't they get to the point?

Stokley ignored Dee's behavior and continued. "I've

been looking for a new stylist. Do you think yours could take me on?" she asked.

"Possibly," Dee said.

The agents looked at each other again. "So, what do you do for a living?" Stokley asked, leaning forward.

"I'm a fashion stylist."

"Oh, so you know a lot of famous people yourself?" Stokley asked.

"I've met a few," Dee said.

"Probably some infamous people, too, huh?" Stokley chuckled.

Dee frowned. She didn't know what this woman wanted but she prayed for her to get to the point. Dee longed to state her side of the laundering fiasco and go home but she didn't want to incriminate herself by saying too much too fast. That was the only reason she kept playing this little game with them. Otherwise, she would have gone off thirty minutes ago.

"I've known some stylists that wanted to start their own fashion line. Are you gonna do that?" Stokley asked.

"No. I would rather create my magazine," Dee corrected.

"Fashion magazine? Oh, okay. Have you already started print and distribution?"

"No, but I will," Dee said.

"Cool. So, who's the market?" Stokley asked.

"Everyday professional women between the ages of twenty-eight and forty-two," Dee said.

"Great. I can get some pointers from it then."

Dee looked her over again. "I think so."

Stokley laughed. "I know. This type of job doesn't allow for much glitz and glamour. My sister pursued a career as a makeup artist and her life seems so much easier. I admire you."

"Thank you," Dee said. "You know, you don't have to change careers to be glamorous. That's the purpose of my magazine. To show every woman how to look their best no matter what." Dee smiled. The police station wasn't her ideal method of promotion, but she figured she might as well promote the magazine wherever she could.

Stokley nodded. "Yeah. I look forward to your magazine. When will it be out?"

"I give it another six to eight months."

Stokley frowned. "Why is it taking so long?"

"Because I need to get more money for it," Dee said.

"How are you getting it now?" Stokley asked.

Dee opened her mouth, and then closed it. She hadn't anticipated the question coming to her this way. She looked down at the table and tried to think fast.

"Savings," Dee said.

"Really? That's funny 'cuz your bank records show you deposited one hundred and twenty-thousand dollars into your account a couple of weeks ago. Out of the blue, you put that much in the account?" Agent Monroe asked.

Dee nodded. She should have stuck with her original answer to the question. Now she was going to look like a liar.

"So, you're saying that, in one day, you managed to save one hundred and twenty-thousand dollars?" Monroe asked.

"Well, I had help saving it," Dee said, looking down.

"Who helped you, Deidre?" Stokley asked.

"An investor," she said.

"What's his name?" Monroe asked.

"I'm not supposed to give his name. Part of the agreement is his identity will remain anonymous," Dee said. She knew her excuse sounded lame but it was the best she could come up with on short notice.

Stokley raised her eyebrow at Agent Monroe, who stood to the side. As if on cue, he stepped forward.

"Deidre, a few days ago, we found Bobbie Mitchell in the Grand Hyatt Hotel parking lot. He'd been shot twice in the stomach," Monroe said.

Dee gasped and covered her mouth. Fear trickled down her spine. No wonder he never transferred the money or returned her calls. She couldn't tell what was going on but she prayed she would not be next. "Oh my gosh! Is he dead?"

"He's in the hospital, in stable condition," Monroe said. Dee breathed a small sigh of relief.

"When we found him, he had a note in his phone to transfer two hundred-thousand dollars into your account. We also saw notes and records showing you've met with him before and he gave you one hundred and twenty-thousand dollars," Monroe said. He pulled a photo out of his folder and slid it in front of Dee.

"Here's a picture of you and Dwayne Shoreshire, his former business partner, at a dinner a few months ago," Monroe said. He leaned on the table. "We know Bobbie was giving you money, Deidre. We need you to be honest about it. You and Dwayne tried to kill him to get more money."

Dee's eyes widened. "What?! No!"

Stokley put her hand over Dee's hand. "It's okay. You have dreams. You have goals. You want to make them come true."

"Yeah, but…" Dee tried to explain but Stokley interrupted her.

"These guys showed you a way to make that happen. It was supposed to be one hundred and twenty-thousand dollars, but Dwayne wanted more. You didn't wanna hurt anybody," Stokley said to Dee.

"No, it wasn't Dwayne…" Dee said.

Monroe jumped in. "So, you figured you could keep the money to cover the magazine costs *and* get in on the action. You asked Bobbie to cut you in on his deals and he refused. Why not get a piece of the pie instead of being a small funnel for the whole operation?" Monroe asked.

Dee shook her head.

"C'mon. We have to know the truth, Deidre, or we won't be able to save you," Monroe said.

"Save me? What do you mean?" Dee asked.

"Someone's bound to come after you once word spreads that you tried to kill Bobbie. The guy may seem like a dope but he's quite connected to the streets," Monroe said.

"Me? No one should come after me. I didn't do anything," Dee said.

"That's not what the streets will say. Besides, the people he's involved with usually shoot first and ask questions later. You know what I mean?" Stokley asked.

Dee's mouth dropped in horror. She couldn't believe it. She didn't understand how her life could have ended up here. Dee wanted to start her magazine. That's it. And for that dream, she may get killed. Sitting there talking to the agents was surreal. "I would never try to kill someone over money! I don't have to," Dee said, crossing her arms.

"See, that's good. You're telling me you're not really a violent person. That's why you hired someone to do it. The judge may be a little more lenient because of that alone," Stokley said.

Dee's nostrils flared. "That's it. I want a lawyer."

"If you tell us what happened…" Monroe started but, this time Dee interrupted.

"I said I want a lawyer!" Dee said, hitting her hand on the table.

∞

"You should have called me immediately!" Monica yelled at Dee.

Monica had rushed to the station to pick Dee up, after she'd spent an hour with Agents Stokley and Monroe. When Monica picked her up, she practically fell inside of the car. Monica drove Dee back to the bank to get her car as she filled her in.

"I didn't have time. They pounced on me like tigers," Dee said.

"Well, let my lawyer take care of everything from here," Monica said. "But I have one thing to say. I told you so."

Dee threw her head back on the headrest. "Monica, I really don't wanna hear this right now!"

"If you had listened to me, you wouldn't be in this predicament."

Dee rolled her eyes. "You know what? There was so much going on, I may have still gotten caught up."

"How?" Monica asked.

"Even though the issue with Dwayne, the company and the money laundering happened almost seven years ago, they were still tailing Bobbie. They had a hunch he was still involved in it. So they followed him to Florida. They also think Bobbie and Dwayne are still in cahoots." Dee turned to Monica in her seat. "Dwayne has been giving Bobbie thousands of dollars since they stopped working together. The last transaction they found was a couple of months ago. I can't believe all this has been happening behind my back."

"Well, does that mean they're still in business together,

even though they're not in business together?" Monica asked.

"It has to be. I guess Dwayne told me all those crazy things about Bobbie to keep me from suspecting he was still dealing dirty. Oooh. Just wait 'til I talk to him. He's gonna get more than a piece of my mind."

"I don't know, Dee. You might wanna be careful. If Dwayne is involved in all this, he may be kinda dangerous. You know what I mean?" Monica asked.

"Don't worry. I'll handle it."

"You told me that last time. Look at what happened."

Dee sucked her teeth. Monica pulled her car beside Dee's car in the bank parking lot. Dee tried to jump out of the car but Monica placed her hand over Dee's arm. Dee looked over at her.

"I meant what I said, Dee. You need to be careful."

"I will. Promise," Dee said. She hopped out of the car and made a beeline to Dwayne's house. When she reached his door, she pounded away at it and waited, listening for footsteps. She didn't hear anything. She pounded again. Finally, she heard footsteps and the door opened.

"Hey. I was just going to call you," Dwayne said.

"Great. I'm glad to hear you weren't planning to flee the state again," Dee said, allowing her anger to erupt. She pushed her way past him into his house.

Dwayne stared at her, confused. "What are you talking about?"

"I'm talking about your whole little money operation."

"What money operation?"

"Your money laundering operation!" Dee exploded. "I can't believe you've been lying to me all this time. Do you even have a legitimate business, or is Tasha a front?"

"Tasha is my client and finance is my business. Where did you hear all this other stuff from?" Dwayne said.

"Antony told me. He told me about your legal troubles in Texas."

"You're basing this on something you heard from a gossip? You can't believe everything you hear."

"Oh, really? I guess that's why the federal agents decided to pay me a visit today. They questioned me for a full hour, Dwayne. Did they hear the same rumor, too?"

Dwayne sat down and dropped his head.

"Dee, it's not what you think. Okay? It's just that…" Dwayne picked up a couch pillow and threw it across the room. "I got caught up in some things I had a hard time getting out of when I was in Texas."

"What things? Dwayne, for once tell me the truth! Because now I'm involved," Dee shouted.

Dwayne stood up from the couch. He walked over to the window to look at his quiet neighborhood…a sharp contrast from the upheaval he'd experienced in Texas seven years ago. He took a minute to collect himself before he finally told her the truth.

"Bobbie and I were in business together for two years. The first year the business was thriving. We had five major clients and our profit was almost a million for the year. Things were going great," Dwayne said. "In the second year, Bobbie came to me about someone who wanted us to work with his money. He had hundreds of thousands of dollars he had obtained illegally and he wanted us to invest it in stocks and businesses to keep the authorities from finding it."

"Why didn't you report him? Bobbie? Both of them?" Dee asked.

Dwayne turned around and faced Dee. "Bobbie left out the illegal part when he first talked to me about it. We were both bringing in clients and we don't do background checks on people before we work with them. I didn't question Bobbie because I trusted my partner."

Dee plopped down on his couch and sighed.

"Within four months of working with this client, the police visited our office with a warrant asking to see our books. I was obviously concerned because it was my business they were tearing apart," Dwayne said, pointing at his chest. "And I had no idea what they were looking for. As it turned out, we were not only laundering money for a crooked client, but we were fixing the books too. Bobbie kept a second set of books and the police found all the discrepancies."

Dee's mouth dropped open. She wished Dwayne was lying but somehow she believed his story. She did, however, still have questions.

"If you guys stopped working together seven years ago, why are you still giving Bobbie money?" Dee asked.

Dwayne sat down next to Dee. "Ever since we parted ways, I've been trying to get away from Bobbie. When he went to prison, I hoped that would be it. I could start over. But as soon as he got out, he started following me, doing whatever he could to disrupt my life, job, relationships. Whenever I move, he's right behind me. I've been paying him to keep him from telling people about the problems we had in Texas. I was paying him to keep him from ruining my life again."

Now that Dwayne had bared his soul, Dee had many emotions running through her. She felt relieved that Dwayne had come clean, but she also felt bad that she had doubted him. She felt very foolish for doing business with Bobbie when she'd already been warned about him. Then it hit her. Since she'd accepted money from Bobbie, she wondered if he would harass her the way he'd harassed Dwayne. She didn't have thousands of dollars in hush money to give him. Dee didn't want to, but she knew what she had to do next.

"Dwayne, I have something I need to tell you. I think I'm gonna need your help."

CHAPTER 31

Monica

Monica expected Tony to hold a grudge against her for refusing to attend his Indianapolis game. After his behavior for the past several months, she knew he would continue to give her the silent treatment, but to her surprise he'd come home in a positive mood. He bought gifts for her and the kids. He was actually very nice.

Part of her didn't trust his new attitude. As much as they had been through, she felt like this was the sun before the clouds. But she decided to force herself to believe everything would work out. She didn't ask him about his behavior, nor did she ask him for details on his whereabouts. Monica waited for the camera to tell the real story. After Tony's third day home, it was finally time to find out what the camera had captured.

As Monica sat at her vanity table brushing her short, black hair, she thought about the day ahead. She planned to remove the hidden camera she'd placed in Tony's car. She was so nervous about what she would see the acid in her stomach bubbled over. She brushed her hair, waiting for Marianna to leave the house. No one else was there and once her nanny left, no one would see her sneak into the garage to get the camera. While she brushed, she thought about Dee and her legal issues. She hadn't heard from her since she dropped her off at the bank, which concerned her a little bit. She hoped Dee would follow her lawyer's advice.

When she'd stopped brushing her hair and put the brush down, her eyes fell on a five-year-old photo of her and Tony. They both wore broad smiles in the picture. They looked so happy, as if they had their whole lives ahead of them and nothing could change that. No one would guess he'd started another family elsewhere. Monica winced and looked away from the photo. The paternity issue still stung.

Before Monica could shed any tears, her phone rang.

"Hello?" Monica answered, clearing her throat.

"Did something happen at the opening?" Stephanie asked without a greeting.

Monica shook her head. "What do you mean?"

"The opening for Janet's restaurant? Did I miss something?" Stephanie asked again.

"A lot of politicians, athletes, and entertainers were there. You were there. I don't understand your question. Why do you ask?" Monica asked.

"Because I'm on the Internet right now and somebody's blowing up the message boards about you and an unidentified man in a heated lip-lock!" Stephanie said.

Monica's heart dropped. She'd tried to forget that part

of the night, hoping Robert and the girls would forget as well. Obviously that wasn't going to happen. Up until then she hadn't told anybody, not even Dee and Stephanie, about the kiss, but, deep down Monica knew those girls would spread the word and she would have to explain.

"Oh my gosh!"

"Yeah. Where is this coming from?" Stephanie asked.

Monica paused for a second. Although she didn't want to admit it, she knew she had to tell the truth. "A couple of the college interns working the event walked in on Robert kissing me," Monica admitted. She grimaced saying the words.

"What?! I knew it. I should've been keeping my eye on you."

"It was a spur of the moment thing. Neither one of us expected that to happen," Monica said. "This is awful."

"I told you there were some leftover feelings there," Stephanie said.

"I think we got caught up in the moment. He saw I was upset about everything that's been happening with Tony and wanted to comfort me," Monica said.

"And that's what he did, huh?" Stephanie asked.

Monica rolled her eyes. "C'mon. It wasn't that serious. He got a little out of hand with it. That's all."

"Yeah. Well, you know what this means," Stephanie said.

"It's only a matter of hours before Tony finds out," Monica said.

"Lie!" Stephanie suggested.

"Thanks a lot, Stephanie. My marriage is in bad enough shape. I can't make it worse by lying."

"Why not?! He lied to you. I say, if there's no proof, there's no problem. It's the interns' words against yours," Stephanie reasoned. "Is Tony home yet?"

"He's been home for a couple of days. He's at practice," Monica said.

"Is he speaking to you now?" Stephanie asked.

"Yeah, he's actually very happy, but not for long," Monica said sarcastically. She hung her head. "I need to go and call Robert."

"Be careful," Stephanie said.

Monica ended the call and dialed Robert's number right away.

It had been a couple of days since Robert had left to go back to California. Because they'd crossed dangerous territory the night of the opening, Monica hesitated to call him. She didn't know how to address the kiss, but it had to be mentioned. Bringing it up would create a lot of awkwardness, but not only because they gotten caught. The feelings it brought to the surface had a lot to do with the discomfort as well. The truth was she missed him, and that scared her as much as people finding out about the liplock. As she waited for Robert to pick up, she paced her bedroom floor. She stopped when he answered.

"Hi, Robert. It's Monica."

"Hey. How's it going? I was thinking about you today."

"Oh, really? Well, I hope they were good thoughts because you won't be happy about the reason I'm calling."

"What is it?" Robert asked.

Monica took a deep breath. "You remember the girls that walked in on us at the opening?"

"Yeah," Robert said slowly.

"Well, they're spreading news about what happened all over the Internet," Monica said. "I told you they would talk."

Robert sighed. "Well, that is unfortunate."

"Unfortunate? Any day now my husband is going to hear about this. He's gonna hit the roof!"

"What do you want me to say, Monica? I'm sorry it's happening like this," Robert asked.

"What do you mean 'happening like this'?"

"This is what I meant, Monica. Something like this was bound to happen," Robert said. "I still love you and I will always love you. If I move to Tampa, I don't know that I'll be able to control these feelings."

Robert's words rendered her speechless. Deep down, she loved him, too, and perhaps she always would. Yet she prided herself on being the type of woman that handled things the right way. She couldn't make any commitments to him; she already had a commitment to Tony. As tough as it was sometimes, Monica took her wedding vows seriously. She planned to honor her part. She needed to stick with Tony.

"I'm in a sticky situation. I have to honor my commitments and my family. Anything less than that would be inexcusable," Monica said.

"So you're saying no matter what happens, we could never be?" Robert said.

"Robert…" Monica started.

"It's okay. You don't have to say anything. I know I put you in an awkward position, but I want you to know that however things play out, I am here for you," Robert said.

Monica had to swallow the lump in her throat. "Thank you. That means a lot to me."

"Are you gonna be okay dealing with Tony?" he asked.

"Yeah. I just have to think about how I'm going to handle this. I'll know better when I look at the video," Monica said.

"What video?"

"I bought a camera and put it in Tony's car to see if he's up to something. I plan to watch it today."

"Whoa! You did what?"

"I put a camera in his car."

"Damn, Monica. It's like that?"

"Well, what else am I supposed to do? I need to know what he's up to. I'm certain he's not telling me the full truth."

"Since you bought it, I guess you might as well watch it, right? Hey, listen. I have to go. I'll call you a little later to check on you, okay?"

"Okay."

"Stay out of trouble," Robert said, laughing.

"Yeah, right." Monica hung up, glad they were able to end their call on a positive note. Robert had a point, though. As long as she'd already bought the camera, she might as well watch the video.

Monica tipped to the top of her stairs and listened for noise.

"Marianna!" she called out. No answer. She trotted downstairs and stepped out of the side door. After sprinting to the garage where the Lamborghini awaited Tony's return from practice, Monica opened the car door and reached into the backseat. She leaned in, feeling feverishly for the little pen camera. She almost panicked when she couldn't find it. After leaning all the way into the backseat and feeling with both hands, Monica finally found it.

I hope it recorded at a good angle, Monica thought. She swiped the camera and darted into the office. She sat down at the desk and turned on the computer. As she plugged the device into the computer, she felt hot. She was overcome with anxiety and fear about what she was about to see. Monica felt those bubbles gathering in her stomach again. Deciding she had to see the video, she pushed her anxiety aside and pressed the "play" button.

The color picture showed the space between the two front seats, the dashboard and the windshield. She fast-forwarded through footage of no one in the car. When the picture showed Tony getting in and cranking up the car, she clicked "play" again. After about thirteen minutes of her husband driving down the street and changing radio stations, she smiled, happy to see the video was boring. She clicked the fast forward button, positive there was nothing else to see. Then Tony stopped the car and a female got into the passenger seat. Monica stopped the video to rewind it back and watch the beginning of the woman's entrance.

At first she couldn't make out the woman but she waited, hoping the mystery woman would move into the camera's range. When she leaned forward, Monica could see her long, red hair and medium-brown skin. She could also see her reach over and plant a kiss on Tony's lips. Monica's face burned as hot as a poker.

She stopped the video, stood up and paced the floor for about fifteen minutes thinking about all the things she could do. Torture Tony? That sounded good. He deserved to suffer after lying to her. Too bad she didn't have any grits around the house. It was just as well. No use putting herself and Tony on the six o'clock news.

Divorce him? She swallowed hard. Even after the video and their rough year together, something about that word didn't sit right with her. She'd invested so much time into this man, this family, this house and this lifestyle. Why should she be the one to walk away?

Monica dropped down into one of the chairs. She imagined moving again. Fending off reporters who wanted details about their failed marriage. Scaling back on her lifestyle. Sharing custody of the kids—with Tony and the other woman. *Oh, no*, Monica thought. She closed her eyes and shook her head. There was no way she could let this happen. She had to find a way to salvage her marriage.

Her biggest problem was she didn't know how to save the marriage. She'd tried counseling but Tony didn't want to go. She'd tried talking to him but he didn't think anything was wrong with the way things were going. Monica knew one thing: their situation was very wrong and they needed to fix it. She was determined to make him see that.

The sound of the front door opening interrupted her thoughts. Tony strolled past the office and found her standing in the middle of the floor.

"Oh, hey. What's up?" Tony offered a half-cocked smile before continuing to rummage through the mail.

"Nothing much. Just catching up on things. Watching videos," Monica said, grinding her teeth.

"Really? Anything I might know?"

"I don't know, but you've got to take a look at this one video. It's an unbelievable play. C'mon." Monica walked back behind the desk and motioned for Tony to follow. Looking a little reluctant, Tony walked into the office and followed her behind the desk. When Monica saw him coming, she clicked the "play" button. Tony's eyes widened as he focused on the scene unraveling in front of him.

"What is this?" he asked.

"Don't you remember?" she asked.

"You hid a camera in my car! Why would you do that?!"

"Because I had a feeling you were lying to me! Apparently, I was right."

"Turn that off! Give me that!" Tony reached for the camera pen but Monica snatched it away from him.

"No. You told me you were through with Jessica. I want to know what's going on!" Monica shouted.

"Listen. It's not as bad as you think," Tony said, still reaching for the camera.

"Oh no? Is this her? I thought you didn't talk to her anymore. So I guess this means you lied, huh? It is your baby."

Tony didn't answer. He ran his hand over his face and tried to walk away. She grabbed his arm.

"I want an answer, Tony, and I want it now! Are you still with her?"

"I'm as much with her as you are with Robert," Tony said.

Monica stepped back as if she'd been struck off balance. *Oh, no! He heard about the kiss*, Monica thought.

"Yeah, I guess you thought I didn't know about that one. All your little secret meetings and phone conversations. People talk. I know what's going on. You must think I'm a fool." Tony looked her up and down.

"I'm not cheating on you with him. He's a college friend. I saw him. We talked. I don't have a baby with the man," Monica said. She looked in his face for recognition about the kiss but she didn't see it. Since she didn't see it, she continued without mentioning it.

"I don't even wanna hear that, Monica. 'Cuz if it was that innocent, why didn't you tell me about him? Instead, I gotta hear about it in the streets."

"Because I didn't want you to overreact. And I don't care what you think happened with him. That still doesn't give you the right to be with her. Not while we're supposed to be working on our marriage."

"How is this working on it? Sneaking behind my back. I don't wanna be the only one working on it, while you have a man on the side. What's the matter? You think you made the wrong choice?"

"For the last time, I'm not seeing Robert! He introduced me to my client." Monica huffed.

"No man does you a favor like that unless he wants something or he's already getting it from you. If he hasn't gotten you yet, he was planning on broaching the subject later. As much as you guys talked on the phone, it was going to be more sooner than later," Tony said.

"How do you know how much we talked on the phone? Were you checking my phone records or something?" Monica asked.

Tony stared at her.

"Oh, I don't believe this! How could you do that?" Monica shouted.

"The same way you planted a camera in my car!" Tony

yelled. "You going around here hiding your conversations, getting defensive every time I ask you a question about them. I needed to know what you were doing."

"That gave you no right to snoop on my phone!" Monica said.

Tony walked closer to her. "Correction. That's my phone! I pay the damn bill every month. As a matter of fact, I pay for everything up in here and if I wanna check up on what I'm paying for, I will. There ain't nothing you can do about it. Now is there?" Tony asked, jumping up in Monica's face.

Monica pushed past Tony and stormed upstairs. When she slammed the bedroom door behind her, she paced again. She couldn't believe he was talking to her that way. She birthed his children. Yet he stood in front of her talking like she was some chick on the street he bought. Worst of all, he made her confront the fact she'd allowed him to think he'd bought her.

Monica heard the front door close. One of their cars screeched out of the driveway and down the street. Sure Tony was gone, she picked up the telephone.

Within an hour of her and Tony's argument, Dee and Stephanie sat on Monica's bed. They listened to the details of the argument while Dee stayed fixated on the camera.

"All I got to say is can I use this when you're finished?" Dee asked.

"Sure. I shouldn't need it anymore. I'm so disgusted," Monica said. "You guys didn't have to come over."

Stephanie handed Monica a cup of chamomile tea.

"Of course we did. That's what we're supposed to do," Stephanie said. Monica smiled at Stephanie and took the tea.

"Oh, I had to come over here to see what Mr. Hatcher was up to. This is trifling. Just trifling," Dee said.

"Tell me about it. And you know what's worse? I asked him if the boy was his and he didn't even answer," Monica said.

"That's probably 'cuz it is," Dee said.

Monica shook her head. "I can't believe I tried to believe his story. I must have been an idiot."

"No, you weren't an idiot. You were trying to give your husband the benefit of the doubt. It's not your fault that he took advantage of your trust," Stephanie said. "You did the right thing."

Monica chuckled. "You know he actually had the nerve to try to turn everything around on me?"

"How?" Dee asked.

"He accused me of cheating with Robert."

Dee and Stephanie exchanged looks.

"What?" Monica asked. "Oh, c'mon."

"Well, how long do you think you guys could've gone on like that?" Stephanie asked. "You kissed the man for goodness sakes."

"Wait a minute! You kissed him?" Dee asked.

"Thanks, Stephanie," Monica said.

Stephanie shrugged.

"When did this happen, Ms. Goody Two Shoes?"

Dee asked, moving closer to Monica to hear the details.

"At Janet's opening, but it was no big deal. It was one little kiss. That's all. Okay?" Monica said.

Dee raised her eyebrows.

"I wasn't going to cheat on Tony."

"That sounds good, but in the real world, you were right on the verge. It was just a matter of time," Stephanie said.

Although Monica and Robert's association had caused some snags, it had brought her some positive changes. There's no telling how long it would have taken her to start working on her PR business if he hadn't come along. She now had people wanting to work with her and she had him to thank for it. No matter what anyone said, a part of her felt like it was worth knowing him.

"Whatever," Monica said.

"What are you going to do now?" Dee asked.

"I don't know. I have a lot to think about. Like if this Jessica girl can convince Tony to leave me." Monica grimaced.

Stephanie shook her head. "As cocky as Tony is, I don't think he really wants to leave. I think he sees the effect of his actions, but feels too inadequate to fix it. All he needs is to calm down and take some time to look inside himself. Then, he'll find the inner strength to move back toward his family."

Dee rolled her eyes. "When did you become Dr. Phil?" Dee asked.

"I'm not. I'm trying to offer some support. Besides, this is great practice for motherhood. You know the whole nurturing thing? I'm getting pretty good at it, don't you think?"

"You are amazing. Our friend is in crisis and you still find a way to make this about you. I can't believe you're so selfish," Dee said.

"I'm not selfish!"

"Listen, ladies. I really don't feel like playing referee with y'all right now, okay?" Monica said.

"Sorry," Stephanie said.

"My bad," Dee said. "Hey. Why don't we go to the movies?"

"Oh, I don't feel like going out," Monica answered.

"I think it's a good idea," Stephanie said.

"It'll temporarily take your mind off your problems. C'mon. Let's go," Dee said, standing up.

"No. Seriously, Dee. I'm not up for it. I wanna lie here and sleep my troubles away."

Dee sighed. "Well, I'll get going then. I have to start preparing for court anyway. Will you guys be there?"

"Yeah, I'll still make it," Monica said.

"Me, too," Stephanie said.

"Okay. I'll see you later. Call me if you need anything." Dee walked out of the bedroom door. Stephanie turned to Monica.

"Are you sure you're okay?"

"Yeah, I'll be fine. As a matter of fact, you can go

ahead and go, too. I'm gonna take a nap," Monica said.

"You're positive?" Stephanie asked. "'Cuz I don't have anything else to do today."

"Yes. Go." Monica shooed her away.

After her friends left, Monica rolled over. She heard the phone ring. At first, she waited a few minutes, expecting Marianna to answer it. Then, she remembered Marianna wasn't there. She reached over and picked up the cordless phone.

"Hello?"

There was silence for three seconds.

"Hello?" Monica said.

The person hung up. Monica replaced the phone on the cradle and sighed. *Looks like I'll be changing my phone number tomorrow.*

CHAPTER 32

Stephanie

S tephanie had reached the tail end of her publicity campaign for Operation Baby. She had the message boards and blogs on fire, and Pamela Waters had written about her and Levin in her column a few different times. When she was at Janet's restaurant opening and heard Monica say Pamela was there, she had almost broken her neck trying to find Pamela. Unfortunately, she had never found her that night. She had really wanted to introduce herself to the woman; see if she could fill her with more stories about her and Levin's relationship. She particularly wanted to give her more details about the "baby."

Since that didn't work out, Stephanie had to hope Pamela somehow had heard about her attendance at the opening and had covered it in her gossip column. She sat on her bed, hunched over her laptop and lost in concentration. She stifled her yawns and tried her hardest to fight sleep. She refused to give in to her tired eyes. Instead, she scanned the web pages, looking for pictures of Janet's restaurant opening, specifically the pictures Brian the photographer, had snapped of her.

"Yes, there it is," Stephanie said out loud in her bedroom. She found the picture of her covering her stomach. It appeared in Pamela Waters' infamous column with a caption reading, "Levin's Love Child." Stephanie cheesed.

"Wheee!" she said with self-satisfaction.

In the entertainment industry, rumors always spread fast but Stephanie put in a lot of work to make sure the details of her and Levin's impending parenthood had spread even faster than normal. Her work had paid off; even her friends had reported the headlines back to her. *Levin, Fiancée Expecting Baby*, the news screamed.

Stephanie continued to surf the net, searching for more evidence of her work when her phone rang. It was Levin and his voice sounded small—distant, even.

"What's wrong? Is everything okay?" Stephanie asked.

"Did you tell anybody about the baby?" Levin asked.

"No. Why?" Stephanie glanced around her room, as if to see if someone could hear her.

"People keep coming up to me asking about it."

"Maybe someone in your camp said something," Stephanie offered.

"I didn't tell anyone in my camp but Victor and I know he ain't telling. He wishes he didn't even know."

Stephanie dropped her head and her shoulders. She felt a little disappointed. Although her plan had succeeded, she still wanted Levin to want the "baby." Secretly, she wanted him to shout the news from the highest mountaintops. Instead, he hid the news, like he didn't want to accept it. But Stephanie refused to allow her attitude to betray her inner worries. She would make him happy about it.

"Oh, that's just as well. Sometimes the worst rumors come from people close to you, you know?"

"I don't know who could've said something. Victor is really pissed about the news getting out," Levin said.

Stephanie frowned. She grew tired of Victor butting his nose into places it didn't belong. After she finished Operation Baby, she needed to begin Operation Eliminate Victor because no one should have that much control over another person's life. "Who cares? That's his problem."

"I have to care, Stephanie."

"Why?!"

"Because he's my manager. You know what's worse? He thinks someone is purposely spreading the news to ruin my career."

"That's ridiculous. There's more to life than your career, Levin," Stephanie said. "Don't worry about it. Just let people talk."

"Unfortunately, I can't do that. In addition to asking me about you and the baby, they're asking about Felicia. I hate being put on the spot. I don't like explaining this stuff to people. If I say the wrong thing, I could get put on front street. I've never been in this situation before."

Levin had a point. He'd spent most of his time hopping from woman to woman. Not long enough to explain anything; he never had to. Stephanie had stuck around him longer than any woman in the past five years—a fact she hadn't missed. She hoped he didn't ask her to pretend they weren't together for the sake of his image.

"What did your publicist tell you to say?" Stephanie asked.

"She told me to say nothing for the time being but the media is relentless. Even the Internet has gotten out of control. There are people on there, telling everybody about us through the blogs and message boards. It's spreading like crazy."

Stephanie couldn't help smiling on her end. She was glad he was seeing all of her hard work.

"Levin, all the gossip and image stuff has nothing to do with you and me. Remember? You said that," Stephanie said.

"Yeah, I did."

"We should be enjoying this time together, preparing for our baby." After a couple of seconds, he spoke.

"You're right. How's everything going?" Levin said. He still sounded distracted.

"I went to the doctor yesterday and everything is looking really good. I went to the library and picked out books on baby names."

"Really? Which ones were you looking at?"

"Well, if it's a girl, I'm thinking Lalani. If it's a boy, I'm thinking Levin."

"That's really sweet, baby," he said in a small moment

of affection. "Listen, I gotta get going. I'll head that way Monday, aight?"

"How long will you be here?"

"Only a couple of days. Then, I have to fly to Mexico to start the movie."

"Okay. I love you."

"Love you, too."

He may be irritated now but he'll come around, she thought as she hung up. She reached over to retrieve her secret notebook off of her nightstand. There she kept the full layout of her plan. She opened the book and reviewed her tasks and outcomes. Tell Levin she was pregnant. Check. Tell Natalie about the baby. Check. Spread the rumor on the Internet. Check. Send tips to the media outlets. Check. Purchase pregnancy stuff. Check. Now all she had to do was wait a couple more weeks and tell Levin she lost the baby. By then he would be so distraught he would stay with her and really try to work it out. No man would leave his lady after a miscarriage. He'd really look like a jerk then. And if he did leave her, she could always spread more rumors about him. She already had the media contacts to do it. Stephanie had to laugh to herself. *Why hadn't I thought of all this sooner?*

She did have one snag. She didn't know how to pull off a fake miscarriage. Should she tell him she fell? As she sat on her bed trying to figure it out, her stomach growled and rumbled. She rubbed her forehead and felt beads of sweat gathering around her hairline. Filled with unexplained nausea, she moved her notebook and laptop to the side and trudged to the bathroom. She leaned over her toilet, waiting for something to come up but nothing happened.

I thought those sausages smelled funny last night, Stephanie thought. Next time, she'd follow her gut and avoid eating something she knew wasn't right, but she'd had a strange craving for meat lately. She'd also been feeling sick often. Catching the flu now would be a nightmare. When she was sick, colds had a way of zapping all of her energy and thinking power. She needed that to get through the rest of her plan.

For now, it looked like she would have to pay the price of the faulty sausages. She curled herself into a ball on the bathroom floor, moaning and cradling her stomach. For fifteen minutes, she waited for something to come up. Still nothing. After waiting and waiting to vomit, she stood up and stumbled out of the bathroom, thinking lying down might help. When she reached her bedroom door, she doubled over and threw up on her cream-colored carpet, turning it "chocolate milkshake" brown.

∞

By the time Levin arrived in town, Stephanie still felt under the weather. In fact, she felt worse. She couldn't understand why she had gotten sick all of a sudden. Monica had recommended she visit her doctor, Dr. Andrew Tisdale. He worked her in the same day she called, ran a few tests and told her they would call her within a day or two. In the meantime, she prepared for Levin's arrival. She still had work to do with him.

Despite her efforts to clean up, Levin jumped back when Stephanie opened her door. He immediately noticed her condition.

"Are you okay? You look a little pale," he said.

Oh, no. I must be slipping, she thought. Stephanie thought she'd covered up her illness. She wore a short Dina Bar-El dress with Manolo Blahnik heels, thinking a sexy look would mask everything. Levin, however, always picked up on the slightest change in mood or circumstance. It's one of the things she loved about him but also one of the things that made her "baby" plan a challenge. If she let her guard down, he would detect her scheme.

"I'm great. I think I may be catching a little cold but I've taken something for it," Stephanie said.

"Are you sure you still want to go out? Maybe you should stay in. It can't be good to be sick while you're pregnant," Levin said.

Stephanie nodded her head. They had to go out. She'd picked the perfect place. The Open Table, Janet's new restaurant, had become a major attraction since Monica had helped her open it. Entertainers, reporters and other public figures frequented the new hot spot. Stephanie made sure they had a reservation there. People would see them together as a couple. It helped reinforce their family vibe.

"Yeah, of course. I'm fine. I have the sniffles. That's all. Come on. Let's go." Stephanie grabbed Levin's arm and pulled him out of the door.

Once they reached the restaurant, everything fell into place. They talked. They laughed. Occasionally, she would pull out her compact mirror to see the people in the restaurant gawking at them and pointing. *Perfect*, she thought. She almost gave herself an imaginary pat on the back, but she had to stop short when she saw an unexpected visitor.

"Excuse me." Levin and Stephanie looked up to find a tall woman with long, black hair. Her light blue mini dress barely covered her hourglass figure. She had a Sharpie and a piece of paper in her hand. "Hello. My name is Elise. I am such a big fan of yours. Would you mind signing this paper for me?"

"Not at all," Levin said. He grabbed the paper and pen and wrote his autograph.

"My name is spelled E-L-I-S-E." As she spelled her name, she leaned over Levin's shoulder revealing her cleavage. Levin's eyes shifted up and her chest immediately greeted them. Stephanie's face turned red.

Levin handed her the paper and pen, as he and the woman held eye contact. "Thank you," she said.

At that moment, Stephanie hit the table so hard that half the room stopped and looked in their direction. The woman looked at Stephanie. "You're welcome," Stephanie said.

"Stephanie? What are you doing?" Levin asked, scanning the room to see all the people staring at them.

"I'm letting your 'fan' know that we appreciate her support. And now, I'm sure she doesn't mind leaving us be while we finish a quiet dinner together." Stephanie smiled. "Thank you."

The woman frowned, turned around and walked off. Levin stared at Stephanie. "Are you crazy?"

"No." Stephanie pointed at the woman, who was now turning the corner. "She's crazy for coming up here to seduce you in front of me. And you."

"What about me?" Levin asked.

"You sat there and ogled her chest like they were a two-piece snack on your plate. Did you forget I was here, Levin?"

"No. I was trying to be friendly."

"That was more than friendly. That was 'meet me tonight at the hotel,'" Stephanie said.

"Man, I don't wanna hear all of this."

This was not the night Stephanie had planned. And it was going south all because of some tramp who felt the need to bring her legs and cleavage over to meet Levin. Maybe she didn't get the memo that Stephanie was his woman and the mother of his unborn child. So what the latter wasn't true? She still needed to respect Stephanie's position. As if the night wasn't already shot, Stephanie was in for another unexpected visitor.

"Hey, y'all! I thought that was you."

Stephanie turned around to follow the voice and saw Natalie.

Oh my gosh, Stephanie thought. "Hey, girl! What are you doing here?" Stephanie asked. She really hoped to finish talking to Levin alone.

"I'm out with DJ Rock. Girl, did I tell you I was seeing him?" Stephanie shook her head but Natalie barely noticed. "He is wonderful and special. I think he might be the one, you know what I mean?"

Stephanie couldn't believe her friend continued to talk nonstop about her new relationship in the middle of their private dinner.

"Yeah, I do," Stephanie answered in a short terse voice, hoping her friend would catch a hint and leave. Instead, Natalie stood there, shaking her head and beaming at the atmosphere. She sighed.

"Isn't this place breathtaking?" Natalie asked.

"Yeah," Stephanie said.

"I heard it was even more amazing the night of the opening," Natalie said.

"Yes, it was." *Please go away*, Stephanie thought. She didn't want to be rude to her friend, but she really wanted Natalie to let her finish working on her plan. They could chitchat tomorrow.

"Boy, I am so happy to see the two of you together. Almost as happy as I was when you told me about the baby," Natalie said, resting her hand on Stephanie's shoulder.

Stephanie silently gasped. In that moment, she thought she saw her life crumble right before her eyes, or more like the life she tried to build with Levin. She'd told Natalie about the baby, but never told her not to mention their conversation to Levin. Now she wished she had. Stephanie cringed on the inside but she pretended like nothing happened on the outside. She didn't even look at Levin. After unwittingly dropping a bomb on Stephanie's scheme, Natalie readied herself to leave.

"Well, I have to go. Rock is waiting for me. It's good to see you guys. We should all go out to dinner sometime." Then Natalie walked off.

Stephanie still couldn't bring herself to look at Levin. For the second time she'd been caught in a lie, and she didn't know how to fix it. The waiter came to the table and placed the bill in front of Levin. He picked it up, glanced at the amount, slid his American Express Black Card in the billfold and placed it back on the table. Although he didn't speak a word, his actions rang as loud as sirens. He was simmering under the surface. After fiddling with the bill, he finally put his elbows on the table and crossed his arms.

"I can't figure out for the life of me why you keep lying to me. Can you explain that to me?"

Stephanie had to think quickly. She didn't want to admit to another lie. She thought she'd use another excuse.

"She must have read it on the Internet or heard it on the radio," Stephanie said.

Levin sucked his teeth.

"I'm serious. I didn't tell her. She's mistaken."

"Then why didn't you correct her?"

"Because I didn't want to make her feel bad," Stephanie said.

Levin rolled his eyes. "Why do I have the feeling you're not telling me the truth right now?"

"I don't know, Levin, but I am."

Stephanie maintained her position with Levin, but in her head she was cursing Natalie out. Why couldn't she have said hello and kept moving? Now she was stuck trying to convince Levin she hadn't lied to him. By the time the waiter returned Levin's credit card back to him, it looked like the argument was going to die down. Unfortunately, it turned into the calm before the storm. Stephanie and Levin argued all the way back to her condo. He couldn't understand why she had lied to him when he asked her if she'd told anybody about the baby. She sensed he might suspect something was up. To distract him, she pouted and whined, aiming to make him feel bad for her.

They stepped into her condo, still arguing.

"All I'm saying, Stephanie, is this is the second time I've caught you in a lie. What else are you lying about?"

"Nothing. I simply don't remember telling Natalie. She called a couple of days after I got back from New York and I don't know. Maybe I told her. But if I did, can you blame me, Levin? I was excited. People are usually excited about something like this."

"What are you saying?" Levin asked.

"I'm saying it would be nice if you showed some enthusiasm about it. It's your baby and you act like there's a problem."

"There's no problem. I just feel like…" He stopped in mid sentence as if preventing himself from saying something he might regret later.

"Like what?" Stephanie asked.

"Like I'm being pressured or…"

Stephanie interrupted him. "Trapped? Is that what you think I did? You think I trapped you? Go ahead and say it. Be a man about yours. If you think I trapped you, go ahead and say it!"

Levin sighed and looked at Stephanie. "I'm not saying you trapped me. Okay? I'm saying this is a surprise and I have so much going on right now." Levin reached out for Stephanie's hand but she pulled it away.

"C'mon, baby. Don't be like that. I'm sorry."

"I think you should leave now." Stephanie's lower lip quivered.

"But I just got here," Levin said.

"I'm not feeling like company anymore."

"Well, could I at least use your bathroom first?" he asked.

She waved him away. He walked down the hall, while Stephanie stepped into the living room. She flopped down on her couch and tried to determine her next move. Task two had blown up in her face since Natalie had opened her big mouth in front of Levin. She thought

about allowing him to feel sorry for his apathetic attitude toward the "baby." That should get things back on
track. He'd already apologized. She could ride this wave
until morning and then, pretend she'd forgiven him for
his callousness.

Stephanie reached for her TV remote and noticed the
red light on her cordless phone blinking in rapid succession. She turned to see her phone, alerting her she
had messages.

She picked it up and pressed a button to listen. In the
first message, Dee wanted to know if she could borrow
Stephanie's diamond earrings for her upcoming court
appearance. The next two messages came from companies
selling extended automobile warranties and mortgage
services. The last message came from Dr. Tisdale's office.

*Hello. This message is for Ms. Stephanie Robinson. We've
received the results from your tests and everything is normal.
However, your tests have revealed you are three weeks' pregnant. Please call us back Monday through Friday between
the hours of eight a.m. to five p.m. to discuss prenatal care.
Thank you. ...Beep.*

She jumped up and clasped her hands over her mouth.
Did she hear them right? She was pregnant. If she didn't
believe dreams came true before, she definitely believed
it now. Here she was playing a game, faking a pregnancy,
only to find out she'd been pregnant for weeks. This
gave her renewed hope for getting past the Natalie fiasco.
Stephanie hopped from the living room to the hallway,

peeping around the corner to look for Levin. She didn't see him, so she figured she'd check on him.

"Levin?" Stephanie called.

He didn't answer.

As she turned the corner, she still didn't see or hear him, but she did see the light coming from the open bathroom. She approached it and looked in.

"Levin?" Stephanie called again.

Levin sat on the closed toilet lid, reading. She walked inside to make out the book in his hand. To her horror, she saw him reading her secret notebook—the one with her "baby" plan. She'd left it on the bathroom counter before she'd left for dinner with him and he'd found it. Her excitement turned into panic. She took a deep breath.

"Levin, I can explain everything." Her voice shook, betraying her fear.

He looked up at her.

"It's not that bad. Really." She had hoped she could do better than that, but right then, she couldn't. She had to concentrate to keep from wetting her drawers.

"This was a game?" Levin asked, hurt and disbelief seeping into his voice.

"No, it wasn't. I promise," Stephanie said.

"You're not pregnant, are you?" he asked.

"Yes, I am! I can prove it."

"I don't wanna hear it!" Levin yelled. He threw the notebook at Stephanie and pushed past her to leave the bathroom.

Stephanie stumbled, barely catching the notebook. When she regained her balance, she ran behind him and tugged at his arm but he shook her off.

"Please, Levin, I can explain this," she cried, grabbing him again.

He shoved her backward so hard she had to grab the couch to break her fall. She'd never seen him so angry. It scared her but she felt like she couldn't let him go. She'd worked so hard. They'd come so far. She couldn't imagine letting him walk out of the door and never seeing him again. She refused to go through all of this for nothing. And what about their baby? It deserved to have both of them in his or her life. Whatever the problems were, they would work it out. They had to work it out.

But for now, Levin seemed as angry as ever. "I can't believe I've been with you for almost a year and had no idea you were so scandalous."

Stephanie stood up straight. "Scandalous? And what do you call all those chicks you be taking back to the VIP at the club? I'm scandalous, Levin? I'm just trying to make a life with you," Stephanie said, wiping her tear-stained face.

"How do you do that lying to me all the time?"

"I'm not lying!"

"Then what do you call this?"

"But I am pregnant, Levin! Just listen." She rushed over to her phone to retrieve the message.

"I'm not listening to anything! From now on I won't believe nothing else you have to say, Stephanie!"

Levin opened her front door and looked back at her. "Nothing!" He slammed the door behind him.

"Levin!" Stephanie yelled.

She hugged her notebook and sobbed. How did this happen? She knew her plan had risks, but, those risks seemed small compared to landing the man of her dreams. Now she had a price to pay for all her conniving.

What am I going to do now? Stephanie asked herself. Unable to answer, she curled up on her couch with her notebook and cried herself to sleep.

CHAPTER 33

Monica

On a gorgeous Wednesday afternoon, the trees swayed back and forth in response to the gentle breeze. It looked as if the white as cotton clouds gathered and shifted to create undiscovered shapes, even though earth was really the one moving. The blue sky looked bluer than usual against the soft, white ruffles. The sun shined but not at a beaming rate. It was more of a light gleam, enough to complement the many roses, gardenias, lilies and tulips in Monica's garden. Whenever Monica felt down, she loved to walk to the back of their house and sit amongst all the beauty earth had given her. With the way the weather turned out, Mother Earth must have approved of her decision to do so. She almost instantly felt better.

So far, it had turned into a peaceful day. The children had school and Tony had left early for his away game. He hadn't said anything before leaving but Monica didn't worry. They probably both needed more time to cool off. At least, she'd found time to prop her feet up, lie back and allow the sunrays to caress her face. She closed her eyes and dozed off, thoroughly enjoying the quiet until Marianna ran outside with the cordless phone.

"Mrs. Hatcher. Phone for you," Marianna said.

Monica opened her eyes and stared at the phone as if she'd spotted a bug. She sighed and leaned forward to grab it. "Thanks." She turned to it and answered.

"Hello."

"He won't take my calls or let me into his hotel room!"

At first Monica couldn't make out the person on the other end of the hysteria, but when she thought about it, she was able to put two and two together, which equaled Stephanie.

"Stephanie? Who? Levin?" Monica asked.

"Yes," Stephanie whined.

"Why is he not answering your calls?"

"All day I've tried to reach him, but he won't even return my calls. I went to his hotel but the front desk won't allow me to go up. He's angry with me." Stephanie burst into tears. Monica could hear her friend heaving into the receiver.

"Did you guys have a fight or something? Maybe he needs to cool off."

"No. I need to talk to him now!"

"Stephanie, I know you're stuck on him but don't you think this might be the reason you guys are having so many problems? Give the man some space," Monica reasoned.

"You don't understand." Stephanie sniffled.

"Understand what?"

"He thinks I'm not really pregnant."

"Why would he think that? Did you tell him you weren't?"

"No."

"Well, are you pregnant?"

"Yes."

Monica sighed impatiently. "Girl, I'm gonna need more information because I'm not understanding where this is going. Why would he think you're not pregnant?"

Stephanie broke down and told Monica what she'd done. "I sorta created a plan to get Levin to commit to me."

"Plan? What kinda plan?" Monica asked.

"I told him I was pregnant. I also got people on the internet and the media to start talking about it. At the time I wasn't, but now I am."

"That's what you did with my media contacts?" she asked.

Stephanie didn't answer.

Monica was horrified, wondering what on earth would drive her friend to do something so extreme and stupid. "Oh, Stephanie. If I had known I wouldn't have given you the list of media," Monica said. "I would have given you the number to a crisis hotline. How could you do something like that?"

"Victor is the one that put him up to telling people he was seeing Felicia. It wasn't really true. Levin really wanted to be with me. I only wanted to make it easier for him to see it."

"So you faked a pregnancy?" Monica asked. Her friend's

logic amazed her sometimes. She was far from stupid, but at any time she could do something that a normal person would think twice about attempting. But not her. She'd keep going full speed ahead with no regard for the consequences.

"That's the thing. I'm pregnant now but he found the book I wrote everything down in."

"Oh, Stephanie."

"I know it sounds bad but I need to get to him. He needs to know I really am pregnant."

"What do you want me to do about it? I've got my own problems to deal with."

"Do you think you could talk to him for me? Let him know what's up. I would be indebted to you forever." Stephanie whined.

"I don't wanna get involved in this. It's your mess. You need to clean it up," Monica said.

"I'm going to but first I have to tell him the truth. How am I supposed to do that if I can't even reach him?" Stephanie asked. "Please, Monica, if you want, I won't ask you for anything else. Please help me with this."

Monica tried to make it a rule not to judge her friends' decisions, but Stephanie's behavior took the cake. It was hard to hide her absolute disgust for her actions and it was just like Stephanie to want someone else to help her clean it up. She also had a hard time wanting to assist her friend. Not only did she disapprove of her actions, she hated getting in the middle of other people's relationships. She was nobody's relationship expert. Her own marriage was struggling, for goodness sakes. But then, she thought about the innocent baby involved. It didn't ask to be in this situation. It wasn't the child's fault her mother was as nutty as ten fruitcakes. When Monica thought about it that way, her heart softened and she made a decision she usually wouldn't make.

"Okay. Maybe in a week, I'll give him a call. That way he'll have time to cool down."

"No! He leaves today. He'll be on location with his movie. He'll probably be hard to reach then. Please," Stephanie begged.

"Errrr. Okay, okay. I'll try to reach him today and see if I can talk to him."

"Thank you, Monica. You are a life saver and a true friend."

Stephanie hung up and left Monica wondering what she'd gotten herself into.

∞

Stephanie wasn't lying. Levin was very hard to get on the phone. Monica had tried calling him eight times, and each time it went to his voicemail. She thought about leaving a message, but figured if she had, he'd guess why she was calling and ignore the message. The last time she'd called she'd decided to take a trip down to his hotel. She entered the lobby and headed straight for the front desk, where a scrawny, pimply-faced kid stood there shuffling through papers. Monica approached the desk and began her song and dance.

"Hello. I am terribly sorry to bother you but I'm here to see someone but I forgot which room they are in. If I give you the name, could you point me in the right direction?" Monica asked.

"No, ma'am. We are not allowed to disclose any information about a customer," the clerk said.

"What if I really need to talk to them?"

He shook his head. "The best I can do is take the person's name and try calling them and find out if they want to give you that information."

Monica sighed. "Okay. His name is Levin Young."

"Okay. Give me one second." The clerk disappeared around the corner. He returned and picked up the phone to call the room. Monica tapped her French manicured nails on the hotel front desk, waiting for an answer. The clerk held the phone for about a minute, then shot her an apologetic smile.

"I'm sorry, ma'am. Mr. Young is not available right now and it is standard protocol we verify a guest before letting them go up or disclosing any information to them," the clerk said.

Monica sighed. She didn't want to do this, but it looked like she had no choice. She had to use whatever tool she had. "Listen. My name is Monica Hatcher and my husband is Tony T. Hatcher. He plays for the Tampa Bay

Buccaneers. Have you ever heard of him?" Monica asked.

The clerk's eyes widened. "Yes, I have. It's a pleasure to meet you, Mrs. Hatcher."

She nodded. "The thing is Levin and Tony are very good friends. In fact they're planning to go into business together. Anyhoo, my husband needed to get some really important documents to him before Levin left for Mexico. Since my husband is already on the road, he couldn't do it. So he sent me here." Monica leaned forward. "Now these papers are very, very important. I would hate to have to tell my husband you guys wouldn't let me give them to Levin because of some simple little protocol. Why, I can't imagine what kind of stink that would cause, could you?" Monica asked.

"No, ma'am." The clerk looked over his shoulder. "I tell you what. I'll let you up and if there's a problem, call down here for me. My name is James." He stuck his chest out and smiled wide.

"Well, thank you, James. I really appreciate it. You have been so professional and courteous. I'm going to make sure I tell your supervisor what a great asset you are to this hotel," Monica said.

"Thank you, Mrs. Hatcher," James cheesed.

After James gave her the hotel room number, Monica headed for the elevators. She stepped onto Levin's floor and saw a security guard standing outside of his door. As she strolled down the hall, she psyched herself up for what she would have to say to get past "Bubba."

She approached the door and stood in front of him. "Excuse me. I need to have a word with Levin. Could you let him know I'm here?" Monica asked, looking up at the towering security guard.

"No visitors," the guard said.

"Yes, I understand that but I'm not a visitor. I'm a friend and I need to see him before he leaves," Monica said.

"No visitors," the guard repeated.

Is this dude retarded? Monica thought.

"It'll only take a minute but I have to see him," Monica said, standing with her left hip poked out.

The guard removed his sunglasses and looked down at Monica. "Listen. Levin is busy getting ready for his flight. He doesn't have time for any groupies so you'll have to catch him the next time he's in town like all the others."

Monica's mouth fell open and she saw red. This guard must have lost his mind. He had no right to talk to her that way. "Who the hell do you think you're talking to?! Do you know who I am?"

"I don't care who you are. Get like Michael Jackson and beat it!" the guard yelled.

Before Monica could lay into the guard, Levin's hotel door cracked open and he peeped out.

"Levin," Monica said, smiling.

"Monica? What are you doing here?" Levin said.

"I need to talk to you."

Levin opened his door all the way to let Monica in. "It's okay, Brody. She's aight."

Brody stepped aside and allowed Monica to pass. She rolled her eyes at the guard and stepped into Levin's hotel room. Monica walked past the three suitcases near the door to sit on the couch in front of the window. Levin sat next to her and sighed. Monica opened her mouth to speak but Levin held up his hand. She stopped.

"Monica, before you start. I know why you're here and I can appreciate why you're here, but I don't have anything to say to Stephanie," Levin said.

"Levin, believe me. I completely understand why you would be disgusted by what Stephanie did. I was shocked as well when she told me what she did."

He raised an eyebrow. "You didn't know?"

"I had no clue," Monica said. "But trust me, she really is pregnant now. I know. We have the same doctor."

Levin shook his head. "I don't have time to deal with all these games. She's been lying to me for a long time and I'm tired of it. I have to go shoot this movie and I'm going to focus on that right now."

"But don't you want to be a part of your baby's life?"

"Sure. If she turns out to be pregnant and it's mine, I'll take care of it. The baby won't want for anything."

"If it's yours? C'mon, Levin. You know she's not with anybody else."

"And how do I know that? Oh, I forgot. She's been so damn honest about everything else," Levin said.

"Look. I know what she did was wrong. I was mortified when she told me but the only reason she did it was because she wanted you. You may not realize it but for the past twelve months, we couldn't talk to her for five minutes without your name coming up. The sun rose and set on you. This is about love. She loves you."

Levin stood up. "No."

"No?"

"No. This isn't about love. This is about a woman who is so insecure she would do anything to keep a man, even if it's deceitful. This is about a woman who would date anybody in the industry that'll pay her bills. Oh, don't think I haven't heard about her. And last but not least, this is about a woman who lies to me. What am I supposed to do with that?"

Monica wracked her brain for an answer but she couldn't think of anything. He made a lot of sense. To top it all off, she couldn't blame him for being angry with Stephanie. Her friend had really dug a hole for herself on this one. Oh, well. At least, Monica could tell her she gave it her best. She took it as far as she could. Stephanie would have to do the rest. Looking up at Levin, Monica could tell he wasn't going to listen to much more.

She stood up beside Levin. "Okay. I guess I'll be going now. Have a safe trip and good luck on the movie."

"Thanks." Levin gave Monica a hug.

Monica passed the mean guard and stepped onto the elevator. She pulled out her phone and dialed Stephanie's number. Stephanie must have been waiting for the call because she answered within the first ring.

"Hello?" she said, sounding out of breath.

"Hey, Stephanie."

"Did you talk to Levin? Did you tell him everything?!" Stephanie asked eager to hear how the talk had turned out.

"Yes, I did," Monica said. She paused, reluctant to go on. She knew this was not the news her friend wanted to hear and hated to be the one to tell her.

"Well?" Stephanie asked.

"Maybe you should give him some time. He's still a little upset. Let him go to his movie. Once he gets a little distance between him and the situation, he may be able to hear what you have to say, but right now, Stephanie, he doesn't want to hear anything."

For a minute, Stephanie didn't respond, which concerned Monica. She spoke again. "You don't wanna get too worked up about this. Get some rest and I'll call you later. Okay?"

"Okay," Stephanie said.

Monica hung up, hoping Stephanie would relax and allow things to blow over.

In the meantime she had some personal issues of her own to handle. While Tony had left for his away games, she figured this would give her time to think. For eight years, she'd put her own dreams aside for her family, while Tony had spent the whole time thinking about himself. She needed to figure out where she wanted to go with her marriage.

Once she ended her call with Stephanie, Monica jumped into her car and dialed her parents' number. While she waited for her mother to answer, she pulled off to head home. After a few rings, her mother answered in her usual "why are you bothering me" tone.

"Hello, Mother. Are you busy?" Monica asked.

"I'm always busy. What do you want?" Corlene asked.

Of course. There's a lot to do when you don't work, Monica thought. "I'm calling because I wanted to ask a favor." Monica dreaded having to tell her mother what was going on in her marriage, but she knew she would have to do it. She took a deep breath. "Tony and I are having some issues, and I need to get the kids away. I really need some time to think. Their school is over in a couple of days. I wanted to know if you would be willing to keep the kids for a couple of weeks."

Corlene didn't immediately respond. There was a lengthening silence on her side of the phone. Monica hoped her mother would agree, because she really didn't feel like begging.

"Mother?"

"Yes," Corlene said.

"Will you keep them?"

"Of course, we'll keep them but don't 'think' too long," Corlene said.

"It's just a couple of weeks." Monica rolled her eyes.

"What's the problem? Another woman?"

It was Monica's turn to lapse into silence.

"That's what I thought. Either way, I hope you're not thinking about leaving. No woman with any sense would leave in your situation."

"Well, it's not about other women, Mother. It's about me."

"And the children. And the money and the status. I'm going to need you to woman up," Corlene said.

Monica's ears began to burn. "You know what? I don't get you. For eight years, you've berated Tony left and right. Now that we're having problems, you're telling me I have to stay?"

"Monica, it's no secret men aren't as evolved as women. We can't hold them to the same standards we hold ourselves. But there's one thing we can do. We have the power to make them jump through hoops. We can make them do anything we want. This is a great opportunity for you. Use his guilt to get more of what you want. Torture him forever if you want, but never, ever leave the money."

Monica couldn't believe this was her mother's logic. Her words of wisdom. Her motto for life. She'd said it as if nothing else mattered. There were so many other things in life that mattered. It angered and saddened her that her mother was so one-dimensional. She was angry her mother would suggest she remain with Tony for the money and the money only. What about trust, love and respect? In that moment, Monica was convinced there was no way possible her mother had ever been truly happy. The expensive houses, cars and trinkets couldn't have possibly given Corlene the fulfillment she needed. Monica believed her mother was utterly miserable, and she felt sorry for her.

"Fine, Mother. I have to go. I'll get them packed and on their way soon."

By the time she hung up, Monica was pulling into her driveway. She walked into her house and saw Marianna passing through the foyer with a basket of clothes. It dawned on her that so much had been happening in their house and Marianna probably had no clue. She needed to explain to her they were going through some changes. She stopped her.

"Hey, Marianna. I need to talk to you. Could we step in here for a minute?" Monica pointed to the kitchen nook.

"Sure, Mrs. Hatcher."

They walked into the kitchen and Monica pointed to a chair. Marianna and Monica took their seats.

"First, let me say you are a gem, and we feel very lucky to have you with us. In many ways it's like you are a part of our family," Monica said.

"Thank you, Mrs. Hatcher. You are the nicest people I've ever worked for and I'm grateful to work with you," Marianna said.

Monica smiled. "I'm glad. I brought you in here because I wanted to let you know there are some things going on between Mr. Hatcher and me. The children don't know it yet, but we are having some problems and I'm going to need your help in keeping the kids happy, comfortable and secure. I would really appreciate it if you could help me keep them as stable as possible."

Marianna placed her hand to her mouth. "Oh my gosh.

I'm sorry to hear about you and Mr. Hatcher. I do hope you all can work things out, but I will be happy to make sure the kids continue to thrive, despite everything going on," Marianna said.

"Thank you," Monica said, patting her hand. "I appreciate it. Well, that's all. I'm going to send the kids to my mother's house for a few weeks so things can settle down and I can get my head clear. Could you start getting their luggage together?"

"Sure, Mrs. Hatcher. I'll put these away." Marianna stood up, grabbed her basket and walked toward the laundry room. Monica sighed and trod upstairs to lie down. After all the drama of the day, she was bushed. She fell on her bed and drifted to sleep. It took awhile for her to rest peacefully. Stephanie's sadness and her mother's words haunted her consciousness, but somewhere along the way, she managed to gain some peace.

Six hours later, her phone snatched her right out of her sleep. She jumped up and fumbled for the phone.

"Hello?" Monica answered the phone groggy and disoriented.

"Are you Monica Hatcher?"

"Yes. Yes. Who is this?"

"I'm calling about Stephanie Robinson. She listed you as an emergency contact."

Monica turned on her light. "What? Why? What's going on?"

"Ms. Robinson was admitted to the hospital for hemorrhaging. She had a miscarriage."

CHAPTER 34

Around 8:30 in the morning people filed into the courtroom. Monica had had a hard time making it to the courthouse. She'd stayed with Stephanie for a few hours. She didn't get home from the hospital until 1:50 a.m. After a few hours of sleep, she had to wake back up and come out to support Dee. It would be an understatement to say Monica was exhausted. Somehow she made it to the courthouse in time to hear Judge Anderson call the court to order. Dee sat in one of the first few benches with Dwayne, while a visibly bruised and battered Bobbie sat at the defendant's table. He had a bandage on his head and his arm was in a sling. Monica scurried up front to sit next to Dee and Dwayne.

"Sorry I'm late," Monica whispered.

"Oh, don't worry about it. How's Stephanie?" Dee asked.

"She looked kinda bad last night but she's hanging in there. I'm gonna go see her after this."

Their conversation was interrupted when the judge asked Bobbie to rise for his arraignment. He stood up, wobbling along the way. Though Bobbie had boosted himself up to be the big man in town, he was a mere fraction of that standing in front of the judge. His shoulders drooped and he held his head down the whole time while his charges were being read to him. Bobbie was looking at twelve years in prison for three counts of money laundering. In eight years, he could receive parole.

Monica would have felt sorry for him if his activities hadn't caused others so much frustration and false hope.

When the issue of bail had come up, the lawyer had asked for a low bail because the chances of Bobbie's fleeing were small given his physical condition. The judge kept it higher because of his past and his dangerous connections. In the end, the bail was set at two hundred and fifty-thousand dollars.

Bobbie didn't move or make a sound. He turned as he was led out of the courtroom. He glanced over and looked straight into Dwayne's eyes. The two men held eye contact for about six seconds, but it was the longest six seconds ever. If they had been on the streets, Monica was sure they would have come to blows. Luckily they were in a courtroom where Bobbie was led in the opposite direction and plenty of police were around.

Dee, Dwayne and Monica walked out of the building onto the steps.

"Well, do you guys feel a little better about everything now that Bobbie's in custody?" Monica asked.

"A little, but I hate the thought that I might have to testify against him later. I feel like I'm setting myself up for problems. What if he comes after me like he did you?" Dee said, looking at Dwayne.

"I don't think that'll happen," Dwayne said.

"How do you know?" Dee asked.

"For one, he wants to get at me and that's what all this was about in the beginning. And two, I won't let him harass you," Dwayne said.

"I saw that look you guys gave each other in the courtroom. That was chilling. If we hadn't been in court, I would have run as fast as I could," Monica said, chuckling a little.

"And that might have been the right thing to do. But I'm not sweating that dude," Dwayne said.

"Let me get going. I have to go check on Stephanie," Monica said.

"Tell her I said take it easy and I'll see her soon," Dee said.

"Okay."

Dee and Dwayne walked to his car, where he opened the passenger door for her. As Monica watched them together, she hoped Dwayne was right in believing Bobbie wouldn't come after Dee again. With a character like his, there was really no telling.

Monica drove to the hospital on fumes, stomach fumes to be exact. She hadn't eaten much since yesterday, and the sleep she missed was threatening to catch up with her even as she drove. She pulled into the hospital parking lot and made a beeline to the vending machines.

She grabbed a Nestea, opened it and gulped half of the bottle down right then. It felt so good going down. Once she felt like she'd partially eliminated the hunger pangs coming, Monica searched for the elevator. She found it around the corner and walked on.

After the short ride to the second floor, Monica stepped off the hospital elevator. Her eyes began to sting from little sleep and her right temple throbbed. *Great. I solve one problem and have another one*, Monica thought. She reached Room 212, leaned her head against the wall, and closed her eyes. After days of stress and unrest, the idea of sleep sounded good to her.

She jumped up straight when a nurse walked by. The nurse looked her up and down.

"Are you all right?" the nurse asked.

Monica nodded her head. *Let me move before someone puts me in the next room*, she thought.

Monica slowly opened the door and tiptoed inside. Stephanie lay in her hospital bed, staring at the television. She turned around when she heard Monica enter the room. A small smile struggled across her face. Monica could see the dark circles lingering under her eyes, but overall she looked a little better than she did the previous night. Monica dropped her purse and Nestea bottle. She sat on the side of Stephanie's bed.

"Hey, honey! How you feeling?"

"I'm good." Stephanie leaned forward. "How was Dee's day at the courthouse? I wish I could have been there."

"Yeah. Dee said hello and she'll see you soon. The judge was pretty stern with Bobbie, which is what he needed. It looks like Dee doesn't have to worry about going to prison like she originally thought, which is great because I can't see her in prison," Monica said.

"Me, neither. Her trying to put on lashes in the little mirror." Monica and Stephanie broke into laughter. Monica nodded her head and wiped the tears running from her eyes.

"I'm just glad they got him and she can now start moving on," Monica said.

"I know. Does Dee still plan to do the magazine thing?" Stephanie asked.

"Yeah, but I think she's going to put it on hold. It won't look good to the police for her to immediately pick back up and start building when they just confiscated thousands of dollars from her. They might think she's hiding more money," Monica said.

"Is she?" Stephanie asked, cocking her head to the side.

Monica shrugged. "She might be."

"Wouldn't you?" Stephanie asked.

"No, I don't think it's worth going to prison for."

"Awww. The police won't even notice some of the money is missing. Even if they did, they're not going to put her in jail for a couple thousand dollars."

Stephanie never ceased to amaze Monica. After all she'd been through, she was still able to take such a nonchalant attitude toward dishonesty. She was losing the man of her dreams and had lost her baby because she'd insisted on living with twisted logic. She still didn't get it but, given her delicate situation, Monica opted not to preach to her. She chose a more diplomatic stance.

"Money or no money. Dee plans to be a lot more careful about whom she trusts from now on. If she'd listened to Dwayne in the beginning, she wouldn't be in this situation," Monica said.

"Dwayne lied! She could've still gotten caught up."

Monica knew what Stephanie meant but she chose the lesser of the two evils.

"But she could've avoided the problems she had. It would've been more responsible for her to refrain from doing business with someone she didn't know."

Stephanie shook her head. "Monica, everybody lies."

"Not necessarily." Monica frowned.

"What about Tony?"

The words sliced into Monica like a sword. For the last few days, Monica had been running around so much doing for others she hadn't found time to mull over her problems with Tony. She'd spent more time planning Janet's event, tending to her children, and solving her friends' problems. But right then she had to face those problems head-on and they were pretty ugly.

Seeing the hurt on Monica's face, Stephanie tried to recant. "What I meant was nobody's perfect," she said.

The two women lapsed into silence for several minutes. Trying to let the awkward moment pass, Monica scanned the room for something to talk about. Her eyes rested on a large arrangement of red roses, pink Gerbera daisies, and white lilies.

"Who are those from?" Monica asked.

Stephanie smiled wide and winked. "Who do you think?"

Monica raised her eyebrows. "Are you serious?"

Suddenly, all the weariness in Stephanie's face disappeared, as her words flew from her mouth like lightning. "Levin came to see me! It was perfect, Monica. He got here around six this morning. He gave me a hug, squeezing me really tight. And he smelled so good."

Monica rolled her eyes.

"Anyway, he dropped off the flowers."

"What did he say?"

"He asked how I was doing and did I need anything. We talked about us and where we're going from here."

"Where exactly are you all going from here?"

"We're going to talk about it more when he gets back from shooting his movie." Stephanie nodded. "I think we'll be back together."

"Well, that sounds good and all," Monica commented. "But that doesn't mean he's ready to forgive and forget." She really wanted her friend to learn from this situation and grow smarter from it, but it didn't look like she would. Watching Stephanie bubble over with excitement reminded Monica of the way she'd been acting for the past year. It was like nothing was going to change.

"I know. I'm glad he came. That's all," Stephanie said,

flopping back against the pillow. She stared at Monica. "I won't do anything like that again."

"Good," Monica said firmly.

In her hospital bed, Stephanie rolled over on her side to sleep. Monica patted her on the shoulder and said, "I'm going to go now. I'll let Dee know how you're doing, but I'll come back when you're ready to go." Stephanie nodded and Monica headed toward the door. When she reached for the handle, Monica stopped to turn back around.

"You know, you did pretty good with the whole media thing. You think you might wanna job?"

"No." Stephanie pouted.

Monica sucked her teeth. "That's what I thought."

∞

When Monica left the hospital, she didn't go to Dee's house immediately. Instead she went home, where she was able to catch up on some much needed rest. A few hours of sleep and she felt like a new woman. She showered and changed clothes. Then she left again to visit Dee's house. Monica pulled into Dee's driveway and saw Dwayne's car. She knocked on the door. Dwayne answered.

"Monica!"

"Hi, Dwayne. Did you guys come right here after court?"

"No. We stopped to have lunch. How is Stephanie?"

"She's doing really good. She's trying to keep her spirit up but…I know she's going to need a lot of support."

"Well, whatever you guys need, I'm happy to help," Dwayne offered.

"Thanks, Dwayne. I appreciate that."

She followed him through the foyer into Dee's living room. The television was on a sports show. Dee came downstairs. She looked relaxed and comfortable now that the court had cleared her and Dwayne of charges for the illegal money activities and Bobbie's brutal attack. "Don't you look rested?" Monica asked.

"Girl, I didn't know I would but I really do feel better already," Dee said.

"So, you're not worried anymore about him trying to getcha later?" Monica asked.

"I would be lying if I said I wasn't worried about it a little bit," she said. "He knows bad people. Wouldn't that make him connected enough to have someone else get at me, even while he's in prison? I think I still need to be on alert."

"If he was that connected, he wouldn't have gotten caught in the first place. Or shot up himself," Monica said.

"That's true." Dee bit her lip. "Didn't he look awful? Whoever got him, got him good. He looked like it hurt him to breathe. Didn't it, Dwayne?"

Dwayne blinked fast. "Uh. Yeah. He was in pretty bad shape."

"Did they ever find out who shot Bobbie?" Monica asked, looking from Dee to Dwayne.

"No. They think it was a robbery," Dee said, reaching for a glass of wine while looking at Dwayne.

"Are they sure?" Monica asked, also waiting for Dwayne to respond.

"His wallet was taken. It seems like he was robbed." Dwayne pushed his hands in his pockets and shrugged.

The women nodded. He hung his head and turned toward the couch to watch TV.

Monica faced Dee. "I guess, but he did so many people wrong. Look at all the people he victimized."

"Yeah, but none of his victims were ruthless or vengeful. Seriously, who would've had the gall to try to do him in?"

Dee and Monica looked at each other and shrugged. In the spirit of their relief, the two friends clinked glasses and downed their wine. Dwayne did his best to ignore their Bobbie conversation. He was lucky they didn't suspect anything. Who knew that the guy would do such a sloppy job? He reached for the remote and turned up the volume, listening to the Buccaneers talk about their upcoming game with the Titans.

ABOUT THE AUTHOR

Jaye Cheríe is editor and publisher of Entertainment Wire, an online entertainment medium devoted to news, reviews, and interviews. She has photographed, interviewed, and written articles on entertainers and personalities, such as *CSI: New York* actor Hill Harper, TLC member and reality show star Chilli, singer Eric Benét, and comedian J. Anthony Brown. She is the author of *The Golddigger's Club* and *The Cost of Love and Sanity*.

If you enjoyed "The Golddigger's Club,"
be sure to check out

The Cost of
Love and Sanity

by Jaye Cheríe
Coming soon from Strebor Books

CHAPTER 1

"Uh um," the VP of Operations, Mr. Eugene Sims, stood behind his executive chair and cleared his throat. The room acknowledged him with silent cooperation. "Surely, you all are wondering why I've called this meeting. Everyone is in a hurry to get out of here and enjoy their New Year's. Nevertheless, we have a pressing issue to discuss before the first of next month." He frowned.

"As you all know, our numbers are down twenty percent this quarter after being down nineteen percent last quarter. We've lost contracts. We aren't getting as many good people placed with our present clients and this is affecting our business." He leaned on the chair. "Golden

Burch has been looking for a sales professional for four months. We haven't sent him anyone in four months!" the VP raised his voice, allowing his aggravation to erupt like a volcano.

For a second, you could hear a rat pee on cotton. Alexis Carter, one of three junior recruitment managers, blinked four times in rapid succession. Until Mr. Sims' outburst she'd been fighting hard to stay awake. She should have made herself a cup of tea that morning or at least stopped somewhere and bought a tea. A tea and two sunrisers. She could smell the steaming hot, peppered sausage, melted cheese and buns burning up her fingers as she pushed one into her mouth. Her stomach growled in response to her food fantasy. She quickly placed her hand over her stomach and looked to her left and her right to see if anyone heard it. Nobody showed any signs they did.

Suddenly, Dan Reece, a coordinator, raised his hand, looking like a fifth-grader about to ask his teacher if he could go to the bathroom.

"What?" Mr. Sims zeroed in on Dan.

"We haven't sent over any sales candidates because none of them fit their qualifications," Dan said.

"And what did you do about that?"

Dan fell silent, searching his colleagues' faces for ideas about what to say next. When no one offered him a lifeline, he answered on his own, sitting up straight in his chair. "Well, I...I called everyone I could in our database."

"And?" the VP said, without blinking.

Dan swallowed. This meeting was going further downhill by the minute.

"And no one matched," Dan said.

The VP pointed toward the embarrassed employee. "This is my point. As bad as the economy is, with all the people out there looking for jobs, all we're doing is making excuses. We're not doing everything we can to find the candidates. That's not gonna cut it."

Alex sat back in her chair. She knew this talk would come. The year started with a bang and ended with a whimper. She'd hoped their tongue lashing wouldn't come today, especially since her stomach seemed intent on gearing up for a second growl.

"Last year, we launched the Referral Program. Whatever happened to that? I heard it a couple of times in the meetings but not one person has mentioned anything about it since." Mr. Sims walked toward the right side of the room. "What about other ideas? Has anyone even attempted to find other ways to solve this problem?"

In an effort to look productive in this train wreck of a meeting, Alex answered. "I've had my people making triple the calls, to unemployed candidates as well as employed ones. I figured maybe some people are ready for a career upgrade."

She saw Dan smirk out of the corner of her eye.

Mr. Sims nodded. "Well, Alex, we'll have to continue finding ways to recruit. It's the company's goal to find people jobs, right?"

"Right," the room said in unison.

"Good. I'm glad we agree on something. In the meantime, we're going to have to make some changes." Mr. Sims scanned the board room. "The company will have to let someone go in a few months."

Everyone looked around at each other, except Alex. She couldn't see herself on the chopping block and, most importantly, she wouldn't see herself on the chopping block. She'd exceeded her recruitment numbers over the past two years. She became one of their top recruitment managers her first month there. *This can't apply to me. I'll make sure of it.*

"We'll be observing you guys. We should be making a decision around March or April. Until then, come up with ways to help our clients. Immediately. I'll be watching."

After a few minutes of uncomfortable silence and exchanged glances, Mr. Sims dismissed the executive staff from the boardroom. Alex sped away from the low chatters and panicked expressions and headed toward the elevator. Courtney Davis and Romero Martinez filed behind her.

"Wow!" Romero said. "I guess we'd really better get on the ball, huh? We need to work harder at protecting the image of the company."

"Forget the image of the company! I need to keep my job," said Courtney. As Alex watched her talk, she thought about Courtney's uncle—the CEO Mark Davis. Somehow, Alex didn't think the spunky redhead had anything to worry about.

Courtney bounced off the elevator onto the third floor.

Romero shook his head and said what they were both thinking. "Like she's gonna get fired. I hope they don't get carried away with the rest of us. I have a kid in private school." Romero narrowed his eyes and wrinkled his forehead.

"This only means it's really time to buckle down," Alex said.

Romero's eyes stared off into the empty space. "Yeah. I suppose you're right."

The bell rang and the elevator doors opened to Alex's floor. She turned toward the door and raised her foot to step off.

"Hey!"

She turned back toward Romero.

"Thanks."

Alex forced a smile and nodded.

"Say. Did you get my email?" Romero asked.

Her brain flashed back to the email she had received from him yesterday. Romero had asked her to attend an art exhibit with him. Refusing to allow recognition of the email to cross her face, Alex feigned ignorance. "What email?"

"Oh, I sent you an email about the art exhibit downtown tomorrow. I wanted to know if you would like to go check it out with me?" Romero asked, smiling.

Alex took a deep breath. She hated to tell him no. He really was a nice guy—but not the guy for her. Besides, she'd been seeing Phillip for about six months now. Even though she and Phillip were far from heading toward the wedding chapel, she couldn't see making a run for Romero.

She snapped her fingers. "You know what? I already have plans with my friend."

"Oh, yes. Yes, of course," he said, lowering his head slightly.

"But thank you. Thank you for the invite."

"Sure. Maybe some other time," Romero said.

"Maybe." Alex stepped forward and the elevator door closed behind her.

She shook her head. *Not a chance.* Romero wanted more than she could possibly give him and she did not believe in dating nice guys because they were, well nice. Besides, any romance between them would spark unwanted office gossip. Employees already had enough food for thought with the coming layoff. She had to concentrate on how to keep upper management off her back and what she wanted to do for New Year's Eve.

Alex steered East onto Camelot Drive determined to release all thoughts of the emergency meeting. The crisp air seeped through the small cracks between her car doors, while hot air swished through the air vents, blowing her dark brown, shoulder-length hair off her neck. Christmas lights still lined most of the houses in her subdivision. Each house Alex passed seemed to outshine the one before it. Her house, on the other hand, fit into the small group without holiday decorations. As she pulled her black

Lexus up to the two-story home, Alex couldn't help but notice the lack of holiday spirit there. She should have been embarrassed but she had an excuse; she'd been too busy at work to bother with decorations and she didn't feel like asking Phillip to do anything these days.

The man initially represented himself as the perfect gentleman—patient, polite and thoughtful. But, over the last couple of months, Phillip had become impatient and a little selfish. Suddenly, his time and objectives took precedence over anything she had to do. Yet, he liked to present reasons for his requests as if they made more sense. He would have probably told her she didn't need light decorations because she had no children around to appreciate them.

Phillip's car was already parked in her driveway. Alex switched off her ignition and looked at his car, then, at the front door. She longed to go inside, eat, take a shower and curl up in bed with the TV remote instead of feigning interest in conversation with him. Maybe the night wouldn't drag out too long. Maybe she could stop him before he harped on the problems with public education or government. She opened her car door and pushed herself out. Walking past Phillip's silver Audi, she placed her hand on top of the car. The cool hood indicated he'd been there awhile.

Upon opening the door, she smelled steak, rice, tomatoes and okra. *I hate okra and he knows this.* She sighed and placed her briefcase on the table in her foyer. Alex rounded the corner to see Phillip bent forward into the cabinet.

"Hey. What's up?" Alex asked, forcing herself to sound chipper.

His face emerged, showing neatly framed facial hair. "Nothing," Phillip said. He stood straight. "Did you bring some salt with you?"

"No," Alex said, sitting down on a stool.

He frowned and closed the cabinet door. "I thought you said you would stop to get some on your way home."

"No, I didn't say that."

"Yes, you did."

"No, I didn't." Alex furrowed her brow.

"Is it that you didn't say it or is it that you don't remember saying it?"

"I didn't say it, Phillip. I didn't even know I needed any."

"It's your house! You don't ever check to see what you need in your house."

Alex's blood boiled to 103 degrees. She pressed her fingertips to her temples and took a deep breath. "I don't have a problem with missing salt. You do."

He shrugged and tossed his hands up in the air. "Fine. I hope you don't mind the tomatoes and okra being bland because there wasn't enough seasoning."

"Since you didn't go to the store to get it, I'm sure it's fine." Alex rolled her eyes. She hated it when Phillip overdramatized things. It was salt. Not gold.